EMERSON'S ESSAYS

Essays by

RALPH WALDO
EMERSON

WITH INTRODUCTION BY IRWIN EDMAN

First and Second Series Complete in One Volume

NEW YORK: THOMAS Y. CROWELL COMPANY

Published 1926, by

THOMAS Y. CROWELL COMPANY, INC.

introduction copyright 1951 by Thomas Y. Crowell Company, Inc.

ISBN 0-8152-0001-3

Printed in the United States of America

EMERSON AS UNREQUIRED READING

BY IRWIN EDMAN

T HE ESSAY has almost vanished from the world of modern writing, and it is hard to realize what a power it was in the hands of Emerson and what a power his essays still hold for the modern reader. It has always been astonishing to find in obscure corners of Europe that Emerson is being read, sometimes because he has been for a century identified as the deeper voice of America, but more often for the same reason that he has devoted readers up and down this country, often in obscure hamlets and among those not generally given to literature or philosophy.

Since I find myself often at unexpected or perhaps stolen moments of leisure turning to Emerson, I think I have discovered what are the pleasures of Emerson for the reader rather than for the student, the moralist, or the philosopher. For I do not read Emerson professionally. For disclosures of the nature and signature of things, I prefer, on the whole, more explicit, more literal, and more analytic thinkers. I read and reread Emerson because he is that almost extinct species, the reflective man of letters, the meditative essayist, the thoughtful writer of a prose which has, without any of the more patent devices of verse, the magical effects of poetry.

v

What is an essay, and how in a certain mode was Emerson one of its masters? The essay is an adventure in ideas, an exploration of a theme, a sortie of reflection. It is not an article; it is not an explication. The essay is an idea reflected through a personal medium. It is the form of literature in which the part counts, perhaps, more than the whole, and in which the part that counts most is the sentence. It is the mode of writing in which, when the whole does count, it counts most as a tone, an atmosphere; mood and attitude are more important than explicit structure, than pedestrian reasoned argument. The essayist himself is remembered no less than his subject, even when he is not talking about himself. When Emerson, for instance, calls the particular piece of writing "Politics" or "Plato" or "Friendship" or "Compensation," there is an Emersonian melody, a spiritual signature, a quality of personality that remains after the subject of the essay is forgotten and even after the theme remains only vaguely in one's head.

But in a writer, especially of essays, it is a singular combination of things that gives the total atmosphere, the pervasive quality, the residual aroma or flavor. In Emerson it is the bright flash of eternity, the vista of the timeless caught in a sunburst of words. It is in the sentence that reads like the mystic avowal of an oracle or an inspired sage. It is, indeed, in the single sentence or in the single paragraph that Emerson is at his best.

But a writer is identified in quality by his recurrent motifs, by the mood he engenders. Prose, even eloquent prose, is not mere music and would be vacuous if it were. Emerson is all of a piece, all of one temperament, and to turn to him at some late, quiet hour of the night is to come inevitably, familiarly, and with quickening excitement upon his familiar themes or, more accurately, his variations upon a theme. Over all, one might say, is the Over Soul. Emerson is an arch Platonist. To him the world about us is the visible appearance of what is invisible; things in time are symbols of essences in eternity; the life, the vitality, the soul in us is the life, the soul of the universe. To the odd-moment reader of Emerson, this is one of his special enchantments; we look into one of his pages and we have intimations of an Empyrean, glimpses of the eternal; we are lifted out of the provincialisms of time as well as of space and have a vivid sense of an authentic spiritual world, and often by the sheer magic of a paragraph come to feel that we live, move, and have our being in the wide universe of spirit, all radiance, all beauty, all good.

There is another theme of Emerson's which comes not from the Greeks but which breathes a native American air. It is suggested by the title of his essay, "Self Reliance," but the idea appears in essays whose headings do not in the least suggest it, as in the famous lecture called "The American Scholar." It is the notion of the great adventure, the fresh exploration, the open sea that beckons the soul of each individual, that soul which is the special instance of universal divinity, eternal creation. Emerson saw the expanding commercialism, the rampant materialism of an America already given over to things; his words ring with a celebration of the living person, the unquenchable free spirit.

To open Emerson anywhere is to open a window admitting a fresh reviving air. Whether the title be "Friendship" or "The Poet" or "Manners" or "Love," one feels one's self vivified by a warm conviction of vitality, and to have glimpses of experience forever opening upon fresh experience, to feel newborn into a new-made world.

It is clear why young people in Emerson's day, and why those dulled in their ardors by habit or convention, why those oppressed by the rigidities and recurrences of diurnal living returned with delight to Emerson. In his pages young people in young America found a voice that spoke to them of how much remained to be done, how much of freshness and morning there still was in the world. To older people in an older America and in a still older Europe, his essays reiterate the theme of the recurrent miracle of creation that takes place each day in the soul as it took place in the first dawn of man or of earth, or of civilization, or of art.

It is not always easy on reflection to accept without reservation Emerson's romantic faith that every day is the beginning of a fresh era, that every soul has God-like potential in it, that every act is the free act of a spirit untrammeled by necessity, by convention, by the past. But the point is not whether or not Emerson successfully argues his faith. For he does not argue at all. What is important, what is enkindling, is that he communicates his belief. He makes one feel the possibility of escape from the rigidities of habits in action, from dogmas in religion, from academic imitation in art, from colonialism in culture, from idolatry to the past. He makes contagious a sense of freedom and creativeness. He breathes into the reader, in the literal sense inspires the reader, with a belief in himself, in the future. He makes the reader aware of fresh potentialities in the self and of fresh new fields for achievement. All this he accomplishes not by argument, but by eloquence and by art.

A good many of us today are inclined, in a world menaced by standardization, by regimentation and indoctrination, to smile a little condescendingly at Emerson's bland assurance, his passionate if quiet belief in the individual, in the divine promise in every human being. There is attractiveness enough in the notion of independence, of freedom, of integrity to one's own creative soul. But contemporary men are too much aware of brute facts, of necessary conditions and of the hard discipline of causes and consequences. Freshness, novelty, spontaneity are wonderfully persuasive. But the condition of man, we know, has a history, and the future of man is not a creation out of nothing, but a reconstruction of a past. Yet for all the chastening to which modern intelligence has submitted itself, perhaps because of that chastening, Emerson comes as a voice of renewal. "Man," he says in "The Over Soul," "will calmly front the morrow in the negligency of that trust which carries Good with it, and so has already the whole future in the bottom of its heart." In a time when we have begun to take too literally the constrictions of nature and society Emerson speaks to us radiantly, releasingly (in the essay on "Self Reliance") : "We are now men and must accept in the highest mind the same transcendent destiny; and not minors and invalids in a protected corner, not cowards fleeing before a revolution, but guides, redeemers and benefactors, obeying the Almighty effort and advancing on Chaos and the Dark."

One may not agree, but one cannot help suspending disagreement when one reads such exhilarating utterance. Nor can one resist the wholeheartedness, the generosity of insight of such a passage as this from "Friendship" : "The essence of friendship is entirety, a total magnanimity and trust." Perhaps as we grow older we find it harder to believe with Emerson that every day is a new experience, unique in wonder and creation. But to read him is to retrieve that youthful sense of being ever in sight of a new continent, the vision of a beckoning dream. He manages to be optimistic without seeming smug. He turns even the recognized facts of disappointment in love to good account: "There are moments when affections rule the man and make his happiness dependent on a person or persons. . . . That which is beautiful and attractive in such relations must be succeeded and supplemented only by what is more beautiful, and so on forever."

Even the abstractions in Emerson have a glow and his images are a festival. It is by these that we are persuaded to a sense of the greatness in each of us, the greatness which is a part of the living creativeness in Nature. One need not study Emerson systematically to be made a sharer in this felt glory, this lifting hope; in some burst of metaphor, in some daring suggestion, it haunts each heightened page.

BIOGRAPHICAL NOTE

OLIVER WENDELL HOLMES has said that to educate a boy properly we must begin with his great-grandfather; and then he gives us the number of great-grandfathers at the sixth remove as thirty-two. It is interesting and profitable, therefore, to consider the record of a family whose grandfathers, and grandmothers too, were famous in themselves, and rendered historic by the birth of Ralph Waldo Emerson.

The two English streams—the Emersons and Bulkeleys —which united on American soil, originated in Yorkshire and Bedfordshire respectively. The first Emerson who came to America was a clergyman who settled in the town of Ipswich, Massachusetts, in 1635. From him to Ralph Waldo Emerson there is but one break in the line of clergymen. His son Joseph was the pioneer minister in Mendon, Massachusetts, and when driven from that place by the Indians, settled in Concord. The union of the two English streams was effected when he married Elizabeth, granddaughter of Peter Bulkeley of Concord, a descendant of the rectors of Odell in Bedfordshire. Edward and Peter Bulkeley were stanch Puritans; the former gained the praise of Walsingham, and the latter the enmity of Archbishop Laud. As a result of this enmity Peter left England and came to Cambridge, and then pushed on to the river Musketaquid, Meadow River, then in New Hampshire, and there purchased land from the Indians, which became the town of Concord, Massa-chusetts.

The centres of New England culture were Cambridge, Concord, and Boston, and the atmosphere of these places was the native element of Emerson's immediate ancestry. Joseph Emerson's son, Edward, married Rebecca Waldo, from whom our genial scholar derived his picturesque name. Although he was not a minister he was next thing to it, as he was deacon of the First Church in New-bury. His son Joseph was a distinguished scholar, gradu-ating from Harvard College in 1717. He was minister in Malden for nearly a half century; and married Mary, daughter of Rev. Samuel Moody of York, Maine. Of his three sons, who were ministers, William was a patriot minister of Concord. He built the Old Manse. At the outbreak of the Revolution he entered the army as chap-lain, and soon died of fever. His son William graduated at Harvard College and began his ministry at Harvard, Massachusetts. In 1796, he married Ruth Haskins of Boston, and after returning with her to his rural home he wrote in his Journal : "We are poor and cold. and have little meal, and little wood, and little meat; but, thank God, courage enough." In 1799, he was invited to preach before the First Church in Boston, and soon after be-came its minister. The church stood on Cornhill, now Washington Street, where the Rogers Building stands, not far from the corner of State Street. The old gambrel-roofed parish house stood in the centre of nearly an acre of land on Summer Street, where is now the corner of Chauncey Street. In this house Ralph Waldo Emerson, the second of five boys was born on the 25th of May, 1803.

This New England home had all the characteristics of the best in old England. It was a home of plain living and high thinking, in which intelligence, courage, thrift, and industry were mellowed and sanctified by deep religious conviction. These influences remind us of those which surrounded Burns and Carlyle in Scotland, and Coleridge and Wordsworth in England, and it is not surprising therefore that these men were those whom Emerson came to love with magnanimity and praise with eloquence. The characteristics which the young lad early revealed were those which gave him distinction in later life. The child was father of the man, although, as in the case of Wordsworth, his genius matured somewhat slowly. In his early days he was thus saved from becoming either a prig or a prodigy. Early sorrow may have been an important element in the forming of his character, as it was in that of Coleridge. His father died in 1811, and the family many times in the following years had the experience which the father and mother had in the early days at Harvard, Massachusetts,—they were "poor and cold, with little meal, and little wood, and little meat; but, thank God, courage enough." The courage and self-denial of the noble mother and gracious aunt enabled the children to be fed, clothed, and liberally educated. The family removed to Beacon Street, and lived where the Athenæum now stands. Here they kept boarders, the mother doing the housework and the aunt Mary consoling them with stories of heroic endurance; "scorn trifles, lift your aims," was the tone of her discourse. It was such experiences, we must believe, that developed, perhaps too early, the self-sufficing power of solitude, and made the lad shy and isolated, a creature "moving about in worlds not realized." One of his school-fellows describes him when at the Latin School as "a spiritual looking boy in blue nankeen, whose image more than any other is still deeply stamped upon my mind, as I then saw him and loved him, I knew not why, and thought him so angelic and remarkable."

Barrie says, "It does not matter much what happens to one after he is twelve." The elements which went into Emerson's early life of hardship in the home, the school, and the university were evolved into these noble utterances on Love, Friendship, Manners, Heroism, etc., which have formed, sustained, and consoled so many in England and America. Speaking of his own home influences, Carlyle says: "Misery was early training the rugged boy into a Stoic, that one day he might be the assurance of a Scottish man. Ours was not a joyful life, yet a safe and quiet one; above most others, or any other I have witnessed, a wholesome one. We were taciturn, rather than talkative, but if little was said, that little had generally a meaning." Emerson says: "What is the hoop that holds them stanch? It is the iron band of poverty, of necessity, of austerity, which, excluding them from the sensual enjoyments which make other boys too early old, has directed their activity into safe and right channels, and made them, despite themselves, reverers of the grand, the beautiful, and the good. The angels that

dwell with them, and are weaving laurels of life upon
their youthful brows, are Toil and Want, and Truth and
Mutual Faith."

Emerson was able to enter college on receiving the
appointment of President's freshman; this position, and
that of waiter at Commons, secured for him his room
free of charge and three-fourths of his board. At the
same time his brother William, who was teaching in
Maine, was contributing to the support of the family.
Later, Emerson took the Boylston prize for declamation;
this he carried home to his mother with the hope that
it would buy her a new shawl, but he was disappointed,
as it went to pay the baker's bill. Like many others,
Emerson thought that his college course did but little for
him; the subjects and methods were not to his taste. In
one of his later journals he speaks of the "instinct which
leads a youth who has no faculty for mathematics, and
weeps over the impossible Analytical Geometry, to console his defeats with Chaucer and Montaigne, with Plutarch and Plato at night. The boy at college apologizes
for not learning the tutor's tasks : but stronger nature gives
him Otway and Massinger to read, or betrays him into a
stroll to Mount Auburn in study hours." This reminds
us of the criticisms of Wordsworth and Tennyson on the
spirit at Cambridge in their day. Wordsworth, deploring
the absence of simplicity and dignity, says :—

> Mine eyes were crossed by butterflies, ears vexed
> By chattering popinjays; the inner heart
> Seemed trivial, and the impresses without
> Of a too gaudy region.

Therefore he sought the companionship of the great teachers :—

> Beside the pleasant mill of Trompington
> I laughed with Chaucer in the hawthorn shade;
> Heard him, while birds were warbling, tell his tales
> Of amorous passion. And that gentle Bard,
> Chosen of the Muses for their Page of State,
> Sweet Spencer . . . .
> I called him Brother, Englishman, and Friend.

Tennyson in a poem in the "Memoir" says:—

> Your doctors, and your proctors, and your deans,
> Shall not avail you when the Daybeam sports
> New risen o'er awakened Albion. No!
> . . . Because your manner sorts
> Not with this age wherefrom ye stand apart,
> Because the lips of little children preach
> Against you, you that do profess to teach,
> And teach us nothing, feeding not the heart.

Emerson on leaving college followed teaching for a time, but that occupation did not satisfy him, although he was successful in the very line in which he thought college teaching defective, that of inspiration. He gave his pupils selections from the great poets to read at home, and then made them subjects of discussion in the class. He believed in mere literature. Although he could not yet hitch his wagon to a star, he kept the star in view, and it soon opened up its soul to him, for he afterward said of this time: "I was already writing every night in my chamber, my first thoughts on morals and the beautiful laws of Compensation and of individual genius, which to observe and illustrate have given sweetness to many hours

of my life." Assuredly he was beginning to reveal the
one great gift, the vital soul of the poet and philosopher;
for at this time he wrote, on returning to his home in
Canterbury Lane, Roxbury, perhaps as a farewell to the
drudgery of teaching where he says, "we clung to the safe
and cold details of languages, geography, arithmetic, and
chemistry":—

> O when I am safe in my sylvan home,
> I tread on the pride of Greece and Rome;
> And when I am stretched beneath the pines,
> When the evening star so holy shines,
> I laugh at the love and the pride of man,
> At the sophist schools, and the learned clan;
> For what are they all, in their high conceit,
> When man in the bush with God may meet?

So he gave up teaching and prepared to take his place
in the profession which so many of his ancestors had
adorned.

The atmosphere of Boston and Cambridge was the
bracing one of civil and religious freedom, and the lamp
of the scholar was kept burning. Dr. Holmes says: "We
may count as symbols of the three hills of this 'darling
town of ours,' as Emerson called it, and say that each
had its beacon; civil liberty lighted the torch on one
summit, religious freedom caught the flame and shone
from the second, and the lamp of the scholar burned
steadily on the third. . . . The two high-caste religions of
that day were white-handed Unitarianism, and ruffled-
shirt Episcopalianism. What called itself 'Society' was
chiefly distributed between them." But after a time the
young idealist found the materialism of creed and ob-

servance even in the Unitarian Second Church a positive
impediment to the highest spiritual growth. He said
"Forms are as essential as bodies, but to exalt particular
forms, to adhere to one form a moment after it is outgrown is unreasonable, and it is alien to the spirit of
Christ." His teaching seemed to be that as soon as a
form became instinct with spirit it could be discarded;
the lower was implied in the higher. We are not surprised at this from one whose teachers had been Plato,
Montaigne, Plutarch, and Shakespeare,—one so beautiful
in spirit and so sincere in thought and action. While
he was deciding upon his duty to the church he married
Miss Ellen Louise Tucker, a woman of remarkable beauty,
grace, and buoyancy of spirit. Of her he wrote:—

> This morn I climbed the misty hill,
> And roamed the pastures through;
> How danced thy form before my path,
> Amid the deep-eyed dew!
>
> When the redbird spread his sable wing,
> And showed his side of flame;
> When the rosebud ripened to the rose
> In both I read thy name.

Her health, never robust, soon began to decline, and
in February, 1831, she who had been to him a bright
revelation of the best nature of woman passed "'to where
beyond these voices there is peace." In the following year
he ceased his ministrations in the church. The bereave-
ment and the struggle had cost him dearly in the matter
of physical strength, and to seek restoration he planned
his first visit to Europe.

At the time of Emerson's visit to Europe, the old order which had prevailed in the last century in politics, art, and religion, was giving way to the new. The elements in the great revolutionary movement which was making for the new spirit were the democratic in Burns, Cowper, and Wordsworth; the transcendental in Hegel, Goethe and Coleridge; the mediæval, which in Scott took the direction of art, and in Newman, religion; while the revolutionary reaction in Byron and Shelley, and the scientific attitude in Lyell and Darwin were startling the world. Lowell says: "To what end visit Europe, if people carry with them their old parochial horizon? . . . The wise man travels to discover himself." That Emerson was wise is seen by the fact that the men whom he sought and by whom he was revealed to himself were Mill, Landor, Coleridge, Wordsworth, and Carlyle, although he visited Naples, Rome, and Paris. His meeting with Carlyle was the most significant perhaps of all, in that it gave us the incomparable correspondence between the two men during a period of forty years. He found Carlyle in the wilds of Craigenputtock, that "Solitude almost Druidical."

Of this visit Carlyle writes: "He seemed to be one of the most loveable creatures in himself we had ever looked on. He stayed till next day with us, and talked and heard talk to his heart's content, and left us all really sad to part with him. Jane says that it is the first journey since Noah's Deluge undertaken to Craigenputtock for such a purpose." Emerson says of this pilgrimage: "A white day in my years, I found the youth I sought in Scotland—and good and wise and pleasant he seems to me.

. . . I never saw more amiableness than in his countenance."

On arriving at Liverpool, ready for the return voyage,
he wrote in his journal, September 1, 1833: "I thank God
who has led me through this European scene—this last
schoolroom in which He has pleased to instruct me—
in safety and pleasure; and has brought me to the shore,
and to the ship that steers westward. He has shown me
the men I wished to see, Landor, Coleridge, Carlyle,
Wordsworth; He has thereby comforted and confirmed
me in my convictions. Many things I owe to the sight
of these men."

On his return he went to live with his mother in Newton.
He was in great demand as a lecturer; the lecture platform now became his pulpit, and his period of literary
activity began in earnest. His first lectures were upon
scientific subjects, which he treated in a true Words-
worthian fashion, for he believed that the time of which
the poet of Rydal had prophesied in 1800 had come; that
science was ready to put on the form of flesh and blood,
and that it was the duty of the poet "to lend his divine
spirit to aid the transformation and to welcome the Being
thus produced as a dear and genuine inmate of the household of man." Emerson revealed to us the truth of
Wordsworth's famous definition of poetry, "The breath
and finer spirit of all knowledge; the impassioned expression which is in the countenance of all science." Here
we have a poet working under such conditions that he
may speak out, and his utterance was this:—

> "Striving to be man, the worm
> Mounts through all the spires of form."

Emerson's ideas in regard to Evolution are revealed by
Tennyson when he says :—

> The Lord let the house of a brute to the soul of a man
>   And the man said, 'Am I your debtor?'
> And the Lord—'Not yet; but make it as clean as you can,
>   And then I will let you a better.'

He soon passed to the consideration of such literary
and philosophical subjects as Milton, Michael Angelo,
Burke, and others, in which we find the great work of
his life.

After the death of his brilliant brother Edward, com-
memorated in "In Memoriam," the family moved to Concord in October, 1834, and established a home at the
Old Manse. Here was situation beautiful for prospect
for the eye that cannot choose but see. A place where so
many sights reminded him of the early days of the
Revolution must naturally stir the patriot's heart. The
feelings thus aroused were revealed in the address which
he gave on the second centennial anniversary of the
town, September, 1835. On the anniversary of the Concord Fight in April, 1836,

> By the rude bridge that arched the flood,

he read the poem which Dr. Garnett says, "was destined
like the shot he celebrates, to be heard round the world."

A few days after the former address he married Miss
Lydia Jackson, of Plymouth, Massachusetts, and took up
his abode in "the plain, square, wooden house which
sheltered him to the last." In 1836 his brother Charles
died, and he wrote to Carlyle, "I have put so much dependence on his gifts, that we made but one man to-

gether; for I needed never to do what he could do by
noble nature much better than I." In this year was published his first great work, "Nature." This startled and
confused the public, which found Wordsworth too vague
and mystical. Dr. Holmes says, "No writer is more
deeply imbued with the spirit of Wordsworth than Emerson, as we cannot fail to see in turning the pages of
'Nature.'" Emerson was now to repeat the experience of
Wordsworth, and suffer ridicule at the hands of those who
would not give themselves the trouble of comprehending
him. Another startling act of his was to edit Carlyle's
"Sartor Resartus," to which he contributed a Preface.

An event occurred at Cambridge, in August, 1837,
which Lowell says "was without any former parallel in
our literary annals, a scene to be always treasured in
.he memory for its picturesqueness and its inspiration."
This was the address entitled "The American Scholar."
It is Emerson's literary creed, and it sounded the warning which we have been slow to heed. He calls upon "the
sluggard intellect of this continent to look from under its
iron lids and fill the postponed expectations of the world
with something better than the exertions of mechanical
skill." The following year he disturbed the ministers as
much as he had previously the poets and philosophers.
This he did in his address before the senior class in the
Divinity College, Cambridge. Transcendentalism made
its clearest and most emphatic utterance in his lecture,
"The Transcendentalist." In this he said: "What is
properly called Transcendentalism among us is Idealism;
Idealism as it appears in 1842. As thinkers, mankind
have ever divided into two sects—Materialists and

Idealists." He now contributed much prose and verse to
the accredited organ of these Idealists, the *Dial*, and his
associates were Theodore Parker, Alcott, Channing, and
others. He had been casting his poetry in the form of
prose; he now uses the instrument of verse, the various
stops of which he never quite mastered, and yet in many
poems, such as "Threnody," "Walden," "The Rhodora,"
"The Song of Nature," "The Sphinx," we have profound
insight, noble music, impassioned feeling, grace, and
beauty.

In 1841 his first volume of Essays was published. The
first essay was on History, and the last on Art, but perhaps the most inspiring of all was that entitled "The Over
Soul," which might be entitled "Emerson's Vision," or
the "Overflow of Spiritual Imagination." This year
brought affliction to the home. His little boy only five
years old, "that domesticated sunbeam," passed away.
This event is the subject of that lament so full of dignity
and pathos—"Threnody," which Dr. Garnett calls a
Greek funeral monument.

He now began to take an active part in the great questions relating to slavery, as is seen in his address given at
Concord in 1844. This year saw the second series of
Essays published, and two years later his Poems were
brought together in a single volume. In October, 1847,
he sailed for Europe, and during this visit he delivered
many courses of lectures in England and Scotland and
found everywhere enthusiastic listeners. Soon after his
return from England he gathered for publication those
English lectures included in the volume "Representative
Men." His lectures still continued to be a distinct feature

of every Lyceum course, and his impressions of the English people after repeated delivery were collected in 1856, in the volume "English Traits."

From this time Emerson's genius ripened and sweetened, until he "stood on the heights of his life with a glimpse of heights that are higher." In him poetry and philosophy met as they have not in any American, with the possible exception of Hawthorne, and it is not easy to determine where he is most poetic, in his verse or in his prose. He lived close to the soul of things, and his voice was the voice of a prophet. He had all the apparent carelessness of form which we find in Wordsworth, and yet this is the secret of his art—mere spirit, revealing itself with the felicity and power of musical utterance. His interests spanned the total of humanity, and humanity began to see in him one of the far-shining children of men. He did not have to pass unrecognized in his own land as so many great teachers before him had to do. The noble disciples whom he gathered about him, though not always judicious in their praise, were always sincere. The tribute which Lowell pays to his master is as sane as it is graceful: "We look upon him as one of the few men of genius whom our age has produced, and there needs no better proof of it than his masculine faculty of fecundating other minds. Search for his eloquence in his books, and you will miss it; but meanwhile you will find that it has kindled all your thoughts. . . . A diction at once so rich and so homely as his, I know not where to match in these days of writing by the page; it is like homespun cloth of gold. The many cannot miss his meaning, and only the few can find it. It is the open secret of all true genius. It is wholesome to angle in those profound pools, though one be rewarded with nothing more than the leap of a fish that flashes his freckled side in the sun, and as suddenly absconds in the dark and dreamy waters again."

Sainte-Beuve has defined a true classic as "an author who has enriched the human mind, increased its treasure, and caused it to advance a step; who has discovered some moral and not equivocal truth, or revealed some eternal passion in the heart where all seemed known and discovered; who has expressed his thought, observation, or invention, in no matter what form, only provided it is broad and great, refined and sensible, sane and beautiful in itself; who has spoken to all in his own peculiar style, a style which is found to be also that of the whole world, a style new and old, easily contemporary with all time." We should not be unwilling to have Emerson judged by this standard. Like all great writers, Emerson has suffered from the unwise plaudits of the sect and coterie, and the churlish denunciations of the partisan, but he is sure to speak to us who listen, and say with gentle and serene assurance :—

> What is true at last will tell;
> Few at first will place thee well;
> Some too low would have thee shine,
> Some too high—no fault of thine—
>   Hold thine own, and make thy will!
> Year will graze the heel of year,
> But seldom comes the poet here,
>   And the Critic's rarer still.

One may consider it a fortunate event in life to have heard the splendidly fearless, tenderly sympathetic, and eminently just estimate of Emerson by Matthew Arnold, on that evening in the old Tremont Temple, when the eloquent and gracious Wendell Phillips introduced him as "one who would hew to the line no matter in whose face the chips flew." In his noble introduction, after paying tribute to those whose voices haunted the Oxford of his youth,—Newman, Carlyle, and Goethe,—Arnold said: "And beside those voices, there came to us, in that old Oxford time, a voice also from this side of the Atlantic,— a clear and pure voice, which for my ear, at any rate, brought a strain as new and moving, and unforgettable, as the strain of Newman or Carlyle or Goethe. . . . He was your Newman, your man of soul and genius visible to you in the flesh, speaking to your bodily ears, a present object for your heart and imagination. That is surely the most potent of all influences! nothing can come up to it. Emerson is the friend and aider of those who would live in the spirit. . . . As Wordsworth's poetry is, in my judgment, the most important work done in verse, in our language, during the present century, so Emerson's "Essays" are, I think, the most important work done in prose. . . . I figure him to my mind as visible upon earth still, as still standing here by Boston Bay, or at his own Concord, in his habit as he lived, but of heightened stature and shining features, with one hand stretched out towards the East, to our laden and laboring England; the other towards the ever-growing West, to his own dearly loved America—great, intellectual, sensual, avaricious America.

To us he shows for guidance his lucid freedom, his cheerfulness and hope; to you his dignity, delicacy, serenity, elevation."

ANDREW J. GEORGE

CONTENTS

FIRST SERIES

SECOND SERIES

Emerson's Essays

First Series

HISTORY

'There is no great and no small
To the Soul that maketh all:
And where it cometh, all things are;
And it cometh everywhere.

I am owner of the sphere,
Of the seven stars and the solar year,
Of Caesar's hand, and Plato's brain,
Of Lord Christ's heart, and Shakespeare's strain.

THERE is one mind common to all individual men. Every man is an inlet to the same and to all of the same. He that is once admitted to the right of reason is made a freeman of the whole estate. What Plato has thought, he may think; what a saint has felt, he may feel; what at any time has befallen any man, he can understand. Who hath access to this universal mind is a party to all that is or can be done, for this is the only and sovereign agent.

Of the works of this mind history is the record. Its genius is illustrated by the entire series of days. Man

is explicable by nothing less than all his history.
Without hurry, without rest, the human spirit goes
forth from the beginning to embody every faculty,
every thought, every emotion which belongs to it, in
appropriate events. But always the thought is prior
to the fact; all the facts of history preëxist in the
mind as laws. Each law in turn is made by circumstances predominant, and the limits of nature give
power to but one at a time. A man is the whole encyclopædia of facts. The creation of a thousand forests is in one acorn, and Egypt, Greece, Rome, Gaul,
Britain, America, lie folded already in the first man.
Epoch after epoch, camp, kingdom, empire, republic,
democracy, are merely the application of his manifold
spirit to the manifold world.

This human mind wrote history, and this must
read it. The Sphinx must solve her own riddle. If
the whole of history is in one man, it is all to be
explained from individual experience. There is a relation between the hours of our life and the centuries
of time. As the air I breathe is drawn from the great
repositories of nature, as the light on my book is
yielded by a star a hundred millions of miles distant,
as the poise of my body depends on the equilibrium
of centrifugal and centripetal forces, so the hours
should be instructed by the ages and the ages explained by the hours. Of the universal mind each
individual man is one more incarnation. All its properties consist in him. Every step in his private experience flashes a light on what great bodies of men
have done, and the crises of his life refer to national
crises. Every revolution was first a thought in one

man's mind, and when the same thought occurs to another man, it is the key to that era. Every reform was once a private opinion, and when it shall be a private opinion again it will solve the problem of the age. The fact narrated must correspond to something in me to be credible or intelligible. We, as we read, must become Greeks, Romans, Turks, priest and king, martyr and executioner; must fasten these images to some reality in our secret experience, or we shall see nothing, learn nothing, keep nothing. What befell Asdrubal or Cæsar Borgia is as much an illustration of the mind's powers and depravations as what has befallen us. Each new law and political movement has meaning for you. Stand before each of its tablets and say, "Here is one of my coverings; under this fantastic, or odious, or graceful mask did my Proteus nature hide itself." This remedies the defect of our too great nearness to ourselves. This throws our own actions into perspective; and as crabs, goats, scorpions, the balance and the water-pot lose all their meanness when hung as signs in the zodiac, so I can seen my own vices without heat in the distant persons of Solomon, Alcibiades, and Catiline.

It is the universal nature which gives worth to particular men and things. Human life, as containing this, is mysterious and inviolable, and we hedge it round with penalties and laws. All laws derive hence their ultimate reason; all express at last reverence for some command of this supreme, illimitable essence. Property also holds of the soul, covers great spiritual facts, and instinctively we at first hold to it with swords and laws and wide and complex combinations. The obscure consciousness of this fact is the light of all our day, the claim of claims; the plea for education, for justice, for charity; the foundation of friendship and love and of the heroism and grandeur which belong to acts of self-reliance. It is remarkable that involuntarily we always read as superior beings. Universal history, the poets, the romancers, do not in their stateliest pictures,—in the sacerdotal, the imperial palaces, in the triumphs of will or of genius, —anywhere lose our ear, anywhere make us feel that we intrude, that this is for our betters; but rather is it true that in their grandest strokes we feel most at home. All that Shakspeare says of the king, yonder slip of a boy that reads in the corner feels to be true of himself. We sympathize in the great moments of history, in the great discoveries, the great resistances, the great prosperities of men;—because there law was enacted, the sea was searched, the land was found, or the blow was struck, *for us,* as we ourselves in that place would have done or applauded.

So is it in respect to condition and character. We honor the rich because they have externally the freedom, power, and grace which we feel to be proper to man, proper to us. So all that is said of the wise man by stoic or oriental or modern essayist, describes to each reader his own idea, describes his unattained but attainable self. All literature writes the character of the wise man. All books, monuments, pictures, conversation, are portraits in which he finds the lineaments he is forming. The silent and the loud praise him and accost him, and he is stimulated wherever he moves, as by personal allusions. A wise and good soul therefore never needs look for allusions personal and laudatory in discourse. He hears the commendation, not of himself, but, more sweet, of that character he seeks, in every word that is said concerning character, yea further in every fact that befalls,—in the running river and the rustling corn. Praise is looked, homage tendered, love flows, from mute nature, from the mountains and the lights of the firmament.

These hints, dropped as it were from sleep and night, let us use in broad day. The student is to read history actively and not passively; to esteem his own life the text, and books the commentary. Thus compelled, the muse of history will utter oracles, as never to those who do not respect themselves. I have no expectation that any man will read history aright who thinks that what was done in a remote age, by men whose names have resounded far, has any deeper sense than what he is doing to-day.

The world exists for the education of each man. There is no age or state of society or mode of action in history to which there is not somewhat corresponding in his life. Every thing tends in a wonderful manner to abbreviate itself and yield its whole virtue to him. He should see that he can live all history in his own person. He must sit at home with might and main and not suffer himself to be bullied by kings or empires, but know that he is greater than all the geography and all the government of the world; he must transfer the point of view from which history is commonly read, from Rome and Athens and London, to himself, and not deny his conviction that he is the Court, and if England or Egypt have any thing to say to him he will try the case; if not let them forever be silent. He must attain and maintain that lofty sight where facts yield their secret sense, and poetry and annals are alike. The instinct of the mind, the purpose of nature, betrays itself in the use we make of the signal narrations of history. Time dissipates to shining ether the solid angularity of facts. No anchor, no cable, no fences avail to keep a fact a fact. Babylon and Troy, and Tyre, and even early Rome are passing already into fiction. The Garden of Eden, the Sun standing still in Gibeon, is poetry thenceforward to all nations. Who cares what the fact was, when we have thus made a constellation of it to hang in heaven an immortal sign? London and Paris and New York must go the same way. "What is history," said Napoleon, "but a fable agreed upon?" This life of ours is stuck round with Egypt, Greece, Gaul, England, War, Colonization, Church, Court and Commerce, as with so many flowers and wild ornaments grave and gay. I will not make more account of them. I believe in Eternity. I can find Greece, Palestine, Italy, Spain and the Islands, —the genius and creative principle of each and of all eras, in my own mind.

We are always coming up with the facts that have moved us in history in our private experience and verifying them here. All history becomes subjective; in other words there is properly no History, only Biography. Every mind must know the whole lesson for itself,—must go over the whole ground. What it does not see, what it does not live, it will not know. What the former age has epitomized into a formula or rule for manipular convenience, it will lose all the good of

verifying for itself, by means of the wall of that rule.
Somewhere or other, some time or other, it will demand
and find compensation for that loss, by doing the work
itself. Ferguson discovered many things in astronomy
which had long been known. The better for him.

History must be this or it is nothing. Every law
which the state enacts indicates a fact in human nature;
that is all. We must in our own nature see the necessary reason for every fact,—see how it could and must
be. So stand before every public every private work;
before an oration of Burke, before a victory of Napoleon, before a martyrdom of Sir Thomas More, of
Sidney, of Marmaduke Robinson; before a French
Reign of Terror, and a Salem hanging of witches;
before a fanatic Revival and the Animal Magnetism in
Paris, or in Providence. We assume that we under
like influence should be alike affected, and should
achieve the like; and we aim to master intellectually the
steps and reach the same height or the same degradation that our fellow, our proxy has done.

All inquiry into antiquity,—all curiosity respecting
the pyramids, the excavated cities, Stonehenge, the
Ohio Circles, Mexico, Memphis, is the desire to do
away this wild, savage, and preposterous There or
Then, and introduce in its place the Here and the Now.
It is to banish the *not me* and supply the *me*. It is to
abolish difference and restore unity. Belzoni digs and
measures in the mummy-pits and pyramids of Thebes
until he can see the end of the difference between the
monstrous work and himself. When he has satisfied
himself, in general and in detail, that it was made by
such a person as himself, so armed and so motived, and

to ends to which he himself in given circumstances should also have worked, the problem is solved; his thought lives along the whole line of temples and sphinxes and catacombs, passes through them all like a creative soul with satisfaction, and they live again to the mind, or are *now*.

A Gothic cathedral affirms that it was done by us and not done by us. Surely it was by man, but we find it not in our man. But we apply ourselves to the history of its production. We put ourselves into the place and historical state of the builder. We remember the forest dwellers, the first temples, the adherence to the first type, and the decoration of it as the wealth of the nation increased; the value which is given to wood by carving led to the carving over the whole mountain of stone of a cathedral. When we have gone through this process, and added thereto the Catholic Church, its cross, its music, its processions, its Saints' days and image-worship, we have as it were been the man that made the minster; we have seen how it could and must be. We have the sufficient reason.

The difference between men is in their principle of association. Some men classify objects by color and size and other accidents of appearance; others by intrinsic likeness, or by the relation of cause and effect. The progress of the intellect consists in the clearer vision of causes, which overlooks surface differences. To the poet, to the philosopher, to the saint, all things are friendly and sacred, all events profitable all days holy, all men divine. For the eye is fastened on the life, and slights the circumstance. Every chemical substance, every plant, every animal in its growth, teaches the unity of cause, the variety of appearance.

Why, being as we are, surrounded by this all-creating nature, soft and fluid as a cloud or the air, should we be such hard pedants, and magnify a few forms? Why should we make account of time, or of magnitude, or of figure? The soul knows them not, and genius, obeying its law, knows how to play with them as a young child plays with greybeards and in churches. Genius studies the causal thought, and far back in the womb of things sees the rays parting from one orb, that diverge, ere they fall, by infinite diameters. Genius watches the monad through all his masks as he performs the metempsychosis of nature. Genius detects through the fly, through the caterpillar, through the grub, through the egg, the constant type of the individual; through countless individuals the fixed species; through many species the genus; through all genera the steadfast type; through all the kingdoms of organized life the eternal unity. Nature is a mutable cloud which is always and never the same. She casts the same thought into troops of forms, as a poet makes twenty fables with one moral. Beautifully shines a spirit through the bruteness and toughness of matter. Alone omnipotent, it converts all things to its own end. The adamant streams into softest but precise form before it, but whilst I look at it its outline and texture are changed altogether. Nothing is so fleeting as form. Yet never does it quite deny itself. In man we still trace the rudiments or hints of all that we esteem badges of servitude in the lower races; yet in him they enhance his nobleness and grace; as Io, in

Æschylus, transformed to a cow, offends the imagination, but how changed when as Isis in Egypt she meets Jove, a beautiful woman with nothing of the metamorphosis left but the lunar horns as the splendid ornament of her brows.

The identity of history is equally intrinsic, the diversity equally obvious. There is, at the surface, infinite variety of things; at the centre there is simplicity and unity of cause. How many are the acts of one man in which we recognize the same character. See the variety of the sources of our information in respect to the Greek genius. Thus at first we have the *civil history* of that people, as Herodotus, Thucydides, Xenophon, Plutarch have given it—a very sufficient account of what manner of persons they were and what they did. Then we have the same soul expressed for us again in their *literature;* in poems, drama, and philosophy: a very complete form. Then we have it once more in their *architecture*—the purest senuous beauty—the perfect medium never overstepping the limit of charming propriety and grace. Then we have it once more in *sculpture,*—the "tongue on the balance of expression," those forms in every action at every age of life, ranging through all the scale of condition, from god to beast, and never transgressing the ideal serenity, but in convulsive exertion, the liege of order and of law. Thus, of the genius of one remarkable people we have a fourfold representation— the most various expression of one moral thing: and to the senses what more unlike than an ode of Pindar, a marble Centaur, the peristyle of the Parthenon, and the last actions of Phocion? Yet do these varied external expressions proceed from one national mind.

Every one must have observed faces and forms which, without any resembling feature, make a like impression on the beholder. A particular picture or copy of verses, if it do not awaken the same train of images, will yet superinduce the same sentiment as some wild mountain walk, although the resemblance is nowise obvious to the senses, but is occult and out of the reach of the understanding. Nature is an endless combination and repetition of a very few laws. She hums the old well known air through innumerable variations.

Nature is full of a sublime family likeness throughout her works. She delights in startling us with resemblances in the most unexpected quarters. I have seen the head of an old sachem of the forest which at once reminded the eye of a bald mountain summit, and the furrows of the brow suggested the strata of the rock. There are men whose manners have the same essential splendor as the simple and awful sculpture on the friezes of the Parthenon and the remains of the earliest Greek art. And there are compositions of the same strain to be found in the books of all ages. What is Guido's Rospigliosi Aurora but a morning thought, as the horses in it are only a morning cloud. If any one will but take pains to observe the variety of actions to which he is equally inclined in certain moods of mind, and those to which he is averse, he will see how deep is the chain of affinity.

A painter told me that nobody could draw a tree without in some sort becoming a tree; or draw a child by studying the outlines of its form merely,— but, by watching for a time his motions and plays, the painter enters into his nature and can then draw him at will in every attitude. So Roos "entered into the inmost nature of a sheep." I knew a draughtsman employed in a public survey who found that he could not sketch the rocks until their geological structure was first explained to him.

What is to be inferred from these facts but this: that in a certain state of thought is the common origin of very diverse works? It is the spirit and not the fact that is identical. By descending far down into the depths of the soul, and not primarily by a painful acquisition of many manual skills, the artist attains the power of awakening other souls to a given activity.

It has been said that "common souls pay with what they do, nobler souls with that which they are." And why? Because a soul living from a great depth of being, awakens in us by its actions and words, by its very looks and manners, the same power and beauty that a gallery of sculpture or of pictures are wont to animate.

Civil history, natural history, the history of art and the history of literature,—all must be explained from individual history, or must remain words. There is nothing but is related to us, nothing that does not interest us,—kingdom, college, tree, horse, or iron shoe, the roots of all things are in man. It is in the soul that architecture exists. Santa Croce and the Dome of St. Peter's are lame copies after a divine model. Strasburg Cathedral is a material counterpart of the soul of Erwin of Steinbach. The true poem is the poet's mind; the true ship is the ship-builder. In the man, could we lay him open, we should see the reason for the last flourish and tendril of his work, as every spine and tint in the sea-shell preëxist in the secreting organs of the fish. The whole of heraldry and of chivalry is in courtesy. A man of fine manners shall pronounce your name with all the ornament that titles of nobility could ever add.

The trivial experience of every day is always verifying some old prediction to us and converting into things for us also the words and signs which we had heard and seen without heed. Let me add a few examples, such as fall within the scope of every man's observation, of trivial facts which go to illustrate great and conspicuous facts.

A lady with whom I was riding in the forest said to me that the woods always seemed to her *to wait,* as if the genii who inhabited them suspended their deeds until the wayfarer had passed onward. This is precisely the thought which poetry has celebrated in the dance of the fairies, which breaks off on the approach of human feet. The man who has seen the rising moon break out of the clouds at midnight, has been present like an archangel at the creation of light and of the world. I remember that being abroad one summer day in the fields, my companion pointed out to me a broad cloud, which might extend a quarter of a mile parallel to the horizon, quite accurately in the form of a cherub as painted over churches,—a round block in the centre, which it was easy to animate with eyes and mouth, supported on either side by wide stretched symmetrical wings. What appears once in the atmosphere may appear often, and it was undoubtedly the archetype of that familiar ornament. I have seen in the sky a chain of summer lightning which at once revealed to me that the Greeks drew from nature when they painted the thunderbolt in the hand of Jove. I have seen a snowdrift along the sides of the stone wall which obviously gave the idea of the common architectural scroll to abut a tower.

By simply throwing ourselves into new circumstances we do continually invent anew the orders and the ornaments of architecture, as we see how each people merely decorated its primitive abodes. The Doric temple still presents the semblance of the wooden cabin in which the Dorian dwelt. The Chinese pagoda is plainly a Tartar tent. The Indian and Egyptian temples still betray the mounds and subterranean houses of their forefathers. "The custom of making houses and tombs in the living rock" (says Heeren in his Researches on the Ethiopians), "determined very naturally the principal character of the Nubian Egyptian architecture to the colossal form which it assumed. In these caverns already prepared by nature, the eye was accustomed to dwell on huge shapes and masses, so that when art came to the assistance of nature it could not move on a small scale without degrading itself. What would statues of the usual size, or neat porches and wings have been, associated with those gigantic halls before which only Colossi could sit as watchmen or lean on the pillars of the interior?"

The Gothic church plainly originated in a rude adaptation of the forest trees, with all their boughs, to a festal or solemn arcade; as the bands about the cleft pillars still indicate the green withes that tied them. No one can walk in a road cut through pine woods, without being struck with the architectural appearance of the grove, especially in winter, when the barrenness of all other trees shows the low arch of the Saxons. In the woods in a winter afternoon one will see as readily the origin of the stained glass window, with which the Gothic cathedrals are adorned, in the colors of the western sky seen through the bare and crossing branches of the forest. Nor can any lover of nature enter the old piles of Oxford and the English cathedrals, without feeling that the forests overpowered the mind of the builder, and that his chisel, his saw and plane still reproduced its ferns, its spikes of flowers, its locust, its pine, its oak, its fir, its spruce.

The Gothic cathedral is a blossoming in stone subdued by the insatiable demand of harmony in man. The mountain of granite blooms into an eternal flower, with the lightness and delicate finish as well as the aërial proportions and perspective of vegetable beauty.

In like manner all public facts are to be individualized, all private facts are to be generalized. Then at once History becomes fluid and true, and Biography deep and sublime. As the Persian imitated in the slender shafts and capitals of his architecture the stem and flower of the lotus and palm, so the Persian court in its magnificent era never gave over the Nomadism of its barbarous tribes, but travelled from Ecbatana, where the spring was spent, to Susa in summer and to Babylon for the winter.

In the early history of Asia and Africa, Nomadism and Agriculture are the two antagonist facts. The geography of Asia and of Africa necessitated a nomadic life. But the nomads were the terror of all

those whom the soil or the advantages of a market had
induced to build towns.   Agriculture therefore was a
religious injunction, because of the perils of the state
from nomadism.   And in these late and civil countries of England and America the contest of these pro-
pensities still fights out the old battle in each individual.
We are all rovers and all fixtures by turns, and pretty
rapid turns.   The nomads of Africa are constrained
to wander, by the attacks of the gad-fly, which drives
the cattle mad, and so compels the tribe to emigrate
in the rainy season and drive off the cattle to the
higher sandy regions.   The nomads of Asia follow
the pasturage from month to month.   In America and
Europe the nomadism is of trade and curiosity.   A
progress certainly, from the gad-fly of Astaboras to
the Anglo and Italo-mania of Boston Bay.   The difference between men in this respect is the faculty of
rapid domestication, the power to find his chair and
bed everywhere, which one man has and another has
not.   Some men have so much of the Indian left, have
constitutionally such habits of accommodation that at
sea, or in the forest, or in the snow, they sleep as
warm, and dine with as good appetite, and associate as
happily as in their own house.   And to push this old
fact still one degree nearer, we may find it a representative of a permanent fact in human nature.   The intellectual nomadism is the faculty of objectiveness or of
eyes which everywhere feed themselves.   Who hath
such eyes, everywhere falls into easy relations with his
fellow-men.   Every man, every thing is a prize, a
study, a property to him, and this love smooths his
brow, joins him to men, and makes him beautiful and

beloved in their sight. His house is a wagon; he roams through all latitudes as easily as a Calmuc.

Every thing the individual sees without him corresponds to his states of mind, and every thing is in turn intelligible to him, as his onward thinking leads him into the truth to which that fact or series belongs.

The primeval world, the Fore-World, as the Germans say, I can dive to it in myself as well as grope for it with researching fingers in catacombs, libraries, and the broken reliefs and torsos of ruined villas.

What is the foundation of that interest all men feel in Greek history, letters, art and poetry, in all its periods from the heroic or Homeric age down to the domestic life of the Athenians and Spartans, four or five centuries later? This period draws us because we are Greeks. It is a state through which every man in some sort passes. The Grecian state is the era of the bodily nature, the perfection of the senses,—of the spiritual nature unfolded in strict unity with the body. In it existed those human forms which supplied the sculptor with his models of Hercules, Phœbus, and Jove; not like the forms abounding in the streets of modern cities, wherein the face is a confused blur of features, but composed of incorrupt, sharply defined and symmetrical features, whose eye-sockets are so formed that it would be impossible for such eyes to squint and take furtive glances on this side and on that, but they must turn the whole head.

The manners of that period are plain and fierce. The reverence exhibited is for personal qualities; courage, address, self-command, justice, strength, swiftness, a loud voice, a broad chest. Luxury is not known, nor elegance. A sparse population and want make every man his own valet, cook, butcher and soldier, and the habit of supplying his own needs educates the body to wonderful performances. Such are 'the Agamemnon and Diomed of Homer, and not far different is the picture Xenophon gives of himself and his compatriots in the Retreat of the Ten Thousand. "After the army had crossed the river Teleboas in Armenia, there fell much snow, and the troops lay miserably on the ground covered with it. But Xenophon arose naked, and taking an axe, began to split wood; whereupon others rose and did the like." Throughout his army seemed to be a boundless liberty of speech. They quarrel for plunder, they wrangle with the generals on each new order, and Xenophon is as sharp-tongued as any and sharper tongued than most, and so gives as good as he gets. Who does not see that this is a gang of great boys, with such a code of honor and such lax discipline as great boys have?

The costly charm of the ancient tragedy, and indeed of all the old literature, is that the persons speak simply,—speak as persons who have great good sense without knowing it, before yet the reflective habit has become the predominant habit of the mind. Our admiration of the antique is not admiration of the old, but of the natural. The Greeks are not reflective, but perfect in their senses, perfect in their health, with the finest physical organization in the world. Adults acted with the simplicity and grace of boys. They made vases, tragedies and statues, such as healthy senses should—that is, in good taste. Such things have continued to be made in all ages, and are now, wherever a healthy physique exists; but, as a class, from their superior organization, they have surpassed all. They combine the energy of manhood with the engaging unconsciousness of childhood. Our reverence for them is our reverence for childhood. Nobody can reflect upon an unconscious act with regret or contempt. Bard or hero cannot look down on the word or gesture of a child. It is as great as they. The attraction of these manners is that they belong to man, and are known to every man in virtue of his being once a child; besides that there are always individuals who retain these characteristics. A person of childlike genius and inborn energy is still a Greek, and revives our love of the Muse of Hellas. A great boy, a great girl with good sense is a Greek. Beautiful is the love of nature in the Philoctetes. But in reading those fine apostrophes to sleep, to the stars, rocks, mountains, and waves, I feel time passing away as an ebbing sea. I feel the eternity of man, the identity of his thought. The Greek had it seems the same fellow-beings as I. The sun and moon, water and fire, met his heart precisely as they meet mine. Then the vaunted distinction between Greek and English, between Classic and Romantic schools, seems superficial and pedantic. When a thought of Plato becomes a thought to me,—when a truth that fired the soul of Pindar fires mine, time is no more. When I feel that we two meet in a perception, that our two souls are tinged with the same hue, and do as it were run into one, why should I measure degrees of latitude, why should I count Egyptian years?

The student interprets the age of chivalry by his own age of chivalry, and the days of maritime ad-

venture and circumnavigation by quite parallel miniature experiences of his own.   To the sacred history of
the world he has the same key.   When the voice of a
prophet out of the deeps of antiquity merely echoes
to him a sentiment of his infancy, a prayer of his
youth, he then pierces to the truth through all the confusion of tradition and the caricature of institutions.

Rare, extravagant spirits come by us at intervals,
who disclose to us new facts in nature.   I see that
men of God have always from time to time walked
among men and made their commission felt in the
heart and soul of the commonest hearer.   Hence evi-
dently the tripod, the priest, the priestess inspired by
the divine afflatus.

Jesus astonishes and overpowers sensual people.
They cannot unite him to history, or reconcile him with
themselves.   As they come to revere their intuitions
and aspire to live holily, their own piety explains every
fact, every word.

How easily these old worships of Moses, of Zoroaster, of Menu, of Socrates, domesticate themselves
in the mind.   I cannot find any antiquity in them.
They are mine as much as theirs.

Then I have seen the first monks and anchorets,
without crossing seas or centuries.   More than once
some individual has appeared to me with such negligence of labor and such commanding contemplation,
a haughty beneficiary begging in the name of God, as
made good to the nineteenth century Simeon the Styl-
ite, the Thebais, and the first Capuchins.

The priestcraft of the East and West, of the Magian,
Brahmin, Druid, and Inca, is expounded in the individ-

ual's private life. The cramping influence of a hard
formalist on a young child, in repressing his spirits and
courage, paralyzing the understanding, and that without producing indignation, but only fear and obedience,
and even much sympathy with the tyranny,—is a
familiar fact, explained to the child when he becomes a
man, only by seeing that the oppressor of his youth is
himself a child tyrannized over by those names and
words and forms of whose influence he was merely the
organ to the youth. The fact teaches him how Belus
was worshipped and how the Pyramids were built,
better than the discovery by Champollion of the names
of all the workmen and the cost of every tile. He finds
Assyria and the Mounds of Cholula at his door, and
himself has laid the courses.

Again, in that protest which each considerate person makes against the superstition of his times, he repeats step for step the part of old reformers, and in
the search after truth finds, like them, new perils to
virtue. He learns again what moral vigor is needed
to supply the girdle of a superstition. A great licen-
tiousness treads on the heels of a reformation. How
many times in the history of the world has the Luther
of the day had to lament the decay of piety in his
own household. "Doctor," said his wife to Martin
Luther, one day, "how is it that whilst subject to papacy
we prayed so often and with such fervor, whilst now
we pray with the utmost coldness and very seldom?"

The advancing man discovers how deep a property
he hath in literature,—in all fable as well as in all
history. He finds that the poet was no odd fellow
who described strange and impossible situations, but

that universal man wrote by his pen a confession true for one and true for all. His own secret biography he finds in lines wonderfully intelligible to him, dotted down before he was born. One after another he comes up in his private adventures with every fable of Æsop, of Homer, of Hafiz, of Ariosto, of Chaucer, of Scott, and verifies them with his own head and hands.

The beautiful fables of the Greeks, being proper creations of the Imagination and not of the Fancy, are universal verities. What a range of meanings and what perpetual pertinence has the story of Prometheus! Beside its primary value as the first chapter of the history of Europe (the mythology thinly veiling authentic facts, the invention of the mechanic arts and the migration of colonies), it gives the history of religion, with some closeness to the faith of later ages. Prometheus is the Jesus of the old mythology. He is the friend of man; stands between the unjust "justice" of the Eternal Father and the race of mortals, and readily suffers all things on their account. But where it departs from the Calvinistic Christianity and exhibits him as the defier of Jove, it represents a state of mind which readily appears wherever the doctrine of Theism is taught in a crude, objective form, and which seems the self-defence of man against this untruth, namely, a discontent with the believed fact that a God exists, and a feeling that the obligation of reverence is onerous. It would steal if it could the fire of the Creator, and live apart from him and independent of him. The Prometheus Vinctus is the romance of skepticism. Not less true to all time are the details of that stately apologue. Apollo kept the flocks of

Admetus, said the poets. Every man is a divinity in disguise, a god playing the fool. It seems as if heaven had sent its insane angels into our world as to an asylum, and here they will break out in their native music and utter at intervals the words they have heard in heaven; then the mad fit returns and they mope and wallow like dogs. When the gods come among men, they are not known. Jesus was not; Socrates and Shakspeare were not. Antæus was suffocated by the gripe of Hercules, but every time he touched his mother earth his strength was renewed. Man is the broken giant, and in all his weakness both his body and his mind are invigorated by habits of conversation with nature. The power of music, the power of poetry, to unfix and as it were clap wings to all solid nature, interprets the riddle of Orpheus, which was to his childhood an idle tale. The philosophical perception of identity through endless mutations of form makes him know the Proteus. What else am I who laughed or wept yesterday, who slept last night like a corpse, and this morning stood and ran? And what see I on any side but the transmigrations of Proteus? I can symbolize my thought by using the name of any creature, of any fact, because every creature is man agent or patient. Tantalus is but a name for you and me. Tantalus means the impossibility of drinking the waters of thought which are always gleaming and waving within sight of the soul. The transmigration of souls: that too is no fable. I would it were; but men and women are only half human. Every animal of the barn-yard, the field and the forest, of the earth and of the waters that are under the earth, has con-

trived to get a footing and to leave the print of its
features and form in some one or other of these up
right, heaven-facing speakers.   Ah, brother, hold fast
to the man and awe the beast; stop the ebb of thy
soul,—ebbing downward into the forms into whose
habits thou hast now for many years slid.   As near
and proper to us is also that old fable of the Sphinx,
who was said to sit in the road-side and put riddles
to every passenger.   If the man could not answer, she
swallowed him alive.   If he could solve the riddle,
the Sphinx was slain.   What is our life but an endless flight of winged facts or events!   In splendid
variety these changes come, all putting questions to
the human spirit.   Those men who cannot answer by
a superior wisdom these facts or questions of time,
serve them.   Facts encumber them, tyrannize over
them, and make the men of routine, the men of *sense,*
in whom a literal obedience to facts has extinguished
every spark of that light by which man is truly man.
But if the man is true to his better instincts or sentiments, and refuses the dominion of facts, as one that
comes of a higher race; remains fast by the soul and
sees the principle, then the facts fall aptly and supple
into their places; they know their master, and the
meanest of them glorifies him.

See in Goethe's Helena the same desire that every
word should be a thing.   These figures, he would say,
these Chirons, Griffins, Phorkyas, Helen and Leda, are
somewhat, and do exert a specific influence on the mind.
So far then are they eternal entities, as real to-day as
in the first Olympiad.   Much revolving them he writes
out freely his humor, and gives them body to his own

imagination. And although that poem be as vague and fantastic as a dream, yet it is much more attractive than the more regular dramatic pieces of the same author, for the reason that it operates a wonderful relief to the mind from the routine of customary images, —awakens the reader's invention and fancy by the wild freedom of the design, and by the unceasing succession of brisk shocks of surprise.

The universal nature, too strong for the petty nature of the bard, sits on his neck and writes through his hand; so that when he seems to vent a mere caprice and wild romance, the issue is an exact allegory. Hence Plato said that "poets utter great and wise things which they do not themselves understand." All the fictions of the Middle Age explain themselves as a masked or frolic expression of that which in grave earnest the mind of that period toiled to achieve. Magic and all that is ascribed to it is manifestly a deep presentiment of the powers of science. The shoes of swiftness, the sword of sharpness, the power of subduing the elements, of using the secret virtues of minerals, of understanding the voices of birds, are the obscure efforts of the mind in a right direction. The preternatural prowess of the hero, the gift of perpetual youth, and the like, are alike the endeavor of the human spirit "to bend the shows of things to the desires of the mind."

In Perceforest and Amadis de Gaul a garland and a rose bloom on the head of her who is faithful, and fade on the brow of the inconstant. In the story of the Boy and the Mantle even a mature reader may be surprised with a glow of virtuous pleasure at the triumph of the gentle Genelas; and indeed all the postulates of elfin annals, that the fairies do not like to be named; that their gifts are capricious and not to be trusted; that who seeks a treasure must not speak; and the like I find true in Concord, however they might be in Cornwall or Bretagne.

Is it otherwise in the newest romance? I read the Bride of Lammermoor. Sir William Ashton is a mask for a vulgar temptation, Ravenswood Castle a fine name for proud poverty, and the foreign mission of state only a Bunyan disguise for honest industry. We may all shoot a wild bull that would toss the good and beautiful, by fighting down the unjust and sensual. Lucy Ashton is another name for fidelity, which is always beautiful and always liable to calamity in this world.

But along with the civil and metaphysical history of man, another history goes daily forward,—that of the external world,—in which he is not less strictly implicated. He is the compend of time; he is also the correlative of nature. The power of man consists in the multitude of his affinities, in the fact that his life is intertwined with the whole chain of organic and inorganic being. In the age of the Cæsars out from the Forum at Rome proceeded the great highways north, south, east, west, to the centre of every province of the empire, making each market-town of Persia, Spain, and Britain pervious to the soldiers of the capital: so out of the human heart go as it were highways to the heart of every object in nature, to reduce it under the dominion of man. A man is a bundle of relations, a knot of roots, whose flower and fruitage is the world. All his faculties refer to natures out of him and pre-

dict the world he is to inhabit, as the fins of the fish
foreshow that water exists, or the wings of an eagle
in the egg presuppose air. Insulate and you destroy
him. He cannot live without a world. Put Napoleon
in an island prison, let his faculties find no men to act
on, no Alps to climb, no stake to play for, and he would
beat the air, and appear stupid. Transport him to large
countries, dense population, complex interests and antagonist power, and you shall see that the man Napoleon, bounded that is by such a profile and outline, is not
the virtual Napoleon. This is but Talbot's shadow;

> His substance is not here.
> For what you see is but the smaller part
> And least proportion of humanity;
> But were the whole frame here,
> It is of such a spacious, lofty pitch,
> Your roof were not sufficient to contain it.
>
> *Henry VI.*

Columbus needs a planet to shape his course upon.
Newton and Laplace need myriads of age and thick-
strown celestial areas. One may say a gravitating solar
system is already prophesied in the nature of Newton's
mind. Not less does the brain of Davy or of Gay Lus-
sac, from childhood exploring the affinities and repul-
sions of particles, anticipate the laws of organization.
Does not the eye of the human embryo predict the
light? the ear of Handel predict the witchcraft of har-
monic sound? Do not the constructive fingers of
Watt, Fulton, Whittemore, Arkwright, predict the
fusible, hard, and temperable texture of metals, the
properties of stone, water, and wood? the lovely attributes of the maiden child predict the refinements and

decorations of civil society? Here also we are reminded of the action of man on man. A mind might
ponder its thought for ages and not gain so much self-
knowledge as the passion of love shall teach it in a day.
Who knows himself before he has been thrilled with
indignation at an outrage, or has heard an eloquent
tongue, or has shared the throb of thousands in a
national exultation or alarm? No man can antedate
his experience, or guess what faculty or feeling a new
object shall unlock, any more than he can draw to-day
the face of a person whom he shall see to-morrow for
the first time.

I will not go now behind the general statement to
explore the reason of this correspondency. Let it
suffice that in the light of these two facts, namely, that
the mind is One, and that nature is its correlative,
history is to be read and written.

Thus in all ways does the soul concentrate and reproduce its treasures for each pupil, for each new-born
man. He too shall pass through the whole cycle of
experience. He shall collect into a focus the rays of
nature. History no longer shall be a dull book. It
shall walk incarnate in every just and wise man. You
shall not tell me by languages and titles a catalogue
of the volumes you have read. You shall make me
feel what periods you have lived. A man shall be the
Temple of Fame. He shall walk, as the poets have
described that goddess, in a robe painted all over with
wonderful events and experiences;—his own form and
features by their exalted intelligence shall be that varie-
gated vest. I shall find in him the Foreworld; in his
childhood the Age of Gold, the Apples of Knowledge,

the Argonautic Expedition, the calling of Abraham, the
building of the Temple, the Advent of Christ, Dark
Ages, the Revival of Letters, the Reformation, the discovery of new lands, the opening of new sciences and
new regions in man. He shall be the priest of Pan,
and bring with him into humble cottages the blessings
of the morning stars, and all the recorded benefits of
heaven and earth.

Is there somewhat overweening in this claim? Then
I reject all I have written, for what is the use of pre-
tending to know what we know not? But it is the fault
of our rhetoric that we cannot strongly state one fact
without seeming to belie some other. I hold our actual
knowledge very cheap. Hear the rats in the wall,
see the lizard on the fence, the fungus under foot, the
lichen on the log. What do I know sympathetically,
morally, of either of these worlds of life? As long as
the Caucasian man,—perhaps longer,—these creatures
have kept their counsel beside him, and there is no
record of any word or sign that has passed from one
to the other. Nay, what does history yet record of the
metaphysical annals of man? What light does it shed
on those mysteries which we hide under the names
Death and **Immortality**? Yet every history should be
written in a wisdom which divined the range of our
affinities and looked at facts as symbols. I am
ashamed to see what a shallow village tale our so-
called History is. How many times we must say
Rome, and Paris, and Constantinople! What does
Rome know of rat and lizard? What are Olympiads
and Consulates to these neighboring systems of being?
Nay, what food or experience or succor have they for

the Esquimaux seal-hunter, for the Kanaka in his canoe, for the fisherman, the stevedore, the porter?

Broader and deeper we must write our annals,—from an ethical reformation, from an influx of the ever new, ever sanative conscience,—if we would trulier express our central and wide-related nature, instead of this old chronology of selfishness and pride to which we have too long lent our eyes. Already that day exists for us, shines in on us at unawares, but the path of science and of letters is not the way into nature, but from it, rather. The idiot, the Indian, the child and unschooled farmer's boy come much nearer to these—understand them better than the dissector or the antiquary.

SELF-RELIANCE

Ne te quæsiveris extra.

Man is his own star; and the soul that can
Render an honest and a perfect man,
Commands all light, all influence, all fate;
Nothing to him falls early or too late.
Our acts our angels are, or good or ill,
Our fatal shadows that walk by us still.

Epilogue to Beaumont and Fletcher's Honest Man's Fortune.

Cast the bantling on the rocks,
Suckle him with the she-wolf's teat,
Wintered with the hawk and fox,
Power and speed be hands and feet.

I READ the other day some verses written by an eminent painter which were original and not conventional. Always the soul hears an admonition in such lines, let the subject be what it may. The sentiment they instil is of more value than any thought they may contain. To believe your own thought, to believe that what is true for you in your private heart is true for all men,—that is genius. Speak your latent conviction, and it shall be universal sense; for always the inmost becomes the outmost—and our first thought is rendered back to us by the trumpets of the Last Judgment. Familiar as the voice of the mind is to each, the highest merit we ascribe to Moses, Plato and Milton is that they set at naught books and traditions, and spoke not what men, but what they thought. A man should learn to detect and watch that gleam of light which flashes across his mind from within, more than the lustre of the firmament of bards and sages. Yet he dismisses without notice his thought, because it is his. In every work of genius we recognize our own rejected thoughts; they come back to us with a certain alienated majesty. Great works of art have no more affecting lesson for us than this. They teach us to abide by our spontaneous impression with good-humored inflexibility then most when the whole cry of voices is on the other side. Else to-morrow a stranger will say with masterly good sense precisely what we have thought and felt all the time, and we shall be forced to take with shame our own opinion from another.

There is a time in every man's education when he arrives at the conviction that envy is ignorance; that imitation is suicide; that he must take himself for better for worse as his portion; that though the wide universe is full of good, no kernel of nourishing corn can come to him but through his toil bestowed on that plot of ground which is given to him to till. The power which resides in him is new in nature, and none but he knows what that is which he can do, nor does he know until he has tried. Not for nothing one face, one character, one fact, makes much impression on him, and another none. It is not without preëstablished harmony, this sculpture in the memory. The eye was

placed where one ray should fall, that it might testify
of that particular ray.   Bravely let him speak the utmost syllable of his confession.   We but half express
ourselves, and are ashamed of that divine idea which
each of us represents.   It may be safely trusted as pro-
portionate and of good issues, so it be faithfully imparted, but God will not have his work made manifest
by cowards.   It needs a divine man to exhibit anything
divine.   A man is relieved and gay when he has put
his heart into his work and done his best; but what he
has said or done otherwise shall give him no peace.   It
is a deliverance which does not deliver.   In the attempt
his genius deserts him; no muse befriends; no invention, no hope.

Trust thyself: every heart vibrates to that iron
string.   Accept the place the divine providence has
found for you, the society of your contemporaries,
the connexion of events.   Great men have always done
so, and confided themselves childlike to the genius of
their age, betraying their perception that the Eternal
was stirring at their heart, working through their
hands, predominating in all their being.   And we are
now men, and must accept in the highest mind the
same transcendent destiny; and not pinched in a corner,
not cowards fleeing before a revolution, but redeemers
and benefactors, pious aspirants to be noble clay under
the Almighty effort let us advance on Chaos and the
Dark.

What pretty oracles nature yields us on this text
in the face and behavior of children, babes, and even
brutes.   That divided and rebel mind, that distrust of
a sentiment because our arithmetic has computed the

strength and means opposed to our purpose, these have not. Their mind being whole, their eye is as yet unconquered, and when we look in their faces, we are disconcerted. Infancy conforms to nobody; all conform to it; so that one babe commonly makes four or five out of the adults who prattle and play to it. So God has armed youth and puberty and manhood no less with its own piquancy and charm, and made it enviable and gracious and its claims not to be put by, if it will stand by itself. Do not think the youth has no force, because he cannot speak to you and me. Hark! in the next room who spoke so clear and emphatic? It seems he knows how to speak to his contemporaries. Good Heaven! it is he! it is that very lump of bashfulness and phlegm which for weeks has done nothing but eat when you were by, and now rolls out these words like bell-strokes. It seems he knows how to speak to his contemporaries. Bashful or bold then, he will know how to make us seniors very unnecessary.

The nonchalance of boys who are sure of a dinner, and would disdain as much as a lord to do or say aught to conciliate one, is the healthy attitude of human nature. How is a boy the master of society; independent, irresponsible, looking out from his corner on such people and facts as pass by, he tries and sentences them on their merits, in the swift, summary way of boys, as good, bad, interesting, silly, eloquent, troublesome. He cumbers himself never about consequences, about interest; he gives an independent, genuine verdict. You must court him; he does not court you. But the man is as it were clapped into jail by his consciousness. As soon as he has once acted or spoken with eclat he is a committed person, watched by the sympathy or the hatred of hundreds, whose affections must now enter into his account. There is no Lethe for this. Ah, that he could pass again into his neutral, godlike independence! Who can thus lose all pledge and, having observed, observe again from the same unaffected, unbiased, unbribable, unaffrighted innocence, must always be formidable, must always engage the poet's and the man's regards. Of such an immortal youth the force would be felt. He would utter opinions on all passing affairs, which being seen to be not private but necessary, would sink like darts into the ear of men and put them in fear.

These are the voices which we hear in solitude, but they grow faint and inaudible as we enter into the world. Society everywhere is in conspiracy against the manhood of every one of its members. Society is a joint-stock company, in which the members agree, for the better securing of his bread to each shareholder, to surrender the liberty and culture of the eater. The virtue in most request is conformity. Self-reliance is its aversion. It loves not realities and creators, but names and customs.

Whoso would be a man, must be a nonconformist. He who would gather immortal palms must not be hindered by the name of goodness, but must explore if it be goodness. Nothing is at last sacred but the integrity of our own mind. Absolve you to yourself, and you shall have the suffrage of the world. I remember an answer which when quite young I was prompted to make to a valued adviser who was wont to importune me with the dear old doctrines of the church. On my

saying, What have I to do with the sacredness of traditions, if I live wholly from within? my friend suggested,—"But these impulses may be from below, not
from above." I replied, "They do not seem to me to
be such; but if I am the devil's child, I will live then
from the devil." No law can be sacred to me but that
of my nature. Good and bad are but names very readily transferable to that or this; the only right is what
is after my constitution; the only wrong what is against
it. A man is to carry himself in the presence of all
opposition as if every thing were titular and ephemeral
but he. I am ashamed to think how easily we capitulate
to badges and names, to large societies and dead institutions. Every decent and well-spoken individual affects and sways me more than is right. I ought to go
upright and vital, and speak the rude truth in all ways.
If malice and vanity wear the coat of philanthropy,
shall that pass? If an angry bigot assumes this bountiful cause of Abolition, and comes to me with his last
news from Barbadoes, why should I not say to him,
"Go love thy infant; love thy wood-chopper; be good-
natured and modest; have that grace; and never varnish
your hard, uncharitable ambition with this incredible
tenderness for black folk a thousand miles off. Thy
love afar is spite at home." Rough and graceless
would be such greeting, but truth is handsomer than
the affectation of love. Your goodness must have some
edge to it,—else it is none. The doctrine of hatred
must be preached, as the counteraction of the doctrine
of love, when that pules and whines. I shun father
and mother and wife and brother when my genius calls
me. I would write on the lintels of the door-post,

Whim. I hope it is somewhat better than whim at last, but we cannot spend the day in explanation. Expect me not to show cause why I seek or why I exclude company. Then, again, do not tell me, as a good man did to-day, of my obligation to put all poor men in good situations. Are they *my* poor? I tell thee, thou foolish philanthropist, that I grudge the dolalr, the dime, the cent I give to such men as do not belong to me and to whom I do not belong. There is a class of persons to whom by all spiritual affinity I am bought and sold; for them I will go to prison if need be; but your miscellaneous popular charities; the education at college of fools; the building of meeting-houses to the vain end to which many now stand; alms to sots, and the thousandfold Relief Societies;—though I confess with shame I sometimes succumb and give the dollar, it is a wicked dollar, which by-and-by I shall have the manhood to withhold.

Virtues, are, in the popular estimate, rather the exception than the rule. There is the man *and* his virtues. Men do what is called a good action, as some piece of courage or charity, much as they would pay a fine in expiation of daily non-appearance on parade. Their works are done as an apology or extenuation of their living in the world,—as invalids and the insane pay a high board. Their virtues are penances. I do not wish to expiate, but to live. My life is not an apology, but a life. It is for itself and not for a spectacle. I much prefer that it should be of a lower strain, so it be genuine and equal, than that it should be glittering and unsteady. I wish it to be sound and sweet, and not to need diet and bleeding. My life should be unique; it should be an alms, a battle, a conquest, a medicine. I ask primary evidence that you are a man, and refuse this appeal from the man to his actions. I know that for myself it makes no difference whether I do or forbear those actions which are reckoned excellent. I cannot consent to pay for a privilege where I have intrinsic right. Few and mean as my gifts may be, I actually am, and do not need for my own assurance or the assurance of my fellows any secondary testimony.

What I must do is all that concerns me, not what the people think. This rule, equally arduous in actual and in intellectual life, may serve for the whole distinction between greatness and meanness. It is the harder because you will always find those who think they know what is your duty better than you know it. It is easy in the world to live after the world's opinion; it is easy in solitude to live after our own; but the great man is he who in the midst of the crowd keeps with perfect sweetness the independence of solitude.

The objection to conforming to usages that have become dead to you is that it scatters your force. It loses your time and blurs the impression of your character. If you maintain a dead church, contribute to a dead Bible Society, vote with a great party either for the Government or against it, spread your table like base housekeepers,—under all these screens I have difficulty to detect the precise man you are. And of course so much force is withdrawn from your proper life. But do your thing, and I shall know you. Do your work, and you shall reinforce yourself. A man must consider

what a blindman's-buff is this game of conformity.
If I know your sect I anticipate your argument.   I
hear a preacher announce for his text and topic the expediency of one of the institutions of his church.   Do I
not know beforehand that not possibly can he say a new
and spontaneous word?   Do I not know that with all
this ostentation of examining the grounds of the institution he will do no such thing?   Do I not know that
he is pledged to himself not to look but at one side, the
permitted side, not as a man, but as a parish minister?
He is a retained attorney, and these airs of the bench
are the emptiest affectation.   Well, most men have
bound their eyes with one or another handkerchief, and
attached themselves to some one of these communities
of opinion.   This conformity makes them not false in
a few particulars, authors of a few lies, but false in all
particulars.   Their every truth is not quite true.
Their two is not the real two, their four not the real
four: so that every word they say chagrins us and we
know not where to begin to set them right.   Meantime
nature is not slow to equip us in the prison-uniform of
the party to which we adhere.   We come to wear one
cut of face and figure, and acquire by degrees the
gentlest asinine expression.   There is a mortifying experience in particular, which does not fail to wreak
itself also in the general history; I mean "the foolish
face of praise," the forced smile which we put on in
company where we do not feel at ease, in answer to
conversation which does not interest us.   The muscles,
not spontaneously moved but moved by a low usurping
wilfulness, grow tight about the outline of the face, and

make the most disagreeable sensation; a sensation of rebuke and warning which no brave young man will suffer twice.

For non-conformity the world whips you with its displeasure. And therefore a man must know how to estimate a sour face. The bystanders look askance on him in the public street or in the friend's parlor. If this aversation had its origin in contempt and resistance like his own he might well go home with a sad countenance; but the sour faces of the multitude, like their sweet faces, have no deep cause—disguise no god, but are put on and off as the wind blows and a newspaper directs. Yet is the discontent of the multitude more formidable than that of the senate and the college. It is easy enough for a firm man who knows the world to brook the rage of the cultivated classes. Their rage is decorous and prudent, for they are timid, as being very vulnerable themselves. But when to their feminine rage the indignation of the people is added, when the ignorant and the poor are aroused, when the unintelligent brute force that lies at the bottom of society is made to growl and mow, it needs the habit of magnanimity and religion to treat it godlike as a trifle of no concernment.

The other terror that scares us from self-trust is our consistency; a reverence for our past act or word because the eyes of others have no other data for computing our orbit than our past acts, and we are loath to disappoint them.

But why should you keep your head over your shoulder? Why drag about this monstrous corpse of your memory, lest you contradict somewhat you have stated in this or that public place? Suppose you should contradict yourself; what then? It seems to be a rule of wisdom never to rely on your memory alone, scarcely even in acts of pure memory, but to bring the past for judgment into the thousand-eyed present, and live ever in a new day. Trust your emotion. In your metaphysics you have denied personality to the Deity, yet when the devout motions of the soul come, yield to them heart and life, though they should clothe God with shape and color. Leave your theory, as Joseph his coat in the hand of the harlot, and flee.

A foolish consistency is the hobgoblin of little minds, adored by little statesmen and philosophers and divines. With consistency a great soul has simply nothing to do. He may as well concern himself with his shadow on the wall. Out upon your guarded lips! Sew them up with packthread, do. Else if you would be a man speak what you think to-day in words as hard as cannon balls, and to-morrow speak what to-morrow thinks in hard words again, though it contradict every thing you said to-day. Ah, then, exclaim the aged ladies, you shall be sure to be misunderstood! Misunderstood! It is a right fool's word. Is it so bad then to be misunderstood? Pythagoras was misunderstood, and Socrates, and Jesus, and Luther, and Copernicus, and Galileo, and Newton, and every pure and wise spirit that ever took flesh. To be great is to be misunderstood.

I suppose no man can violate his nature. All the sallies of his will are rounded in by the law of his being, as the inequalities of Andes and Himmaleh are insignificant in the curve of the sphere. Nor does it

matter how you gauge and try him. A character is
like an acrostic or Alexandrian stanza;—read it forward, backward, or across, it still spells the same thing.
In this pleasing contrite wood-life which God allows
me, let me record day by day my honest thought without prospect or retrospect, and, I cannot doubt, it will
be found symmetrical, though I mean it not and see it
not. My book should smell of pines and resound with
the hum of insects. The swallow over my window
should interweave that thread or straw he carries in his
bill into my web also. We pass for what we are.
Character teaches above our wills. Men imagine that
they communicate their virtue or vice only by overt actions, and do not see that virtue or vice emit a breath
every moment.

Fear never but you shall be consistent in whatever
variety of actions, so they be each honest and natural
in their hour. For of one will, the actions will be
harmonious, however unlike they seem. These varieties are lost sight of when seen at a little distance, at
a little height of thought. One tendency unites them
all. The voyage of the best ship is a zigzag line of a
hundred tacks. This is only microscopic criticism.
See the line from a sufficient distance, and it straight-
ens itself to the average tendency. Your genuine action will explain itself and will explain your other genuine actions. Your conformity explains nothing.
Act singly, and what you have already done singly will
justify you now. Greatness always appeals to the
future. If I can be great enough now to do right and
scorn eyes, I must have done so much right before as
to defend me now. Be it how it will, do right now.

Always scorn appearances and you always may. The force of character is cumulative. All the foregone days of virtue work their health into this. What makes the majesty of the heroes of the senate and the field, which so fills the imagination? The consciousness of a train of great days and victories behind. There they all stand and shed an united light on the advancing actor. He is attended as by a visible escort of angels to every man's eye. That is it which throws thunder into Chatham's voice, and dignity into Washington's port, and America into Adams's eye. Honor is venerable to us because it is no ephemeris. It is always ancient virtue. We worship it to-day because it is not of to-day. We love it and pay it homage because it is not a trap for our love and homage, but is self-dependent, self-derived, and therefore of an old immaculate pedigree, even if shown in a young person.

I hope in these days we have heard the last of conformity and consistency. Let the words be gazetted and ridiculous henceforward. Instead of the gong for dinner, let us hear a whistle from the Spartan fife. Let us bow and apologize never more. A great man is coming to eat at my house. I do not wish to please him: I wish that he should wish to please me. I will stand here for humanity, and though I would make it kind, I would make it true. Let us affront and reprimand the smooth mediocrity and squalid contentment of the times, and hurl in the face of custom and trade and office, the fact which is the upshot of all history, that there is a great responsible Thinker and Actor moving wherever moves a man; that a true man belongs to no other time or place, but is the centre of

things. Where he is, there is nature. He measures
you and all men and all events. You are constrained
to accept his standard. Ordinarily, every body in society reminds us of somewhat else, or of some other
person. Character, reality, reminds you of nothing
else; it takes place of the whole creation. The man
must be so much that he must make all circumstances
indifferent—put all means into the shade. This all
great men are and do. Every true man is a cause,
a country, and an age; requires infinite spaces and
numbers and time fully to accomplish his thought;—
and posterity seem to follow his steps as a procession.
A man Cæsar is born, and for ages after we have a
Roman Empire. Christ is born, and millions of minds
so grow and cleave to his genius that he is confounded
with virtue and the possible of man. An institution is
the lengthened shadow of one man; as, the Reformation, of Luther; Quakerism, of Fox; Methodism, of
Wesley; Abolition, of Clarkson. Scipio, Milton called
"the height of Rome"; and all history resolves itself
very easily into the biography of a few stout and earnest persons.

Let a man then know his worth, and keep things
under his feet. Let him not peep or steal, or skulk
up and down with the air of a charity-boy, a bas-
tard, or an interloper in the world which exists for
him. But the man in the street, finding no worth
in himself which corresponds to the force which built
a tower or sculptured a marble god, feels poor when
he looks on these. To him a palace, a statue, or a
costly book have an alien and forbidding air, much like
a gay equipage, and seem to say like that, "Who are

you, sir?" Yet they all are his, suitors for his notice, petitioners to his faculties that they will come out and take possession. The picture waits for my verdict; it is not to command me, but I am to settle its claim to praise. That popular fable of the sot who was picked up dead drunk in the street, carried to the duke's house, washed and dressed and laid in the duke's bed, and, on his waking, treated with all obsequious ceremony like the duke, and assured that he had been insane —owes its popularity to the fact that it symbolizes so well the state of man, who is in the world a sort of sot, but now and then wakes up, exercises his reason and finds himself a true prince.

Our reading is mendicant and sycophantic. In history our imagination makes fools of us, plays us false. Kingdom and lordship, power and estate, are a gaudier vocabulary than private John and Edward in a small house and common day's work: but the things of life are the same to both: the sum total of both is the same. Why all this deference to Alfred and Scanderbeg and Gustavus? Suppose they were virtuous; did they wear out virtue? As great a stake depends on your private act to-day as followed their public and renowned steps. When private men shall act with original views, the lustre will be transferred from the actions of kings to those of gentlemen.

The world has indeed been instructed by its kings, who have so magnetized the eyes of nations. It has been taught by this colossal symbol the mutual reverence that is due from man to man. The joyful loyalty with which men have everywhere suffered the king, the noble, or the great proprietor to walk among

them by a law of his own, make his own scale of men
and things and reverse theirs, pay for benefits not with
money but with honor, and represent the Law in his
person, was the hieroglyphic by which they obscurely
signified their consciousness of their own right and
comeliness, the right of every man.

The magnetism which all original action exerts is
explained when we inquire the reason of self-trust
Who is the Trustee? What is the aboriginal Self,
on which a universal reliance may be grounded? What
is the nature and power of that science-baffling star,
without parallax, without calculable elements, which
shoots a ray of beauty even into trivial and impure
actions, if the least mark of independence appear? The
inquiry leads us to that source, at once the essence of
genius, the essence of virtue, and the essence of life,
which we call Spontaneity or Instinct. We denote this
primary wisdom as Intuition, whilst all later teachings
are tuitions. In that deep force, the last fact behind
which analysis cannot go, all things find their common origin. For the sense of being which in calm
hours rises, we know not how, in the soul, is not diverse from things, from space, from light, from time,
from man, but one with them and proceedeth obviously
from the same source whence their life and being also
proceedeth. We first share the life by which things
exist and afterwards see them as appearances in nature
and forget that we have shared their cause. Here is
the fountain of action and the fountain of thought.
Here are the lungs of that inspiration which giveth man
wisdom, of that inspiration of man which cannot be
denied without impiety and atheism. We lie in the lap

of immense intelligence, which makes us organs of its
activity and receivers of its truth.   When we discern
justice, when we discern truth, we do nothing of ourselves, but allow a passage to its beams.   If we ask
whence this comes, if we seek to pry into the soul that
causes—all metaphysics, all philosophy is at fault.   Its
presence or its absence is all we can affirm.   Every man
discerns between the voluntary acts of his mind and
his involuntary preceptions.   And to his involuntary
preceptions he knows a perfect respect is due.   He may
err in the expression of them, but he knows that these
things are so, like day and night, not to be disputed.
All my wilful actions and acquisitions are but roving;
—the most trivial reverie, the faintest native emotion,
are domestic and divine.   Thoughtless people contradict as readily the statement of perceptions as of opinions, or rather much more readily; for they do not distinguish between perception and notion.   They fancy
that I choose to see this or that thing.   But perception
is not whimsical, but fatal.   If I see a trait, my children will see it after me, and in course of time all
mankind,—although it may chance that no one has seen
it before me.   For my perception of it is as much a
fact as the sun.

The relations of the soul to the divine spirit are so
pure that it is profane to seek to interpose helps.   It
must be that when God speaketh he should communicate, not one thing, but all things; should fill the world
with his voice; should scatter forth light, nature, time,
souls, from the centre of the present thought; and new
date and new create the whole.   Whenever a mind is
simple and receives a divine wisdom, then old things

pass away,—means, teachers, texts, temples fall; it lives now, and absorbs past and future into the present hour. All things are made sacred by relation to it,—one thing as much as another. All things are dissolved to their centre by their cause, and in the universal miracle petty and particular miracles disappear. This is and must be. If therefore a man claims to know and speak of God and carries you backward to the phraseology of some old mouldered nation in another country, in another world, believe him not. Is the acorn better than the oak which is its fulness and completion? Is the parent better than the child into whom he has cast his ripened being? Whence then this worship of the past? The centuries are conspirators against the sanity and majesty of the soul. Time and space are but physiological colors which the eye maketh, but the soul is light; where it is, is day; where it was, is night; and history is an impertinence and an injury if it be any thing more than a cheerful apologue or parable of my being and becoming.

Man is timid and apologetic; he is no longer upright; he dares not say "I think," "I am," but quotes some saint or sage. He is ashamed before the blade of grass or the blowing rose. These roses under my window make no reference to former roses or to better ones; they are for what they are; they exist with God to-day. There is no time to them. There is simply the rose; it is perfect in every moment of its existence. Before a leaf-bud has burst, its whole life acts; in the full-blown flower there is no more; in the leafless root there is no less. Its nature is satisfied and it satisfies nature in all moments alike. There is no time to it.

But man postpones or remembers; he does not live in the present, but with reverted eye laments the past, or, heedless of the riches that surround him, stands on tiptoe to foresee the future. He cannot be happy and strong until he too lives with nature in the present, above time.

This should be plain enough. Yet see what strong intellects dare not yet hear God himself unless he speak the phraseology of I know not what David, or Jeremiah, or Paul. We shall not always set so great a price on a few texts, on a few lives. We are like children who repeat by rote the sentences of grandames and tutors, and, as they grow older, of the men of talents and character they chance to see,—painfully recollecting the exact words they spoke; afterwards, when they come into the point of view which those had who uttered these sayings, they understand them and are willing to let the words go; for at any time they can use words as good when occasion comes. So was it with us, so will it be, if we proceed. If we live truly, we shall see truly. It is as easy for the strong man to be strong, as it is for the weak to be weak. When we have new perception, we shall gladly disburthen the memory of its hoarded treasures as old rubbish. When a man lives with God, his voice shall be as sweet as the murmur of the brook and the rustle of the corn.

And now at last the highest truth on this subject remains unsaid; probably cannot be said; for all that we say is the far off remembering of the intuition. That thought, by what I can now nearest approach to say it, is this. When good is near you, when you have life in yourself,—it is not by any known or appointed way; you shall not discern the foot-prints of any other, you shall not see the face of man; you shall not hear any name;—the way, the thought, the good, shall be wholly strange and new. It shall exclude all other being. You take the way from man, not to man. All persons that ever existed are its fugitive ministers. There shall be no fear in it. Fear and hope are alike beneath it. It asks nothing. There is somewhat low even in hope. We are then in vision. There is nothing that can be called gratitude, nor properly joy. The soul is raised over passion. It seeth identity and eternal causation. It is a perceiving that Truth and Right are. Hence it becomes a Tranquillity out of the knowing that all things go well. Vast spaces of nature; the Atlantic Ocean, the South Sea; vast intervals of time, years, centuries, are of no account. This which I think and feel underlay that former state of life and circumstances, as it does underlie my present and will always all circumstances, and what is called life and what is called death.

Life only avails, not the having lived. Power ceases in the instant of repose; it resides in the moment of transition from a past to a new state, in the shooting of the gulf, in the darting to an aim. This one fact the world hates, that the soul *becomes;* for that forever degrades the past; turns all riches to poverty, all reputation to a shame; confounds the saint with the rogue; shoves Jesus and Judas equally aside. Why then did we prate of self-reliance? Inasmuch as the soul is present there will be power not confident but agent. To talk of reliance is a poor external way of speaking. Speak rather of that which relies because it works

and is. Who has more soul than I masters me, though
he should not raise his finger. Round him I must revolve by the gravitation of spirits. Who has less I
rule with like facility. We fancy it rhetoric when we
speak of eminent virtue. We do not yet see that virtue
is Height, and that a man or a company of men, plastic
and permeable to principles, by the law of nature must
overpower and ride all cities, nations, kings, rich men,
poets, who are not.

This is the ultimate fact which we so quickly reach
on this, as on every topic, the resolution of all into
the ever-blessed ONE. Virtue is the governor, the
creator, the reality. All things real are so by so much
virtue as they contain. Hardship, husbandry, hunting,
whaling, war, eloquence, personal weight, are somewhat, and engage my respect as examples of the soul's
presence and impure action. I see the same law working in nature for conservation and growth. The poise
of a planet, the bended tree recovering itself from the
strong wind, the vital resources of every animal and
vegetable, are also demonstrations of the self-sufficing
and therefore self-relying soul. All history, from its
highest to its trivial passages is the various record of
this power.

Thus all concentrates; let us not rove; let us sit at
home with the cause. Let us stun and astonish the intruding rabble of men and books and institutions by a
simple declaration of the divine fact. Bid them take
the shoes from off their feet, for God is here within.
Let our simplicity judge them, and our docility to our
own law demonstrate the poverty of nature and fortune
beside our native riches.

But now we are a mob. Man does not stand in awe of man, nor is the soul admonished to stay at home, to put itself in communication with the internal ocean, but it goes abroad to beg a cup of water of the urns of men. We must go alone. Isolation must precede true society. I like the silent church before the service begins, better than any preaching. How far off, how cool, how chaste the persons look, begirt each one with a precinct or sanctuary. So let us always sit. Why should we assume the faults of our friend, or wife, or father, or child, because they sit around our hearth, or are said to have the same blood? All men have my blood and I have all men's. Not for that will I adopt their petulance or folly, even to the extent of being ashamed of it. But your isolation must not be mechanical, but spiritual, that is, must be elevation. At times the whole world seems to be in conspiracy to importune you with emphatic trifles. Friend, client, child, sickness, fear, want, charity, all knock at once at thy closet door and say, "Come out unto us."—Do not spill thy soul; do not all descend; keep thy state; stay at home in thine own heaven; come not for a moment into their facts, into their hubbub of conflicting appearances, but let in the light of thy law on their confusion. The power men possess to annoy me I give them by a weak curiosity. No man can come near me but through my act. "What we love that we have, but by desire we bereave ourselves of the love."

If we cannot at once rise to the sanctities of obedience and faith, let us at least resist our temptations, let us enter into the state of war and wake Thor and Woden, courage and constancy, in our Saxon breasts.

This is to be done in our smooth times by speaking the truth. Check this lying hospitality and lying affection. Live no longer to the expectation of these deceived and deceiving people with whom we converse. Say to them, O father, O mother, O wife, O brother, O friend, I have lived with you after appearances hitherto. Henceforward I am the truth's. Be it known unto you that henceforward I obey no law less than the eternal law. I will have no covenants but proximities. I shall endeavor to nourish my parents, to support my family, to be the chaste husband of one wife,—but these relations I must fill after a new and unprecedented way. I appeal from your customs. I must be myself. I cannot break myself any longer for you, or you. If you can love me for what I am, we shall be happier. If you cannot, I will still seek to deserve that you should. I must be myself. I will not hide my tastes or aversions. I will so trust that what is deep is holy, that I will do strongly before the sun and moon whatever inly rejoices me and the heart appoints. If you are noble, I will love you; if you are not, I will not hurt you and myself by hypocritical attentions. If you are true, but not in the same truth with me, cleave to your companions; I will seek my own. I do this not selfishly but humbly and truly. It is alike your interest, and mine, and all men's, however long we have dwelt in lies, to live in truth. Does this sound harsh to-day? You will soon love what is dictated by your nature as well as mine, and if we follow the truth it will bring us out safe at last.—But so may you give these friends pain. Yes, but I cannot sell my liberty and my power, to save their sensibility. Besides, all persons have their moments of reason, when they look out into the region of absolute truth; then will they justify me and do the same thing.

The populace think that your rejection of popular standards is a rejection of all standard, and mere antinomianism; and the bold sensualist will use the name of philosophy to gild his crimes. But the law of consciousness abides. There are two confessionals, in one or the other of which we must be shriven. You may fulfil your round of duties by clearing yourself in the *direct* or in the *reflex* way. Consider whether you have satisfied your relations to father, mother, cousin, neighbor, town, cat and dog; whether any of these can upbraid you. But I may also neglect this reflex standard and absolve me to myself. I have my own stern claims and perfect circle. It denies the name of duty to many offices that are called duties. But if I can discharge its debts it enables me to dispense with the popular code. If any one imagines that this law is lax, let him keep its commandment one day.

And truly it demands something godlike in him who has cast off the common motives of humanity and has ventured to trust himself for a task-master. High be his heart, faithful his will, clear his sight, that he may in good earnest be doctrine, society, law, to himself, that a simple purpose may be to him as strong as iron necessity is to others.

If any man consider the present aspects of what is called by distinction *society,* he will see the need of these ethics. The sinew and heart of man seem to be drawn out, and we are become timorous desponding whimperers. We are afraid of truth, afraid of fortune, afraid of death, and afraid of each other. Our age yields no great and perfect persons. We want men and women who shall renovate life and our social state, but we see that most natures are insolvent; cannot satisfy their own wants, have an ambition out of all proportion to their practical force, and so do lean and beg day and night continually. Our housekeeping is mendicant, our arts, our occupations, our marriages, our religion we have not chosen, but society has chosen for us. We are parlor soldiers. The rugged battle of fate, where strength is born, we shun.

If our young men miscarry in their first enterprises they lose all heart. If the young merchant fails, men say he is *ruined*. If the finest genius studies at one of our colleges, and is not installed in an office within one year afterwards, in the cities or suburbs of Boston or New York, it seems to his friends and to himself that he is right in being disheartened and in complaining the rest of his life. A sturdy lad from New Hampshire or Vermont, who in turn tries all the professions, who *teams it, farms it, peddles,* keeps a school, preaches edits a newspaper, goes to Congress, buys a township, and so forth, in successive years, and always like a cat falls on his feet, is worth a hundred of these city dolls. He walks abreast with his days and feels no shame in not "studying a profession," for he does not postpone his life, but lives already. He has not one chance, but a hundred chances. Let a stoic arise who shall reveal the resources of man and tell men they are not leaning willows, but can and must detach themselves; that with the exercise of self-trust, new powers shall appear; that a man is the word made flesh, born to shed healing to the nations, that he should be ashamed of our compassion, and that the moment he acts from himself, tossing the laws, the books, idolatries and customs out of the window,—we pity him no more but thank and revere him;—and that teacher shall restore the life of man to splendor and make his name dear to all History.

It is easy to see that a greater self-reliance—a new respect for the divinity in man—must work a revolution in all the offices and relations of men; in their religion; in their education; in their pursuits; their modes of living; their association; in their property; in their speculative views.

1. In what prayers do men allow themselves! That which they call a holy office is not so much as brave and manly. Prayer looks abroad and asks for some foreign addition to come through some foreign virtue, and loses itself in endless mazes of natural and supernatural, and mediatorial and miraculous. Prayer that craves a particular commodity—anything less than all good, is vicious. Prayer is the contemplation of the facts of life from the highest point of view. It is the soliloquy of a beholding and jubilant soul. It is the spirit of God pronouncing his works good. But prayer as a means to effect a private end is theft and meanness. It supposes dualism and not unity in nature and consciousness. As soon as the man is at one with God, he will not beg. He will then see prayer in all action. The prayer of the farmer kneeling in his field to weed it, the prayer of the rower kneeling with the stroke of his oar, are true prayers heard throughout nature, though for cheap ends. Caratach, in Fletcher's

Bonduca, when admonished to inquire the mind of the god Audate, replies,

> His hidden meaning lies in our endeavors;
> Our valors are our best gods.

Another sort of false prayers are our regrets. Discontent is the want of self-reliance: it is infirmity of will. Regret calamities if you can thereby help the sufferer; if not, attend your own work and already the evil begins to be repaired. Our sympathy is just as base. We come to them who weep foolishly and sit down and cry for company, instead of imparting to them truth and health in rough electric shocks, putting them once more in communication with the soul. The secret of fortune is joy in our hands. Welcome evermore to gods and men is the self-helping man. For him all doors are flung wide Him all tongues greet, all honors crown, all eyes follow with desire. Our love goes out to him and embraces him because he did not need it. We solicitously and apologetically caress and celebrate him because he held on his way and scorned our disapprobation. The gods love him because men hated him. "To the persevering mortal," said Zoroaster, "the blessed Immortals are swift."

As men's prayers are a disease of the will, so are their creeds a disease of the intellect. They say with those foolish Israelites, "Let not God speak to us, lest we die. Speak thou, speak any man with us, and we will obey." Everywhere I am bereaved of meeting God in my brother, because he has shut his own temple doors and recites fables merely of his brother's, or his brother's God. Every new mind is a new classifica-

tion.   If it prove a mind of uncommon activity and
power, a Locke, a Lavoisier, a Hutton, a Bentham, a
Spurzheim, it imposes its classification on other men,
and lo! a new system.   In proportion always to the
depth of the thought, and so to the number of the objects it touches and brings within reach of the pupil, is
his complacency.   But chiefly is this apparent in creeds
and churches, which are also classification of some
powerful mind acting on the great elemental thought
of Duty and man's relation to the Highest.   Such is
Calvinism, Quakerism, Swedenborgianism.   The pupil
takes the same delight in subordinating every thing to
the new terminology that a girl does who has just
learned botany in seeing a new earth and new seasons
thereby.   It will happen for a time that the pupil will
feel a real debt to the teacher—will find his intellectual
power has grown by the study of his writings.   This
will continue until he has exhausted his master's mind.
But in all unbalanced minds the classification is idolized,
passes for the end and not for a speedily exhaustible
means, so that the walls of the system blend to their
eye in the remote horizon with the walls of the universe; the luminaries of heaven seem to them hung on
the arch their master built.   They cannot imagine how
you aliens have any right to see—how you can see;
"It must be somehow that you stole the light from us."
They do not yet perceive that light, unsystematic, in-
domitable, will break into any cabin, even into theirs.
Let them chirp awhile and call it their own.   If they
are honest and do well. presently their neat new pin-
fold will be too strait and low, will crack, will lean.
will rot and vanish, and the immortal light, all young

and joyful, million-orbed, million-colored, will beam
over the universe as on the first morning.

2. It is for want of self-culture that the idol of
Travelling, the idol of Italy, of England, of Egypt,
remains for all educated Americans. They who made
England, Italy, or Greece venerable in the imagination,
did so not by rambling round creation as a moth round
a lamp, but by sticking fast where they were, like an
axis of the earth. In manly hours we feel that duty is
our place and that the merry men of circumstance
should follow as they may. The soul is no traveller :
the wise man stays at home with the soul, and when his
necessities, his duties, on any occasion call him from
his house, or into foreign lands, he is at home still and
is not gadding abroad from himself, and shall make
men sensible by the expression of his countenance that
he goes, the missionary of wisdom and virtue, and
visits cities and men like a sovereign and not like an
interloper or a valet.

I have no churlish objection to the circumnavigation of the globe for the purposes of art, of study, and
benevolence, so that the man is first domesticated, or
does not go abroad with the hope of finding somewhat
greater than he knows. He who travels to be amused
or to get somewhat which he does not carry, travels
away from himself, and grows old even in youth among
old things. In Thebes, in Palmyra, his will and mind
have become old and dilapidated as they. He carries
ruins to ruins.

Travelling is a fool's paradise. We owe to our
first journeys the discovery that place is nothing. At
home I dream that at Naples, at Rome, I can be intoxi-

cated with beauty and lose my sadness. I pack my trunk, embrace my friends, embark on the sea and at last wake up in Naples, and there beside me is the stern Fact, the sad self, unrelenting, identical, that I fled from. I seek the Vatican and the palaces. I affect to be intoxicated with sights and suggestions, but I am not intoxicated. My giant goes with me wherever I go.

3. But the rage of travelling is itself only a symptom of a deeper unsoundness affecting the whole intellectual action. The intellect is vagabond, and the universal system of education fosters restlessness. Our minds travel when our bodies are forced to stay at home. We imitate; and what is imitation but the travelling of the mind? Our houses are built with foreign taste; our shelves are garnished with foreign ornaments; our opinions, our tastes, our whole minds, lean, and follow the Past and the Distant, as the eyes of a maid follow her mistress. The soul created the arts wherever they have flourished. It was in his own mind that the artist sought his model. It was an application of his own thought to the thing to be done and the conditions to be observed. And why need we copy the Doric or the Gothic model? Beauty, convenience, grandeur of thought and quaint expression are as near to us as to any, and if the American artist will study with hope and love the precise thing to be done by him, considering the climate, the soil, the length of the day, the wants of the people, the habit and form of the government, he will create a house in which all these will find themselves fitted, and taste and sentiment will be satisfied also.

Insist on yourself; never imitate. Your own gift

you can present every moment with the cumulative
force of a whole life's cultivation; but of the adopted
talent of another you have only an extemporaneous
half possession. That which each can do best, none
but his Maker can teach him. No man yet knows
what it is, nor can, till that person has exhibited it.
Where is the master who could have taught Shakspeare? Where is the master who could have instructed
Franklin, or Washington, or Bacon, or Newton?
Every great man is an unique. The Scipionism of
Scipio is precisely that part he could not borrow. If
anybody will tell me whom the great man imitates
in the original crisis when he performs a great act,
I will tell him who else than himself can teach him.
Shakspeare will never be made by the study of Shakspeare. Do that which is assigned thee and thou canst
not hope too much or dare too much. There is at this
moment, there is for me an utterance bare and grand as
that of the colossal chisel of Phidias, or trowel of the
Egyptians, or the pen of Moses or Dante, but different
from all these. Not possibly will the soul, all rich, all
eloquent, with thousand-cloven tongue, deign to repeat
itself; but if I can hear what these patriarchs say, surely
I can reply to them in the same pitch of voice; for the
ear and the tongue are two organs of one nature.
Dwell up there in the simple and noble regions of thy
life, obey thy heart and thou shalt reproduce the Fore-
world again.

4. As our Religion, our Education, our Art look
abroad, so does our spirit of society. All men plume
themselves on the improvement of society, and no man
improves.

Society never advances. It recedes as fast on one side as it gains on the other. Its progress is only apparent like the workers of a treadmill. It undergoes continual changes; it is barbarous, it is civilized, it is christianized, it is rich, it is scientific; but this change is not amelioration. For every thing that is given something is taken. Society acquires new arts and loses old instincts. What a contrast between the well-clad, reading, writing, thinking American, with a watch, a pencil and a bill of exchange in his pocket, and the naked New Zealander, whose property is a club, a spear, a mat and an undivided twentieth of a shed to sleep under. But compare the health of the two men and you shall see that his aboriginal strength, the white man has lost. If the traveller tell us truly, strike the savage with a broad axe and in a day or two the flesh shall unite and heal as if you struck the blow into soft pitch, and the same blow shall send the white to his grave.

The civilized man has built a coach, but has lost the use of his feet. He is supported on crutches, but lacks so much support of muscle. He has got a fine Geneva watch, but he has lost the skill to tell the hour by the sun. A Greenwich nautical almanac he has, and so being sure of the information when he wants it, the man in the street does not know a star in the sky. The solstice he does not observe; the equinox he knows as little; and the whole bright calendar of the year is without a dial in his mind. His note-books impair his memory; his libraries overload his wit; the insurance-office increases the number of accidents; and it may be a question whether machinery does not encumber;

whether we have not lost by refinement some energy, by a christianity entrenched in establishments and forms some vigor of wild virtue. For every stoic was a stoic; but in Christendom where is the Christian?

There is no more deviation in the moral standard than in the standard of height or bulk. No greater men are now than ever were. A singular equality may be observed between the great men of the first and of the last ages; nor can all the science, art, religion, and philosophy of the nineteenth century avail to educate greater men than Plutarch's heroes, three or four and twenty centuries ago. Not in time is the race progressive. Phocion, Socrates, Anaxagoras, Diogenes, are great men, but they leave no class. He who is really of their class will not be called by their name, but be wholly his own man, and in his turn the founder of a sect. The arts and inventions of each period are only its costumes and do not invigorate men. The harm of the improved machinery may compensate its good. Hudson and Behring accomplished so much in their fishing-boats as to astonish Parry and Franklin, whose equipment exhausted the resources of science and art. Galileo, with an opera-glass, discovered a more splendid series of facts than any one since. Columbus found the New World in an undecked boat. It is curious to see the periodical disuse and perishing of means and machinery which were introduced with loud laudation a few years or centuries before. The great genius returns to essential man. We reckoned the improvements of the art of war among the triumphs of science, and yet Napoleon conquered Europe by the Bivouac, which consisted of falling back on naked valor and disencumbering it of all aids. The Emperor held it impossible to make a perfect army, says Las Cases, "without abolishing our arms, magazines, commissaries and carriages, until, in imitation of the Roman custom, the soldier should receive his supply of corn, grind it in his hand-mill and bake his bread himself."

Society is a wave. The wave moves onward, but the water of which it is composed does not. The same particle does not rise from the valley to the ridge. Its unity is only phenomenal. The persons who make up a nation to-day, die, and their experience with them.

And so the reliance on Property, including the reliance on governments which protect it, is the want of self-reliance. Men have looked away from themselves and at things so long that they have come to esteem what they call the soul's progress, namely, the religious, learned and civil institutions as guards of property, and they deprecate assaults on these, because they feel them to be assaults on property. They measure their esteem of each other by what each has, and not by what each is. But a cultivated man becomes ashamed of his property, ashamed of what he has, out of new respect for his being. Especially he hates what he has if he sees that it is accidental,—came to him by inheritance, or gift, or crime; then he feels that it is not having; it does not belong to him, has no root in him, and merely lies there because no revolution or no robber takes it away. But that which a man is, does always by necessity acquire, and what the man acquires, is permament and living property, which does not wait the beck of rulers, or mobs, or revolutions, or fire, or storm, or bankruptcies, but perpetually renews itself wherever the man is put. "Thy lot or portion of life," said the Caliph Ali, "is seeking after thee; therefore be at rest from seeking after it." Our dependence on these foreign goods leads us to our slavish respect for numbers. The political parties meet in numerous conventions; the greater the concourse and with each new uproar of announcement, The delegation from Essex! The Democrats from New Hampshire! The Whigs of Maine! the young patriot feels himself stronger than before by a new thousand of eyes and arms. In like manner the reformers summon conventions and vote and resolve in multitude. But not so O friends! will the God deign to enter and inhabit you, but by a method precisely the reverse. It is only as a man puts off from himself all external support and stands alone that I see him to be strong and to prevail. He is weaker by every recruit to his banner. Is not a man better than a town? Ask nothing of men, and, in the endless mutation, thou only firm column must presently appear the upholder of all that surrounds thee. He who knows that power is in the soul, that he is weak only because he has looked for good out of him and elsewhere, and, so perceiving, throws himself unhesitatingly on his thought, instantly rights himself, stands in the erect position, commands his limbs, works miracles; just as a man who stands on his feet is stronger than a man who stands on his head.

So use all that is called Fortune. Most men gamble with her, and gain all, and lose all, as her wheel rolls. But do thou leave as unlawful these winnings, and deal with Cause and Effect, the chancellors of God. In the Will work and acquire, and thou hast chained the wheel of Chance, and shalt always drag her after thee. A political victory, a rise of rents, the recovery of your sick or the return of your absent friend, or some other quite external event raises your spirit, and you think good days are preparing for you. Do not believe it. It can never be so. Nothing can bring you peace but yourself. Nothing can bring you peace but the triumph of principles.

COMPENSATION

EVER since I was a boy I have wished to write a discourse on Compensation; for it seemed to me when very young that on this subject Life was ahead of theology and the people knew more than the preachers taught. The documents too from which the doctrine is to be drawn, charmed my fancy by their endless variety, and lay always before me, even in sleep; for they are the tools in our hands, the bread in our basket, the transactions of the street, the farm and the dwelling-house; the greetings, the relations, the debts and credits, the influence of character, the nature and endowment of all men. It seemed to me also that in it might be shown men a ray of divinity, the present action of the Soul of this world, clean from all vestige of tradition; and so the heart of man might be bathed by an inundation of eternal love, conversing with that which he knows was always and always must be, because it really is now. It appeared moreover that if this doctrine could be stated in terms with any resemblance to those bright intuitions in which this truth is sometimes revealed to us, it would be a star in many dark hours and crooked passages in our journey, that would not suffer us to lose our way.

I was lately confirmed in these desires by hearing a

sermon at church.   The preacher, a man esteemed for
his orthodoxy, unfolded in the ordinary manner the
doctrine of the Last Judgment.   He assumed that judgment is not executed in this world; that the wicked are
successful; that the good are miserable; and then urged
from reason and from Scripture a compensation to be
made to both parties in the next life.   No offence appeared to be taken by the congregation at this doctrine.
As far as I could observe when the meeting broke up
they separated without remark on the sermon.

Yet what was the import of this teaching?   What
did the preacher mean by saying that the good are miserable in the present life?   Was it that houses and
lands, offices, wine, horses, dress, luxury, are had by
unprincipled men, whilst the saints are poor and despised; and that a compensation is to be made to these
last hereafter, by giving them the like gratifications another day,—bank-stock and doubloons, venison and
champagne?   This must be the compensation intended
for what else?   Is it that they are to have leave to pray
and praise? to love and serve men?   Why, that they
can do now.   The legitimate inference the disciple
would draw was, "We are to have *such* a good time as
the sinners have now";—or, to push it to its extreme
import,—"You sin now, we shall sin by-and-by; we
would sin now, if we could; not being successful we expect our revenge tomorrow."

The fallacy lay in the immense concession that the
bad are successful; that justice is not done now.   The
blindness of the preacher consisted in deferring to the
base estimate of the market of what constitutes a manly
success, instead of confronting and convicting the world

from the truth; announcing the Presence of the Soul; the omnipotence of the Will; and so establishing the standard of good and ill, of success and falsehood, and summoning the dead to its present tribunal.

I find a similar base tone in the popular religious works of the day and the same doctrines assumed by the literary men when occasionally they treat the related topics. I think that our popular theology has gained in decorum, and not in principle, over the superstitions it has displaced. But men are better than this theology. Their daily life gives it the lie. Every ingenuous and aspiring soul leaves the doctrine behind him in his own experience, and all men feel sometimes the falsehood which they cannot demonstrate. For men are wiser than they know. That which they hear in schools and pulpits without afterthought, if said in conversation would probably be questioned in silence. If a man dogmatize in a mixed company on Providence and the divine laws, he is answered by a silence which conveys well enough to an observer the dissatisfaction of the hearer, but his incapacity to make his own statement.

I shall attempt in this and the following chapter to record some facts that indicate the path of the law of Compensation; happy beyond my expectation if I shall truly draw the smallest arc of this circle.

POLARITY, or action and reaction, we meet in every part of nature; in darkness and light, in heat and cold; in the ebb and flow of waters; in male and female; in the inspiration and expiration of plants and animals; in the systole and diastole of the heart; in the undulations of fluids and of sound; in the centrifugal and centri-

petal gravity; in electricity, galvanism, and chemical affinity.   Superinduce magnetism at one end of a needle,
the opposite magnetism takes place at the other end.   If
the south attracts, the north repels.   To empty here,
you must condense there.   An inevitable dualism bi-
sects nature, so that each thing is a half, and suggests
another thing to make it whole; as, spirit, matter; man,
woman; subjective, objective; in, out; upper, under;
motion, rest; yea, nay.

Whilst the world is thus dual, so is every one of its
parts.   The entire system of things gets represented in
every particle.   There is somewhat that resembles the
ebb and flow of the sea, day and night, man and woman
in a single needle of the pine, in a kernel of corn, in each
individual of every animal tribe.   The reaction, so
grand in the elements, is repeated within these small
boundaries.   For example, in the animal kingdom the
physiologist has observed that no creatures are favorites, but a certain compensation balances every gift and
every defect.   A surplusage given to one part is paid
out of a reduction from another part of the same creature.   If the head and neck are enlarged, the trunk and
extremities are cut short.

The theory of the mechanic forces is another example.   What we gain in power is lost in time, and
the converse.   The periodic or compensating errors of
the planets is another instance.   The influences of climate and soil in political history are another.   The cold
climate invigorates.   The barren soil does not breed fe-
vers, crocodiles, tigers, or scorpions.

The same dualism underlies the nature and condition
of man.   Every excess causes a defect; every defect an

excess. Every sweet hath its sour; every evil its good.
Every faculty which is a receiver of pleasure has an
equal penalty put on its abuse. It is to answer for its
moderation with its life. For every grain of wit there
is a grain of folly. For every thing you have missed,
you have gained something else; and for every thing
you gain, you lose something. If riches increase, they
are increased that use them. If the gatherer gathers
too much, nature takes out of the man what she puts
into his chest; swells the estate, but kills the owner.
Nature hates monopolies and exceptions. The waves
of the sea do not more speedily seek a level from their
loftiest tossing than the varieties of condition-tend to
equalize themselves. There is always some levelling
circumstance that puts down the overbearing, the
strong, the rich, the fortunate, substantially on the same
ground with all others. Is a man too strong and fierce
for society and by temper and position a bad citizen,—
a morose ruffian, with a dash of the pirate in him?—
nature sends him a troop of pretty sons and daughters
who are getting along in the dame's classes at the village school, and love and fear for them smooths his
grim scowl to courtesy. Thus she contrives to intener-
ate the granite and felspar, takes the boar out and puts
the lamb in and keeps her balance true.

The farmer imagines power and place are fine things.
But the President has paid dear for his White House.
It has commonly cost him all his peace, and the best of
his manly attributes. To preserve for a short time so
conspicuous an appearance before the world, he is content to eat dust before the real masters who stand erect
behind the throne. Or do men desire the more substan-

tial and permanent grandeur of genius? Neither has
this an immunity. He who by force of will or of
thought is great and overlooks thousands, has the responsibility of overlooking. With every influx of light
comes new danger. Has he light? he must bear witness to the light, and always outrun that sympathy
which gives him such keen satisfaction, by his fidelity
to new revelations of the incessant soul. He must hate
father and mother, wife and child. Has he all that
the world loves and admires and covets?—he must cast
behind him their admiration and afflict them by faith-
fulness to his truth and become a byword and a hissing.

This Law writes the laws of the cities and nations.
It will not be baulked of its end in the smallest iota. It
is in vain to build or plot or combine against it. Things
refuse to be mismanaged long. *Res nolunt diu male
administrari.* Though no checks to a new evil appear,
the checks exist, and will appear. If the government
is cruel, the governor's life is not safe. If you tax too
high, the revenue will yield nothing. If you make the
criminal code sanguinary, juries will not convict.
Nothing arbitrary, nothing artificial can endure. The
true life and satisfactions of man seem to elude the utmost rigors or felicities of condition and to establish
themselves with great indifferency under all varieties of
circumstance. Under all governments the influence of
character remains the same,—in Turkey and New England about alike. Under the primeval despots of
Egypt, history honestly confesses that man must have
been as free as culture could make him.

These appearances indicate the fact that the universe
is represented in every one of its particles. Every

thing in nature contains all the powers of nature.
Every thing is made of one hidden stuff; as the naturalist sees one type under every metamorphosis, and regards a horse as a running man, a fish as a swimming
man, a bird as a flying man, a tree as a rooted man.
Each new form repeats not only the main character of
the type, but part for part all the details, all the aims,
furtherances, hindrances, energies and whole system of
every other. Every occupation, trade, art, transaction,
is a compend of the world and a correlative of every
other. Each one is an entire emblem of human life;
of its good and ill, its trials, its enemies, its course and
its end. And each one must somehow accommodate
the whole man and recite all his destiny.

The world globes itself in a drop of dew. The mi-
croscope cannot find the animalcule which is less perfect
for being little. Eyes, ears, taste, smell, motion, resistance, appetite, and organs of reproduction that take
hold on eternity,—all find room to consist in the small
creature. So do we put our life into every act. The
true doctrine of omnipresence is that God reappears
with all his parts in every moss and cobweb. The value
of the universe contrives to throw itself into every
point. If the good is there, so is the evil; if the affinity, so the repulsion; if the force, so the limitation.

Thus is the universe alive. All things are moral.
That soul which within us is a sentiment, outside of us
is a law. We feel its inspirations; out there in history
we can see its fatal strength. It is almighty. All nature feels its grasp. "It is in the world, and the world
was made by it." It is eternal but it enacts itself in
time and space. Justice is not postponed. A perfect

equity adjusts its balance in all parts of life. Οἱ κύβοι Διὸς ἀεὶ εὐπίπτουσι. The dice of God are always loaded. The world looks like a multiplication-table, or a mathematical equation, which, turn it how you will, balances itself. Take what figure you will, its exact value, nor more nor less, still returns to you. Every secret is told, every crime is punished, every virtue rewarded, every wrong redressed, in silence and certainty. What we call retribution is the universal necessity by which the whole appears wherever a part appears. If you see smoke, there must be fire. If you see a hand or a limb, you know that the trunk to which it belongs is there behind.

Every act rewards itself, or in other words integrates itself, in a twofold manner: first in the thing, or in real nature; and secondly in the circumstance, or in apparent nature. Men call the circumstance the retribution. The casual retribution is in the thing and is seen by the soul. The retribution in the circumstance is seen by the understanding; it is inseparable from the thing, but is often spread over a long time and so does not become distinct until after many years. The specific stripes may follow late after the offence, but they follow because they accompany it. Crime and punishment grow out of one stem. Punishment is a fruit that unsuspected ripens within the flower of the pleasure which concealed it. Cause and effect, means and ends, seed and fruit, cannot be severed; for the effect already blooms in the cause, the end preexists in the means, the fruit in the seed.

Whilst thus the world will be whole and refuses to

be disparted, we seek to act partially, to sunder, to appropriate; for example,—to gratify the senses we sever the pleasure of the senses from the needs of the character. The ingenuity of man has been dedicated to the solution of one problem,—how to detach the sensual sweet, the sensual strong, the sensual bright, etc., from the moral sweet, the moral deep, the moral fair; that is, again, to contrive to cut clean off this upper surface so thin as to leave it bottomless; to get a *one end,* without an *other end.* The soul says, Eat; the body would feast. The soul says, The man and woman shall be one flesh and one soul; the body would join the flesh only. The soul says, Have dominion over all things to the ends of virtue; the body would have the power over things to its own ends.

The soul strives amain to live and work through all things. It would be the only fact. All things shall be added unto it,—power, pleasure, knowledge, beauty. The particular man aims to be somebody; to set up for himself; to truck and higgle for a private good; and, in particulars, to ride that he may ride; to dress that he may be dressed; to eat that he may eat; and to govern, that he may be seen. Men seek to be great; they would have offices, wealth, power, and fame. They think that to be great is to get only one side of nature,—the sweet, without the other side,—the bitter.

Steadily is this dividing and detaching counteracted. Up to this day it must be owned no projector has had the smallest success. The parted water reunites behind our hand. Pleasure is taken out of pleasant things, profit out of profitable things, power out of strong things, the moment we seek to separate them from the whole. We can no more halve things and get the sensual good, by itself, than we can get an inside that shall have no outside, or a light without a shadow. "Drive out nature with a fork, she comes running back."

Life invests itself with inevitable conditions, which the unwise seek to dodge, which one and another brags that he does not know, brags that they do not touch him;—but the brag is on his lips, the conditions are in his soul. If he escapes them in one part they attack him in another more vital part. If he has escaped them in form and in the appearance, it is because he has resisted his life and fled from himself, and the retribution is so much death. So signal is the failure of all attempts to make this separation of the good from the tax, that the experiment would not be tried,—since to try it is to be mad,—but for the circumstance that when the disease began in the will, of rebellion and separation, the intellect is at once infected, so that the man ceases to see God whole in each object, but is able to see the sensual allurement of an object and not see the sensual hurt; he sees the mermaid's head but not the dragon's tail, and thinks he can cut off that which he would have from that which he would not have. "How secret art thou who dwellest in the highest heavens in silence, O thou only great God, sprinkling with an unwearied providence certain penal blindnesses upon such as have unbridled desires!" [1]

The human soul is true to these facts in the painting of fable, of history, of law, of proverbs, of conversation. It finds a tongue in literature unawares.

[1] St. Augustine, Confessions, B. I.

Thus the Greeks called Jupiter, Supreme Mind; but having traditionally ascribed to him many base actions, they involuntarily made amends to Reason by tying up the hands of so bad a god. He is made as helpless as a king of England. Prometheus knows one secret which Jove must bargain for; Minerva, another. He cannot get his own thunders; Minerva keeps the key of them:

> Of all the gods, I only know the keys
> That ope the solid doors within whose vaults
> His thunders sleep.

A plain confession of the in-working of the All and of its moral aim. The Indian mythology ends in the same ethics; and indeed it would seem impossible for any fable to be invented and get any currency which was not moral. Aurora forgot to ask youth for her lover, and though so Tithonus is immortal, he is old. Achilles is not quite invulnerable; for Thetis held him by the heel when she dipped him in the Styx and the sacred waters did not wash that part. Siegfried, in the Nibelungen, is not quite immortal, for a leaf fell on his back whilst he was bathing in the Dragon's blood, and that spot which it covered is mortal. And so it always is. There is a crack in every thing God has made. Always it would seem there is this vindictive circumstance stealing in at unawares even into the wild poesy in which the human fancy attempted to make bold holiday and to shake itself free of the old laws,—this back-stroke, this kick of the gun, certifying that the law is fatal; that in nature nothing can be given, all things are sold.

This is that ancient doctrine of Nemesis, who keeps
watch in the Universe and lets no offence go unchas-
tised.   The Furies they said are attendants on Justice,
and if the sun in heaven should transgress his path they
would punish him.   The poets related that stone walls
and iron swords and leathern thongs had an occult sympathy with the wrongs of their owners; that the belt
which Ajax gave Hector dragged the Trojan hero over
the field at the wheels of the car of Achilles, and the
sword which Hector gave Ajax was that on whose
point Ajax fell.   They recorded that when the Tha-
sians erected a statue to Theogenes, a victor in the
games, one of his rivals went to it by night and endeavored to throw it down by repeated blows, until at
last he moved it from its pedestal and was crushed to
death beneath its fall.

This voice of fable has in it somewhat divine.   It
came from thought above the will of the writer.   That
is the best part of each writer which has nothing private in it; that is the best part of each which he does
not know; that which flowed out of his constitution
and not from his too active invention; that which in the
study of a single artist you might not easily find, but
in the study of many you would abstract as the spirit
of them all.   Phidias it is not, but the work of man in
that early Hellenic world that I would know.   The
name and circumstance of Phidias, however convenient for history, embarrasses when we come to the highest criticism.   We are to see that which man was tending to do in a given period, and was hindered, or, if
you will, modified in doing, by the interfering volitions

of Phidias, of Dante, of Shakspeare, the organ whereby man at the moment wrought.

Still more striking is the expression of this fact in the proverbs of all nations, which are always the literature of Reason, or the statements of an absolute truth without qualification. Proverbs, like the sacred books of each nation, are the sanctuary of the Intuitions. That which the droning world, chained to appearances, will not allow the realist to say in his own words, it will suffer him to say in proverbs without contradiction. And this law of laws, which the pulpit, the senate and the college deny, is hourly preached in all markets and all languages by flights of proverbs, whose teaching is as true and as omnipresent as that of birds and flies.

All things are double, one against another.—Tit for tat; an eye for an eye; a tooth for a tooth; blood for blood; measure for measure; love for love.—Give, and it shall be given you.—He that watereth shall be watered himself.—What will you have? quoth God; pay for it and take it.—Nothing venture, nothing have.— Thou shalt be paid exactly for what thou hast done, no more, no less.—Who does not work shall not eat.— Harm watch, harm catch.—Curses always recoil on the head of him who imprecates them.—If you put a chain around the neck of a slave, the other end fastens itself around your own.—Bad counsel confounds the adviser. —The devil is an ass.

It is thus written, because it is thus in life. Our action is overmastered and characterized above our will by the law of nature. We aim at a petty end quite aside from the public good, but our act arranges itself by irresistible magnetism in a line with the poles of the world.

A man cannot speak but he judges himself. With his will or against his will he draws his portrait to the eye of his companions by every word. Every opinion reacts on him who utters it. It is a thread-ball thrown at a mark, but the other end remains in the thrower's bag. Or, rather, it is a harpoon thrown at the whale, unwinding, as it flies, a coil of cord in the boat, and, if the harpoon is not good, or not well thrown, it will go nigh to cut the steersman in twain or to sink the boat.

You cannot do wrong without suffering wrong. "No man had ever a point of pride that was not injurious to him," said Burke. The exclusive in fashionable life does not see that he excludes himself from enjoyment, in the attempt to appropriate it. The exclusionist in religion does not see that he shuts the door of heaven on himself, in striving to shut out others. Treat men as pawns and ninepins and you shall suffer as well as they. If you leave out their heart, you shall lose your own. The senses would make things of all persons; of women, of children, of the poor. The vulgar proverb, "I will get it from his purse or get it from his skin," is sound philosophy.

All infractions of love and equity in our social relations are speedily punished. They are punished by Fear. Whilst I stand in simple relations to my fellowman, I have no displeasure in meeting him. We meet as water meets water, or as two currents of air mix, with perfect diffusion and interpenetration of nature. But as soon as there is any departure from simplicity and attempt at halfness, or good for me that is not good

for him, my neighbor feels the wrong; he shrinks from
me as far as I have shrunk from him; his eyes no longer
seek mine; there is war between us; there is hate in him
and fear in me.

All the old abuses in society, the great and universal
and the petty and particular, all unjust accumulations
of property and power, are avenged in the same manner. Fear is an instructor of great sagacity and the
herald of all revolutions. One thing he always teaches,
that there is rottenness where he appears. He is a car-
rion crow, and though you see not well what he hovers
for, there is death somewhere. Our property is timid,
our laws are timid, our cultivated classes are timid.
Fear for ages has boded and mowed and gibbered over
government and property. That obscene bird is not
there for nothing. He indicates great wrongs which
must be revised.

Of the like nature is that expectation of change which
instantly follows the suspension of our voluntary activity. The terror of cloudless noon, the emerald of
Polycrates, the awe of prosperity, the instinct which
leads every generous soul to impose on itself tasks of a
noble asceticism and vicarious virtue, are the tremblings
of the balance of justice through the heart and mind of
man.

Experienced men of the world know very well that
it is best to pay scot and lot as they go along, and
that a man often pays dear for a small frugality. The
borrower runs in his own debt. Has a man gained
any thing who has received a hundred favors and rendered none? Has he gained by borrowing, through
indolence or cunning, his neighbor's wares, or horses,

or money? There arises on the deed the instant acknowledgment of benefit on the one part and of debt on the other; that is, of superiority and inferiority. The transaction remains in the memory of himself and his neighbor; and every new transaction alters according to its nature their relation to each other. He may soon come to see that he had better have broken his own bones than to have ridden in his neighbor's coach, and that "the highest price he can pay for a thing is to ask for it."

A wise man will extend this lesson to all parts of life, and know that it is always the part of prudence to face every claimant and pay every just demand on your time, your talents, or your heart. Always pay; for first or last you must pay your entire debt. Persons and events may stand for a time between you and justice, but it is only a postponement. You must pay at last your own debt. If you are wise you will dread a prosperity which only loads you with more. Benefit is the end of nature. But for every benefit which you receive, a tax is levied. He is great who confers the most benefits. He is base,—and that is the one base thing in the universe,—to receive favors and render none. In the order of nature we cannot render benefits to those from whom we receive them, or only seldom. But the benefit we receive must be rendered again, line for line, deed for deed, cent for cent, to somebody. Beware of too much good staying in your hand. It will fast corrupt and worm worms. Pay it away quickly in some sort.

Labor is watched over by the same pitiless laws. Cheapest, says the prudent, is the dearest labor. What we buy in a broom, a mat, a wagon, a knife, is some application of good sense to a common want. It is best to pay in your land a skilful gardener, or to buy good sense applied to gardening; in your sailor, good sense applied to navigation; in the house, good sense applied to cooking, sewing, serving; in your agent, good sense applied to accounts and affairs. So do you multiply your presence, or spread yourself throughout your estate. But because of the dual constitution of things, in labor as in life there can be no cheating. The thief steals from himself. The swindler swindles from himself. For the real price of labor is knowledge and virtue, whereof wealth and credit are signs. These signs, like paper money, may be counterfeited or stolen, but that which they represent, namely, knowledge and virtue, cannot be counterfeited or stolen. These ends of labor cannot be answered but by real exertions of the mind, and in obedience to pure motives. The cheat, the defaulter, the gambler, cannot extort the benefit, cannot extort the knowledge of material and moral nature which his honest care and pains yield to the operative. The law of nature is, Do the thing, and you shall have the power; but they who do not the thing have not the power.

Human labor, through all its forms, from the sharpening of a stake to the construction of a city or an epic, is one immense illustration of the perfect compensation of the universe. Everywhere and always this law is sublime. The absolute balance of Give and Take, the doctrine that every thing has its price, and if that price is not paid, not that thing but something else is obtained, and that it is impossible to get anything without its price, is not less sublime in the columns of a ledger than in the budgets of states, in the laws of light and darkness, in all the action and re-action of nature. I cannot doubt that the high laws which each man sees ever implicated in those proc-esses with which he is conversant, the stern ethics which sparkle on his chisel-edge, which are measured out by his plumb and foot-rule, which stand as mani-fest in the footing of the shop-bill as in the history of a state,—do recommend to him his trade, and though seldom named, exalt his business to his imagination.

The league between virtue and nature engages all things to assume a hostile front to vice. The beau-tiful laws and substances of the world persecute and whip the traitor. He finds that things are arranged for truth and benefit, but there is no den in the wide world to hide a rogue. Commit a crime, and the earth is made of glass. There is no such thing as concealment. Commit a crime, and it seems as if a coat of snow fell on the ground, such as reveals in the woods the track of every partridge and fox and squirrel and mole. You cannot recall the spoken word, you cannot wipe out the foot-track, you cannot draw up the ladder, so as to leave no inlet or clew. Always some damning circumstance transpires. The laws and substances of nature, water, snow, wind, gravitation, become penalties to the thief.

On the other hand the law holds with equal sure-ness for all right action. Love, and you shall be loved. All love is mathematically just, as much as the two sides of an algebraic equation. The good man has ab-solute good, which like fire turns every thing to its own

nature, so that you cannot do him any harm; but as
the royal armies sent against Napoleon, when he approached cast down their colors and from enemies became friends, so do disasters of all kinds, as sickness,
offence, poverty, prove benefactors.

> Winds blow and waters roll
> Strength to the brave and power and deity,
> Yet in themselves are nothing.

The good are befriended even by weakness and defect. As no man had ever a point of pride that was
not injurious to him, so no man had ever a defect that
was not somewhere made useful to him. The stag
in the fable admired his horns and blamed his feet,
but when the hunter came, his feet saved him, and afterwards, caught in the thicket, his horns destroyed
him. Every man in his lifetime needs to thank his
faults. As no man thoroughly understands a truth until first he has contended against it, so no man has a
thorough acquaintance with the hindrances or talents
of men until he has suffered from the one and seen the
triumph of the other over his own want of the same.
Has he a defect of temper that unfits him to live in society? Thereby he is driven to entertain himself alone
and acquire habits of self-help; and thus, like the
wounded oyster, he mends his shell with pearl.

Our strength grows out of our weakness. Not until we are pricked and stung and sorely shot at, awakens
the indignation which arms itself with secret forces.
A great man is always willing to be little. Whilst he
sits on the cushion of advantages, he goes to sleep.
When he is pushed, tormented, defeated, he has a

chance to learn something; he has been put on his wits,
on his manhood; he has gained facts; learns his ignorance; is cured of the insanity of conceit; has got moderation and real skill. The wise man always throws
himself on the side of his assailants. It is more his
interest than it is theirs to find his weak point. The
wound cicatrizes and falls off from him like a dead skin
and when they would triumph, lo! he has passed on invulnerable. Blame is safer than praise. I hate to be
defended in a newspaper. As long as all that is said
is said against me, I feel a certain assurance of success.
But as soon as honied words of praise are spoken for
me I feel as one that lies unprotected before his enemies.
In general, every evil to which we do not succumb
is a benefactor. As the Sandwich Islander believes
that the strength and valor of the enemy he kills passes
into himself, so we gain the strength of the temptation
we resist.

The same guards which protect us from disaster,
defect and enmity, defend us, if we will, from selfishness and fraud. Bolts and bars are not the best
of our institutions, nor is shrewdness in trade a mark
of wisdom. Men suffer all their life long under the
foolish superstition that they can be cheated. But
it is as impossible for a man to be cheated by any
one but himself, as for a thing to be and not to be
at the same time. There is a third silent party to all
our bargains. The nature and soul of things takes
on itself the guaranty of the fulfilment of every contract, so that honest service cannot come to loss. If
you serve an ungrateful master, serve him the more.
Put God in your debt. Every stroke shall be repaid.

The longer the payment is withholden, the better for you; for compound interest on compound interest is the rate and usage of this exchequer.

The history of persecution is a history of endeavors to cheat nature, to make water run up hill, to twist a rope of sand. It makes no difference whether the actors be many or one, a tyrant or a mob. A mob is a society of bodies voluntarily bereaving themselves of reason and traversing its work. The mob is man voluntarily descending to the nature of the beast. Its fit hour of activity is night. Its actions are insane, like its whole constitution. It persecutes a principle; it would whip a right; it would tar and feather justice, by inflicting fire and outrage upon the houses and persons of those who have these. It resembles the prank of boys, who run with fire-engines to put out the ruddy aurora streaming to the stars. The inviolate spirit turns their spite against the wrong-doers. The martyr cannot be dishonored. Every lash inflicted is a tongue of fame; every prison a more illustrious abode; every burned book or house enlightens the world; every suppressed or expunged word reverberates through the earth from side to side. The minds of men are at last aroused; reason looks out and justifies her own and malice finds all her work in vain. It is the whipper who is whipped and the tyrant who is undone.

Thus do all things preach the indifference of circumstances. The man is all. Every thing has two sides, a good and an evil. Every advantage has its tax. I learn to be content. But the doctrine of com-

pensation is not the doctrine of indifferency. The
thoughtless say, on hearing these representations,—
What boots it to do well? there is one event to good and
evil; if I gain any good I must pay for it; if I lose any
good I gain some other; all actions are indifferent.

There is a deeper fact in the soul than compensation, to wit, its own nature. The soul is not a compensation, but a life. The soul *is*. Under all this
running sea of circumstance, whose waters ebb and
flow with perfect balance, lies the aboriginal abyss of
real Being. Existence, or God, is not a relation or
a part, but the whole. Being is the vast affirmative,
excluding negation, self-balanced, and swallowing up
all relations, parts and times within itself. Nature,
truth, virtue, are the influx from thence. Vice is the
absence or departure of the same. Nothing, Falsehood,
may indeed stand as the great Night or shade on which
as a back-ground the living universe paints itself forth;
but no fact is begotten by it; it cannot work, for it is
not. It cannot work any good; it cannot work any
harm. It is harm inasmuch as it is worse not to be
than to be.

We feel defrauded of the retribution due to evil
acts, because the criminal adheres to his vice and
contumacy and does not come to a crisis or judgment
anywhere in visible nature. There is no stunning con-
futation of his nonsense before men and angels. Has
he therefore outwitted the law? Inasmuch as he carries the malignity and the lie with him he so far de-
creases from nature. In some manner there will be a
demonstration of the wrong to the understanding also;

but, should we not see it, this deadly deduction makes square the eternal account.

Neither can it be said, on the other hand, that the gain of rectitude must be bought by any loss. There is no penalty to virtue; no penalty to wisdom; they are proper additions of being. In a virtuous action I properly *am;* in a virtuous act I add to the world; I plant into deserts conquered from Chaos and Nothing and see the darkness receding on the limits of the horizon. There can be no excess to love, none to knowledge, none to beauty, when these attributes are considered in the purest sense. The soul refuses all limits. It affirms in man always an Optimism, never a Pessimism.

His life is a progress, and not a station. His instinct is trust. Our instinct uses "more" and "less" in application to man, always of the *presence of the soul,* and not of its absence; the brave man is greater than the coward; the true, the benevolent, the wise, is more a man and not less, than the fool and knave. There is therefore no tax on the good of virtue, for that is the incoming of God himself, or absolute existence, without any comparative. All external good has its tax, and if it came without desert or sweat, has no root in me, and the next wind will blow it away. But all the good of nature is the soul's, and may be had if paid for in nature's lawful coin, that is, by labor which the heart and the head allow. I no longer wish to meet good I do not earn, for example to find a pot of buried gold, knowing that it brings with it new responsibility. I do not wish more external goods,—neither possessions, nor honors, nor powers, nor persons. The gain is ap-

parent; the tax is certain.   But there is no tax on the
knowledge that the compensation exists and that it is not
desirable to dig up treasure.   Herein I rejoice with a
serene eternal peace.   I contract the boundaries of possible mischief.   I learn the wisdom of St. Bernard,
"Nothing can work me damage except myself; the
harm that I sustain I carry about with me, and never
am a real sufferer but by my own fault."

In the nature of the soul is the compensation for
the inequalities of condition.   The radical tragedy of
nature seems to be the distinction of More and Less.
How can Less not feel the pain; how not feel indignation or malevolence towards More?   Look at those
who have less faculty, and one feels sad and knows not
well what to make of it.   Almost he shuns their eye;
he fears they will upbraid God.   What should they do?
It seems a great injustice.   But see the facts nearly
and these mountainous inequalities vanish.   Love reduces them as the sun melts the iceberg in the sea.   The
heart and soul of all men being one, this bitterness of
His and *Mine* ceases.   His is mine.   I am my brother
and my brother is me.   If I feel overshadowed and
outdone by great neighbors, I can get love; I can still
receive; and he that loveth maketh his own the grandeur
he loves.   Thereby I make the discovery that my
brother is my guardian, acting for me with the friend-
liest designs, and the estate I so admired and envied is
my own.   It is the eternal nature of the soul to appropriate and make all things its own.   Jesus and
Shakspeare are fragments of the soul, and by love I
conquer and incorporate them in my own conscious do-

main. His virtue,—is not that mine? His wit.—if it cannot be made mine, it is not wit.

Such also is the natural history of calamity. The changes which break up at short intervals the prosperity of men are advertisements of a nature whose law is growth. Evermore it is the order of nature to grow, and every soul is by this intrinsic necessity quitting its whole system of things, its friends and home and laws and faith, as the shellfish crawls out of its beautiful but stony case, because it no longer admits of its growth, and slowly forms a new house. In proportion to the vigor of the individual these revolutions are frequent, until in some happier mind they are incessant and all worldly relations hang very loosely about him, becoming as it were a transparent fluid membrane through which the living form is always seen, and not, as in most men, an indurated heterogeneous fabric of many dates and of no settled character, in which the man is imprisoned. Then there can be enlargement, and the man of to-day scarcely recognizes the man of yesterday. And such should be the outward biography of man in time, a putting off of dead circumstances day by day, as he renews his raiment day by day. But to us, in our lapsed estate, resting, not advancing, resisting, not coöperating with the divine expansion, this growth comes by shocks.

We cannot part with our friends. We cannot let our angels go. We do not see that they only go out that archangels may come in. We are idolators of the old. We do not believe in the riches of the soul, in its proper eternity and omnipresence. We do not believe there is any force in to-day to rival or re-create that beautiful yesterday. We linger in the ruins of the old tent where once we had bread and shelter and organs, nor believe that the spirit can feed, cover, and nerve us again. We cannot again find aught so dear, so sweet, so graceful. But we sit and weep in vain. The voice of the Almighty saith, "Up and onward forevermore!" We cannot stay amid the ruins. Neither will we rely on the New; and so we walk ever with reverted eyes, like those monsters who look backwards.

And yet the compensations of calamity are made apparent to the understanding also, after long intervals of time. A fever, a mutilation, a cruel disappointment, a loss of wealth, a loss of friends, seems at the moment unpaid loss, and unpayable. But the sure years reveal the deep remedial force that underlies all facts. The death of a dear friend, wife, brother, lover, which seemed nothing but privation, somewhat later assumes the aspect of a guide or genius; for it commonly operates revolutions in our way of life, terminates an epoch of infancy or of youth which was waiting to be closed, breaks up a wonted occupation, or a household, or style of living, and allows the formation of new ones more friendly to the growth of character. It permits or constrains the formation of new acquaintances and the reception of new influences that prove of the first importance to the next years; and the man or woman who would have remained a sunny gardenflower, with no room for its roots and too much sunshine for its head, by the falling of the walls and the neglect of the gardener is made the banian of the forest, yielding shade and fruit to wide neighborhoods of men.

SPIRITUAL LAWS

WHEN the act of reflection takes place in the mind, when we look at ourselves in the light of thought, we discover that our life is embosomed in beauty. Behind us, as we go, all things assume pleasing forms, as clouds do far off. Not only things familiar and stale, but even the tragic and terrible are comely as they take their place in the pictures of memory. The river-bank, the weed at the waterside, the old house, the foolish person,—however neglected in the passing,—have a grace in the past. Even the corpse that has lain in the chambers has added a solemn ornament to the house. The soul will not know either deformity or pain. If in the hours of clear reason we should speak the severest truth, we should say that we had never made a sacrifice. In these hours the mind seems so great that nothing can be taken from us that seems much. All loss, all pain, is particular; the universe remains to the heart unhurt. Distress never, trifles never abate our trust. No man ever stated his griefs as lightly as he might. Allow for exaggeration in the most patient and sorely ridden hack that was ever driven. For it is only the finite that has wrought and suffered; the infinite lies stretched in smiling repose.

The intellectual life may be kept clean and healthful if man will live the life of nature and not import into his mind difficulties which are none of his. No man need be perplexed in his speculations. Let him do and say what strictly belongs to him, and though very ignorant of books, his nature shall not yield him any intellectual obstructions and doubts. Our young people are diseased with the theological problems of original sin, origin of evil, predestination and the like. These never presented a practical difficulty to any man, —never darkened across any man's road who did not go out of his way to seek them. These are the soul's mumps and measles and whooping-coughs, and those who have not caught them cannot describe their health or prescribe the cure. A simple mind will not know these enemies. It is quite another thing that he should be able to give account of his faith and expound to another the theory of his self-union and freedom. This requires rare gifts. Yet without this self-knowledge there may be a sylvan strength and integrity in that which he is. "A few strong instincts and a few plain rules" suffice us.

My will never gave the images in my mind the rank they now take. The regular course of studies, the years of academical and professional education have not yielded me better facts than some idle books under the bench at the Latin school. What we do not call education is more precious than that which we call so. We form no guess, at the time of receiving a thought, of its comparative value. And education often wastes its effort in attempts to thwart and baulk this natural magnetism, which with sure discrimination selects its own.

In like manner our moral nature is vitiated by any interference of our will. People represent virtue as a struggle, and take to themselves great airs upon their attainments, and the question is everywhere vexed when a noble nature is commended, Whether the man is not better who strives with temptation. But there is no merit in the matter. Either God is there or he is not there. We love characters in proportion as they are impulsive and spontaneous. The less a man thinks or knows about his virtues the better we like him. Timoleon's victories are the best victories, which ran and flowed like Homer's verses, Plutarch said. When we see a soul whose acts are all regal, graceful and pleasant as roses, we must thank God that such things can be and are, and not turn sourly on the angel and say "Crump is a better man with his grunting resistance to all his native devils."

Not less conspicuous is the preponderance of nature over will in all practical life. There is less intention in history than we ascribe to it. We impute deep-laid far-sighted plans to Cæsar and Napoleon; but the best of their power was in nature, not in them. Men of an extraordinary success, in their honest moments, have always sung "Not unto us, not unto us." According to the faith of their times they have built altars to Fortune, or to Destiny, or to St. Julian. Their success lay in their parallelism to the course of thought, which found in them an unobstructed channel; and the wonders of which they were the visible conductors seemed to the eye their deed. Did the wires generate the galvanism? It is even true that there was less in them on which they could reflect than in another; as the virtue of a pipe is to be smooth and hollow. That which externally seemed will and immovableness was willingness and self-annihilation. Could Shakspeare give a theory of Shakspeare? Could ever a man of prodigious mathematical genius convey to others any insight into his methods? If he could communicate that secret instantly it would lose all its exaggerated value, blending with the daylight and the vital energy the power to stand and to go.

The lesson is forcibly taught by these observations that our life might be much easier and simpler than we make it, that the world might be a happier place than it is, that there is no need of struggles, convulsions, and despairs, of the wringing of the hands and the gnashing of the teeth; that we miscreate our own evils. We interfere with the optimism of nature, for whenever we get this vantage-ground of the past, or of a wiser mind in the present, we are able to discern that we are begirt with spiritual laws which execute themselves.

The face of external nature teaches the same lesson with calm superiority. Nature will not have us fret and fume. She does not like our benevolence or our learning much better than she likes our frauds and wars. When we come out of the caucus, or the bank, or the Abolition Convention, or the Temperance meeting, or the Transcendental club into the fields and woods, she says to us. "So hot? my little sir."

We are full of mechanical actions. We must needs intermeddle and have things in our own way, until the sacrifices and virtues of society are odious. Love should make joy; but our benevolence is unhappy.

Our Sunday schools and churches and pauper-societies are yokes to the neck. We pain ourselves to please nobody. There are natural ways of arriving at the same ends at which these aim, but do not arrive. Why should all virtue work in one and the same way? Why should all give dollars? It is very inconvenient to us country folk, and we do not think any good will come of it. We have not dollars. Merchants have. Let them give them. Farmers will give corn. Poets will sing. Women will sew. Laborers will lend a hand. The children will bring flowers. And why drag this dead weight of a Sunday school over the whole Christendom? It is natural and beautiful that childhood should inquire and maturity should teach; but it is time enough to answer questions when they are asked. Do not shut up the young people against their will in a pew and force the children to ask them questions for an hour against their will.

If we look wider, all things are alike; laws and letters and creeds and modes of living seem a travestie of truth. Our society is encumbered by ponderous machinery, which resembles the endless aqueducts which the Romans built over hill and dale and which are superseded by the discovery of the law that water rises to the level of its source. It is a Chinese wall which any nimble Tartar can leap over. It is a standing army, not so good as a peace. It is a graduated, titled, richly appointed Empire, quite superfluous when Town-meetings are found to answer just as well.

Let us draw a lesson from nature, which always works by short ways. When the fruit is ripe, it falls. When the fruit is despatched, the leaf falls. The cir-

cuit of the waters is mere falling. The walking or
man and all animals is a falling forward. All our
manual labor and works of strength, as prying, split-
ting, digging, rowing and so forth, are done by dint
of continual falling, and the globe, earth, moon, comet,
sun, star, fall forever and ever.

The simplicity of the universe is very different from
the simplicity of a machine. He who sees moral nature out and out and thoroughly knows how knowledge is acquired and character formed, is a pedant.
The simplicity of nature is not that which may easily
be read, but is inexhaustible. The last analysis can
no wise be made. We judge of a man's wisdom by his
hope, knowing that the perception of the inexhaustible-
ness of nature is an immortal youth. The wild fer-
tility of nature is felt in comparing our rigid names
and reputations with our fluid consciousness. We pass
in the world for sects and schools, for erudition and
piety, and we are all the time jejune babes. One sees
very well how Pyrrhonism grew up. Every man sees
that he is that middle point whereof every thing may be
affirmed and denied with equal reason. He is old, he
is young, he is very wise, he is altogether ignorant.
He hears and feels what you say of the seraphim, and
of the tin-pedlar. There is no permanent wise man
except in the figment of the stoics. We side with the
hero, as we read or paint, against the coward and robber; but we have been ourselves that coward and robber, and shall be again, not in the low circumstance, but
in comparison with the grandeurs possible to the soul.

A little consideration of what takes place around
us every day would show us that a higher law than

that of our will regulates events; that our painful labors are very unnecessary and altogether fruitless; that only in our easy, simple, spontaneous action are we strong, and by contenting ourselves with obedience we become divine. Belief and love,—a believing we love will relieve us of a vast load of care. O my brothers, God exists. There is a soul at the centre of nature and over the will of every man, so that none of us can wrong the universe. It has so infused its strong enchantment into nature that we prosper when we accept its advice, and when we struggle to wound its creatures our hands are glued to our sides, or they beat our own breasts. The whole course of things goes to teach us faith. We need only obey. There is a guidance for each of us, and by lowly listening we shall hear the right word. Why need you choose so painfully your place and occupation and associates and modes of action and entertainment? Certainly there is a possible right for you that precludes the need of balance and wilful election. For you there is a reality, a fit place and congenial duties. Place yourself in the middle of the stream of power and wisdom which flows into you as life, place yourself in the full centre of that flood, then you are without effort impelled to truth, to right and a perfect contentment. Then you put all gainsayers in the wrong. Then you are the world, the measure of right, of truth, of beauty. If we will not be marplots with our miserable interferences, the work, the society, letters, arts, science, religion of men would go on far better than now, and the Heaven predicted from the beginning of the world; and still predicted from the bottom of the heart, would organize *it*self, as do now the rose and the air and the sun.

I say, *do not choose;* but that is a figure of speech by which I would distinguish what is commonly called *choice* among men, and which is a partial act, the choice of the hands, of the eyes, of the appetites, and not a whole act of the man. But that which I call right or goodness, is the choice of my constitution; and that which I call heaven, and inwardly aspire after, is the state of circumstances desirable to my constitution; and the action which I in all my years tend to do, is the work for my faculties. We must hold a man amenable to reason for the choice of his daily craft or profession. It is not an excuse any longer for his deeds that they are the custom of his trade. What business has he with an evil trade? Has he not a *calling* in his character?

Each man has his own vocation. The talent is the call. There is one direction in which all space is open to him. He has faculties silently inviting him thither to endless exertion. He is like a ship in a river; he runs against obstructions on every side but one; on that side all obstruction is taken away and he sweeps serenely over God's depths into an infinite sea. This talent and this call depend on his organization, or the mode in which the general soul incarnates itself in him. He inclines to do something which is easy to him and good when it is done, but which no other man can do. He has no rival. For the more truly he consults his own powers, the more difference will his work exhibit from the work of any other. When he is true and faithful his ambition is exactly proportioned to his powers. The height of the pinnacle is determined by the breadth of the base. Every man has this call of the power to do somewhat unique, and no man has any other call. The pretence that he has another call, a summons by name and personal election and outward "signs that mark him extraordinary and not in the roll of common men," is fanaticism, and betrays obtuseness to perceive that there is one mind in all the individuals, and no respect of persons therein.

By doing his work he makes the need felt which he can supply. He creates the taste by which he is enjoyed. He provokes the wants to which he can minister. By doing his own work he unfolds himself. It is the vice of our public speaking that it has not abandonment. Somewhere, not only every orator but every man should let out all the length of all the reins; should find or make a frank and hearty expression of what force and meaning is in him. The common experience is that the man fits himself as well as he can to the customary details of that work or trade he falls into, and tends it as a dog turns a spit. Then he is a part of the machine he moves; the man is lost. Until he can manage to communicate himself to others in his full stature and proportion as a wise and good man, he does not yet find his vocation. He must find in that an outlet for his character, so that he may justify himself to their eyes for doing what he does. If the labor is trivial, let him by his thinking and character make it liberal. Whatever he knows and thinks, whatever in his apprehension is worth doing, that let him communicate, or men will never know and honor him aright. Foolish, whenever you take the meanness and formality of that thing you do, instead of converting it into the obedient spiracle of your character and aims.

We like only such actions as have already long had the praise of men, and do not perceive that anything man can do may be divinely done. We think greatness entailed or organized in some places or duties, in certain offices or occasions, and do not see that Paganini can extract rapture from a catgut, and Eulenstein from a jews-harp, and a nimble-fingered lad out of shreds of paper with his scissors, and Landseer out of swine, and a hero out of the pitiful habitation and company in which he was hidden. What we call obscure condition or vulgar society is that condition and society whose poetry is not yet written, but which you shall presently make as enviable and renowned as any. Accept your genius and say what you think. In our estimates let us take a lesson from kings. The parts of hospitality, the connection of families, the impressiveness of death, and a thousand other things, royalty makes its own estimate of, and a royal mind will. To make habitually a new estimate,—that is elevation.

What a man does, that he has. What has he to do with hope or fear? In himself is his might. Let him regard no good as solid but that which is in his nature and which must grow out of him as long as he exists. The goods of fortune may come and go like summer leaves; let him play with them and scatter them on every wind as the momentary signs of his infinite productiveness.

He may have his own. A man's genius, the quality that differences him from every other, the susceptibility to one class of influences, the selection of what is fit for him, the rejection of what is unfit, determines for him the character of the universe. As a man thinketh so is he, and as a man chooseth so is he and so is nature. A man is a method, a progressive arrangement; a selecting principle, gathering his like to him wherever he goes. He takes only his own out of the multiplicity that sweeps and circles round him. He is like one of those booms which are set out from the shore on rivers to catch drift-wood, or like the loadstone amongst splinters of steel. Those facts, words, persons, which dwell in his memory without his being able to say why, remain because they have a relation to him not less real for being as yet unapprehended. They are symbols of value to him as they can interpret parts of his consciousness which he would vainly seek words for in the conventional images of books and other minds. What attracts my attention shall have it, as I will go to the man who knocks at my door, whilst a thousand persons as worthy go by it, to whom I give no regard. It is enough that these particulars speak to me. A few anecdotes, a few traits of character, manners, face, a few incidents, have an emphasis in your memory out of all proportion to their apparent significance if you measure them by the ordinary standards. They relate to your gift. Let them have their weight, and do not reject them and cast about for illustration and facts more usual in literature. Respect them, for they have their origin in deepest nature. What your heart thinks great, is great. The soul's emphasis is always right.

Over all things that are agreeable to his nature and genius the man has the highest right. Everywhere he may take what belongs to his spiritual estate, nor can

he take anything else though all doors were open, nor
can all the force of men hinder him from taking so
much.   It is vain to attempt to keep a secret from one
who has a right to know it.   It will tell itself.   That
mood into which a friend can bring us is his dominion
over us.   To the thoughts of that state of mind he has
a right.   All the secrets of that state of mind he can
compel.   This is a law which statesmen use in practice.
All the terrors of the French Republic, which held
Austria in awe, were unable to command her diplomacy.
But Napoleon sent to Vienna M. de Narbonne, one of
the old noblesse, with the morals, manners and name of
that interest, saying, that it was indispensable to send to
the old aristocracy of Europe, men of the same connexion, which in fact, constitutes a sort of free-
masonry.   M. Narbonne in less than a fortnight pene-
trated all the secrets of the Imperial Cabinet.

A mutual understanding is ever the firmest chain.
Nothing seems so easy as to speak and to be understood.   Yet a man may come to find *that* the strongest
of defences and of ties,—that he has been understood;
and he who has received an opinion may come to find
it the most inconvenient of bonds.

If a teacher have any opinion which he wishes to
conceal, his pupils will become as fully indoctrinated
into that as into any which he publishes.   If you pour
water into a vessel twisted into coils and angles, it is
vain to say, I will pour it only into this or that;—it
will find its own level in all.   Men feel and act the consequences of your doctrine without being able to show
how they follow.   Show us an arc of the curve, and a

good mathematician will find out the whole figure.
We are always reasoning from the seen to the unseen.
Hence the perfect intelligence that subsists between wise
men of remote ages. A man cannot bury his meanings so deep in his book but time and like-minded men
will find them. Plato had a secret doctrine, had he?
What secret can he conceal from the eyes of Bacon? of
Montaigne? of Kant? Therefore Aristotle said of his
works, "They are published and not published."

No man can learn what he has not preparation for
learning, however near to his eyes is the object. A
chemist may tell his most precious secrets to a carpenter, and he shall be never the wiser,—the secrets
he would not utter to a chemist for an estate. God
screens us evermore from premature ideas. Our eyes
are holden that we cannot see things that stare us in the
face, until the hour arrives when the mind is ripened,
—then we behold them, and the time when we saw them
not is like a dream.

Not in nature but in man is all the beauty and worth
he sees. The world is very empty, and is indebted to
this gilding, exalting soul for all its pride. "Earth fills
her lap with splendors" *not her own.* The vale of
Tempe, Tivoli and Rome are earth and water, rocks
and sky. There are as good earth and water in a thousand places, yet how unaffecting!

People are not the better for the sun and moon, the
horizon and the trees; as it is not observed that the
keepers of Roman galleries or the valets of painters
have any elevation of thought, or that librarians are
wiser men than others. There are graces in the de-

meanor of a polished and noble person which are lost
upon the eye of a churl.   These are like the stars whose
light has not yet reached us.

He may see what he maketh.   Our dreams are the
sequel of our waking knowledge.   The visions of the
night always bear some proportion to the vision of the
day.   Hideous dreams are only exaggerations of the
sins of the day.   We see our own evil affections embodied in bad physiognomies.   On the alps the traveller sometimes sees his own shadow magnified to a
giant, so that every gesture of his hand is terrific.
"My children," said an old man to his boys scared by a
figure in the dark entry, "my children, you will never
see anything worse than yourselves."   As in dreams,
so in the scarcely less fluid events of the world every
man sees himself in colossal, without knowing that it
is himself that he sees.   The good which he sees compared to the evil which he sees, is as his own good to his
own evil.   Every quality of his mind is magnified in
some one acquaintance, and every emotion of his heart
in some one.   He is like a quincunx of trees, which
counts five, east, west, north, or south; or an initial,
medial, and terminal acrostic.   And why not?   He
cleaves to one person and avoids another, according
to their likeness or unlikeness to himself, truly seeking
himself in his associates and moreover in his trade, and
habits, and gestures, and meats, and drinks; and comes
at last to be faithfully represented by every view you
take of his circumstances.

He may read what he writeth.   What can we see or
acquire but what we are?   You have seen a skilful man
reading Virgil.   Well, that author is a thousand books

to a thousand persons. Take the book into your two hands and read your eyes out; you will never find what I find. If any ingenious reader would have a monopoly of the wisdom or delight he gets, he is as secure now the book is Englished, as if it were imprisoned in the Pelews tongue. It is with a good book as it is with good company. Introduce a base person among gentlemen: it is all to no purpose: he is not their fellow. Every society protects itself. The company is perfectly safe, and he is not one of them, though his body is in the room.

What avails it to fight with the eternal laws of mind, which adjust the relation of all persons to each other by the mathematical measure of their havings and beings? Gertrude is enamored of Guy; how high, how aristocratic, how Roman his mien and manners! to live with him were life indeed: and no purchase is too great; and heaven and earth are moved to that end. Well, Gertrude has Guy: but what now avails how high, how aristocratic, how Roman his mien and manners, if his heart and aims are in the senate, in the theatre and in the billiard room, and she has no aims, no conversation that can enchant her graceful lord?

He shall have his own society. We can love nothing but nature. The most wonderful talents, the most meritorious exertions really avail very little with us; but nearness or likeness of nature,—how beautiful is the ease of its victory! Persons approach us, famous for their beauty, for their accomplishments, worthy of all wonder for their charms and gifts: they dedicate their whole skill to the hour and the company; with very imperfect result. To be sure it would be very ungrate-

ful in us not to praise them very loudly.   Then, when
all is done. a person of related mind, a brother or sister
by nature, comes to us so softly and easily, so nearly
and intimately, as if it were the blood in our proper
veins, that we feel as if some one was gone, instead of
another having come: we are utterly relieved and refreshed: it is a sort of joyful solitude.   We foolishly
think in our days of sin that we must court friends by
compliance to the customs of society, to its dress, its
breeding, and its estimates.   But later if we are so
happy we learn that only that soul can be my friend
which I encounter on the line of my own march, that
soul to which I do not decline and which does not decline to me, but, native of the same celestial latitude,
repeats in its own all my experience.   The scholar and
the prophet forget themselves and ape the customs and
costumes of the man of the world to deserve the smile
of beauty.   He is a fool and follows some giddy girl,
and not with religious, ennobling passion a woman with
all that is serene, oracular and beautiful in her soul.
Let him be great, and love shall follow him.   Nothing
is more deeply punished than the neglect of the affinities
by which alone society should be formed, and the insane levity of choosing associates by others' eyes.

He may set his own rate.   It is an universal maxim
worthy of all acceptation that a man may have that
allowance he takes.   Take the place and attitude to
which you see your unquestionable right and all men
acquiesce.   The world must be just.   It always leaves
every man, with profound unconcern, to set his own
rate.   Hero or driveller, it meddles not in the matter.
It will certainly accept your own measure of your do-

ing and being. whether you sneak about and deny your own name, or whether you see your work produced to the concave sphere of the heavens, one with the revolu tion of the stars.

The same reality pervades all teaching. The man may teach by doing, and not otherwise. If he can communicate himself he can teach, but not by words. He teaches who gives, and he learns who receives. There is no teaching until the pupil is brought into the same state or principle in which you are; a trans-fusion takes place; he is you and you are he; then is a teaching, and by no unfriendly chance or bad com-pany can he ever quite lose the benefit. But your prop-ositions run out of one ear as they ran in at the other. We see it advertised that Mr. Grand will deliver an or-ation on the Fourth of July, and Mr. Hand before the Mechanics' Association, and we do not go thither, be-cause we know that these gentlemen will not communi-cate their own character and being to the company. If we had reason to expect such a communication we should go through all inconvenience and opposition. The sick would be carried in litters. But a public or-ation is an escapade, a non-committal, an apology, a gag, and not a communication, not a speech, not a man.

A like Nemesis presides over all intellectual works. We have yet to learn that the thing uttered in words is not therefore affirmed. It must affirm itself, or no forms of grammar and no plausibility can give it evi-dence and no array of arguments. The sentence must also contain its own apology for being spoken.

The effect of any writing on the public mind is

mathematically measurable by its depth of thought.
How much water does it draw? If it awaken you to
think; if it lift you from your feet with the great voice
of eloquence; then the effect is to be wide, slow, permanent, over the minds of men; if the pages instruct
you not, they will die like flies in the hour. The way
to speak and write what shall not go out of fashion
is to speak and write sincerely. The argument which
has not power to reach my own practice, I may well
doubt will fail to reach yours. But take Sidney's
maxim: "Look in thy heart, and write." He that
writes to himself writes to an eternal public. That
statement only is fit to be made public which you have
come at in attempting to satisfy your own curiosity.
The writer who takes his subject from his ear and not
from his heart should know that he has lost as much
as he seems to have gained, and when the empty book
has gathered all its praise, and half the people say,—
"what poetry! what genius!" it still needs fuel to make
fire. That only profits which is profitable. Life alone
can impart life; and though we should burst we can
only be valued as we make ourselves valuable. There
is no luck in literary reputation. They who make up
the final verdict upon every book are not the partial and
noisy readers of the hour when it appears, but a court
as of angels, a public not to be bribed, not to be en-
treated and not to be overawed, decides upon every
man's title to fame. Only those books come down
which deserve to last. All the gilt edges, vellum and
morocco, all the presentation-copies to all the libraries
will not preserve a book in circulation beyond its intrinsic date. It must go with all Walpole's Noble and

Royal Authors to its fate. Blackmore, Kotzebue, or Pollok may endure for a night, but Moses and Homer stand forever. There are not in the world at any one time more than a dozen persons who read and understand Plato:—never enough to pay for an edition of his works; yet to every generation these come duly down, for the sake of those few persons, as if God brought them in his hand. "No book," said Bentley, "was ever written down by any but itself." The permanence of all books is fixed by no effort, friendly or hostile, but by their own specific gravity, or the intrinsic importance of their contents to the constant mind of man. "Do not trouble yourself too much about the light on your statue," said Michael Angelo to the young sculptor; "the light of the public square will test its value."

In like manner the effect of every action is measured by the depth of the sentiment from which it proceeds. The great man knew not that he was great. It took a century or two for that fact to appear. What he did, he did because he must: he used no election: it was the most natural thing in the world, and grew out of the circumstances of the moment. But now, everything he did, even to the lifting of his finger or the eating of bread, looks large, all-related, and is called an institution.

These are the demonstrations in a few particulars of the genius of nature: they show the direction of the stream. But the stream is blood: every drop is alive. Truth has not single victories: all things are its organs, not only dust and stones, but errors and lies. The laws of disease, physicians say, are as beautiful as the laws of health. Our philosophy is affirmative and readily accepts the testimony of negative facts, as every shadow points to the sun. By a divine necessity every fact in nature is constrained to offer its testimony.

Human character does evermore publish itself. It will not be concealed. It hates darkness—it rushes into light. The most fugitive deed and word, the mere air of doing a thing, the intimated purpose, expresses character. If you act you show character; if you sit still you show it; if you sleep you show it. You think because you have spoken nothing when others spoke, and have given no opinion on the times, on the church, on slavery, on the college, on parties and persons, that your verdict is still expected with curiosity as a reserved wisdom. Far otherwise; your silence answers very loud. You have no oracle to utter, and your fellow-men have learned that you cannot help them; for oracles speak. Doth not wisdom cry and understanding put forth her voice?

Dreadful limits are set in nature to the powers of dissimulation. Truth tyrannizes over the unwilling members of the body. Faces never lie, it is said. No man need be deceived who will study the changes of expression. When a man speaks the truth in the spirit of truth, his eye is as clear as the heavens. When he has base ends and speaks falsely, the eye is muddy and sometimes asquint.

I have heard an experienced counsellor say that he never feared the effect upon a jury of a lawyer who does not believe in his heart that his client ought to have a verdict. If he does not believe it his unbelief will appear to the jury, despite all his protestations.

and will become their unbelief. This is that law whereby a work of art, of whatever kind, sets us in the same state of mind wherein the artist was when he made it. That which we do not believe we cannot adequately say, though we may repeat the words never so often. It was this conviction which Swedenborg expressed when he described a group of persons in the spiritual world endeavoring in vain to articulate a proposition which they did not believe; but they could not, though they twisted and folded their lips even to indignation.

A man passes for that he is worth. Very idle is all curiosity concerning other peoples' estimate of us, and idle is all fear of remaining unknown. If a man know that he can do anything,—that he can do it better than any one else,—he has a pledge of the acknowledgment of that fact by all persons. The world is full of judgment-days, and into every assembly that a man enters, in every action he attempts, he is gauged and stamped. In every troop of boys that whoop and run in each yard and square, a new comer is as well and accurately weighed in the balance in the course of a few days and stamped with his right number, as if he had undergone a formal trial of his strength, speed and temper. A stranger comes from a distant school, with better dress, with trinkets in his pockets, with airs and pretensions; an old boy sniffs thereat and says to himself, "It's of no use; we shall find him out to-morrow." "What hath he done?" is the divine question which searches men and transpierces every false reputation. A fop may sit in any chair of the world nor be distinguished for his hour from Homer and Washington;

but there can never be any doubt concerning the respective ability of human beings when we seek the truth. Pretension may sit still, but cannot act. Pretension never feigned an act of real greatness. Pretension never wrote an Iliad, nor drove back Xerxes, nor christianized the world, nor abolished slavery.

Always as much virtue as there is, so much appears; as much goodness as there is, so much reverence it commands. All the devils respect virtue. The high, the generous, the self-devoted sect will always instruct and command mankind. Never a sincere word was utterly lost. Never a magnanimity fell to the ground. Always the heart of man greets and accepts it unexpectedly. A man passes for that he is worth. What he is engraves itself on his face, on his form, on his fortunes, in letters of light which all men may read but himself. Concealment avails him nothing; boasting nothing. There is confession in the glances of our eyes; in our smiles; in salutations; and the grasp of hands. His sin bedaubs him, mars all his good impression. Men know not why they do not trust him; but they do not trust him. His vice glasses his eye demeans his cheek, pinches the nose, sets the mark of the beast on the back of the head, and writes O fool! fool! on the forehead of a king.

If you would not be known to do anything, never do it. A man may play the fool in the drifts of a desert, but every grain of sand shall seem to see. He may be a solitary eater, but he cannot keep his foolish counsel. A broken complexion, a swinish look, ungenerous acts and the want of due knowledge,—all blab. Can a cook, a Chiffinch, an Iachimo be mistaken for

Zeno or Paul? Confucius exclaimed, "How can a man be concealed! How can a man be concealed!"

On the other hand, the hero fears not that if he withhold the avowal of a just and brave act it will go unwitnessed and unloved. One knows it, himself,— and is pledged by it to sweetness of peace and to nobleness of aim which will prove in the end a better proclamation of it than the relating of the incident. Virtue is the adherence in action to the nature of things, and the nature of things makes it prevalent. It consists in a perpetual substitution of being for seeming, and with sublime propriety God is described as saying, I AM.

The lesson which these observations convey is, Be, and not seem. Let us acquiesce. Let us take our bloated nothingness out of the path of the divine circuits. Let us unlearn our wisdom of the world. Let us lie low in the Lord's power and learn that truth alone makes rich and great.

If you visit your friend, why need you apologize for not having visited him, and waste his time and deface your own act? Visit him now. Let him feel that the highest love has come to see him, in thee its lowest organ. Or why need you torment yourself and friend by secret self-reproaches that you have not assisted him or complimented him with gifts and salutations heretofore? Be a gift and a benediction. Shine with real light and not with the borrowed reflection of gifts. Common men are apologies for men; they bow the head, they excuse themselves with prolix reasons they accumulate appearances because the substance is not.

We are full of these superstitions of sense, the worship of magnitude. God loveth not size: whale and minnow are of like dimension. But we call the poet inactive, because he is not a president, a merchant, or a porter. We adore an institution, and do not see that it is founded on a thought which we have. But real action is in silent moments. The epochs of our life are not in the visible facts of our choice of a calling, our marriage, our acquisition of an office, and the like, but in a silent thought by the wayside as we walk; in a thought which revises our entire manner of life and says, "Thus hast thou done, but it were better thus." And all our after years, like menials, do serve and wait on this, and according to their ability to execute its will. This revisal or correction is a constant force, which, as a tendency, reaches through our lifetime. The object of the man, the aim of these moments, is to make daylight shine through him, to suffer the law to traverse his whole being without obstruction, so that on what point soever of his doing your eye falls it shall report truly of his character, whether it be his diet, his house, his religious forms, his society, his mirth, his vote, his opposition. Now he is not homogeneous, but heterogeneous, and the ray does not traverse; there are no thorough lights, but the eye of the beholder is puzzled, detecting many unlike tendencies and a life not yet at one.

Why should we make it a point with our false modesty to disparage that man we are and that form of being assigned to us? A good man is contented. I love and honor Epaminondas, but I do not wish to be Epaminondas. I hold it more just to love the world of this hour than the world of his hour. Nor can you, if I am true, excite me to the least uneasiness by saying, "he acted and thou sittest still." I see action to be good, when the need is, and sitting still to be also good. Epaminondas, if he was the man I take him for, would have sat still with joy and peace, if his lot had been mine. Heaven is large, and affords space for all modes of love and fortitude. Why should we be busy-bodies and super-serviceable? Action and inaction are alike to the true. One piece of the tree is cut for a weathercock and one for the sleeper of a bridge; the virtue of the wood is apparent in both.

I desire not to disgrace the soul. The fact that I am here certainly shows me that the soul had need of an organ here. Shall I not assume the post? Shall I skulk and dodge and duck with my unseasonable apologies and vain modesty and imagine my being here impertinent? less pertinent than Epaminondas or Homer being there? and that the soul did not know its own needs? Besides, without any reasoning on the matter, I have no discontent. The good soul nourishes me alway, unlocks new magazines of power and enjoyment to me every day. I will not meanly decline the immensity of good, because I have heard that it has come to others in another shape.

Besides, why should we be cowed by the name of Action? 'T is a trick of the senses,—no more. We know that the ancestor of every action is a thought. The poor mind does not seem to itself to be any thing unless it have an outside badge,—some Gentoo diet, or Quaker coat, or Calvinistic prayer-meeting, or philanthropic society, or a great donation, or a high office, or, any how, some wild contrasting action to testify that it is somewhat.   The rich mind lies in the sun and sleeps, and is Nature.   To think is to act.

Let us, if we must have great actions, make our own so.   All action is of an infinite elasticity, and the least admits of being inflated with the celestial air until it eclipses the sun and moon.   Let us seek *one* peace by fidelity.   Let me do my duties.   Why need I go gadding into the scenes and philosophy of Greek and Italian history before I have washed my own face or justified myself to my benefactors?   How dare I read Washington's campaigns when I have not answered the letters of my own correspondents?   Is not that a just objection to much of our reading?   It is a pusillanimous desertion of our work to gaze after our neighbors. It is peeping.   Byron says of Jack Bunting,

> He knew not what to say, and so he swore.

I may say it of our preposterous use of books.   He knew not what to do, and so *he read*.   I can think of nothing to fill my time with, and I find the Life of Brant.   It is a very extravagant compliment to pay to Brant, or to General Schuyler, or to General Washington.   My time should be as good as their time: my world, my facts, all my net of relations, as good as theirs, or either of theirs.   Rather let me do my work so well that other idlers if they choose may compare my texture with the texture of these and find it identical with the best.

This over-estimate of the possibilities of Paul and Pericles, this under-estimate of our own, comes from a neglect of the fact of an identical nature. Bonaparte knew but one Merit, and rewarded in one and the same way the good soldier, the good astronomer, the good poet, the good player. Thus he signified his sense of a great fact. The poet uses the names of Cæsar, of Tamerlane, of Bonduca, of Belisarius; the painter uses the conventional story of the Virgin Mary, of Paul, of Peter. He does not therefore defer to the nature of these accidental men, of these stock heroes. If the poet write a true drama, then he is Cæsar, and not the player of Cæsar; then the self-same strain of thought, emotion as pure, wit as subtle, motions as swift, mounting, extravagant, and a heart as great, self-sufficing, dauntless, which on the waves of its love and hope can uplift all that is reckoned solid and precious in the world, palaces, gardens, money, navies, kingdoms,—marking its own incomparable worth by the slight it casts on these gauds of men;—these are all his, and by the power of these he rouses the nations. But the great names cannot stead him, if he have not life himself. Let a man believe in God, and not in names and places and persons. Let the great soul incarnated in some woman's form, poor and sad and single, in some Dolly or Joan, go out to service and sweep chambers and scour floors, and its effulgent daybeams cannot be muffled or hid, but to sweep and scour will instantly appear supreme and beautiful actions, the top and radiance of human life, and all people will get mops and brooms; until, lo, suddenly the great soul has enshrined itself in some other form and done some other deed, and that is now the flower and head of all living nature.

We are the photometers, we the irritable gold-leaf and tinfoil that measure the accumulations of the subtle element. We know the authentic effects of the true fire through every one of its million disguises.

LOVE

EVERY soul is a celestial Venus to every other soul. The heart has its sabbaths and jubilees in which the world appears as a hymeneal feast, and all natural sounds and the circle of the seasons are erotic odes and dances. Love is omnipresent in nature as motive and reward. Love is our highest word and the synonym of God.

Every promise of the soul has innumerable fulfilments; each of its joys ripens into a new want. Nature, uncontainable, flowing, forelooking, in the first sentiment of kindness anticipates already a benevolence which shall lose all particular regards in its general light. The introduction to this felicity is in a private and tender relation of one to one, which is the enchantment of human life; which, like a certain divine rage and enthusiasm, seizes on man at one period and works a revolution in his mind and body; unites him to his race, pledges him to the domestic and civic relations, carries him with new sympathy into nature, enhances the power of the senses, opens the imagination, adds to his character heroic and sacred attributes, establishes marriage and gives permanence to human society.

The natural association of the sentiment of love with the heyday of the blood seems to require that in order to portray it in vivid tints, which every youth and maid should confess to be true to their throbbing experience, one must not be too old. The delicious fancies of youth reject the least savor of a mature philosophy, as chilling with age and pedantry their purple bloom. And therefore I know I incur the imputation of unnecessary hardness and stoicism from those who compose the Court and Parliament of Love. But from these formidable censors I shall appeal to my seniors. For, it is to be considered that this passion of which we speak, though it begin with the young, yet forsakes not the old, or rather suffers no one who is truly its servant to grow old, but makes the aged participators of it not less than the tender maiden, though in a different and nobler sort. For it is a fire that kindling its first embers in the narrow nook of a private bosom, caught from a wandering spark out of another private heart, glows and enlarges until it warms and beams upon multitudes of men and women, upon the universal heart of all, and so lights up the whole world and all nature with its generous flames. It matters not therefore whether we attempt to describe the passion at twenty, at thirty, or at eighty years. He who paints it at the first period will lose some of its later, he who paints it at the last, some of its earlier traits. Only it is to be hoped that by patience and the muses' aid we may attain to that inward view of the law which shall describe a truth ever young, ever beautiful, so central that it shall commend itself to the eye at whatever angle beholden.

And the first condition is that we must leave a too close and lingering adherence to the actual, to facts, and study the sentiment as it appeared in hope, and not in history. For each man sees his own life defaced ana disfigured, as the life of man is not to his imagination. Each man sees over his own experience a certain slime of error, whilst that of other men looks fair and ideal. Let any man go back to those delicious relations which make the beauty of his life, which have given him sincerest instruction and nourishment, he will shrink and shrink. Alas! I know not why, but infinite compunctions embitter in mature life all the remembrances of budding sentiment, and cover every beloved name. Every thing is beautiful seen from the point of the intellect, or as truth. But all is sour if seen as experience. Details are always melancholy; the plan is seemly and noble. It is strange how painful is the actual world—the painful kingdom of time and place. There dwells care and canker and fear. With thought, with the ideal, is immortal hilarity, the rose of joy. Round it all the muses sing. But with names and persons and the partial interests of to-day and yesterday is grief.

The strong bent of nature is seen in the proportion which this topic of personal relations usurps in the conversation of society. What do we wish to know of any worthy person so much as how he has sped in the history of this sentiment? What books in the circulating libraries circulate? How we glow over these novels of passion, when the story is told with any spark of truth and nature! And what fastens attention, in the intercourse of life, like any passage betraying affection between two parties? Perhaps we never saw them before and never shall meet them again. But we see them exchange a glance or betray a deep emotion, and we are no longer strangers. We understand them and take the warmest interest in the development of the ro mance. All mankind love a lover. The earliest demonstrations of complacency and kindness are nature's most winning pictures. It is the dawn of civility and grace in the coarse and rustic. The rude village boy teazes the girls about the school-house door;—but to-day he comes running into the entry and meets one fair child arranging her satchel: he holds her books to help her, and instantly it seems to him as if she removed herself from him infinitely, and was a sacred precinct. Among the throng of girls he runs rudely enough, but one alone distances him: and these two little neighbors, that were so close just now, have learned to respect each other's personality. Or who can avert his eyes from the engaging, half-artful, half-artless ways of school-girls who go into the country shops to buy a skein of silk or a sheet of paper, and talk half an hour about nothing with the broad-faced, good-natured shop-boy. In the village they are on a perfect equality, which love delights in, and without any coquetry the happy, affectionate nature of woman flows out in this pretty gossip. The girls may have little beauty, yet plainly do they establish between them and the good boy the most agreeable, confiding relations; what with their fun and their earnestness, about Edgar and Jonas and Almira, and who was invited to the party, and who danced at the dancing-school, and when the singing-school would begin, and other nothings concerning which the parties cooed. By-and-by that boy wants a wife, and very truly and heartily will he know where to find a sincere and sweet mate, without any risk such as Milton deplores as incident to scholars and great men.

I have been told that my philosophy is unsocial and that in public discourses my reverence for the intellect makes me unjustly cold to the personal relations. But now I almost shrink at the remembrance of such disparaging words. For persons are love's world, and the coldest philosopher cannot recount the debt of the young soul wandering here in nature to the power of love, without being tempted to unsay, as treasonable to nature, aught derogatory to the social instincts. For, though the celestial rapture falling out of heaven seizes only upon those of tender age, and although a beauty overpowering all analysis or comparison and putting us quite beside ourselves we can seldom see after thirty years, yet the remembrance of these visions outlasts all other remembrances, and is a wreath of flowers on the oldest brows. But here is a strange fact; it may seem to many men, in revising their experience, that they have no fairer page in their life's book than the delicious memory of some passage wherein affection contrived to give a witchcraft, surpassing the deep attraction of its own truth, to a parcel of accidental and trival circumstances. In looking backward they may find that several things which were not the charm have more reality to this groping memory than the charm itself which embalmed them. But be our experience in particulars what it may, no man ever forgot the visitations of that power to his heart and brain, which created all things new; which was the dawn in him of music, poetry and art; which made the face of nature radiant with purple light, the morning and the night

varied enchantments; when a single tone of one voice
could make the heart beat, and the most trivial circumstance associated with one form is put in the amber
of memory; when he became all eye when one was
present, and all memory when one was gone; when the
youth becomes a watcher of windows and studious of a
glove, a veil, a ribbon, or the wheels of a carriage; when
no place is too solitary and none too silent for him who
has richer company and sweeter conversation in his new
thoughts than any old friends, though best and purest,
can give him; for, the figures, the motions, the words
of the beloved object are not, like other images, written
in water, but, as Plutarch said, "enamelled in fire," and
make the study of midnight.

Thou art not gone being gone, where e'er thou art,
Thou leav'st in him thy watchful eyes, in him thy loving
    heart.

In the noon and the afternoon of life we still throb at
the recollection of days when happiness was not happy
enough, but must be drugged with the relish of pain
and fear; for he touched the secret of the matter who
said of love,

    All other pleasures are not worth its pains:

and when the day was not long enough, but the night
too must be consumed in keen recollections; when the
head boiled all night on the pillow with the generous
deed it resolved on; when the moonlight was a pleasing
fever and the stars were letters and the flowers ciphers
and the air was coined into song; when all business

seemed an impertinence, and all the men and women running to and fro in the streets, mere pictures.

The passion re-makes the world for the youth. It makes all things alive and significant. Nature grows conscious. Every bird on the boughs of the tree sings now to his heart and soul. Almost the notes are articulate. The clouds have faces as he looks on them. The trees of the forest, the waving grass and the peeping flowers have grown intelligent; and almost he fears to trust them with the secret which they seem to invite. Yet nature soothes and sympathizes. In the green solitude he finds a dearer home than with men.

> Fountain-heads and pathless groves,
> Places which pale passion loves,
> Moonlight walks, when all the fowls
> Are safely housed, save bats and owls,
> A midnight bell, a passing groan,
> These are the sounds we feed upon.

Behold there in the wood the fine madman! He is a palace of sweet sounds and sights; he dilates; he is twice a man; he walks with arms akimbo; he soliloquizes; he accosts the grass and trees; he feels the blood of the violet, the clover and the lily in his veins; and he talks with the brook that wets his foot.

The causes that have sharpened his perceptions of natural beauty have made him love music and verse. It is a fact often observed, that men have written good verses under the inspiration of passion, who cannot write well under any other circumstances.

The like force has the passion over all his nature. It expands the sentiment; it makes the clown gentle

and gives the coward heart.   Into the most pitiful and
abject it will infuse a heart and courage to defy the
world, so only it have the countenance of the beloved
object.   In giving him to another it still more gives
him to himself.   He is a new man, with new perceptions, new and keener purposes, and a religious solemnity of character and aims.   He does not longer apper-
tain to his family and society.   *He* is somewhat.   *He*
is a person.   *He* is a soul.

And here let us examine a little nearer the nature
of that influence which is thus potent over the human
youth.   Let us approach and admire Beauty, whose
revelation to man we now celebrate,—beauty, welcome
as the sun wherever it pleases to shine, which pleases
everybody with it and with themselves.   Wonderful
is its charm.   It seems sufficient to itself.   The lover
cannot paint his maiden to his fancy poor and solitary.
Like a tree in flower, so much soft, budding, informing
loveliness is society for itself; and she teaches his eye
why Beauty was ever painted with Loves and Graces
attending her steps.   Her existence makes the world
rich.   Though she extrudes all other persons from his
attention as cheap and unworthy, she indemnifies him
by carrying out her own being into somewhat impersonal, large, mundane, so that the maiden stands to
him for a representative of all select things and virtues.
For that reason the lover sees never personal resemblances in his mistress to her kindred or to others.   His
friends find in her a likeness to her mother, or her sisters, or to persons not of her blood.   The lover sees
no resemblance except to summer evenings and diamond
mornings, to rainbows and the song of birds.

Beauty is ever that divine thing the ancients esteemed it. It is, they said, the flowering of virtue. Who can analyze the nameless charm which glances from one and another face and form? We are touched with emotions of tenderness and complacency, but we cannot find whereat this dainty emotion, this wandering gleam, point. It is destroyed for the imagination by any attempt to refer it to organization. Nor does it point to any relations of friendship or love that society knows and has, but, as it seems to me, to a quite other and unattainable sphere, to relations of transcendent delicacy and sweetness, a true faerie land; to what roses and violets hint and foreshow. We cannot get at beauty. Its nature is like opaline doves'-neck lustres, hovering and evanescent. Herein it resembles the most excellent things, which all have this rainbow character, defying all attempts at appropriation and use. What else did Jean Paul Richter signify, when he said to music, "Away! away! thou speakest to me of things which in all my endless life I have not found and shall not find." The same fact may be observed in every work of the plastic arts. The statue is then beautiful when it begins to be incomprehensible, when it is passing out of criticism and can no longer be defined by compass and measuring wand, but demands an active imagination to go with it and to say what it is in the act of doing. The god or hero of the sculptor is always represented in a transition *from* that which is representable to the senses, *to* that which is not. Then first it ceases to be a stone. The same remark holds of painting. And of poetry the success is not attained when it lulls and satisfies, but when it astonishes and fires us with new endeavors after the unattainable.   Concerning it Landor inquires "whether it is not to be referred to some purer state of sensation and existence."

So must it be with personal beauty which love worships.   Then first is it charming and itself when it dissatisfies us with any end; when it becomes a story without an end; when it suggests gleams and visions and not earthly satisfactions; when it seems

> too bright and good,
> For human nature's daily food;

when it makes the beholder feel his unworthiness; when he cannot feel his right to it, though he were Cæsar; he cannot feel more right to it than to the firmament and the splendors of a sunset.

Hence arose the saying, "If I love you, what is that to you?"   We say so, because we feel that what we love is not in your will, but above it.   It is the radiance of you and not you.   It is that which you know not in yourself and can never know.

This agrees well with that high philosophy of Beauty which the ancient writers delighted in; for they said that the soul of man, embodied here on earth, went roaming up and down in quest of that other world of its own, out of which it came into this, but was soon stupefied by the light of the natural sun, and unable to see any other objects than those of this world, which are but shadows of real things.   Therefore the Deity sends the glory of youth before the soul, that it may avail itself of beautiful bodies as aids to its recollection of the celestial good and fair; and the man beholding such a person in the female sex runs to her and finds the highest joy in contemplating the form, movement and intelligence of this person, because it suggests to him the presence of that which indeed is within the beauty, and the cause of the beauty.

If however, from too much conversing with material objects, the soul was gross, and misplaced its satisfaction in the body, it reaped nothing but sorrow; body being unable to fulfil the promise which beauty holds out; but if, accepting the hint of these visions and suggestions which beauty makes to his mind, the soul passes through the body and falls to admire strokes of character, and the lovers contemplate one another in their discourses and their actions, then they pass to the true palace of beauty, more and more inflame their love of it, and by this love extinguishing the base affection, as the sun puts out the fire by shining on the hearth, they become pure and hallowed. By coversation with that which is in itself excellent, magnanimous, lowly, and just, the lover comes to a warmer love of these nobilities, and a quicker apprehension of them. Then he passes from loving them in one to loving them in all, and so is the one beautiful soul only the door through which he enters to the society of all true and pure souls. In the particular society of his mate he attains a clearer sight of any spot, any taint which her beauty has contracted from this world, and is able to point it out, and this with mutual joy that they are now able, without offence, to indicate blemishes and hindrances in each other, and give to each all help and comfort in curing the same. And, beholding in many souls the traits of the divine beauty, and separating in each soul that which is divine from the taint which it has contracted in the world, the lover ascends to the highest beauty, to the love and knowledge of the Divinity, by steps on this ladder of created souls.

Somewhat like this have the truly wise told us of love in all ages. The doctrine is not old, nor is it new. If Plato, Plutarch and Apuleius taught it, so have Petrarch, Angelo and Milton. It awaits a truer unfolding in opposition and rebuke to that subterranean prudence which presides at marriages with words that take hold of the upper world, whilst one eye is eternally boring down into the cellar; so that its gravest discourse has ever a slight savor of hams and powdering-tubs. Worst, when the snout of this sensualism intrudes into the education of young women, and withers the hope and affection of human nature by teaching that marriage signifies nothing but a housewife's thrift, and that woman's life has no other aim.

But this dream of love, though beautiful, is only one scene in our play. In the procession of the soul from within outward, it enlarges its circles ever, like the pebble thrown into the pond, or the light proceeding from an orb. The rays of the soul alight first on things nearest, on every utensil and toy, on nurses and domestics, on the house and yard and passengers, on the circle of household acquaintance, on politics and geography and history. But by the necessity of our constitution things are ever grouping themselves according to higher or more interior laws. Neighborhood, size, numbers, habits, persons, lose by degrees their power over us. Cause and effect, real affinities, the longing for harmony between the soul and the circumstance, the high progressive, idealizing instinct,

these predominate later, and ever the step backward
from the higher to the lower relations is impossible.
Thus even love, which is the deification of persons, must
become more impersonal every day.   Of this at first it
gives no hint.   Little think the youth and maiden who
are glancing at each other across crowded rooms with
eyes so full of mutual intelligence,—of the precious
fruit long hereafter to proceed from this new, quite external stimulus.   The work of vegetation begins first
in the irritability of the bark and leaf-buds.   From ex-
changing glances, they advance to acts of courtesy, of
gallantry, then to fiery passion, to plighting troth and
marriage.   Passion beholds its object as a perfect unit.
The soul is wholly embodied, and the body is wholly
ensouled.

> Her pure and eloquent blood
> Spoke in her cheeks, and so distinctly wrought,
> That one might almost say her body thought.

Romeo, if dead, should be cut up into little stars
to make the heavens fine.   Life, with this pair, has no
other aim, asks no more, than Juliet,—than Romeo.
Night, day, studies, talents, kingdoms, religion, are all
contained in this form full of soul, in this soul which
is all form.   The lovers delight in endearments, in
avowals of love, in comparisons of their regards.
When alone, they solace themselves with the remembered image of the other.   Does that other see the same
star; the same melting cloud, read the same book, feel
the same emotion, that now delight me?   They try
and weigh their affection, and adding up all costly advantages, friends, opportunities, properties, exult in dis-

covering that willingly, joyfully, they would give all as
a ransom for the beautiful, the beloved head, not one
hair of which shall be harmed.   But the lot of humanity is on these children.   Danger, sorrow and pain arrive to them as to all.   Love prays.   It makes covenants with Eternal Power in behalf of this dear mate.
The union which is thus effected and which adds a new
value to every atom in nature, for it transmutes every
thread throughout the whole web of relation into a
golden ray, and bathes the soul in a new and sweeter
element, is yet a temporary state.   Not always can
flowers, pearls, poetry, protestations, nor even home in
another heart, content the awful soul that dwells in clay.
It arouses itself at last from these endearments, as
toys, and puts on the harness and aspires to vast and
universal aims.   The soul which is in the soul of each,
craving for a perfect beatitude, detects incongruities,
defects and disproportion in the behavior of the other.
Hence arise surprise, expostulation and pain.   Yet that
which drew them to each other was signs of loveliness,
signs of virtue: and these virtues are there, however
eclipsed.   They appear and reappear and continue to
attract; but the regard changes, quits the sign and attaches to the substance.   This repairs the wounded
affection.   Meantime, as life wears on, it proves a game
of permutation and combination of all possible positions
of the parties, to extort all the resources of each and
acquaint each with the whole strength and weakness
of the other.   For, it is the nature and end of this
relation, that they should represent the human race to
each other.   All that is in the world, which is or ought

to be known, is cunningly wrought into the texture of
man, of woman.

> The person love does to us fit,
> Like manna, has the taste of all in it.

The world rolls: the circumstances vary every hour.
All the angels that inhabit this temple of the body appear at the windows, and all the gnomes and vices also.
By all the virtues they are united. If there be virtue,
all the vices are known as such; they confess and flee.
Their once flaming regard is sobered by time in either
breast, and losing in violence what it gains in extent,
it becomes a thorough good understanding. They re-
sign each other without complaint to the good offices
which man and woman are severally appointed to discharge in time, and exchange the passion which once
could not lose sight of its object, for a cheerful, disengaged furtherance, whether present or absent, of each
other's designs. At last they discover that all which at
first drew them together,—those once sacred features,
that magical play of charms,—was deciduous, had a
prospective end, like the scaffolding by which the house
was built; and the purification of the intellect and the
heart from year to year is the real marriage, foreseen
and prepared from the first, and wholly above their consciousness. Looking at these aims with which two
persons, a man and a woman, so variously and cor-
relatively gifted, are shut up in one house to spend in
the nuptial society forty or fifty years, I do not wonder
at the emphasis with which the heart prophesies this
crisis from early infancy, at the profuse beauty with

which the instincts deck the nuptial bower, and nature
and intellect and art emulate each other in the gifts and
the melody they bring to the epithalamium.

Thus are we put in training for a love which knows
not sex, nor person, nor partiality, but which seeketh
virtue and wisdom everywhere, to the end of increas-
ing virtue and wisdom.   We are by nature observers,
and thereby learners.   That is our permanent state.
But we are often made to feel that our affections are
but tents of a night.   Though slowly and with pain, the
objects of the affections change, as the objects of
thought do.   There are moments when the affections
rule and absorb the man and make his happiness dependent on a person or persons.   But in health the mind
is presently seen again,—its overarching vault, bright
with galaxies of immutable lights, and the warm loves
and fears that swept over us as clouds must lose their
finite character and blend with God, to attain their own
perfection.   But we need not fear that we can lose anything by the progress of the soul.   The soul may be
trusted to the end.   That which is so beautiful and attractive as these relations, must be succeeded and sup-
planted only by what is more beautiful, and so on forever.

FRIENDSHIP

W E have a great deal more kindness than is ever spoken. Maugre all the selfishness that chills like east winds the world, the whole human family is bathed with an element of love like a fine ether. How many persons we meet in houses, whom we scarcely speak to, whom yet we honor, and who honor us! How many we see in the street, or sit with in church, whom, though silently, we warmly rejoice to be with! Read the language of these wandering eye-beams. The heart knoweth.

The effect of the indulgence of this human affection is a certain cordial exhilaration. In poetry and in common speech the emotions of benevolence and complacency which are felt towards others are likened to the material effects of fire; so swift, or much more swift, more active, more cheering, are these fine inward irradiations. From the highest degree of passionate love to the lowest degree of good will, they make the sweetness of life.

Our intellectual and active powers increase with our affection. The scholar sits down to write, and all his years of meditation do not furnish him with one good thought or happy expression; but it is necessary to write a letter to a friend,—and forthwith troops of gentle thoughts invest themselves, on every hand, with

chosen words. See, in any house where virtue and
self-respect abide, the palpitation which the approach of
a stranger causes. A commended stranger is expected
and announced, and an uneasiness betwixt pleasure and
pain invades all the hearts of a household. His arrival
almost brings fear to the good hearts that would welcome him. The house is dusted, all things fly into their
places, the old coat is exchanged for the new, and they
must get up a dinner if they can. Of a commended
stranger, only the good report is told by others, only
the good and new is heard by us. He stands to us for
humanity. He is what we wish. Having imagined
and invested him, we ask how we should stand related
in conversation and action with such a man, and are
uneasy with fear. The same idea exalts conversation
with him. We talk better than we are wont. We have
the nimblest fancy, a richer memory, and our dumb
devil has taken leave for the time. For long hours we
can continue a series of sincere, graceful, rich communications, drawn from the oldest, secretest experience so that they who sit by, of our own kinsfolk and
acquaintance, shall feel a lively surprise at our unusual
powers. But as soon as the stranger begins to intrude
his partialities, his definitions, his defects into the conversation, it is all over. He has heard the first, the last
and best he will ever hear from us. He is no stranger
now. Vulgarity, ignorance, misapprehension are old
acquaintances. Now, when he comes he may get the
order, the dress and the dinner,—but the throbbing of
the heart and the communications of the soul, no more.

Pleasant are these jets of affection which make a
young world for me again. Delicious is a just and

firm encounter of two, in a thought, in a feeling.   How
beautiful, on their approach to this beating heart, the
steps and forms of the gifted and the true!   The moment we indulge our affections, the earth is metamor-
phosed: there is no winter and no night: all tragedies,
all ennuis vanish,—all duties even; nothing fills the proceeding eternity but the forms all radiant of beloved
persons.   Let the soul be assured that somewhere in the
universe it should rejoin its friend, and it would be
content and cheerful alone for a thousand years.

I awoke this morning with devout thanksgiving for
my friends, the old and the new.   Shall I not call God
the Beautiful, who daily showeth himself so to me in
his gifts?   I chide society, I embrace solitude, and yet
I am not so ungrateful as not to see the wise, the lovely
and the noble-minded, as from time to time they pass
my gate.   Who hears me, who understands me, becomes mine,—a possession for all time.   Nor is nature
so poor but she gives me this joy several times, and
thus we weave social threads of our own, a new web
of relations; and, as many thoughts in succession substantiate themselves, we shall by-and-by stand in a new
world of our own creation, and no longer strangers
and pilgrims in a traditionary globe.   My friends have
come to me unsought.   The great God gave them to
me.   By oldest right, by the divine affinity of virtue
with itself, I find them, or rather not I, but the Deity
in me and in them, both deride and cancel the thick
walls of individual character, relation, age, sex circumstance, at which he usually connives, and now
makes many one.   High thanks I owe you, excellent
lovers, who carry out the world for me tc new and

noble depths, and enlarge the meaning of all my
thoughts. These are not stark and stiffened persons,
but the new-born poetry of God,—poetry without
stop,—hymn, ode and epic, poetry still flowing and not
yet caked in dead books with annotation and grammar,
but Apollo and the Muses chanting still. Will these
two separate themselves from me again, or some of
them? I know not, but I fear it not; for my relation
to them is so pure that we hold by simple affinity, and
the Genius of my life being thus social, the same affinity
will exert its energy on whomsoever is as noble as these
men and women, wherever I may be.

I confess to an extreme tenderness of nature on
this point. It is almost dangerous to me to "crush
the sweet poison of misused wine" of the affections.
A new person is to me always a great event and hinders
me from sleep. I have had such fine fancies lately
about two or three persons which have given me delicious hours; but the joy ends in the day; it yields no
fruit. Thought is not born of it; my action is very
little modified. I must feel pride in my friend's accomplishments as if they were mine,—wild, delicate,
throbbing property in his virtues. I feel as warmly
when he is praised, as the lover when he hears applause
of his engaged maiden. We overestimate the conscience of our friend. His goodness seems better than
our goodness, his nature finer, his temptations less.
Every thing that is his, his name, his form, his dress,
books and instruments, fancy enhances. Our own
thought sounds new and larger from his mouth.

Yet the systole and diastole of the heart are not
without their analogy in the ebb and flow of love.

Friendship, like the immortality of the soul, is too good to be believed. The lover, beholding his maiden, half knows that she is not verily that which he worships; and in the golden hour of friendship we are surprised with shades of suspicion and unbelief. We doubt that we bestow on our hero the virtues in which he shines, and afterwards worship the form to which we have ascribed this divine inhabitation. In strictness, the soul does not respect men as it respects itself. In strict science all persons underlie the same condition of an infinite remoteness. Shall we fear to cool our love by facing the fact, by mining for the metaphysical foundation of this Elysian temple? Shall I not be as real as the things I see? If I am, I shall not fear to know them for what they are. Their essence is not less beautiful than their appearance, though it needs finer organs for its apprehension. The root of the plant is not unsightly to science, though for chaplets and festoons we cut the stem short. And I must hazard the production of the bald fact amidst these pleasing reveries, though it should prove an Egyptian skull at our banquet. A man who stands united with his thought conceives magnificently of himself. He is conscious of a universal success, even though bought by uniform particular failures. No advantages, no powers, no gold or force, can be any match for him. I cannot choose but rely on my own poverty more than on your wealth. I cannot make your consciousness tantamount to mine. Only the star dazzles; the planet has a faint, moon-like ray. I hear what you say of the admirable parts and tried temper of the party you praise, but I see well that, for all his purple cloaks, I shall not

like him, unless he is at last a poor Greek like me.   I
cannot deny it, O friend, that the vast shadow of the
Phenomenal includes thee also in its pied and painted
immensity,—thee also, compared with whom all else is
shadow.   Thou art not Being, as Truth is, as Justice
is,—thou art not my soul, but a picture and effigy of
that.   Thou hast come to me lately, and already thou
art seizing thy hat and cloak.   Is it not that the soul
puts forth friends as the tree puts forth leaves, and
presently, by the germination of new buds, extrudes the
old leaf?   The law of nature is alternation forevermore.   Each electrical state superinduces the opposite.
The soul environs itself with friends that it may enter
into a grander self-acquaintance or solitude; and it goes
alone for a season that it may exalt its conversation or
society.   This method betrays itself along the whole
history of our personal relations, the instinct of affection revives the hope of union with our mates, and the
returning sense of insulation recalls us from the chase.
Thus every man passes his life in the search after
friendship, and if he should record his true sentiment,
he might write a letter like this to each new candidate
for his love.

DEAR FRIEND: If I was sure of thee, sure of thy capacity,
sure to match my mood with thine, I should never think
again of trifles in relation to thy comings and goings. I
am not very wise: my moods are quite attainable: and I
respect thy genius: it is to me as yet unfathomed; yet dare I
not presume in thee a perfect intelligence of me, and so thou
art to me a delicious torment.   Thine ever, or never.

Yet these uneasy pleasures and fine pains are for
curiosity and not for life.   They are not to be indulged.

This is to weave cobweb, and not cloth. Our friendships hurry to short and poor conclusions, because we have made them a texture of wine and dreams, instead of the tough fibre of the human heart. The laws of friendship are great, austere and eternal, of one web with the laws of nature and of morals. But we have aimed at a swift and petty benefit, to suck a sudden sweetness. We snatch at the slowest fruit in the whole garden of God, which many summers and many winters must ripen. We seek our friend not sacredly, but with an adulterate passion which would appropriate him to ourselves. In vain. We are armed all over with subtle antagonisms, which, as soon as we meet, begin to play, and translate all poetry into stale prose. Almost all people descend to meet. All association must be a compromise, and, what is worst, the very flower and aroma of the flower of each of the beautiful natures disappears as they approach each other. What a perpetual disappointment is actual society, even of the virtuous and gifted! After interviews have been compassed with long foresight we must be tormented presently by baffled blows, by sudden, unseasonable apathies, by epilepsies of wit and of animal spirits, in the hey-dey of friendship and thought. Our faculties do not play us true, and both parties are relieved by solitude.

I ought to be equal to every relation. It makes no difference how many friends I have and what content I can find in conversing with each, if there be one to whom I am not equal. If I have shrunk unequal from one contest, instantly the joy I find in all the rest becomes mean and cowardly. I should hate myself, if then I made my other friends my asylum.

The valiant warrior famoused for fight,
After a hundred victories, once foiled,
Is from the book of honor razed quite
And all the rest forgot for which he toiled.

Our impatience is thus sharply rebuked.   Bashful‧
ness and apathy are a tough husk in which a delicate
organization is protected from premature ripening
It would be lost if it knew itself before any of the
best souls were yet ripe enough to know and own it.
Respect the *naturlangsamkeit* which hardens the ruby
in a million years, and works in duration in which Alps
and Andes come and go as rainbows.   The good spirit
of our life has no heaven which is the price of rashness.
Love, which is the essence of God, is not for levity, but
for the total worth of man.   Let us not have this childish luxury in our regards, but the austerest worth; let
us approach our friend with an audacious trust in the
truth of his heart, in the breadth, impossible to be over‧
turned, of his foundations.

The attractions of this subject are not to be resisted,
and I leave, for the time, all account of subordinate social benefit, to speak of that select and sacred relation
which is a kind of absolute, and which even leaves the
language of love suspicious and common, so much is
this purer, and nothing is so much divine.

I do not wish to treat friendships daintily, but with
roughest courage.   When they are real, they are not
glass threads or frost-work, but the solidest thing we
know.   For now, after so many ages of experience,
what do we know of nature or of ourselves?   Not
one step has man taken toward the solution of the
problem of his destiny.   In one condemnation of folly

stand the whole universe of men. But the sweet sincerity of joy and peace which I draw from this alliance with my brother's soul is the nut itself whereof all nature and all thought is but the husk and shell. Happy is the house that shelters a friend! It might well be built, like a festal bower or arch, to entertain him a single day. Happier, if he know the solemnity of that relation and honor its law! It is no idle bond, no holiday engagement. He who offers himself a candidate for that covenant comes up, like an Olympian, to the great games where the first-born of the world are the competitors. He proposes himself for contest where Time, Want, Danger, are in the lists, and he alone is victor who has truth enough in his constitution to preserve the delicacy of his beauty from the wear and tear of all these. The gifts of fortune may be present or absent, but all the hap in that contest depends on intrinsic nobleness and the contempt of trifles. There are two elements that go to the composition of friendship, each so sovereign that I can detect no superiority in either, no reason why either should be first named. One is Truth. A friend is a person with whom I may be sincere. Before him I may think aloud. I am arrived at last in the presence of a man so real and equal that I may drop even those most undermost garments of dissimulation, courtesy, and second thought, which men never put off, and may deal with him with the simplicity and wholeness with which one chemical atom needs another. Sincerity is the luxury allowed, like diadems and authority, only to the highest rank, *that* being permitted to speak truth, as having none above it to court or conform unto. Every man alone is sin-

cere. At the entrance of a second person, hypocrisy
begins. We parry and fend the approach of our fellow man by compliments, by gossip, by amusements, by
affairs. We cover up our thought from him under a
hundred folds. I knew a man who under a certain religious frenzy cast off this drapery, and omitting all
compliment and commonplace, spoke to the conscience
of every person he encountered, and that with great
insight and beauty. At first he was resisted, and all
men agreed he was mad. But persisting as indeed he
could not help doing for some time in this course, he
attained to the advantage of bringing every man of his
acquaintance into true relations with him. No man
would think of speaking falsely with him, or of putting him off with any chat of markets or reading-rooms.
But every man was constrained by so much sincerity to
face him, and what love of nature, what poetry, what
symbol of truth he had, he did certainly show him.
But to most of us society shows not its face and eye,
but its side and its back. To stand in true relations
with men in a false age is worth a fit of insanity, is it
not? We can seldom go erect. Almost every man
we meet requires some civility, requires to be humored;
—he has some fame, some talent, some whim of religion or philanthropy in his head that is not to be questioned, and which spoils all conversation with him.
But a friend is a sane man who exercise not my ingenuity, but me. My friend gives me entertainment
without requiring me to stoop, or to lisp, or to mask
myself. A friend therefore is a sort of paradox in
nature. I who alone am, I who see nothing in nature
whose existence I can affirm with equal evidence to my

own, behold now the semblance of my being, in all its
height, variety and curiosity, reiterated in a foreign
form; so that a friend may well be reckoned the masterpiece of nature.

The other element of friendship is Tenderness. We
are holden to men by every sort of tie, by blood, by
pride, by fear, by hope, by lucre, by lust, by hate, by
admiration, by every circumstance and badge and
trifle, but we can scarce believe that so much character
can subsist in another as to draw us by love. Can another be so blessed and we so pure that we can offer
him tenderness? When a man becomes dear to me I
have touched the goal of fortune. I find very little
written directly to the heart of this matter in books.
And yet I have one text which I cannot choose but
remember. My author says, "I offer myself faintly
and bluntly to those whose I effectually am, and tender
myself least to him to whom I am the most devoted."
I wish that friendship should have feet, as well as eyes
and eloquence. It must plant itself on the ground, before it walks over the moon. I wish it to be a little
of a citizen, before it is quite a cherub. We chide the
citizen because he makes love a commodity. It is an
exchange of gifts, of useful loans; it is good neighborhood; it watches with the sick; it holds the pall at
the funeral; and quite loses sight of the delicacies and
nobility of the relation. But though we cannot find
the god under his disguise of a sutler, yet on the other
hand we cannot forgive the poet if he spins his thread
too fine and does not substantiate his romance by the
municipal virtues of justice, punctuality, fidelity and
pity. I hate the prostitution of the name of friend-

ship to signify modish and worldly alliances. I much
prefer the company of ploughboys and tin-pedlars to
the silken and perfumed amity which only celebrates its
days of encounter by a frivolous display, by rides in
a curricle and dinners at the best taverns. The end of
friendship is a commerce the most strict and homely
that can be joined; more strict than any of which we
have experience. It is for aid and comfort through all
the relations and passages of life and death. It is fit
for serene days and graceful gifts and country rambles,
but also for rough roads and hard fare, shipwreck,
poverty and persecution. It keeps company with the
sallies of the wit and the trances of religion. We are
to dignify to each other the daily needs and offices of
man's life, and embellish it by courage, wisdom and
unity. It should never fall into something usual and
settled, but should be alert and inventive and add
rhyme and reason to what was drudgery.

For perfect friendship may be said to require natures
so rare and costly, so well tempered each and so happily adapted, and withal so circumstanced (for even
in that particular, a poet says, love demands that the
parties be altogether paired), that very seldom can its
satisfaction be realized. It cannot subsist in its perfection, say some of those who are learned in this warm
lore of the heart, betwixt more than two. I am not
quite so strict in my terms, perhaps because I have never
known so high a fellowship as others. I please my
imagination more with a circle of godlike men and
women variously related to each other and between
whom subsists a lofty intelligence. But I find this law
of *one to one* peremptory for conversation, which is the

practice and consummation of friendship. Do not mix
waters too much. The best mix as ill as good and
bad. You shall have very useful and cheering discourse at several times with two several men, but let all
three of you come together and you shall not have one
new and hearty word. Two may talk and one may
hear, but three cannot take part in a conversation of
the most sincere and searching sort. In good company
there is never such discourse between two, across the
table, as take place when you leave them alone. In
good company the individuals at once merge their egotism into a social soul exactly coëxtensive with the
several consciousnesses there present. No partialities
of friend to friend, no fondnesses of brother to sister,
of wife to husband, are there pertinent, but quite otherwise. Only he may then speak who can sail on the
common thought of the party, and not poorly limited
to his own. Now this convention, which good sense
demands, destroys the high freedom of great conversation, which requires an absolute running of two souls
into one.

No two men but being left alone with each other
enter into simple relations. Yet it is affinity that determines *which* two shall converse. Unrelated men
give little joy to each other; will never suspect the latent powers of each. We talk sometimes of a great
talent for conversation, as if it were a permanent property in some individuals. Conversation is an evanescent relation,—no more. A man is reputed to have
thought and eloquence; he cannot, for all that, say a
word to his cousin or his uncle. They accuse his silence with as much reason as they would blame the in-

significance of a dial in the shade. In the sun it will
mark the hour. Among those who enjoy his thought
he will regain his tongue.

Friendship requires that rare mean betwixt likeness
and unlikeness that piques each with the presence of
power and of consent in the other party. Let me be
alone to the end of the world, rather than that my
friend should overstep, by a word or a look, his real
sympathy. I am equally baulked by antagonism and
by compliance. Let him not cease an instant to be himself. The only joy I have in his being mine, is that
the *not mine* is *mine*. It turns the stomach, it blots
the daylight; where I looked for a manly furtherance
or at least a manly resistance, to find a mush of concession. Better be a nettle in the side of your friend
than his echo. The condition which high friendship
demands is ability to do without it. To be capable that
high office requires great and sublime parts. There
must be very two, before there can be very one. Let it
be an alliance of two large, formidable natures, mutually beheld, mutually feared, before yet they recognise
the deep identity which, beneath these disparities, unites
them.

He only is fit for this society who is magnanimous.
He must be so to know its law. He must be one who
is sure that greatness and goodness are always economy. He must be one who is not swift to intermeddle
with his fortunes. Let him not dare to intermeddle
with this. Leave to the diamond its ages to grow, nor
expect to accelerate the births of the eternal. Friendship demands a religious treatment. We must not be
wilful, we must not provide. We talk of choosing our

friends, but friends are self-elected. Reverence is a great part of it. Treat your friend as a spectacle. Of course if he be a man he has merits that are not yours, and that you cannot honor if you must needs hold him close to your person. Stand aside. Give those merits room. Let them mount and expand. Be not so much his friend that you can never know his peculiar energies, like fond mammas who shut up their boy in the house until he is almost grown a girl. Are you the friend of your friend's buttons, or of his thought? To a great heart he will still be a stranger in a thousand particulars, that he may come near in the holiest ground. Leave it to girls and boys to regard a friend as property, and to suck a short and all-confounding pleasure, instead of the pure nectar of God.

Let us buy our entrance to this guild by a long probation. Why should we desecrate noble and beautiful souls by intruding on them? Why insist on rash personal relations with your friend? Why go to his house, or know his mother and brother and sisters? Why be visited by him at your own? Are these things material to our covenant? Leave this touching and clawing. Let him be to me a spirit. A message, a thought, a sincerity, a glance from him, I want, but not news, nor pottage. I can get politics and chat and neighborly conveniences from cheaper companions. Should not the society of my friend be to me poetic, pure, universal and great as nature itself? Ought I to feel that our tie is profane in comparison with yonder bar of cloud that sleeps on the horizon, or that clump of waving grass that divides the brook? Let us not vilify, but raise it to that standard. That great defying eye, that scornful beauty of his mien and action, do not pique yourself on reducing, but rather fortify and enhance. Worship his superiorities. Wish him not less by a thought, but hoard and tell them all. Guard him as thy great counterpart; have a princedom to thy friend. Let him be to thee forever a sort of beautiful enemy, untamable, devoutly revered, and not a trivial conveniency to be soon outgrown and cast aside. The hues of the opal, the light of the diamond, are not to be seen if the eye is too near. To my friend I write a letter and from him I receive a letter. That seems to you a little. Me it suffices. It is a spiritual gift, worthy of him to give and of me to receive. It profanes nobody. In these warm lines the heart will trust itself, as it will not to the tongue, and pour out the prophecy of a godlier existence than all the annals of heroism have yet made good.

Respect so far the holy laws of this fellowship as not to prejudice its perfect flower by your impatience for its opening. We must be our own before we can be another's. There is at least this satisfaction in crime, according to the Latin proverb; you can speak to your accomplice on even terms. *Crimen quos inquinat, æquat.* To those whom we admire and love, at first we cannot. Yet the least defect of self-possession vitiates, in my judgment, the entire relation. There can never be deep peace between two spirits, never mutual respect, until in their dialogue each stands for the whole world.

What is so great as friendship, let us carry with what grandeur of spirit we can. Let us be silent,— so we may hear the whisper of the gods. Let us not interfere. Who set you to cast about what you should say to the select souls, or to say anything to such? No matter how ingenious, no matter how graceful and bland. There are innumerable degrees of folly and wisdom, and for you to say aught is to be frivolous. Wait, and thy soul shall speak. Wait until the necessary and everlasting overpowers you, until day and night avail themselves of your lips. The only money of God is God. He pays never with any thing less, or any thing else. The only reward of virtue is virtue: the only way to have a friend is to be one. You shall not come nearer a man by getting into his house. If unlike, his soul only flees the faster from you, and you shall catch never a true glance of his eyes. We see the noble afar off and they repel us; why should we intrude? Late,—very late,—we perceive that no arrangements, no introductions, no consuetudes or habits of society would be of any avail to establish us in such relations with them as we desire—but solely the uprise of nature in us to the same degree it is in them: then shall we meet as water with water: and if we should not meet them then, we shall not want them, for we are already they. In the last analysis, love is only the reflection of a man's own worthiness from other men. Men have sometimes exchanged names with their friends, as if they would signify that in their friend each loved his own soul.

The higher the style we demand of friendship, of course the less easy to establish it with flesh and blood. We walk alone in the world. Friends such as we desire are dreams and fables. But a sublime hope cheers ever the faithful heart, that elsewhere, in other regions

of the universal power, souls are now acting, enduring
and daring, which can love us and which we can love.
We may congratulate ourselves that the period of non-
age, of follies, of blunders and of shame, is passed in
solitude, and when we are finished men we shall grasp
heroic hands in heroic hands. Only be admonished by
what you already see, not to strike leagues of friendship with cheap persons, where no friendship can be.
Our impatience betrays us into rash and foolish alliances which no God attends. By persisting in your
path, though you forfeit the little you gain the great.
You become pronounced. You demonstrate yourself,
so as to put yourself out of the reach of false relations,
and you draw to you the first-born of the world,—those
rare pilgrims whereof only one or two wander in nature
at once and before whom the vulgar great show as
spectres and shadows merely.

Is is foolish to be afraid of making our ties too spiritual as if so we could lose any genuine love. Whatever correction of our popular views we make from
insight, nature will be sure to bear us out in, and though
it seem to rob us of some joy, will repay us with a
greater. Let us feel if we will the absolute insulation
of man. We are sure that we have all in us. We go
to Europe, or we pursue persons, or we read books, in
the instinctive faith that these will call it out and reveal
us to ourselves. Beggars all. The persons are such as
we; the Europe, an old faded garment of dead persons; the books, their ghosts. Let us drop this idolatry. Let us give over this mendicancy. Let us even
bid our dearest friends farewell, and defy them, saying
"Who are you? Unhand me; I will be dependent no

more." Ah! seest thou not, O brother, that thus we part only to meet again on a higher platform, and only be more each other's because we are more our own? A friend is Janus-faced: he looks to the past and the future. He is the child of all my foregoing hours, the prophet of those to come. He is the harbinger of a greater friend. It is the property of the divine to be reproductive.

I do then with my friends as I do with my books. I would have them where I can find them, but I seldom use them. We must have society on our own terms, and admit or exclude it on the slightest cause. I cannot afford to speak much with my friend. If he is great he makes me so great that I cannot descend to converse. In the great days, presentiments hover before me, far before me, in the firmament. I ought then to dedicate myself to them. I go in that I may seize them, I go out that I may seize them. I fear only that I may lose them receding into the sky in which now they are only a patch of brighter light. Then, though I prize my friends, I cannot afford to talk with them and study their visions, lest I lose my own. It would indeed give me a certain household joy to quit this lofty seeking, this spiritual astronomy or search of stars, and come down to warm sympathies with you; but then I know well I shall mourn always the vanishing of my mighty gods. It is true, next week I shall have languid times, when I can well afford to occupy myself with foreign objects; then I shall regret the lost literature of your mind, and wish you were by my side again. But if you come, perhaps you will fill my mind only with new visions; not with yourself but with your lustres, and I shall not be able any more than now to converse with you. So I will owe to my friends this evanescent intercourse. I will receive from them not what they have but what they are. They shall give me that which properly they cannot give me, but which emanates from them. But they shall not hold me by any relations less subtle and pure. We will meet as though we met not, and part as though we parted not.

It has seemed to me lately more possible than I knew, to carry a friendship greatly on one side, without due correspondence on the other. Why should I cumber myself with the poor fact that the receiver is not capacious? It never troubles the sun that some of his rays fall wide and vain into ungrateful space, and only a small part on the reflecting planet. Let your greatness educate the crude and cold companion. If he is unequal he will presently pass away; but thou art enlarged by thy own shining, and no longer a mate for frogs and worms, dost soar and burn with the gods of the empyrean. It is thought a disgrace to love unrequited. But the great will see that true love cannot be unrequited. True love transcends instantly the unworthy object and dwells and broods on the eternal, and when the poor interposed mask crumbles, it is not sad, but feels rid of so much earth and feels its independency the surer. Yet these things may hardly be said without a sort of treachery to the relation. The essence of friendship is entireness, a total magnanimity and trust. It must not surmise or provide for infirmity. It treats its object as a god, that it may deify both.

PRUDENCE

WHAT right have I to write on Prudence, whereof I have little, and that of the negative sort? My prudence consists in avoiding and going without, not in the inventing of means and methods, not in adroit steering, not in gentle repairing. I have no skill to make money spend well, no genius in my economy, and whoever sees my garden discovers that I must have some other garden. Yet I love facts, and hate lubricity and people without perception. Then I have the same title to write on prudence that I have to write on poetry or holiness. We write from aspiration and antagonism, as well as from experience. We paint those qualities which we do not possess. The poet admires the man of energy and tactics; the merchant breeds his son for the church or the bar; and where a man is not vain and egotistic you shall find what he has not by his praise. Moreover it would be hardly honest in me not to balance these fine lyric words of Love and Friendship with words of coarser sound, and whilst my debt to my senses is real and constant, not to own it in passing.

Prudence is the virtue of the senses. It is the science of appearances. It is the outmost action of the inward life. It is God taking thought for oxen. It moves matter after the laws of matter. It is content to seek health of body by complying with physical conditions, and health of mind by the laws of the intellect.

The world of the senses is a world of shows; it does not exist for itself, but has a symbolic character; and a true prudence or law of shows recognizes the co-presence of other laws and knows that its own office is subaltern; knows that it is surface and not centre where it works. Prudence is false when detached. It is legitimate when it is the Natural History of the soul incarnate, when it unfolds the beauty of laws within the narrow scope of the senses.

There are all degrees of proficiency in knowledge of the world. It is sufficient to our present purpose to indicate three. One class lives to the utility of the symbol, esteeming health and wealth a final good. Another class live above this mark to the beauty of the symbol, as the poet and artist and the naturalist and man of science. A third class live above the beauty of the symbol to the beauty of the thing signified; these are wise men. The first class have common sense; the second, taste; and the third, spiritual perception. Once in a long time, a man traverses the whole scale, and sees and enjoys the symbol solidly, then also has a clear eye for its beauty, and lastly, whilst he pitches his tent on this sacred volcanic isle of nature, does not offer to build houses and barns thereon, reverencing the splendor of the God which he sees bursting through each chink and cranny.

The world is filled with the proverbs and acts and winkings of a base prudence, which is a devotion to matter, as if we possessed no other faculties than the palate, the nose, the touch, the eye and ear; a prudence which adores the Rule of Three, which never subscribes, which gives never, which seldom lends, and asks but one question of any project,—Will it bake bread? This is a disease like a thickening of the skin until the vital organs are destroyed. But culture, revealing the high origin of the apparent world and aiming at the perfection of the man as the end, degrades every thing else, as health and bodily life, into means. It sees prudence not to be a several faculty, but a name for wisdom and virtue conversing with the body and its wants. Cultivated men always feel and speak so as if a great fortune, the achievement of a civil or social measure, great personal influence, a graceful and commanding address, had their value as proofs of the energy of the spirit. If a man lose his balance and immerse himself in any trades or pleasures for their own sake, he may be a good wheel or pin, but he is not a cultivated man.

The spurious prudence, making the senses final, is the god of sots and cowards, and is the subject of all comedy. It is nature's joke, and therefore literature's. The true prudence limits this sensualism by admitting the knowledge of an internal and real world. This recognition once made,—the order of the world and the distribution of affairs and times being studied with the co-perception of their subordinate place, will reward any degree of attention. For, our existence, thus apparently attached in nature to the sun and the returning moon and the periods which they mark; so susceptible to climate and to country, so alive to social good and evil, so fond of splendor and so tender to hunger and cold and debt,—reads all its primary lessons out of these books.

Prudence does not go behind nature and ask whence it is? It takes the laws of the world whereby man's being is conditioned, as they are, and keeps these laws that it may enjoy their proper good. It respects space and time, climate, want, sleep, the law of polarity, growth and death. There revolve, to give bound and period to his being on all sides, the sun and moon, the great formalists in the sky: here lies stubborn matter, and will not swerve from its chemical routine. Here is a planted globe, pierced and belted with natural laws and fenced and distributed externally with civil partitions and properties which impose new restraints on the young inhabitant.

We eat of the bread which grows in the field. We live by the air which blows around us and we are poisoned by the air that is too cold or too hot, too dry or too wet. Time, which shows so vacant, indivisible and divine in its coming, is slit and peddled into trifles and tatters. A door is to be painted, a lock to be repaired. I want wood or oil, or meal or salt; the house smokes, or I have a headache; then the tax; and an affair to be transacted with a man without heart or brains, and the stinging recollection of an injurious or very awkward word,—these eat up the hours. Do what we can, summer will have its flies. If we walk in the woods we must feed mosquitos. If we go a-fishing we must expect a wet coat. Then climate is a great impediment to idle persons. We often resolve to give up the care of the weather, but still we regard the clouds and the rain.

We are instructed by these petty experiences which usurp the hours and years. The hard soil and four months of snow make the inhabitant of the northern temperate zone wiser and abler than his fellow who enjoys the fixed smile of the tropics. The islander may ramble all day at will. At night he may sleep on a mat under the moon, and wherever a wild date-tree grows, nature has, without a prayer even, spread a table for his morning meal. The northerner is perforce a householder. He must brew, bake, salt and preserve his food. He must pile wood and coal. But as it happens that not one stroke can labor lay to without some new acquaintance with nature; and as nature is inexhaustibly significant, the inhabitants of these climates have always excelled the southerner in force. Such is the value of these matters that a man who knows other things can never know too much of these. Let him have accurate perceptions. Let him, if he have hands, handle; if eyes, measure and discriminate; let him accept and hive every fact of chemistry, natural history and economics; the more he has, the less is he willing to spare any one. Time is always bringing the occasions that disclose their value. Some wisdom comes out of every natural and innocent action. The domestic man, who loves no music so well as his kitchen clock and the airs which the logs sing to him as they burn on the hearth, has solaces which others never dream of. The application of means to ends ensures victory and the songs of victory not less in a farm or a shop than in the tactics of party or of war. The good husband finds method as efficient in the packing of firewood in a shed or in the harvesting of fruits in the

cellar, as in Peninsular campaigns or the files of the
Department of State.   In the rainy day he builds a
work-bench, or gets his tool-box set in the corner of
the barn-chamber, and stored with nails, gimlet,
pincers, screwdriver and chisel.   Herein he tastes an
old joy of youth and childhood, the cat-like love of
garrets, presses and corn-chambers, and of the conveniences of long housekeeping.   His garden or his
poultry-yard—very paltry places it may be—tells him
many pleasant anecdotes.   One might find argument
for optimism in the abundant flow of this saccharine
element of pleasure in every suburb and extremity of the
good world.   Let a man keep the law,—any law,—and
his way will be strown with satisfactions.   There is
more difference in the quality of our pleasures than
in the amount.

On the other hand, nature punishes any neglect of
prudence.   If you think the senses final, obey their
law.   If you believe in the soul, do not clutch at sensual
sweetness before it is ripe on the slow tree of cause and
effect.   It is vinegar to the eyes to deal with men of
loose and imperfect perception.   Dr. Johnson is reported to have said,—"If the child say he looked out
of this window, when he looked out of that,—whip
him."   Our American character is marked by a more
than average delight in accurate perception, which is
shown by the currency of the by-word, "No mistake."
But the discomfort of unpunctuality, of confusion of
thought about facts, inattention to the wants of to-
morrow, is of no nation.   The beautiful laws of time
and space, once dislocated by our inaptitude, are holes
and dens.   If the hive be disturbed by rash and stupid

hands, instead of honey it will yield us bees. Our
words and actions to be fair must be timely. A gay
and pleasant sound is the whetting of the scythe in the
mornings of June; yet what is more lonesome and sad
than the sound of a whetstone or mower's rifle when
it is too late in the season to make hay? Scatter
brained and "afternoon men" spoil much more than
their own affair in spoiling the temper of those who
deal with them. I have seen a criticism on some paintings, of which I am reminded when I see the shiftless
and unhappy men who are not true to their senses. The
last Grand Duke of Weimar, a man of superior understanding, said: "I have sometimes remarked in the
presence of great works of art, and just now especially
in Dresden, how much a certain property contributes to
the effect which gives life to the figures, and to the life
an irresistible truth. This property is the hitting, in
all the figures we draw, the right centre of gravity. I
mean the placing the figures firm upon their feet, making the hands grasp, and fastening the eyes on the
spot where they should look. Even lifeless figures, as
vessels and stools—let them be drawn ever so correctly
—lose all effect so soon as they lack the resting upon
their centre of gravity, and have a certain swimming
and oscillating appearance. The Raphael in the Dresden gallery (the only great affecting picture which I
have seen) is the quietest and most passionless piece you
can imagine; a couple of saints who worship the Virgin
and child. Nevertheless it awakens a deeper impression than the contortions of ten crucified martyrs. For,
beside all the resistless beauty of form, it possesses in
the highest degree the property of the perpendicularity

of all the figures." This perpendicularity we demand
of all the figures in this picture of life. Let them stand
on their feet, and not float and swing. Let us know
where to find them. Let them discriminate between
what they remember and what they dreamed. Let them
call a spade a spade. Let them give us facts, and honor
their own senses with trust.

But what man shall dare task another with impru-
dence? Who is prudent? The men we call greatest
are least in this kingdom. There is a certain fatal dislocation in our relation to nature, distorting all our
modes of living and making every law our enemy, which
seems at last to have aroused all the wit and virtue in
the world to ponder the question of Reform. We
must call the highest prudence to counsel, and ask why
health and beauty and genius should now be the exception rather than the rule of human nature? We do
not know the properties of plants and animals and the
laws of nature, through our sympathy with the same;
but this remains the dream of poets. Poetry and prudence should be coincident. Poets should be lawgiv-
ers; that is, the boldest lyric inspiration should not chide
and insult, but should announce and lead the civil code
and the day's work. But now the two things seems ir-
reconcilably parted. We have violated law upon law
until we stand amidst ruins, and when by chance we
espy a coincidence between reason and the phenomena,
we are surprised. Beauty should be the dowry of
every man and woman, as invariably as sensation; but
it is rare. Health or sound organization should be universal. Genius should be the child of genius, and
every child should be inspired; but now it is not to be

predicted of any child, and nowhere is it pure. We call partial half lights, by courtesy, genius; talent which converts itself to money; talent which glitters to-day that it may dine and sleep well to-morrow; and society is officered by *men of parts,* as they are properly called, and not by divine men. These use their gifts to refine luxury, not to abolish it. Genius is always ascetic; and piety, and love. Appetite shows to the finer souls as a disease, and they find beauty in rites and bounds that resist it.

We have found out fine names to cover our sensuality withal, but no gifts can raise intemperance. The man of talent affects to call his transgressions of the laws of the senses trivial and to count them nothing considered with his devotion to his art. His art rebukes him. That never taught him lewdness, nor the love of wine, nor the wish to reap where he had not sowed. His art is less for every deduction from his holiness, and less for every defect of common sense. On him who scorned the world, as he said, the scorned world wreaks its revenge. He that despiseth small things will perish by little and little. Goethe's Tasso is very likely to be a pretty fair historical portrait, and that is true tragedy. It does not seem to me so genuine grief when some tyrannous Richard III. oppresses and slays a score of innocent persons, as when Antonio and Tasso, both apparently right, wrong each other. One living after the maxims of this world and consistent and true to them, the other fired with all divine sentiments, yet grasping also at the pleasures of sense, without submitting to their law. That is a grief we all feel, a knot we cannot untie. Tasso's is no infrequent case in modern biography.   A man of genius, of an ardent temperament, reckless of physical laws, self-indulgent, becomes presently unfortunate, querulous, a "discomfortable cousin," a thorn to himself and to others.

The scholar shames us by his bifold life.   Whilst something higher than prudence is active, he is admirable; when common sense is wanted, he is an encumbrance.   Yesterday, Cæsar was not so great; today, Job not so miserable.   Yesterday, radiant with the light of an ideal world in which he lives, the first of men, and now oppressed by wants and by sickness, for which he must thank himself, none is so poor to do him reverence.   He resembles the opium eaters whom travellers describe as frequenting the bazaars of Constantinople, who skulk about all day, the most pitiful drivellers, yellow, emaciated, ragged, sneaking; then at evening, when the bazaars are open, they slink to the opium-shop, swallow their morsel and become tranquil, glorious and great.   And who has not seen the tragedy of imprudent genius struggling for years with paltry pecuniary difficulties, at last sinking, chilled, exhausted and fruitless, like a giant slaughtered by pins?

Is it not better that a man should accept the first pains and mortifications of this sort, which nature is not slack in sending him, as hints that he must expect no other good than the just fruit of his own labor and self-denial?   Health, bread, climate, social position, have their importance, and he will give them their due.   Let him esteem Nature a perpetual counsellor, and her perfections the exact measure of our deviations.   Let him make the night night, and the day day.   Let him control the habit of expense.   Let him see that as much wisdom may be expended on a private economy as on an empire, and as much wisdom may be drawn from it. The laws of the world are written out for him on every piece of money in his hand. There is nothing he will not be the better for knowing, were it only the wisdom of Poor Richard, or the State-street prudence of buying by the acre to sell by the foot; or the thrift of the agriculturist, to stick a tree between whiles, because it will grow whilst he sleeps; or the prudence which consists in husbanding little strokes of the tool, little portions of time, particles of stock and small gains. The eye of prudence may never shut. Iron, if kept at the ironmonger's, will rust; beer, if not brewed in the right state of the atmosphere, will sour; timber of ships will rot at sea, or if laid up high and dry, will strain, warp and dry-rot. Money, if kept by us, yields no rent and is liable to loss; if invested, is liable to depreciation of the particular kind of stock. Strike, says the smith, the iron is white. Keep the rake, says the haymaker, as nigh the scythe as you can, and the cart as nigh the rake. Our Yankee trade is reputed to be very much on the extreme of this prudence. It saves itself by its activity. It takes bank notes,—good, bad, clean, ragged, and saves itself by the speed with which it passes them off. Iron cannot rust, nor beer sour, nor timber rot, nor calicoes go out of fashion, nor money stocks depreciate, in the few swift moments in which the Yankee suffers any one of them to remain in his possession. In skating over thin ice our safety is in our speed.

Let him learn a prudence of a higher strain. Let him learn that every thing in nature, even motes and feathers, go by law and not by luck, and that what he sows he reaps. By diligence and self-command let him put the bread he eats at his own disposal, and not at that of others, that he may not stand in bitter and false relations to other men; for the best good of wealth is freedom. Let him practise the minor virtues. How much of human life is lost in waiting! Let him not make his fellow creatures wait. How many words and promises are promises of conversation! Let his be words of fate. When he sees a folded and sealed scrap of paper float round the globe in a pine ship and come safe to the eye for which it was written, amidst a swarming population; let him likewise feel the admonition to integrate his being across all these distracting forces, and keep a slender human word among the storms, distances and accidents that drive us hither and thither, and, by persistency, make the paltry force of one man reappear to redeem its pledge after months and years in the most distant climates.

We must not try to write the laws of any one virtue, looking at that only. Human nature loves no contradictions, but is symmetrical. The prudence which secures an outward well-being is not to be studied by one set of men, whilst heroism and holiness are studied by another, but they are reconcilable. Prudence concerns the present time, persons, property and existing forms. But as every fact hath its roots in the soul, and, if the soul were changed, would cease to be, or would become some other thing, therefore the proper administration of outward things will always rest on a just apprehension of their cause and origin; that is, the good man will be the wise man, and the single-hearted the politic man. Every violation of truth is not only a sort of suicide in the liar, but is a stab at the health of human society. On the most profitable lies the course of events presently lays a destructive tax; whilst frankness proves to be the best tactics, for it invites frankness, puts the parties on a convenient footing and makes their business a friendship. Trust men and they will be true to you; treat them greatly and they will show themselves great, though they make an exception in your favor to all their rules of trade.

So, in regard to disagreeable and formidable things, prudence does not consist in evasion or in flight, but in courage. He who wishes to walk in the most peaceful parts of life with any serenity must screw himself up to resolution. Let him front the object of his worst apprehension, and his stoutness will commonly make his fears groundless. The Latin proverb says, "in battles the eye is first overcome." The eye is daunted and greatly exaggerates the perils of the hour. Entire self-possession may make a battle very little more dangerous to life than a match at foils or at football. Examples are cited by soldiers, of men who have seen the cannon pointed and the fire given to it, and who have stepped aside from the path of the ball. The terrors of the storm are chiefly confined to the parlor and the cabin. The drover, the sailor, buffets it all day, and his health renews itself at as vigorous a pulse under the sleet as under the sun of June.

In the occurrence of unpleasant things among neighbors, fear comes readily to heart and magnifies the consequence of the other party; but it is a bad counsellor. Every man is actually weak and apparently strong. To

himself he seems weak; to others formidable. You are
afraid of Grim; but Grim also is afraid of you. You
are solicitous of the good will of the meanest person,
uneasy at his ill will. But the sturdiest offender of
your peace and of the neighborhod, if you rip up *his*
claims, is as thin and timid as any; and the peace of
society is often kept, because, as children say, one is
afraid and the other dares not. Far off, men swell,
bully and threaten: bring them hand to hand, and they
are a feeble folk.

It is a proverb that "courtesy costs nothing"; but
calculation might come to value love for its profit.
Love is fabled to be blind, but kindness is necessary
to perception; love is not a hood, but an eye-water.
If you meet a sectary or a hostile partisan, never recognize the dividing lines, but meet on what common
ground remains,—if only that the sun shines and the
rain rains for both,—the area will widen very fast,
and ere you know it, the boundary mountains on which
the eye had fastened have melted into air. If he set
out to contend, almost St. Paul will lie, almost St. John
will hate. What low, poor, paltry, hypocritical people
an argument on religion will make of the pure and
chosen souls. Shuffle they will and crow, crook and
hide, feign to confess here, only that they may brag
and conquer there, and not a thought has enriched either
party, and not an emotion of bravery, modesty, or
hope. So neither should you put yourself in a false
position to your contemporaries by indulging a vein of
hostility and bitterness. Though your views are in
straight antagonism to theirs, assume an identity of

sentiment, assume that you are saying precisely that which all think, and in the flow of wit and love roll out your paradoxes in solid column, with not the infirmity of a doubt. So at least shall you get an adequate deliverance. The natural motions of the soul are so much better than the voluntary ones that you will never do yourself justice in dispute. The thought is not then taken hold of by the right handle, does not show itself proportioned and in its true bearings, but bears extorted, hoarse, and half witness. But assume a consent and it shall presently be granted, since really and underneath their all external diversities, all men are of one heart and mind.

Wisdom will never let us stand with any man or men on an unfriendly footing. We refuse sympathy and intimacy with people, as if we waited for some better sympathy and intimacy to come. But whence and when? To-morrow will be like to-day. Life wastes itself whilst we are preparing to live. Our friends and fellow-workers die off from us. Scarcely can we say we see new men, new women, approaching us. We are too old to regard fashion, too old to expect patronage of any greater or more powerful. Let us suck the sweetness of those affections and consuetudes that grow near us. These old shoes are easy to the feet. Undoubtedly we can easily pick faults in our company, can easily whisper names prouder, and that tickle the fancy more. Every man's imagination hath its friends; and pleasant would life be with such companions. But if you cannot have them on good mutual terms, you cannot have them. If not the Deity but our ambition hews and shapes the new relations, their virtue escapes, as strawberries lose their flavor in garden beds.

Thus truth, frankness, courage, love, humility and all the virtues range themselves on the side of prudence, or the art of securing a present well-being. I do not know if all matter will be found to be made of one element, as oxygen or hydrogen, at last, but the world of manners and actions is wrought of one stuff, and begin where we will we are pretty sure in a short space to be mumbling our ten commandments.

HEROISM

Paradise is under the shadow of swords.
—*Mahomet.*

IN the elder English dramatists, and mainly in the plays of Beaumont and Fletcher, there is a constant recognition of gentility, as if a noble behavior were as easily marked in the society of their age as color is in our American population. When any Rodrigo, Pedro or Valerio enters, though he be a stranger, the duke or governor exclaims, "This is a gentleman," and proffers civilities without end; but all the rest are slag and refuse. In harmony with this delight in personal advantages there is in their plays a certain heroic cast of character and dialogue,—as in Bonduca, Sophocles, the Mad Lover, the Double Marriage,—wherein the speaker is so earnest and cordial and on such deep grounds of character, that the dialogue, on the slightest additional incident in the plot, rises naturally into poetry. Among many texts take the following. The Roman Martius has conquered Athens,—all but the invincible spirits of Sophocles, the duke of Athens, and Dorigen, his wife. The beauty of the latter inflames Martius, and he seeks to save her husband; but Sophocles will not ask his life, although assured that a word will save him, and the execution of both proceeds :—

Valerius. Bid thy wife farewell.

Soph. No, I will take no leave. My Dorigen,
Yonder, above, 'bout Ariadne's crown,
My spirit shall hover for thee. Prithee, haste.

Dor. Stay, Sophocles,—with this tie up my sight;
Let not soft nature so transformed be,
And lose her gentler sexed humanity,
To make me see my lord bleed. So, 't is well;
Never one object underneath the sun
Will I behold before my Sophocles:
Farewell; now teach the Romans how to die.

Mar. Dost know what 't is to die?

Soph. Thou dost not, Martius,
And, therefore, not what 't is to live; to die
Is to begin to live. It is to end
An old, stale, weary work and to commence
A newer and a better. 'T is to leave
Deceitful knaves for the society
Of gods and goodness. Thou thyself must part
At last from all thy garlands, pleasures, triumphs,
And prove thy fortitude what then 't will do.

Val. But art not grieved nor vexed to leave thy life thus?

Soph. Why should I grieve or vex for being sent
To them I ever loved best? Now I'll kneel,
But with my back toward thee: 't is the last duty
This trunk can do the gods.

Mar. Strike, strike, Valerius,
Or Martius' heart will leap out at his mouth.
This is a man, a woman. Kiss thy lord,
And live with all the freedom you were wont.
O love! thou doubly hast afflicted me
With virtue and with beauty. Treacherous heart,
My hand shall cast thee quick into my urn,
Ere thou transgress this knot of piety.

Val. What ails my brother?

Soph. Martius, O Martius,
Thou now hast found a way to conquer me.

Dor. O star of Rome! what gratitude can speak
Fit words to follow such a deed as this?
Mar. This admirable duke, Valerius,
With his disdain of fortune and of death,
Captived himself, has captivated me,
And though my arm hath ta'en his body here,
His soul hath subjugated Martius' soul.
By Romulus, he is all soul, I think;
He hath no flesh, and spirit cannot be gyved,
Then we have vanquished nothing; he is free,
And Martius walks now in captivity.

I do not readily remember any poem, play, sermon, novel or oration that our press vents in the last few years, which goes to the same tune. We have a great many flutes and flageolets, but not often the sound of any fife. Yet Wordsworth's "Laodamia," and the ode of "Dion," and some sonnets, have a certain noble music; and Scott will sometimes draw a stroke like the portrait of Lord Evandale given by Balfour of Burley. Thomas Carlyle, with his natural taste for what is manly and daring in character, has suffered no heroic trait in his favorites to drop from his biographical and historical pictures. Earlier, Robert Burns has given us a song or two. In the Harleian Miscellanies there is an account of the battle of Lutzen which deserves to be read. And Simon Ockley's History of the Saracens recounts the prodigies of individual valor, with admiration all the more evident on the part of the narrator that he seems to think that his place in Christian Oxford requires of him some proper protestations of abhorrence. But if we explore the literature of Heroism we shall quickly come to Plutarch, who is its Doctor and historian. To him we owe the Brasidas, the Dion, the Epaminondas, the Scipio of old, and I must think we are more deeply indebted to him than to all the ancient writers. Each of his "Lives" is a refutation to the despondency and cowardice of our religious and political theorists. A wild courage, a stoicism not of the schools but of the blood, shines in every anecdote, and has given that book its immense fame.

We need books of this tart cathartic virtue more than books of political science or of private economy. Life is a festival only to the wise. Seen from the nook and chimney-side of prudence, it wears a ragged and dangerous front. The violations of the laws of nature by our predecessors and our contemporaries are punished in us also. The disease and deformity around us certify the infraction of natural, intellectual and moral laws, and often violation on violation to breed such compound misery. A lockjaw that bends a man's head back to his heels; hydrophobia that makes him bark at his wife and babes; insanity that makes him eat grass; war, plague, cholera, famine, indicate a cer-tain ferocity in nature, which, as it had its inlet by human crime, must have its outlet by human suffering. Unhappily almost no man exists who has not in his own person become to some amount a stockholder in the sin, and so made himself liable to a share in the expiation.

Our culture therefore must not omit the arming of the man. Let him hear in season that he is born into the state of war, and that the commonwealth and his own well-being require that he should not go danc-ing in the weeds of peace, but warned, self-collected and neither defying nor dreading the thunder, let him take both reputation and life in his hand, and with perfect urbanity dare the gibbet and the mob by the absolute truth of his speech and the rectitude of his behavior.

Towards all this external evil the man within the breast assumes a warlike attitude, and affirms his ability to cope single-handed with the infinite army of enemies. To this military attitude of the soul we give the name of Heroism. Its rudest form is the contempt for safety and ease, which makes the attractiveness of war. It is a self-trust which slights the restraints of prudence, in the plenitude of its energy and power to repair the harms it may suffer. The hero is a mind of such balance that no disturbances can shake his will, but pleasantly and as it were merrily he advances to his own music, alike in frightful alarms and in the tipsy mirth of universal dissoluteness. There is somewhat not philosophical in heroism; there is somewhat not holy in it; it seems not to know that other souls are of one texture with it; it hath pride; it is the extreme of individual nature. Nevertheless we must profoundly revere it. There is somewhat in great actions which does not allow us to go behind them. Heroism feels and never reasons, and therefore is always right; and although a different breeding, different religion and greater intellectual activity would have modified or even reversed the particular action, yet for the hero that thing he does is the highest deed, and is not open to the censure of philosophers or divines. It is the avowal of the unschooled man that he finds a quality in him that is negligent of expense, of

health, of life, of danger, of hatred, of reproach, and
that he knows that his will is higher and more excellent than all actual and all possible antagonists.

Heroism works in contradiction to the voice of mankind and in contradiction, for a time, to the voice of
the great and good. Heroism is an obedience to a
secret impulse of an individual's character. Now to
no other man can its wisdom appear as it does to him,
for every man must be supposed to see a little farther
on his own proper path than any one else. Therefore
just and wise men take umbrage at his act, until after
some little time be past: then they see it to be in uni-
son with their acts. All prudent men see that the action is clean contrary to a sensual prosperity; for every
heroic act measures itself by its contempt of some external good. But it finds its own success at last, and
then the prudent also extol.

Self-trust is the essence of heroism. It is the state
of the soul at war, and its ultimate objects are the last
defiance of falsehood and wrong, and the power to
bear all that can be inflicted by evil agents. It speaks
the truth and it is just. It is generous, hospitable, temperate, scornful of petty calculations and scornful of
being scorned. It persists; it is of an undaunted boldness and of a fortitude not to be wearied out. Its jest
is the littleness of common life. That false prudence
which dotes on health and wealth is the foil, the butt
and merriment of heroism. Heroism, like Plotinus, is
almost ashamed of its body. What shall it say then to
the sugar-plums and cats'-cradles, to the toilet, compliments, quarrels, cards and custard, which rack the
wit of all human society? What joys has kind na-

ture provided for us dear creatures! There seems to be no interval between greatness and meanness. When the spirit is not master of the world, then it is its dupe. Yet the little man takes the great hoax so innocently, works in it so headlong and believing, is born red, and dies gray, arranging his toilet, attending on his own health, laying traps for sweet food and strong wine, setting his heart on a horse or a rifle, made happy with a little gossip or a little praise, that the great soul cannot choose but laugh at such earnest nonsense. "Indeed, these humble considerations make me out of love with greatness. What a disgrace is it to me to take note how many pairs of silk stockings thou hast, namely, these and those that were the peach-colored ones; or to bear the inventory of thy shirts, as one for superfluity, and one other for use."

Citizens, thinking after the laws of arithmetic, consider the inconvenience of receiving strangers at their fireside, reckon narrowly the loss of time and the unusual display: the soul of a better quality thrusts back the unseasonable economy into the vaults of life, and says, I will obey the God, and the sacrifice and the fire he will provide. Ibn Hankal, the Arabian geographer, describes a heroic extreme in the hospitality of Sogd, in Bukharia. "When I was in Sogd I saw a great building, like a palace, the gates of which were open and fixed back to the wall with large nails. I asked the reason, and was told that the house had not been shut, night or day, for a hundred years. Strangers may present themselves at any hour and in whatever number; the master has amply provided for the reception of the men and their animals and is never happier than when they tarry for some time.   Nothing of the kind have I seen in any other country."   The magnanimous know very well that they who give time, or money, or shelter, to the stranger,—so it be done for love and not for ostentation,—do, as it were, put God under obligation to them, so perfect are the compensations of the universe.   In some way the time they seem to lose is redeemed and the pains they seem to take remunerate themselves.   These men fan the flame of human love and raise the standard of civil virtue among mankind.   But hospitality must be for service and not for show, or it pulls down the host.   The brave soul rates itself too high to value itself by the splendor of its table and draperies.   It gives what it hath, and all it hath, but its own majesty can lend a better grace to bannocks and fair water than belong to city feasts.

The temperance of the hero proceeds from the same wish to do no dishonor to the worthiness he has.   But he loves it for its elegancy, not for its austerity.   It seems not worth his while to be solemn and denounce with bitterness flesh-eating or wine-drinking, the use of tobacco, or opium, or tea, or silk, or gold.   A great man scarcely knows how he dines, how he dresses, but without railing or precision his living is natural and poetic.   John Eliot, the Indian Apostle, drank water, and said of wine, "It is a noble, generous liquor and we should be humbly thankful for it, but, as I remember, water was made before it."   Better still is the temperance of King David, who poured out on the ground unto the Lord the water which three of his warriors had brought him to drink, at the peril of their lives.

It is told of Brutus, that when he fell on his sword after the battle of Philippi, he quoted a line of Euripides, "O Virtue! I have followed thee through life, and I find thee at last but a shade." I doubt not the hero is slandered by this report. The heroic soul does not sell its justice and its nobleness. It does not ask to dine nicely and to sleep warm. The essence of greatness is the perception that virtue is enough. Poverty is its ornament. Plenty does not need it, and can very well abide its loss.

But that which takes my fancy most in the heroic class, is the good-humor and hilarity they exhibit. It is a height to which common duty can very well attain, to suffer and to dare with solemnity. But these rare souls set opinion, success, and life at so cheap a rate that they will not soothe their enemies by petitions, or the show of sorrow, but wear their own habitual greatness. Scipio, charged with peculation, refuses to do himself so great a disgrace as to wait for justification, though he had the scroll of his accounts in his hands, but tears it to pieces before the tribunes. Socrates's condemnation of himself to be maintained in all honor in the Prytaneum, during his life, and Sir Thomas More's playfulness at the scaffold, are of the same strain. In Beaumont and Fletcher's "Sea Voyage," Juletta tells the stout captain and his company,—

> *Jul.* Why, slaves, 't is in our power to hang ye.
> *Master.*   Very likely,
> 'T is in our powers, then, to be hanged, and scorn ye.

These replies are sound and whole. Sport is the bloom and glow of a perfect health. The great will

not condescend to take any thing seriously; all must
be as gay as the song of a canary, though it were the
building of cities or the eradication of old and foolish
churches and nations which have cumbered the earth
long thousands of years. Simple hearts put all the
history and customs of this world behind them, and
play their own play in innocent defiance of the Blue-
Laws of the world; and such would appear, could we
see the human race assembled in vision, like little
children frolicking together, though to the eyes of mankind at large they wear a stately and solemn garb of
works and influences.

The interest these fine stories have for us, the power
of a romance over the boy who grasps the forbidden
book under his bench at school, our delight in the
hero, is the main fact to our purpose. All these great
and transcendent properties are ours. If we dilate in
beholding the Greek energy, the Roman pride, it is that
we are already domesticating the same sentiment. Let
us find room for this great guest in our small houses.
The first step of worthiness will be to disabuse us of
our superstitious associations with places and times,
with number and size. Why should these words,
Athenian, Roman, Asia and England, so tingle in the
ear? Let us feel that where the heart is, there the
muses, there the gods sojourn, and not in any geography of fame. Massachusetts, Connecticut River and
Boston Bay you think paltry places, and the ear loves
names of foreign and classic topography. But here
we are:—that is a great fact, and, if we will tarry a
little, we may come to learn that here is best. See to
it only that thyself is here,—and art and nature, hope

and dread, friends, angels and the Supreme Being
shall not be absent from the chamber where thou sittest. Epaminondas, brave and affectionate, does not
seem to us to need Olympus to die upon, nor the
Syrian sunshine. He lies very well where he is.
The Jerseys were handsome ground enough for
Washington to tread, and London streets for the feet
of Milton. A great man illustrates his place, makes his
climate genial in the imagination of men, and its air
the beloved element of all delicate spirits. That country is the fairest which is inhabited by the noblest minds.
The pictures which fill the imagination in reading the
actions of Pericles, Xenophon, Columbus, Bayard, Sidney, Hampden, teach us how needlessly mean our life
is; that we, by the depth of our living, should deck it
with more than regal or national splendor, and act on
principles that should interest man and nature in the
length of our days.

We have seen or heard of many extraordinary young
men who never ripened, or whose performance in actual
life was not extraordinary. When we see their air
and mien, when we hear them speak of society, of
books, of religion, we admire their superiority; they
seem to throw contempt on the whole state of the world;
theirs is the tone of a youthful giant who is sent to
work revolutions. But they enter an active profession
and the forming Colossus shrinks to the common size
of man. The magic they used was the ideal tendencies,
which always makes the Actual ridiculous; but the
tough world has its revenge the moment they put their
horses of the sun to plough in its furrow. They found
no example and no companion, and their heart fainted.

What then? The lesson they gave in their first as-
pirations is yet true; and a better valor and a purer
truth shall one day execute their will and put the
world to shame. Or why should a woman liken herself to any historical woman, and think, because Sap-
pho, or Sévigné, or De Staël, or the cloistered souls
who have had genius and cultivation do not satisfy the
imagination and the serene Themis, none can,—certainly not she. Why not? She has a new and un-
attempted problem to solve, perchance that of the happiest nature that ever bloomed. Let the maiden, with
erect soul, walk serenely on her way, accept the hint
of each new experience, try in turn all the gifts God
offers her that she may learn the power and the charm
that like a new dawn radiating of the deep of space,
her new-born being is. The fair girl who repels interference by a decided and proud choice of influences,
so careless of pleasing, so wilful and lofty, inspires
every beholder with somewhat of her own nobleness.
The silent heart encourages her; O friend, never strike
sail to a fear. Come into port greatly, or sail with
God the seas. Not in vain you live, for every passing
eye is cheered and refined by the vision.

The characteristic of genuine heroism is its persistency. All men have wandering impulses, fits and starts
of generosity. But when you have resolved to be great,
abide by yourself, and do not weakly try to reconcile
yourself with the world. The heroic cannot be the
common, nor the common the heroic. Yet we have
the weakness to expect the sympathy of people in those
actions whose excellence is that they outrun sympathy
and appeal to a tardy justice. If you would serve your

brother, because it is fit for you to serve him, do not take back your words when you find that prudent people do not commend you. Be true to your own act, and congratulate yourself if you have done something strange and extravagant and broken the monotony of a decorous age. It was a high counsel that I once heard given to a young person, "Always do what you are afraid to do." A simple manly character need never make an apology, but should regard its past action with the calmness of Phocion, when he admitted that the event of the battle was happy, yet did not regret his dissuasion from the battle.

There is no weakness or exposure for which we cannot find consolation in the thought,—this is a part of my constitution, part of my relation and office to my fellow-creature. Has nature covenanted with me that I should never appear to disadvantage, never make a ridiculous figure? Let us be generous of our dignity as well as of our money. Greatness once and for ever has done with opinion. We tell our charities, not because we wish to be praised for them, not because we think they have great merit, but for our justification. It is a capital blunder; as you discover when another man recites his charities.

To speak the truth, even with some austerity, to live with some rigor of temperance, or some extremes of generosity, seems to be an asceticism which common good nature would appoint to those who are at ease and in plenty, in sign that they feel a brotherhood with the great multitude of suffering men. And not only need we breathe and exercise the soul by assuming the penalties of abstinence, of debt, of solitude, of un-

popularity, but it behoves the wise man to look with a
bold eye into those rarer dangers which sometimes invade men, and to familiarize himself with disgusting
forms of disease, with sounds of execration, and the
vision of violent death.

Times of heroism are generally times of terror, but
the day never shines in which this element may not
work. The circumstances of man, we say, are historically somewhat better in this country and at this
hour than perhaps ever before. More freedom exists
for culture. It will not now run against an axe at the
first step out of the beaten track of opinion. But whoso
is heroic will always find crises to try his edge. Human virtue demands her champions and martyrs, and
the trial of persecution always proceeds. It is but the
other day that the brave Lovejoy gave his breast to
the bullets of a mob, for the rights of free speech and
opinion, and died when it was better not to live.

I see not any road of perfect peace which a man
can walk, but to take counsel of his own bosom. Let
him quit too much association, let him go home much,
and stablish himself in those courses he approves. The
unremitting retention of simple and high sentiments in
obscure duties is hardening the character to that temper
which will work with honor, if need be in the tumult,
or on the scaffold. Whatever outrages have happened
to men may befall a man again: and very easily in a
republic, if there appear any signs of a decay of religion. Coarse slander, fire, tar and feathers and the
gibbet, the youth may freely bring home to his mind
and with what sweetness of temper he can, and inquire how fast he can fix his sense of duty, braving such

penalties, whenever it may please the next newspaper and a sufficient number of his neighbors to pronounce his opinions incendiary.

It may calm the apprehension of calamity in the most susceptible heart to see how quick a bound Nature has set to the utmost infliction of malice. We rapidly approach a brink over which no enemy can follow us.

> Let them rave:
> Thou art quiet in thy grave.

In the gloom of our ignorance of what shall be, in the hour when we are deaf to the higher voices, who does not envy them who have seen safely to an end their manful endeavor? Who that sees the meanness of our politics but inly congratulates Washington that he is long already wrapped in his shroud, and for ever safe; that he was laid sweet in his grave, the hope of humanity not yet subjugated in him? Who does not sometimes envy the good and brave who are no more to suffer from the tumults of the natural world, and await with curious complacency the speedy term of his own conversation with finite nature? And yet the love that will be annihilated sooner than treacherous has already made death impossible, and affirms itself no mortal but a native of the deeps of absolute and inextinguishable being.

THE OVER-SOUL

But souls that of his own good life partake,
He loves as his own self; dear as his eye
They are to Him: He'll never them forsake:
When they shall die, then God himself shall die:
They live, they live in blest eternity.
                                        —*Henry More.*

THERE is a difference between one and another hour of life in their authority and subsequent effect. Our faith comes in moments; our vice is habitual. Yet there is a depth in those brief moments which constrains us to ascribe more reality to them than to all other experiences. For this reason the argument which is always forthcoming to silence those who conceive extraordinary hopes of man, namely the appeal to experience, is for ever invalid and vain. A mightier hope abolishes despair. We give up the past to the objector, and yet we hope. He must explain this hope. We grant that human life is mean, but how did we find out that it was mean? What is the ground of this uneasiness of ours; of this old discontent? What is the universal sense of want and ignorance, but the fine innuendo by which the great soul makes its enormous claim? Why do men feel that the natural history of man has never been written, but always he is leaving behind what you have said of him, and it becomes old, and books of metaphysics worthless? The philosophy of six thousand years has not searched the chambers and magazines of the soul. In its experiments there has always remained, in the last analysis, a residuum it could not resolve. Man is a stream whose source is hidden. Always our being is descending into us from we know not whence. The most exact calculator has no prescience that somewhat incalculable may not baulk the very next moment. I am constrained every moment to acknowledge a higher origin for events than the will I call mine.

As with events, so is it with thoughts. When I watch that flowing river, which, out of regions I see not, pours for a season its streams into me,—I see that I am a pensioner,—not a cause but a suprised spectator of this ethereal water; that I desire and look up and put myself in the attitude of reception, but from some alien energy the visions come.

The Supreme Critic on all the errors of the past and the present, and the only prophet of that which must be, is that great nature in which we rest as the earth lies in the soft arms of the atmosphere; that Unity, that Over-soul, within which every man's particular being is contained and made one with all other; that common heart of which all sincere conversation is the worship, to which all right action is submission; that overpowering reality which confutes our tricks and talents, and constrains every one to pass for what he is, and to speak from his character and not from his tongue, and which evermore tends to pass into our thought and hand and become wisdom and virtue and power and beauty. We live in succession, in division, in parts, in particles.

Meantime within man is the soul of the whole; the wise silence; the universal beauty, to which every part and particle is equally related; the eternal ONE. And this deep power in which we exist and whose beatitude is all accessible to us, is not only self-sufficing and perfect in every hour, but the act of seeing and the thing seen, the seer and the spectacle, the subject and the object, are one. We see the world piece by piece, as the sun, the moon, the animal, the tree; but the whole, of which these are the shining parts, is the soul. Only by the vision of that Wisdom can the horoscope of the ages be read, and by falling back on our better thoughts, by yielding to the spirit of prophecy which is innate in every man that we can know what it saith. Every man's words who speaks from that life must sound vain to those who do not dwell in the same thought on their own part. I dare not speak for it. My words do not carry its august sense; they fall short and cold. Only itself can inspire whom it will, and behold! their speech shall be lyrical, and sweet, and universal as the rising of the wind. Yet I desire, even by profane words, if sacred I may not use, to indicate the heaven of this deity and to report what hints I have collected of the transcendent simplicity and energy of the Highest Law.

If we consider what happens in conversation, in reveries, in remorse, in times of passion, in surprises, in the instructions of dreams, wherein often we see ourselves in masquerade,—the droll disguises only magnifying and enhancing a real element and forcing it on our distinct notice,—we shall catch many hints that will broaden and lighten into knowledge of the secret of nature. All goes to show that the soul in man is not an organ, but animates and exercises all the organs; is not a function, like the power of memory, of calculation, of comparison,—but uses these as hands and feet; is not a faculty, but a light; is not the intellect or the will, but the master of the intellect and the will;—is the vast background of our being, in which they lie,—an immensity not possessed and that cannot be possessed. From within or from behind, a light shines through us upon things and makes us aware that we are nothing, but the light is all. A man is the façade of a temple wherein all wisdom and all good abide. What we commonly call man, the eating, drinking, planting, counting man, does not, as we know him, represent himself, but misrepresents himself. Him we do not respect, but the soul, whose organ he is, would he let it appear through his action, would make our knees bend. When it breathes through his intellect, it is genius; when it breathes through his will, it is virtue; when it flows through his affection, it is love. And the blindness of the intellect begins when it would be something of itself. The weakness of the will begins when the individual would be something of himself. All reform aims in some one particular to let the great soul have its way through us; in other words, to engage us to obey.

Of this pure nature every man is at some time sensible. Language cannot paint it with his colors. It is too subtle. It is undefinable, unmeasurable; but we know that it pervades and contains us. We know that all spiritual being is in man. A wise old proverb says, "God comes to see us without bell": that is, as there is no screen or ceiling between our heads and the infinite heavens, so is there no bar or wall in the soul, where man, the effect, ceases, and God, the cause, begins. The walls are taken away. We lie open on one side to the deeps of spiritual nature, to all the attributes of God. Justice we see and know, Love, Freedom, Power. These natures no man ever got above, but always they tower over us, and most in the moment when our interests tempt us to wound them.

The sovereignty of this nature whereof we speak is made known by its independency of those limitations which circumscribe us on every hand. The soul circumscribeth all things. As I have said, it contradicts all experience. In like manner it abolishes time and space. The influence of the senses has in most men overpowered the mind to that degree that the walls of time and space have come to look solid, real and insurmountable; and to speak with levity of these limits is, in the world, the sign of insanity. Yet time and space are but inverse measures of the force of the soul. A man is capable of abolishing them both. The spirit sports with time—

> Can crowd eternity into an hour,
> Or stretch an hour to eternity.

We are often made to feel that there is another youth and age than that which is measured from the year of our natural birth. Some thoughts always find us young, and keep us so. Such a thought is the love of the universal and eternal beauty. Every man parts from that contemplation with the feeling that it rather

belongs to ages than to mortal life. The least activity
of the intellectual powers redeems us in a degree from
the influences of time. In sickness, in languor, give us
a strain of poetry or a profound sentence, and we are
refreshed; or produce a volume of Plato or Shakspeare, or remind us of their names, and instantly we
come into a feeling of longevity. See how the deep
divine thought demolishes centuries and millenniums
and makes itself present through all ages. Is the teach
ing of Christ less effective now than it was when first
his mouth was opened? The emphasis of facts and persons to my soul has nothing to do with time. And so
always the soul's scale is one; the scale of the senses
and the understanding is another. Before the great
revelations of the soul, Time, Space and Nature shrink
away. In common speech we refer all things to time,
as we habitually refer the immensely sundered stars to
one concave sphere. And so we say that the Judgment
is distant or near, that the Millennium approaches, that
a day of certain political, moral, social reforms is at
hand, and the like, when we mean that in the nature of
things one of the facts we contemplate is external and
fugitive, and the other is permanent and connate with
the soul. The things we now esteem fixed shall, one
by one, detach themselves like ripe fruit from our experience, and fall. The wind shall blow them none
knows whither. The landscape, the figures, Boston,
London, are facts as fugitive as any institution past, or
any whiff of mist or smoke, and so is society, and so
is the world. The soul looketh steadily forwards, creat-
ing a world always before her, leaving worlds alway be-

hind her.   She has no dates, nor rites, nor persons, nor specialties, nor men.   The soul knows only the soul; all else is idle weeds for her wearing.

After its own law and not by arithmetic is the rate of its progress to be computed.   The soul's advances are not made by gradation, such as can be represented by motion in a straight line, but rather by ascension of state, such as can be represented by metamorphosis,— from the egg to the worm, from the worm to the fly. The growths of genius are of a certain *total* character, that does not advance the elect individual first over John, then Adam, then Richard, and give to each the pain of discovered inferiority, but by every throe of growth the man expands there where he works, passing, at each pulsation, classes, populations, of men.   With each divine impulse the mind rends the thin rinds of the visible and finite, and comes out into eternity, and inspires and expires its air.   It converses with truths that have always been spoken in the world, and becomes conscious of a closer sympathy with Zeno and Arrian than with persons in the house.

This is the law of moral and of mental gain.   The simple rise as by specific levity not into a particular virtue, but into the region of all the virtues.   They are in the spirit which contains them all.   The soul is superior to all the particulars of merit.   The soul requires purity, but purity is not it; requires justice, but justice is not that; requires beneficence, but is somewhat better: so that there is a kind of descent and accommodation felt when we leave speaking of moral nature to urge a virtue which it enjoins.   For, to the soul in her pure action all the virtues are natural, and not painfully acquired. Speak to his heart, and the man becomes suddenly virtuous.

Within the same sentiment is the germ of intellectual growth, which obeys the same law. Those who are capable of humility, of justice, of love, of aspiration, are already on a platform that commands the sciences and arts, speech and poetry, action and grace. For whoso dwells in this moral beatitude does already anticipate those special powers which men prize so highly; just as love does justice to all the gifts of the object beloved. The lover has no talent, no skill, which passes for quite nothing with his enamored maiden, however little she may possess of related faculty; and the heart which abandons itself to the Supreme Mind finds itself related to all its works, and will travel a royal road to particular knowledges and powers. For in ascending to this primary and aboriginal sentiment we have come from our remote station on the circumference instantaneously to the centre of the world, where, as in the closet of God, we see causes, and anticipate the universe, which is but a slow effect.

One mode of the divine teaching is the incarnation of the spirit in a form,—in forms, like my own. I live in society; with persons who answer to thoughts in my own mind, or outwardly express a certain obedience to the great instincts to which I live. I see its presence to them. I am certified of a common nature; and so these other souls, these separated selves, draw me as nothing else can. They stir in me the new emotions we call passion; of love, hatred, fear, admiration, pity; thence come conversation, competition, persuasion, cities and war. Persons are supplementary to the primary teaching of the soul.   In youth we are made for persons.   Childhood and youth see all the world in them. But the larger experience of man discovers the identical nature appearing through them all.   Persons themselves acquaint us with the impersonal.   In all conversation between two persons tacit reference is made, as to a third party, to a common nature.   That third party or common nature is not social; it is impersonal; is God.   And so in groups where debate is earnest, and especially on great questions of thought, the company become aware of their unity; aware that the thought rises to an equal height in all bosoms, that all have a spiritual property in what was said, as well as the sayer. They all wax wiser than they were.   It arches over them like a temple, this unity of thought in which every heart beats with nobler sense of power and duty, and thinks and acts with unusual solemnity.   All are conscious of attaining to a higher selfpossession.   It shines for all.   There is a certain wisdom of humanity which is common to the greatest men with the lowest, and which our ordinary education often labors to silence and obstruct.   The mind is one, and the best minds, who love truth for its own sake, think much less of property in truth.   Thankfully they accept it everywhere, and do not label or stamp it with any man's name, for it is theirs long beforehand.   It is theirs from eternity.   The learned and the studious of thought have no monopoly of wisdom.   Their violence of direction in some degree disqualifies them to think truly.   We owe many valuable observations to people who are not very acute or profound, and who say the thing without effort which we want and have long been hunting in vain. The action of the soul is oftener in that which is felt and left unsaid than in that which is said in any conversation. It broods over every society, and they unconsciously seek for it in each other. We know better than we do. We do not yet possess ourselves, and we know at the same time that we are much more. I feel the same truth how often in my trivial conversation with my neighbors, that somewhat higher in each of us overlooks this by-play, and Jove nods to Jove from behind each of us.

Men descend to meet. In their habitual and mean service to the world, for which they forsake their native nobleness, they resemble those Arabian sheiks who dwell in mean houses and affect an external poverty, to escape the rapacity of the Pacha, and reserve all their display of wealth for their interior and guarded retirements.

As it is present in all persons, so it is in every period of life. It is adult already in the infant man. In my dealing with my child, my Latin and Greek, my accomplishments and my money stead me nothing. They are all lost on him: but as much soul as I have, avails. If I am merely wilful, he gives me a Rowland for an Oliver, sets his will against mine, one for one, and leaves me, if I please, the degradation of beating him by my superiority of strength. But if I renounce my will and act for the soul, setting that up as umpire between us two, out of his young eyes looks the same soul; he reveres and loves with me.

The soul is the perceiver and revealer of truth. We know truth when we see it, let skeptic and scoffer say what they choose. Foolish people ask you, when you have spoken what they do not wish to hear, "How do you know it is truth, and not an error of your own?" We know truth when we see it, from opinion, as we know when we are awake that we are awake. It was a grand sentence of Emanuel Swedenborg, which would alone indicate the greatness of that man's perception,— "It is no proof of a man's understanding to be able to affirm whatever he pleases; but to be able to discern that what is true is true, and that what is false is false, this is the mark and character of intelligence." In the book I read, the good thought returns to me, as every truth will, the image of the whole soul. To the bad thought which I find in it, the same soul becomes a discerning, separating sword, and lops it away. We are wiser than we know. If we will not interfere with our thought, but will act entirely, or see how the thing stands in God, we know the particular thing, and every thing, and every man. For the Maker of all things and all persons stands behind us and casts his dread omniscience through us over things.

But beyond this recognition of its own in particular passages of the individual's experience, it also reveals truth. And here we should seek to reinforce ourselves by its very presence, and to speak with a worthier, loftier strain of that advent. For the soul's communication of truth is the highest event in nature, for it then does not give somewhat from itself, but it gives itself, or passes into and becomes that man whom it enlightens; or, in proportion to that truth he receives, it takes him to itself.

We distinguish the announcements of the soul, its manifestations of its own nature, by the term *Revela-*

tion. These are always attended by the emotion of the sublime. For this communication is an influx of the Divine mind into our mind. It is an ebb of the individual rivulet before the flowing surges of the sea of life. Every distinct apprehension of this central commandment agitates men with awe and delight. A thrill passes through all men at the reception of new truth, or at the performance of a great action, which comes out of the heart of nature. In these communications the power to see is not separated from the will to do, but the insight proceeds from obedience, and the obedience proceeds from a joyful perception. Every moment when the individual feels himself invaded by it, is memorable. Always, I believe, by the necessity of our constitution a certain enthusiasm attends the individual's consciousness of that divine presence. The character and duration of this enthusiasm varies with the state of the individual, from an exstasy and trance and prophetic inspiration,—which is its rarer appearance, to the faintest glow of virtuous emotion, in which form it warms, like our household fires, all the families and associations of men, and makes society possible. A certain tendency to insanity has always attended the opening of the religious sense in men, as if "blasted with excess of light." The trances of Socrates; the "union" of Plotinus; the vision of Porphyry; the conversion of Paul; the aurora of Behmen; the convulsions of George Fox and his Quakers; the illuminations of Swedenborg, are of this kind. What was in the case of these remarkable persons a ravishment, has, in innumerable instances in common life, been exhibited in less striking manner. Fverywhere

the history of religion betrays a tendency to enthusiasm.
The rapture of the Moravian and Quietist; the opening of the internal sense of the Word, in the language
of the New Jerusalem Church; the revival of the Calvinistic churches; the experiences of the Methodists,
are varying forms of that shudder of awe and delight
with which the individual soul always mingles with the
universal soul.

The nature of these revelations is always the same;
they are perceptions of the absolute law. They are
solutions of the soul's own questions. They do not
answer the questions which the understanding asks.
The soul answers never by words, but by the thing
itself that is inquired after.

Revelation is the disclosure of the soul. The popular notion of a revelation, is, that it is a telling of
fortunes. In past oracles of the soul the understanding
seeks to find answers to sensual questions, and under-
takes to tell from God how long men shall exist, what
their hands shall do and who shall be their company,
adding even names and dates and places. But we must
pick no locks. We must check this low curiosity. An
answer in words is delusive; it is really no answer to
the questions you ask. Do not require a description
of the countries towards which you sail. The description does not describe them to you, and to-morrow you
arrive there and know them by inhabiting them. Men
ask of the immortality of the soul, and the employments
of heaven, and the state of the sinner, and so forth.
They even dream that Jesus has left replies to precisely
these interrogatories. Never a moment did that sublime spirit speak in their *patois*. To truth, justice,

love, the attributes of the soul, the idea of immutableness is essentially associated. Jesus, living in these moral sentiments, heedless of sensual fortunes, heeding only the manifestations of these, never made the separation of the idea of duration from the essence of these attributes, never uttered a syllable concerning the duration of the soul. It was left to his disciples to sever duration from the moral elements, and to teach the immortality of the soul as a doctrine, and maintain it by evidences. The moment the doctrine of the immortality is separately taught, man is already fallen. In the flowing of love, in the adoration of humility, there is no question of continuance. No inspired man ever asks this question or condescends to these evidences. For the soul is true to itself, and the man in whom it is shed abroad cannot wander from the present, which is infinite, to a future which would be finite.

These questions which we lust to ask about the future are a confession of sin. God has no answer for them. No answer in words can reply to a question of things. It is not in an arbitrary "decree of God," but in the nature of man, that a veil shuts down on the facts of to-morrow: for the soul will not have us read any other cipher but that of cause and effect. By this veil which curtains events it instructs the children of men to live in to-day. The only mode of obtaining an answer to these questions of the senses is to forego all low curiosity, and, accepting the tide of being which floats us into the secret of nature, work and live, work and live, and all unawares the advancing soul has built and forged for itself a new condition, and the question and the answer are one.

Thus is the soul the perceiver and revealer of truth. By the same fire, serene, impersonal, perfect, which burns until it shall dissolve all things into the waves and surges of an ocean of light,—we see and know each other, and what spirit each is of. Who can tell the grounds of his knowledge of the character of the several individuals in his circle of friends? No man. Yet their acts and words do not disappoint him. In that man, though he knew no ill of him, he put no trust. In that other, though they had seldom met, authentic signs had yet passed, to signify that he might be trusted as one who had an interest in his own character. We know each other very well,—which of us has been just to himself and whether that which we teach or behold is only an aspiration or is our honest effort also.

We are all discerners of spirits. That diagnosis lies aloft in our life or unconscious power, not in the understanding. The whole intercourse of society, its trade, its religion, its friendships, its quarrels,—is one wide judicial investigation of character. In full court, or in small committee, or confronted face to face, accuser and accused, men offer themselves to be judged. Against their will they exhibit those decisive trifles by which character is read. But who judges? and what? Not our understanding. We do not read them by learning or craft. No; the wisdom of the wise man consists herein, that he does not judge them; he lets them judge themselves and merely reads and records their own verdict.

By virtue of this inevitable nature, private will is overpowered, and, maugre our efforts or our imperfections, your genius will speak from you, and mine from me. That which we are, we shall teach, not voluntarily but involuntarily. Thoughts come into our minds through avenues which we never left open, and thoughts go out of our minds through avenues which we never voluntarily opened. Character teaches over our head. The infallible index of true progress is found in the tone the man takes. Neither his age, nor his breeding, nor company, nor books, nor actions, nor talents, nor all together can hinder him from being deferential to a higher spirit than his own. If he have not found his home in God, his manners, his forms of speech, the turn of his sentences, the build, shall I say, of all his opinions will involuntarily confess it, let him brave it out how he will. If he have found his centre, the Deity will shine through him, through all the disguises of ignorance, of ungenial temperament, of unfavorable circumstance. The tone of seeking is one, and the tone of having is another.

The great distinction between teachers sacred or literary; between poets like Herbert, and poets like Pope; between philosophers like Spinoza, Kant and Coleridge,—and philosophers like Locke, Paley, Mackintosh and Stewart; between men of the world who are reckoned accomplished talkers, and here and there a fervent mystic, prophesying half-insane under the infinitude of his thought, is that one class speak *from within,* or from experience, as parties and possessors of the fact; and the other class *from without,* as spectators merely, or perhaps as acquainted with the fact on the evidence of third persons. It is of no use to preach to me from without. I can do that too easily myself.

Jesus speaks always from within, and in a degree that
transcends all others. In that is the miracle. That
includes the miracle. My soul believes beforehand that
it ought so to be. All men stand continually in the
expectation of the appearance of such a teacher. But
if a man do not speak from within the veil, where the
word is one with that it tells of, let him lowly confess it.

The same Omniscience flows into the intellect and
makes what we call genius. Much of the wisdom of
the world is not wisdom, and the most illuminated class
of men are no doubt superior to literary fame, and are
not writers. Among the multitude of scholars and
authors we feel no hallowing presence; we are sensible
of a knack and skill rather than of inspiration; they
have a light and know not whence it comes and call it
their own: their talent is some exaggerated faculty,
some overgrown member, so that their strength is a
disease. In these instances the intellectual gifts do not
make the impression of virtue, but almost of vice; and
we feel that a man's talents stand in the way of his ad-
vancement in truth. But genius is religious. It is a
larger imbibing of the common heart. It is not anomalous, but more like and not less like other men.
There is in all great poets a wisdom of humanity which
is superior to any talents they exercise. The author,
the wit, the partisan, the fine gentleman, does not take
place of the man. Humanity shines in Homer, in
Chaucer, in Spenser, in Shakspeare, in Milton. They
are content with truth. They use the positive degree.
They seem frigid and phlegmatic to those who have
been spiced with the frantic passion and violent colors

ing of inferior but popular writers. For, they are poets by the free course which they allow to the informing soul, which through their eyes beholdeth again and blesses the things which it hath made. The soul is superior to its knowledge, wiser than any of its works. The great poet makes us feel our own wealth, and then we think less of his compositions. His greatest communication to our mind is to teach us to despise all he has done. Shakespeare carries us to such a lofty strain of intelligent activity as to suggest a wealth which beggars his own; and we then feel that the splendid works which he has created, and which in other hours we extol as a sort of self-existent poetry, take no stronger hold of real nature than the shadow of a passing traveller on the rock. The inspiration which uttered itself in Hamlet and Lear could utter things as good from day to day for ever. Why then should I make account of Hamlet and Lear, as if we had not the soul from which they fell as syllables from the tongue?

This energy does not descend into individual life on any other condition than entire possession. It comes to the lowly and simple; it comes to whomsoever will put off what is foreign and proud; it comes as insight; it comes as serenity and grandeur. When we see those whom it inhabits, we are apprised of new degrees of greatness. From that inspiration the man comes back with a changed tone. He does not talk with men with an eye to their opinion. He tries them. It requires of us to be plain and true. The vain traveller attempts to embellish his life by quoting my Lord and the Prince and the Countess, who thus said or did to *him*. The ambitious vulgar show you their spoons and brooches and rings, and preserve their cards and compliments. The more cultivated, in their account of their own experience, cull out the pleasing, poetic circumstance; the visit to Rome, the man of genius they saw; the brilliant friend they know; still further on perhaps the gorgeous landscape, the mountain lights, the mountain thoughts they enjoyed yesterday,—and so seek to throw a romantic color over their life. But the soul that ascendeth to worship the great God is plain and true; has no rose color; no fine friends; no chivalry; no adventures; does not want admiration; dwells in the hour that now is, in the earnest experience of the common day,—by reason of the present moment and the mere trifle having become porous to thought and bibulous of the sea of light.

Converse with a mind that is grandly simple, and literature looks like word-catching. The simplest utterances are worthiest to be written, yet are they so cheap and so things of course, that in the infinite riches of the soul it is like gathering a few pebbles off the ground, or bottling a little air in a phial, when the whole earth and the whole atmosphere are ours. The mere author in such society is like a pickpocket among gentlemen, who has come in to steal a gold button or a pin. Nothing can pass there, or make you one of the circle, but the casting aside your trappings and dealing man to man in naked truth, plain confession and omniscient affirmation.

Souls such as these treat you as gods would, walk as gods in the earth, accepting without any admiration your wit, your bounty, your virtue even, say rather your act of duty, for your virtue they own as their proper blood, royal as themselves, and over-royal, and the father of the gods. But what rebuke their plain fraternal bearing casts on the mutual flattery with which authors solace each other and wound themselves! These flatter not. I do not wonder that these men go to see Cromwell and Christina and Charles the II. and James I. and the Grand Turk. For they are, in their own elevation, the fellows of kings, and must feel the servile tone of conversation in the world. They must always be a godsend to princes, for they confront them, a king to a king, without ducking or concession, and give a high nature the refreshment and satisfaction of resistance, of plain humanity, or even companionship and of new ideas. They leave them wiser and superior men. Souls like these make us feel that sincerity is more excellent than flattery. Deal so plainly with man and woman as to constrain the utmost sincerity and destroy all hope of trifling with you. It is the highest compliment you can pay. Their "highest praising," said Milton, "is not flattery, and their plainest advice is a kind of praising."

Ineffable is the union of man and God in every act of the soul. The simplest person who in his integrity worships God, becomes God; yet for ever and ever the influx of this better and universal self is new and unsearchable. Ever it inspires awe and astonishment. How dear, how soothing to man, arises the idea of God, peopling the lonely place, effacing the scars of our mistakes and disappointments! When we have broken our god of tradition and ceased from our god of rhetoric, then may God fire the heart with his presence. It is the doubling of the heart itself, nay, the infinite

enlargement of the heart with a power of growth to a
new infinity on every side.   It inspires in man an infallible trust.   He has not the conviction, but the sight,
that the best is the true, and may in that thought easily
dismiss all particular uncertainties and fears, and ad-
journ to the sure revelation of time the solution of his
private riddles.   He is sure that his welfare is dear to
the heart of being.   In the presence of law to his mind
he is overflowed with a reliance so universal that it
sweeps away all cherished hopes and the most stable
projects of mortal condition in its flood.   He believes
that he cannot escape from his good.   The things that
are really for thee gravitate to thee.   You are running
to seek your friend.   Let your feet run, but your mind
need not.   If you do not find him, will you not
acquiesce that it is best you should not find him? for
there is a power, which as it is in you, is in him also,
and could therefore very well bring you together, if
it were for the best.   You are preparing with eagerness
to go and render a service to which your talent and your
taste invite you, the love of men and the hope of fame.
Has it not occurred to you that you have no right to
go, unless you are equally willing to be prevented from
going?   O, believe, as thou livest, that every sound
that is spoken over the round world, which thou ought-
est to hear, will vibrate on thine ear.   Every proverb,
every book, every by-word that belongs to thee for aid
or comfort, shall surely come home through open or
winding passages.   Every friend whom not thy fantastic will but the great and tender heart in thee craveth,
shall lock thee in his embrace.   And this because the
heart in thee is the heart of all; not a valve, not a wall,

not an intersection is there anywhere in nature, but one blood rolls uninterruptedly an endless circulation through all men, as the water of the globe is all one sea, and, truly seen, its tide is one.

Let man then learn the revelation of all nature and all thought to his heart; this, namely; that the Highest dwells with him; that the sources of nature are in his own mind, if the sentiment of duty is there. But if he would know what the great God speaketh, he must "go into his closet and shut the door," as Jesus said. God will not make himself manifest to cowards. He must greatly listen to himself, withdrawing himself from all the accents of other men's devotion. Their prayers even are hurtful to him, until he have made his own. Our religion vulgarly stands on numbers of believers. Whenever the appeal is made,—no matter how indirectly,—to numbers, proclamation is then and there made that religion is not. He that finds God a sweet enveloping thought to him never counts his company. When I sit in that presence, who shall dare to come in? When I rest in perfect humility, when I burn with pure love, what can Calvin or Swedenborg say?

It makes no difference whether the appeal is to numbers or to one. The faith that stands on authority is not faith. The reliance on authority measures the decline of religion, the withdrawal of the soul. The position men have given to Jesus, now for many centuries of history, is a position of authority. It characterizes themselves. It cannot alter the eternal facts. Great is the soul, and plain. It is no flatterer, it is no follower; it never appeals from itself. It always believes in itself. Before the immense possibilities of man all mere experience, all past biography, however spotless and sainted, shrinks away. Before that holy heaven which our presentiments foreshow us, we cannot easily praise any form of life we have seen or read of. We not only affirm that we have few great men, but, absolutely speaking, that we have none; that we have no history, no record of any character or mode of living that entirely contents us. The saints and demigods whom history worships we are constrained to accept with a grain of allowance. Though in our lonely hours we draw a new strength out of their memory, yet, pressed on our attention, as they are by the thoughtless and customary, they fatigue and invade. The soul gives itself, alone, original and pure, to the Lonely, Original and Pure, who, on that condition, gladly inhabits, leads and speaks through it. Then is it glad, young and nimble. It is not wise, but it sees through all things. It is not called religious, but it is innocent. It calls the light its own, and feels that the grass grows and the stone falls by a law inferior to, and dependent on, its nature. Behold, it saith, I am born into the great, the universal mind. I, the imperfect, adore my own Perfect. I am somehow receptive of the great soul, and thereby I do overlook the sun and the stars and feel them to be but the fair accidents and effects which change and pass. More and more the surges of everlasting nature enter into me, and I become public and human in my regards and actions. So come I to live in thoughts and act with energies which are immortal. Thus revering the soul, and learning, as the ancients said, that "its beauty is immense," man will come to see that the world is the perennial miracle which the soul worketh, and be less astonished at particular wonders; he will learn that there is no profane history; that all history is sacred; that the universe is represented in an atom, in a moment of time. He will weave no longer a spotted life of shreds and patches, but he will live with a divine unity. He will cease from what is base and frivolous in his own life and be content with all places and any service he can render. He will calmly front the morrow in the negligency of that trust which carries God with it and so hath already the whole future in the bottom of the heart.

CIRCLES

THE eye is the first circle; the horizon which it forms in the second; and throughout nature this primary picture is repeated without end. It is the highest emblem in the cipher of the world. St. Augustine described the nature of God as a circle whose centre was everywhere and its circumference nowhere. We are all our lifetime reading the copious sense of this first of forms. One moral we have already deduced in considering the circular or compensatory character of every human action. Another analogy we shall now trace, that every action admits of being outdone. Our life is an apprenticeship to the truth that around every circle another can be drawn; that there is no end in nature, but every end is a beginning; that there is always another dawn risen on mid-noon, and under every deep a lower deep opens.

This fact, as far as it symbolizes the moral fact of the Unattainable, the flying Perfect, around which the hands of man can never meet, at once the inspirer and the condemner of every success, may conveniently serve us to connect many illustrations of human power in every department.

There are no fixtures in nature. The universe is fluid and volatile. Permanence is but a word of degrees. Our globe seen by God is a transparent law, not a mass of facts. The law dissolves the fact and holds it fluid. Our culture is the predominance of an idea which draws after it all this train of cities and institutions. Let us rise into another idea; they will disappear. The Greek sculpture is all melted away, as if it had been statues of ice: here and there a solitary figure or fragment remaining, as we see flecks and scraps of snow left in cold dells and mountain clefts in June and July. For the genius that created it creates now somewhat else. The Greek letters last a little longer, but are already passing under the same sentence and tumbling into the inevitable pit which the creation of new thought opens for all that is old. The new continents are built out of the ruins of an old planet; the new races fed out of the decomposition of the foregoing. New arts destroy the old. See the investment of capital in aqueducts, made useless by hydraulics; fortifications, by gun-powder; roads and canals, by railways; sails, by steam; steam, by electricity.

You admire this tower of granite, weathering the hurts of so many ages. Yet a little waving hand built this huge wall, and that which builds is better than that which is built. The hand that built can topple it down much faster. Better than the hand and nimbler was the invisible thought which wrought through it; and thus ever, behind the coarse effect, is a fine cause, which, being narrowly seen, is itself the effect of a finer cause. Every thing looks permanent until its secret is known. A rich estate appears to women and children a firm and lasting fact; to a merchant, one easily created out of any materials, and easily lost. An orchard, good till-age, good grounds, seem a fixture, like a gold mine, or a river, to a citizen; but to a large farmer, not much more fixed than the state of the crop. Nature looks provokingly stable and secular, but it has a cause like all the rest; and when once I comprehend that, will these fields stretch so immovably wide, these leaves hang so individually considerable? Permanence is a word of degrees. Every thing is medial. Moons are no more bounds to spiritual power than bat-balls.

The key to every man is his thought. Sturdy and defying though he look, he has a helm which he obeys, which is the idea after which all his facts are classified. He can only be reformed by showing him a new idea which commands his own. The life of man is a self-evolving circle, which, from a ring imperceptibly small, rushes on all sides outwards to new and larger circles, and that without end. The extent to which this generation of circles, wheel without wheel, will go, depends on the force of truth of the individual soul. For it is the inert effort of each thought, having formed itself into a circular wave of circumstance, as for instance an empire, rules of an art, a local usage, a religious rite, to heap itself on that ridge and to solidify and hem in the life. But if the soul is quick and strong it bursts over that boundary on all sides and expands another orbit on the great deep, which also runs up into a high wave, with attempt again to stop and to bind. But the heart refuses to be imprisoned; in its first and narrowest pulses it already tends outward with a vast force and to immense and innumerable expansions.

Every ultimate fact is only the first of a new series. Every general law only a particular fact of some more general law presently to disclose itself. There is no outside, no inclosing wall, no circumference to us. The man finishes his story,—how good! how final! how it puts a new face on all things! He fills the sky. Lo, on the other side rises also a man and draws a circle around the circle we had just pronounced the outline of the sphere. Then already is our first speaker not man, but only a first speaker. His only redress is forthwith to draw a circle outside of his antagonist. And so men do by themselves. The result of to-day, which haunts the mind and cannot be escaped, will presently be abridged into a word, and the principle that seemed to explain nature will itself be included as one example of a bolder generalization. In the thought of to-morrow there is a power to upheave all thy creed, all the creeds, all the literatures of the nations, and marshal thee to a heaven which no epic dream has yet depicted. Every man is not so much a workman in the world as he is a suggestion of that he should be. Men walk as prophecies of the next age.

Step by step we scale this mysterious ladder; the steps are actions, the new prospect is power. Every several result is threatened and judged by that which follows. Every one seems to be contradicted by the new; it is only limited by the new. The new statement is always hated by the old, and, to those dwelling in the old, comes like an abyss of scepticism. But the eye soon gets wonted to it, for the eye and it are effects of one cause; then its innocency and benefit appear, and presently, all its energy spent, it pales and dwindles before the revelation of the new hour.

Fear not the new generalization. Does the fact look

crass and material, threatening to degrade thy theory of spirit? Resist it not; it goes to refine and raise thy theory of matter just as much.

There are no fixtures to men, if we appeal to consciousness. Every man supposes himself not to be fully understood; and if there is any truth in him, if he rests at last on the divine soul, I see not how it can be otherwise. The last chamber, the last closet, he must feel was never opened; there is always a residuum unknown, unanalyzable. That is, every man believes that he has a greater possibility.

Our moods do not believe in each other. To-day I am full of thoughts and can write what I please. I see no reason why I should not have the same thought, the same power of expression, to-morrow. What I write, whilst I write it, seems the most natural thing in the world: but yesterday I saw a dreary vacuity in this direction in which now I see so much; and a month hence, I doubt not, I shall wonder who he was that wrote so many continuous pages. Alas for this infirm faith, this will not strenuous, this vast ebb of a vast flow! I am God in nature; I am a weed by the wall.

The continual effort to raise himself above himself, to work a pitch above his last height, betrays itself in a man's relations. We thirst for approbation, yet cannot forgive the approver. The sweet of nature is love; yet if I have a friend I am tormented by my imperfections. The love of me accuses the other party. If he were high enough to slight me, then could I love him, and rise by my affection to new heights. A man's growth is seen in the successsive choirs of his friends. For every friend whom he loses for truth, he gains a

better. I thought as I walked in the woods and mused
on my friends, why should I play with them this game
of idolatry? I know and see too well, when not voluntarily blind, the speedy limits of persons called high
and worthy. Rich, noble and great they are by the
liberality of our speech, but truth is sad. O blessed
Spirit, whom I forsake for these, they are not thee!
Every personal consideration that we allow costs us
heavenly state. We sell the thrones of angels for a
short and turbulent pleasure.

How often must we learn this lesson? Men cease
to interest us when we find their limitations. The only
sin is limitation. As soon as you once come up with
a man's limitations, it is all over with him. Has he
talents? has he enterprises? has he knowledge? It
boots not. Infinitely alluring and attractive was he to
you yesterday, a great hope, a sea to swim in; now, you
have found his shores, found it a pond, and you care
not if you never see it again.

Each new step we take in thought reconciles twenty
seemingly discordant facts, as expressions of one law.
Aristotle and Plato are reckoned the respective heads of
two schools. A wise man will see that Aristotle Plato-
nizes. By going one step farther back in thought, discordant opinions are reconciled by being seen to be two
extremes of one principle, and we can never go so
far back as to preclude a still higher vision.

Beware when the great God lets loose a thinker on
this planet. Then all things are at risk. It is as when
a conflagration has broken out in a great city, and no
man knows what is safe, or where it will end. There
is not a piece of science but its flank may be turned to-

morrow; there is not any literary reputation, not the so-called eternal names of fame, that may not be revised and condemned. The very hopes of man, the thoughts of his heart, the religion of nations, the manners and morals of mankind are all at the mercy of a new generalization. Generalization is always a new influx of the divinity into the mind. Hence the thrill that attends it.

Valor consists in the power of self-recovery, so that a man cannot have his flank turned, cannot be out-generalled, but put him where you will, he stands. This can only be by his preferring truth to his past apprehension of truth, and his alert acceptance of it from whatever quarter; the intrepid conviction that his laws, his relations to society, his christianity, his world, may at any time be superseded and decease.

There are degrees in idealism. We learn first to play with it academically, as the magnet was once a toy. Then we see in the heyday of youth and poetry that it may be true, that it is true in gleams and fragments. Then, its countenance waxes stern and grand, and we see that it must be true. It now shows itself ethical and practical. We learn that God is; that he is in me; and that all things are shadows of him. The idealism of Berkeley is only a crude statement of the idealism of Jesus, and that again is a crude statement of the fact that all nature is the rapid efflux of goodness executing and organizing itself. Much more obviously is history and the state of the world at any one time directly dependent on the intellectual classification then existing in the minds of men. The things which are dear to men at this hour are so on account of the ideas which have emerged on their mental horizon, and which cause the present order of things, as a tree bears its apples. A new degree of culture would instantly revolutionize the entire system of human pursuits.

Conversation is a game of circles. In conversation we pluck up the *termini* which bound the common of silence on every side. The parties are not to be judged by the spirit they partake and even express under this Pentecost. To-morrow they will have receded from this high-water mark. To-morrow you shall find them stooping under the old pack-saddles. Yet let us enjoy the cloven flame whilst it glows on our walls. When each new speaker strikes a new light, emancipates us from the oppression of the last speaker to oppress us with the greatness and exclusiveness of his own thought, then yields us to another redeemer, we seem to recover our rights, to become men. O, what truths profound and executable only in ages and orbs, are supposed in the announcement of every truth! In common hours, society sits cold and statuesque. We all stand waiting, empty,—knowing, possibly, that we can be full, surrounded by mighty symbols which are not symbols to us, but prose and trivial toys. Then cometh the god and converts the statues into fiery men, and by a flash of his eye burns up the veil which shrouded all things, and the meaning of the very furniture, of cup and saucer, of chair and clock and tester, is manifest. The facts which loomed so large in the fogs of yesterday,—property, climate, breeding, personal beauty and the like, have strangely changed their proportions. All that we reckoned settled shakes and rattles; and literatures, cities, climates, religions, leave their foundations and dance before our eyes.   And yet here again see the swift circumscription!   Good as is discourse, silence is better, and shames it.   The length of the discourse indicates the distance of thought betwixt the speaker and the hearer.   If they were at a perfect understanding in any part, no words would be necessary thereon. If at one in all parts, no words would be suffered.

Literature is a point outside of our hodiernal circle through which a new one may be described.   The use of literature is to afford us a platform whence we may command a view of our present life, a purchase by which we may move it.   We fill ourselves with ancient learning, install ourselves the best we can in Greek, in Punic, in Roman houses, only that we may wiselier see French, English and American houses and modes of living.   In like manner we see literature best from the midst of wild nature, or from the din of affairs, or from a high religion.   The field cannot be well seen from within the field.   The astronomer must have his diameter of the earth's orbit as a base to find the parallax of any star.

Therefore we value the poet.   All the argument and all the wisdom is not in the encyclopædia, or the treatise on metaphysics, or the Body of Divinity, but in the sonnet or the play.   In my daily work I incline to repeat my old steps, and do not believe in remedial force, in the power of change and reform.   But some Petrarch or Ariosto, filled with the new wine of his imagination, writes me an ode or a brisk romance, full of daring thought and action.   He smites and arouses me with his shrill tones, breaks up my whole chain of habits, and I open my eye on my own possibilities.

He claps wings to the sides of all the solid old lumber of the world, and I am capable once more of choosing a straight path in theory and practice.

We have the same need to command a view of the religion of the world. We can never see christianity from the catechism:—from the pastures, from a boat in the pond, from amidst the songs of wood-birds we possibly may. Cleansed by the elemental light and wind, steeped in the sea of beautiful forms which the field offers us, we may chance to cast a right glance back upon biography. Christianity is rightly dear to the best of mankind; yet was there never a young philosopher whose breeding had fallen into the christian church by whom that brave text of Paul's was not specially prized, "Then shall also the Son be subject unto Him who put all things under him, that God may be all in all." Let the claims and virtues of persons be never so great and welcome the instinct of man presses eagerly onward to the impersonal and illimitable, and gladly arms itself against the dogmatism of bigots with this generous word out of the book itself.

The natural world may be conceived of as a system of concentric circles, and we now and then detect in nature slight dislocations which apprize us that this surface on which we now stand is not fixed, but sliding. These manifold tenacious qualities, this chemistry and vegetation, these metals and animals, which seem to stand there for their own sake, are means and methods only, are words of God, and as fugitive as other words. Has the naturalist or chemist learned his craft, who has explored the gravity of atoms and the elective affinities, who has not yet discerned the deeper

law whereof this is only a partial or approximate statement, namely that like draws to like, and that the
goods which belong to you gravitate to you and need
not be pursued with pains and cost? Yet is that statement approximate also, and not final. Omnipresence
is a higher fact. Not through subtle subterranean
channels need friend and fact be drawn to their
counterpart, but, rightly considered, these things proceed from the eternal generation of the soul. Cause
and effect are two sides of one fact.

The same law of eternal procession ranges all that
we call the virtues, and extinguishes each in the light
of a better. The great man will not be prudent in the
popular sense; all his prudence will be so much deduction from his grandeur. But it behoves each to see,
when he sacrifices prudence, to what god he devotes it;
if to ease and pleasure, he had better be prudent still;
if to a great trust, he can well spare his mule and pan-
niers who has a winged chariot instead. Geoffrey
draws on his boots to go through the woods, that his
feet may be safer from the bite of snakes; Aaron never
thinks of such a peril. In many years neither is
harmed by such an accident. Yet it seems to me that
with every precaution you take against such an evil
you put yourself into the power of the evil. I suppose
that the highest prudence is the lowest prudence. Is
this too sudden a rushing from the centre to the verge
of our orbit? Think how many times we shall fall
back into pitiful calculations before we take up our
rest in the great sentiment, or make the verge of to-
day the new centre. Besides, your bravest sentiment is
familiar to the humblest men. The poor and the low

have their way of expressing the last facts of philosophy as well as you. "Blessed be nothing" and "The worse things are, the better they are" are proverbs which express the transcendentalism of common life.

One man's justice is another's injustice; one man's beauty another's ugliness; one man's wisdom another's folly; as one beholds the same objects from a higher point of view. One man thinks justice consists in paying debts, and has no measure in his abhorrence of another who is very remiss in this duty and makes the creditor wait tediously. But that second man has his own way of looking at things; asks himself which debt must I pay first, the debt to the rich, or the debt to the poor? the debt of money, or the debt of thought to mankind, of genius to nature? For you, O broker, there is no other principle but arithmetic. For me, commerce is of trivial import; love, faith, truth of character, the aspiration of man, these are sacred; nor can I detach one duty, like you, from all other duties, and concentrate my forces mechanically on the payment of moneys. Let me live onward; you shall find that, though slower, the progress of my character will liquidate all these debts without injustice to higher claims. If a man should dedicate himself to the payment of notes, would not this be injustice? Owes he no debt but money? And are all claims on him to be postponed to a landlord's or a banker's?

There is no virtue which is final; all are initial. The virtues of society are vices of the saint. The terror of reform is the discovery that we must cast away our virtues, or what we have always esteemed such, into the same pit that has consumed our grosser vices.

> Forgive his crimes, forgive his virtues too,
> Those smaller faults, half converts to the right.

It is the highest power of divine moments that they abolish our contritions also. I accuse myself of sloth and unprofitableness day by day; but when these waves of God flow into me I no longer reckon lost time. I no longer poorly compute my possible achievement by what remains to me of the month or the year; for these moments confer a sort of omnipresence and omnipotence which asks nothing of duration, but sees that the energy of the mind is commensurate with the work to be done, without time.

And thus, O circular philosopher, I hear some reader exclaim, you have arrived at a fine pyrrhonism, at an equivalence and indifference of all actions, and would fain teach us that *if we are true,* forsooth, our crimes may be lively stones out of which we shall construct the temple of the true God.

I am not careful to justify myself. I own I am gladdened by seeing the predominance of the saccharine principle throughout vegetable nature, and not less by beholding in morals that unrestrained inundation of the principle of good into every chink and hole that selfishness has left open, yea into selfishness and sin itself; so that no evil is pure, nor hell itself without its extreme satisfactions. But lest I should mislead any when I have my own head and obey my whims, let me remind the reader that I am only an experimenter. Do not set the least value on what I do, or the least discredit on what I do not, as if I pretended to settle any thing as true or false. I unsettle all things. No facts are to me sacred; none are profane; I simply experiment, an endless seeker with no Past at my back.

Yet this incessant movement and progression which all things partake could never become sensible to us but by contrast to some principle of fixture or stability in the soul. Whilst the eternal generation of circles proceeds, the eternal generator abides. That central life is somewhat superior to creation, superior to knowledge and thought, and contains all its circles. For ever it labors to create a life and thought as large and excellent as itself; but in vain; for that which is made instructs how to make a better.

Thus there is no sleep, no pause, no preservation, but all things renew, germinate and spring. Why should we import rags and relics into the new hour? Nature abhors the old, and old age seems the only disease: all others run into this one. We call it by many names,— fever, intemperance, insanity, stupidity and crime: they are all forms of old age: they are rest, conservatism, appropriation, inertia; not newness, not the way onward. We grizzle every day. I see no need of it. Whilst we converse with what is above us, we do not grow old, but grow young. Infancy, youth, receptive, aspiring, with religious eye looking upward, counts itself nothing and abandons itself to the instruction flowing from all sides. But the man and woman of seventy assume to know all; throw up their hope; renounce aspiration; accept the actual for the necessary and talk down to the young. Let them then become organs of the Holy Ghost; let them be lovers; let them behold truth; and their eyes are uplifted, their wrinkles smoothed, they are perfumed again with hope and power. This old age ought not to creep on a human mind. In nature every moment is new; the past is always swallowed and forgotten; the coming only is sacred. Nothing is secure but life, transition, the energizing spirit. No love can be bound by oath or covenant to secure it against a higher love. No truth so sublime but it may be trivial to-morrow in the light of new thoughts. People wish to be settled: only as far as they are unsettled is there any hope for them.

Life is a series of surprises. We do not guess to-day the mood, the pleasure, the power of to-morrow, when we are building up our being. Of lower states, —of acts of routine and sense, we can tell somewhat, but the masterpieces of God, the total growths and universal movements of the soul, he hideth; they are incalculable. I can know that truth is divine and helpful; but how it shall help me I can have no guess, for *so to be* is the sole inlet of *so to know*. The new position of the advancing man has all the powers of the old, yet has them all new. It carries in its bosom all the energies of the past, yet is itself an exhalation of the morning. I cast away in this new moment all my once hoarded knowledge, as vacant and vain. Now for the first time seem I to know any thing rightly. The simplest words,—we do not know what they mean except when we love and aspire.

The difference between talents and character is adroitness to keep the old and trodden round, and power and courage to make a new road to new and better goals. Character makes an overpowering present, a cheerful, determined hour, which fortifies all the company by making them see that much is possible and excellent that was not thought of. Character dulls the impression of particular events. When we see the conqueror we do not think much of any one battle or success. We see that we had exaggerated the difficulty. It was easy to him. The great man is not convulsible or tormentable. He is so much that events pass over him without much impression. People say sometimes, "See what I have overcome; see how cheerful I am; see how completely I have triumphed over these black events." Not if they still remind me of the black event,—they have not yet conquered. Is it conquest to be a gay and decorated sepulchre, or a half-crazed widow, hysterically laughing? True conquest is the causing the black event to fade and disappear as an early cloud of insignificant result in a history so large and advancing.

The one thing which we seek with insatiable desire is to forget ourselves, to be surprised out of our propriety, to lose our sempiternal memory and to do something without knowing how or why; in short to draw a new circle. Nothing great was ever achieved without enthusiasm. The way of life is wonderful. It is by abandonment. The great moments of history are the facilities of performance through the strength or ideas, as the works of genius and religion. "A man," said Oliver Cromwell, "never rises so high as when he knows not whither he is going." Dreams and drunkenness, the use of opium and alcohol are the semblance and counterfeit of this oracular genius, and hence their dangerous attraction for men. For the like reason they ask the aid of wild passions, as in gaming and war, to ape in some manner these flames and generosities of the heart.

INTELLECT

EVERY substance is negatively electric to that which stands above it in the chemical tables, positively to that which stands below it. Water dissolves wood and iron and salt; air dissolves water; electric fire dissolves air, but the intellect dissolves fire, gravity, laws, method, and the subtlest unnamed relations of nature in its resistless menstruum. Intellect lies behind genius, which is intellect constructive. Intellect is the simple power anterior to all action or construction. Gladly would I unfold in calm degrees a natural history of the intellect, but what man has yet been able to mark the steps and boundaries of that transparent essence? The first questions are always to be asked, and the wisest doctor is gravelled by the inquisitiveness of a child. How can we speak of the action of the mind under any divisions, as of its knowledge, of its ethics, of its works, and so forth, since it melts will into perception, knowledge into act? Each becomes the other. Itself alone is. Its vision is not like the vision of the eye, but is union with the things known.

Intellect and intellection signify to the common ear consideration of abstract truth. The considerations of time and place, of you and me, of profit and hurt tyrannize over most men's minds. Intellect separates the fact considered, from *you,* from all local and personal reference, and discerns it as if it existed for its own sake.   Heraclitus looked upon the affections as dense and colored mists.   In the fog of good and evil affections it is hard for man to walk forward in a straight line.   Intellect is void of affection and sees an object as it stands in the light of science, cool and disengaged. The intellect goes out of the individual, floats over its own personality, and regards it as a fact, and not as *I* and *mine.*   He who is immersed in what concerns person or place cannot see the problem of existence. This the intellect always ponders.   Nature shows all things formed and bound.   The intellect pierces the form, overleaps the wall, detects intrinsic likeness between remote things and reduces all things into a few principles.

The making a fact the subject of thought raises it. All that mass of mental and moral phenomena which we do not make objects of voluntary thought, come within the power of fortune; they constitute the circumstance of daily life; they are subject to change, to fear and hope.   Every man beholds his human condition with a degree of melancholy.   As a ship aground is battered by the waves, so man, imprisoned in mortal life, lies open to the mercy of coming events.   But a truth, separated by the intellect, is no longer a subject of destiny.   We behold it as a god upraised above care and fear.   And so any fact in our life, or any record of our fancies or reflections, disentangled from the web of our unconsciousness, becomes an object impersonal and immortal.   It is the past restored, but embalmed.   A better art than that of Egypt has taken fear and corruption out of it. It is eviscerated of care. It is offered for science. What is addressed to us for contemplation does not threaten us but makes us intellectual beings.

The growth of the intellect is spontaneous in every step. The mind that grows could not predict the times, the means, the mode of that spontaneity. God enters by a private door into every individual. Long prior to the age of reflection is the thinking of the mind. Out of darkness it came insensibly into the marvellous light of to-day. In the period of infancy it accepted and disposed of all impressions from the surrounding creation after its own way. Whatever any mind doth or saith is after a law. It has no random act or word. And this native law remains over it after it has come to reflection or conscious thought. Over it always reigned a firm law. In the most worn, pedantic, introverted self-tormentor's life, the greatest part is incalculable by him, unforeseen, unimaginable, and must be, until he can take himself up by his own ears. What am I? What has my will done to make me that I am? Nothing. I have been floated into this thought, this hour, this connection of events, by might and mind sublime, and my ingenuity and wilfulness have not thwarted, have not aided to an appreciable degree.

Our spontaneous action is always the best. You cannot with your best deliberation and heed come so close to any question as your spontaneous glance shall bring you, whilst you rise from your bed, or walk abroad in the morning after meditating the matter before sleep on the previous night. Always our thinking is a pious reception. Our truth of thought is therefore vitiated

as much by too violent direction given by our will, as
by too great negligence. We do not determine what
we will think. We only open our senses, clear away
as we can all obstruction from the fact, and suffer the
intellect to see. We have little control over our
thoughts. We are the prisoners of ideas. They catch
us up for moments into their heaven and so fully engage us that we take no thought for the morrow, gaze
like children, without an effort to make them our own.
By-and-by we fall out of that rapture, bethink us where
we have been, what we have seen, and repeat as truly
as we can what we have beheld. As far as we can
recall these ecstasies we carry away in the effaceable
memory the result, and all men and all the ages con-
firm it. It is called Truth. But the moment we cease
to report and attempt to correct and contrive, it is not
truth.

If we consider what persons have stimulated and
profited us, we shall perceive the superiority of the
spontaneous or intuitive principle over the arithmetical or logical. The first always contains the second,
but virtual and latent. We want in every man a long
logic; we cannot pardon the absence of it, but it must
not be spoken. Logic is the procession or proportion-
ate unfolding of the intuition; but its virtue is as silent
method; the moment it would appear as propositions
and have a separate value, it is worthless.

In every man's mind, some images, words and facts
remain, without effort on his part to imprint them,
which others forget, and afterwards these illustrate
to him important laws. All our progress is an unfolding, like the vegetable bud. You have first an

instinct, then an opinion, then a knowledge, as the plant has root, bud and fruit. Trust the instinct to the end, though you can render no reason. It is vain to hurry it. By trusting it to the end, it shall ripen into truth and you shall know why you believe.

Each mind has its own method. A true man never acquires after college rules. What you have aggregated in a natural manner surprises and delights when it is produced. For we cannot oversee each other's secret. And hence the differences between men in natural endowment are insignificant in comparison with their common wealth. Do you think the porter and the cook have no anecdotes, no experiences, no wonders for you? Everybody knows as much as the savant. The walls of rude minds are scrawled all over with facts, with thoughts. They shall one day bring a lantern and read the inscriptions. Every man, in the degree in which he has wit and culture, finds his curiosity inflamed concerning the modes of living and thinking of other men, and especially of those classes whose minds have not been subdued by the drill of school education.

This instinctive action never ceases in a healthy mind, but becomes richer and more frequent in its informations through all states of culture. At last comes the era of reflection, when we not only observe, but take pains to observe; when we of set purpose sit down to consider an abstract truth; when we keep the mind's eye open whilst we converse, whilst we read, whilst we act, intent to learn the secret law of some class of facts.

What is the hardest task in the world? To think.

I would put myself in the attitude to look in the eye
an abstract truth, and I cannot. I blench and with-
draw on this side and on that. I seem to know what
he meant who said, No man can see God face to face
and live. For example, a man explores the basis of
civil government. Let him intend his mind without
respite, without rest, in one direction. His best heed
long time avails him nothing. Yet thoughts are flitting before him. We all but apprehend, we dimly
forebode the truth. We say, I will walk abroad, and
the truth will take form and clearness to me. We go
forth, but cannot find it. It seems as if we needed
only the stillness and composed attitude of the library
to seize the thought. But we come in, and are as far
from it as at first. Then, in a moment, and unannounced, the truth appears. A certain wandering light
appears, and is the distinction, the principle, we wanted.
But the oracle comes because we had previously laid
siege to the shrine. It seems as if the law of the intellect resembled that law of nature by which we now
inspire, now expire the breath; by which the heart now
draws in, then hurls out the blood,—the law of undula-
tion. So now you must labor with your brains, and
now you must forbear your activity and see what the
great Soul showeth.

Our intellections are mainly prospective. The immortality of man is as legitimately preached from the
intellections as from the moral volitions. Every intellection is mainly prospective. Its present value is its
least. Inspect what delights you in Plutarch, in Shakspeare, in Cervantes. Each truth that a writer acquires
is a lantern which he instantly turns full on what facts

and thoughts lay already in his mind, and behold, all
the mats and rubbish which had littered his garret become precious. Every trivial fact in his private biography becomes an illustration of this new principle,
revisits the day, and delights all men by its piquancy
and new charm. Men say, where did he get this? and
think there was something divine in his life. But no;
they have myriads of facts just as good, would they
only get a lamp to ransack their attics withal.

We are all wise. The difference between persons is
not in wisdom but in art. I knew, in an academical
club, a person who always deferred to me, who, seeing
my whim for writing, fancied that my experiences had
somewhat superior; whilst I saw that his experiences
were as good as mine. Give them to me and I would
make the same use of them. He held the old; he holds
the new; I had the habit of tacking together the old and
the new which he did not use to exercise. This may
hold in the great examples. Perhaps, if we should
meet Shakspeare we should not be conscious of any
steep inferiority; no, but of a great equality,—only
that he possessed a strange skill of using, of classifying
his facts, which we lacked. For notwithstanding our
utter incapacity to produce anything like Hamlet and
Othello, see the perfect reception this wit and immense
knowledge of life and liquid eloquence find in us all.

If you gather apples in the sunshine, or make hay,
or hoe corn, and then retire within doors and shut
your eyes and press them with your hand, you shall
still see apples hanging in the bright light with boughs
and leaves thereto, or the tasselled grass, or the corn-
flags, and this for five or six hours afterwards. There

lie the impressions on the retentive organ, though you knew it not. So lies the whole series of natural images with which your life has made you acquainted, in your memory, though you know it not, and a thrill of passion flashes light on their dark chamber, and the active power seizes instantly the fit image, as the world of its momentary thought.

It is long ere we discover how rich we are. Our history, we are sure, is quite tame. We have nothing to write, nothing to infer. But our wiser years still run back to the despised recollections of childhood, and always we are fishing up some wonderful article out of that pond; until by-and-by we begin to suspect that the biography of the one foolish person we know is in reality, nothing less than the miniature paraphrase of the hundred volumes of the Universal History.

In the intellect constructive, which we popularly designate by the word Genius, we observe the same balance of two elements as in intellect receptive. The constructive intellect produces thoughts, sentences, poems, plans, designs, systems. It is the generation of the mind, the marriage of thought with nature. To genius must always go two gifts, the thought and the publication. The first is revelation, always a miracle, which no frequency of occurrence or incessant study can ever familiarize, but which must always leave the inquirer stupid with wonder. It is the advent of truth into the world, a form of thought now for the first time bursting into the universe, a child of the old eternal soul, a piece of genuine and immeasurable greatness. It seems, for the time, to inherit all that has yet existed

and to dictate to the unborn. It affects every thought
of man and goes to fashion every institution. But to
make it available it needs a vehicle or art by which it is
conveyed to men. To be communicable it must become
picture or sensible object. We must learn the language
of facts. The most wonderful inspirations die with
their subject if he has no hand to paint them to the
senses. The ray of light passes invisible through space
and only when it falls on an object is it seen. When
the spiritual energy is directed on something outward,
then is it a thought. The relation between it and you
first makes you, the value of you, apparent to me. The
rich inventive genius of the painter must be smothered
and lost for want of the power of drawing, and in our
happy hours we should be inexhaustible poets if once
we could break through the silence into adequate rhyme.
As all men have some access to primary truth, so all
have some art or power of communication in their head,
but only in the artist does it descend into the hand.
There is an inequality, whose laws we do not yet know,
between two men and between two moments of the
same man, in respect to this faculty. In common hours
we have the same facts as in the uncommon or inspired, but they do not sit for their portraits; they
are not detached, but lie in a web. The thought of
genius is spontaneous; but the power of picture or expression, in the most enriched and flowing nature, im-
plies a mixture of will, a certain control over the
spontaneous states, without which no production is possible. It is a conversion of all nature into the rhetoric
of thought, under the eye of judgment, with a strenuous
exercise of choice. And yet the imaginative vocab-

ulary seems to be spontaneous also. It does not flow
from experience only or mainly but from a richer
source. Not by any conscious imitation of particular
forms are the grand strokes of the painter executed,
but by repairing to the fountain-head of all forms in
his mind. Who is the first drawing-master? Without instruction we know very well the ideal of the human form. A child knows if an arm or a leg be distorted in a picture; if the attitude be natural or grand
or mean; though he has never received any instruction
in drawing or heard any conversation on the subject,
nor can himself draw with correctness a single feature.
A good form strikes all eyes pleasantly, long before they
have any science on the subject, and a beautiful face
sets twenty hearts in palpitation, prior to all consideration of the mechanical proportions of the features and
head. We may owe to dreams some light on the fountain of this skill; for as soon as we let our will go and
let the unconscious states ensue, see what cunning
draughtsmen we are! We entertain ourselves with
wonderful forms of men, of women, of animals, of
gardens, of woods and of monsters, and the mystic
pencil wherewith we then draw has no awkwardness
or inexperience, no meagreness or poverty; it can design well and group well; its composition is full of art,
its colors are well laid on and the whole canvas which it
paints is life-like and apt to touch us with terror, with
tenderness, with desire and with grief. Neither are
the artist's copies from experience ever mere copies,
but always touched and softened by tints from this ideal
domain.

The conditions essential to a constructive mind do

not appear to be so often combined but that a good
sentence or verse remains fresh and memorable for
a long time. Yet when we write with ease and come
out into the free air of thought, we seem to be assured
that nothing is easier than to continue this communication at pleasure. Up, down, around, the kingdom of
thought has no enclosures, but the Muse makes us
free of her city. Well, the world has a million writers.
One would think then that good thought would be as
familiar as air and water, and the gifts of each new
hour would exclude the last. Yet we can count all our
good books; nay, I remember any beautiful verse for
twenty years. It is true that the discerning intellect
of the world is always greatly in advance of the creative,
so that there are many competent judges of the best
book, and few writers of the best books. But some of
the conditions of intellectual construction are of rare occurrence. The intellect is a whole and demands integrity in every work. This is resisted equally by a
man's devotion to a single thought and by his ambition
to combine too many.

Truth is our element of life, yet if a man fasten
his attention on a single aspect of truth and apply
himself to that alone for a long time, the truth becomes
distorted and not itself but falsehood; herein resembling the air, which is our natural element and the
breath of our nostrils, but if a stream of the same be
directed on the body for a time, it causes cold, fever,
and even death. How wearisome the grammarian, the
phrenologist, the political or religious fanatic, or indeed any possessed mortal whose balance is lost by the
exaggeration of a single topic. It is incipient insanity.

Every thought is a prison also. I cannot see what you see, because I am caught up by a strong wind and blown so far in one direction that I am out of the hoop of your horizon.

Is it any better if the student, to avoid this offence and to liberalize himself, aims to make a mechanical whole of history, or science, or philosophy, by a numerical addition of all the facts that fall within his vision? The world refuses to be analyzed by addition and subtraction. When we are young we spend much time and pains in filling our note-books with all definitions of Religion, Love, Poetry, Politics, Art, in the hope that in the course of a few years we shall have condensed into our encyclopædia the net value of all the theories at which the world has yet arrived. But year after year our tables get no completeness, and at last we discover that our curve is a parabola, whose arcs will never meet.

Neither by detachment, neither by aggregation is the integrity of the intellect transmitted to its works, but by a vigilance which brings the intellect in its greatness and best state to operate every moment. It must have the same wholeness which nature has. Although no diligence can rebuild the universe in a model by the best accumulation or disposition of details, yet does the world reappear in miniature in every event, so that all the laws of nature may be read in the smallest fact. The intellect must have the like perfection in its apprehension and in its works. For this reason, an index or mercury of intellectual proficiency is the perception of identity. We talk with accomplished persons who appear to be strangers in nature. The cloud, the tree, the turf, the bird, are not theirs, have nothing of them; the world is only their lodging and table. But the poet, whose verses are to be spheral and complete, is one whom nature cannot deceive, whatsoever face of strangeness she may put on. He feels a strict consanguinity, and detects more likeness than variety in all her changes. We are stung by the desire for new thought, but when we receive a new thought it is only the old thought with a new face, and though we make it our own we instantly crave another; we are not really enriched. For the truth was in us before it was reflected to us from natural objects; and the profound genius will cast the likeness of all creatures into every product of his wit.

But if the constructive powers are rare and it is given to few men to be poets, yet every man is a receiver of this descending holy ghost, and may well study the laws of its influx. Exactly parallel is the whole rule of intellectual duty to the rule of moral duty. A self-denial no less austere than the saint's is demanded of the scholar. He must worship truth, and forego all things for that, and choose defeat and pain, so that his treasure in thought is thereby augmented.

God offers to every mind its choice between truth and repose. Take which you please,—you can never have both. Between these, as a pendulum, man oscillates. He in whom the love of repose predominates will accept the first creed, the first philosophy, the first political party he meets,—most likely his father's. He gets rest, commodity and reputation; but he shuts the door of truth. He in whom the love of truth predominates will keep himself aloof from all moorings, and afloat. He will abstain from dogmatism, and recognize all the opposite negations between which, as walls, his being is swung. He submits to the inconvenience of suspense and imperfect opinion, but he is a candidate for truth, as the other is not, and respects the highest law of his being.

The circle of the green earth he must measure with his shoes to find the man who can yield him truth. He shall then know that there is somewhat more blessed and great in hearing than in speaking. Happy is the hearing man: unhappy the speaking man. As long as I hear truth I am bathed by a beautiful element and am not conscious of any limits to my nature. The suggestions are thousandfold that I hear and see. The waters of the great deep have ingress and egress to the soul. But if I speak, I define, I confine and am less. When Socrates speaks, Lysis and Menexenus are afflicted by no shame that they do not speak. They also are good. He likewise defers to them, loves them, whilst he speaks. Because a true and natural man contains and is the same truth which an eloquent man articulates: but in the eloquent man, because he can articulate it, it seems something the less to reside, and he turns to these silent beautiful with the more inclination and respect. The ancient sentence said, Let us be silent, for so are the gods. Silence is a solvent that destroys personality, and gives us leave to be great and universal. Every man's progress is through a succession of teachers, each of whom seems at the time to have a superlative influence, but it at last gives place to a new. Frankly let him accept it all. Jesus says, Leave father, mother, house and lands. and follow me. Who leaves all, re-

ceives more. This is as true intellectually as morally.
Each new mind we approach seems to require an abdica-
tion of all our past and present possessions. A new
doctrine seems at first a subversion of all our opinions,
tastes, and manner of living. Such has Swedenborg,
such has Kant, such has Coleridge, such has Cousin
seemed to many young men in this country. Take
thankfully and heartily all they can give. Exhaust
them, wrestle with them, let them not go until their
blessing be won, and after a short season the dismay
will be overpast, the excess of influence withdrawn, and
they will be no longer an alarming meteor, but one more
bright star shining serenely in your heaven and blending its light with all your day.

But whilst he gives himself up unreservedly to that
which draws him, because that is his own, he is to
refuse himself to that which draws him not, whatsoever fame and authority may attend it, because it is
not his own. Entire self-reliance belongs to the intellect. One soul is a counterpoise of all souls, as a
capillary column of water is a balance for the sea. It
must treat things and books and sovereign genius as
itself also a sovereign. If Æschylus be that man he
is taken for, he has not yet done his office when he has
educated the learned of Europe for a thousand years.
He is now to approve himself a master of delight to me
also. If he cannot do that, all his fame shall avail him
nothing with me. I were a fool not to sacrifice a
thousand Æschyluses to my intellectual integrity.
Especially take the same ground in regard to abstract
truth, the science of the mind. The Bacon, the Spinoza,
the Hume, Schelling, Kant, or whosoever propounds

to you a philosophy of the mind, is only a more or less awkward translator of things in your consciousness which you have also your way of seeing, perhaps of denominating. Say then, instead of too timidly poring into his obscure sense, that he has not succeeded in rendering back to you your consciousness. He has not succeeded; now let another try. If Plato cannot, perhaps Spinoza will. If Spinoza cannot, then perhaps Kant. Any how, when at last it is done, you will find it is no recondite, but a simple, natural, common state which the writer restores to you.

But let us end these didactics. I will not, though the subject might provoke it, speak to the open question between Truth and Love. I shall not presume to interfere in the old politics of the skies; "The cherubim know most; the seraphim love most." The gods shall settle their own quarrels. But I cannot recite, even thus rudely, laws of the intellect, without remembering that lofty and sequestered class who have been its prophets and oracles, the highpriesthood of the pure reason, the *Trismegisti,* the expounders of the principles of thought from age to age. When at long intervals we turn over their abstruse pages, wonderful seems the calm and grand air of these few, these great spiritual lords who have walked in the world,—these of the old religion, —dwelling in a worship which makes the sanctities of christianity look *parvenues* and popular; for "persuasion is in soul, but necessity is in intellect." This band of grandees, Hermes, Heraclitus, Empedocles, Plato, Plotinus, Olympiodorus, Proclus, Synesius and the rest, have somewhat so vast in their logic, so primary in their thinking, that it seems antecedent to all the ordinary distinctions of rhetoric and literatt.re, and to be at once poetry and music and dancing and astronomy and mathematics. I am present at the sowing of the seed of the world. With a geometry of sunbeams the soul lays the foundations of nature. The truth and grandeur of their thought is proved by its scope and applicability, for it commands the entire schedule and inventory of things for its illustration. But what marks its elevation and has even a comic look to us, is the innocent serenity with which these babe-like Jupiters sit in their clouds, and from age to age prattle to each other and to no contemporary. Well assured that their speech is intelligible and the most natural thing in the world, they add thesis to thesis, without a moment's heed of the universal astonishment of the human race below, who do not comprehend their plainest argument; nor do they ever relent so much as to insert a popular or explaining sentence, nor testify the least displeasure or petulance at the dulness of their amazed auditory. The angels are so enamored of the language that is spoken in heaven that they will not distort their lips with the hissing and unmusical dialects of men, but speak their own, whether there be any who understand it or not.

ART

BECAUSE the soul is progressive, it never quite repeats itself, but in every act attempts the production of a new and fairer whole. This appears in works both of the useful and fine arts, if we employ the popular distinction of works according to their aim either at use or beauty. Thus in our fine arts, not imitation but creation is the aim. In landscapes, the painter should give the suggestion of a fairer creation than we know. The details, the prose of nature he should omit and give us only the spirit and splendor. He should know that the landscape has beauty for his eye because it expresses a thought which is to him good: and this because the same power which sees through his eyes is seen in that spectacle; and he will come to value the expression of nature and not nature itself, and so exalt in his copy the features that please him. He will give the gloom of gloom and the sunshine of sunshine. In a portrait he must inscribe the character and not the features, and must esteem the man who sits to him as himself only an imperfect picture or likeness of the aspiring original within.

What is that abridgement and selection we observe in all spiritual activity, but itself the creative impulse? for it is the inlet of that higher illumination which teaches to convey a larger sense by simpler symbols.

What is a man but nature's finer success in self-explication? What is a man but a finer and compacter landscape than the horizon figures; nature's electicism? and what is his speech, his love of painting, love of nature, but a still finer success? all the weary miles and tons of space and bulk left out, and the spirit or moral of it contracted into a musical word, or the most cunning stroke of the pencil?

But the artist must employ the symbols in use in his day and nation to convey his enlarged sense to his fellow-men. Thus the new in art is always formed out of the old. The Genius of the Hour always sets his ineffaceable seal on the work and gives it an inexpressible charm for the imagination. As far as the spiritual character of the period overpowers the artist and finds expression in his work, so far it will always retain a certain grandeur, and will represent to future beholders the Unknown, the Inevitable, the Divine. No man can quite exclude this element of Necessity from his labor. No man can quite emancipate himself from his age and country, or produce a model in which the education, the religion, the politics, usages and arts of his times shall have no share. Though he were never so original, never so wilful and fantastic, he cannot wipe out of his work every trace of the thoughts amidst which it grew. The very avoidance betrays the usage he avoids. Above his will and out of his sight he is necessitated by the air he breathes and the idea on which he and his contemporaries live and toil, to share the manner of his times, without knowing what that manner is. Now that which is inevitable in the work has a higher charm than individual talent can ever give, inasmuch as the artist's pen or chisel seems to have been held and guided by a gigantic hand to inscribe a line in the history of the human race.   This circumstance gives a value to the Egyptian hieroglyphics, to the Indian, Chinese and Mexican idols, however gross and shapeless.   They denote the height of the human soul in that hour, and were not fantastic, but sprung from a necessity as deep as the world.   Shall I now add that the whole extant product of the plastic arts has herein its highest value, *as history;* as a stroke drawn in the portrait of that fate, perfect and beautiful, according to whose ordinations all beings advance to their beatitude?

Thus, historically viewed, it has been the office of art to educate the perception of beauty.   We are immersed in beauty, but our eyes have no clear vision.   It needs, by the exhibition of single traits, to assist and lead the dormant taste.   We carve and paint, or we behold what is carved and painted, as students of the mystery of Form.   The virtue of art lies in detachment, in sequestering one object from the embarrassing variety.   Until one thing comes out from the connection of things, there can be enjoyment, contemplation, but no thought.   Our happiness and unhappiness are unproductive.   The infant lies in a pleasing trance, but his individual character and his practical power depend on his daily progress in the separation of things, and dealing with one at a time.   Love and all the passions concentrate all existence around a single form.   It is the habit of certain minds to give an all-excluding fulness to the object, the thought, the word they alight upon and to make that for the time the deputy of the world. These are the artists, the orators, the leaders of society. The power to detach and to magniiy by detaching is the essence of rhetoric in the hands of the orator and the poet. This rhetoric, or power to fix the momentary eminency of an object, so remarkable in Burke, in Byron, in Carlyle,—the painter and sculptor exhibit in color and in stone. The power depends on the depth of the artist's insight of that object he contemplates. For every object has its roots in central nature, and may of course be so exhibited to us as to represent the world. Therefore each work of genius is the tyrant of the hour and concentrates attention on itself. For the time, it is the only thing worth naming, to do that,—be it a sonnet, an opera, a landscape, a statue, an oration, the plan of a temple, of a campaign, or of a voyage of discovery. Presently we pass to some other object, which rounds itself into a whole as did the first; for example a well laid garden: and nothing seems worth doing but the laying out of gardens. I should think fire the best thing in the world, if I were not acquainted with air, and water, and earth. For it is the right and property of all natural objects, of all genuine talents, of all native properties whatsoever, to be for their moment the top of the world. A squirrel leaping from bough to bough and making the wood but one wide tree for his pleasure, fills the eye not less than a lion, is beautiful, self-sufficing, and stands then and there for nature. A good ballad draws my ear and heart whilst I listen, as much as an epic has done before. A dog, drawn by a master, or a litter of pigs, satisfies and is a reality not less than the frescoes of Angelo. From this succession of excellent objects learn we at last the immensity of the world, the opulence of human nature, which can run out to infinitude in any direction. But I also learn that what astonished and fascinated me in the first work, astonished me in the second work also; that excellence of all things is one.

The office of painting and sculpture seems to be merely initial. The best pictures can easily tell us their last secret. The best pictures are rude draughts of a few of the miraculous dots and lines and dyes which make up the ever-changing "landscape with figures" amidst which we dwell. Painting seems to be to the eye what dancing is to the limbs. When that has educated the frame to self-possession, to nimbleness, to grace, the steps of the dancing-master are better forgotten; so painting teaches me the splendor of color and the expression of form, and as I see many pictures and higher genius in the art, I see the boundless opulence of the pencil, the indifference in which the artist stands free to choose out of the possible forms. If he can draw every thing, why draw any thing? and then is my eye opened to the eternal picture which nature paints in the street, with moving men and children, beggars and fine ladies, draped in red and green and blue and gray; longhaired, grizzled, white-faced, black-faced, wrinkled, giant, dwarf, expanded, elfish,—capped and based by heaven, earth and sea.

A gallery of sculpture teaches more austerely the same lesson. As picture teaches the coloring, so sculpture the anatomy of form. When I have seen fine statues and afterwards enter a public assembly, I understand well what he meant who said, "When I have been reading Homer, all men look like giants." I

too see that painting and sculpture are gymnastics of
the eye, training to the niceties and curiosities of its
function.   There is no statue like this living man, with
his infinite advantage over all ideal sculpture, of perpetual variety.   What a gallery of art have I here!
No mannerist made these varied groups and diverse
original single figures.   Here is the artist himself im-
provising, grim and glad, at his block.   Now one
thought strikes him, now another, and with each moment he alters the whole air, attitude and expression
of his clay.   Away with your nonsense of oil and
easels, of marble and chisels: except to open your eyes
to the witchcraft of eternal art, they are hypocritical
rubbish.

The reference of all production at last to an aboriginal Power explains the traits common to all works
of the highest art, that they are universally intelligible;
that they restore to us the simplest states of mind; and
are religious.   Since what skill is therein shown is the
reappearance of the original soul, a jet of pure light, it
should produce a similar impression to that made by
natural objects.   In happy hours, nature appears to us
one with art; art perfected,—the work of genius.   And
the individual in whom simple tastes and susceptibility to all the great human influences overpowers the accidents of a local and special culture, is the best critic
of art.   Though we travel the world over to find the
beautiful, we must carry it with us, or we find it not.
The best of beauty is a finer charm than skill in
surfaces, in outlines, or rules of art can ever teach,
namely a radiation from the work of art, of human
character,—a wonderful expression through stone, or

canvas, or musical sound, of the deepest and simplest
attributes of our nature, and therefore most intelligible
at last to those souls which have these attributes.   In the
sculptures of the Greeks, in the masonry of the Romans,
and in the pictures of the Tuscan and Venetian masters,
the highest charm is the universal language they speak.
A confession of moral nature, of purity, love, and
hope, breathes from them all.   That which we carry
to them, the same we bring back more fairly illustrated
in the memory.   The traveller who visits the Vatican
and passes from chamber to chamber through galleries
of statues, vases, sarcophagi and candelabra, through
all forms of beauty cut in the richest materials, is in
danger of forgetting the simplicity of the principles out
of which they all sprung, and that they had their origin
from thoughts and laws in his own breast.   He studies
the technical rules on these wonderful remains, but
forgets that these works were not always thus con-
stellated; that they are the contributions of many ages
and many countries; that each came out of the solitary
workshop of one artist, who toiled perhaps in ignorance
of the existence of other sculpture, created his work
without other model save life, household life, and the
sweet and smart of personal relations, of beating
hearts, and meeting eyes; of poverty and necessity and
hope and fear.   These were his inspirations, and these
are the effects he carries home to your heart and mind.
In proportion to his force, the artist will find in his
work an outlet for his proper character.   He must
not be in any manner pinched or hindered by his material, but through his necessity of imparting himself
the adamant will be wax in his hands, and will allow

an adequate communication of himself, in his full
stature and proportion. Not a conventional nature and
culture need he cumber himself with, nor ask what is
the mode in Rome or in Paris, but that house and
weather and manner of living which poverty and the
fate of birth have made at once so odious and so dear,
in the gray unpainted wood cabin, on the corner of a
New Hampshire farm, or in the log hut of the back-
woods, or in the narrow lodging where he has endured
the constraints and seeming of a city poverty,—will,
serve as well as any other condition as the symbol of a
thought which pours itself indifferently through all.

I remember when in my younger days I had heard of
the wonders of Italian painting, I fancied the great
pictures would be great strangers; some surprising combination of color and form; a foreign wonder, barbaric
pearl and gold, like the spontoons and standards of the
militia, which plays such pranks in the eyes and imaginations of schoolboys. I was to see and acquire I
knew not what. When I came at last to Rome and
saw with eyes the pictures, I found that genius left to
novices the gay and fantastic and ostentatious, and
itself pierced directly to the simple and true; that it was
familiar and sincere; that it was the old, eternal fact I
had met already in so many forms; unto which I lived;
that it was the plain *you and me* I knew so well,—had
left at home in so many conversations. I had the same
experience already in a church at Naples. There I saw
that nothing was changed with me but the place, and
said to myself,—"Thou foolish child, hast thou come
out hither, over four thousand miles of salt water, to
find that which was perfect to thee there at home?"—

that fact I saw again in the Academmia at Naples, in the chambers of sculpture, and yet again when I came to Rome and to the paintings of Raphael, Angelo, Sacchi, Titian, and Leonardo da Vinci. "What, old mole! workest thou in the earth so fast?" It had travelled by my side: that which I fancied I had left in Boston was here in the Vatican, and again at Milan and at Paris, and made all travelling ridiculous as a treadmill. I now require this of all pictures, that they domesticate me, not that they dazzle me. Pictures must not be too picturesque. Nothing astonishes men so much as common sense and plain dealing. All great actions have been simple, and all great pictures are.

The Transfiguration, by Raphael, is an eminent example of this peculiar merit. A calm benignant beauty shines over all this picture, and goes directly to the heart. It seems almost to call you by name. The sweet and sublime face of Jesus is beyond praise, yet how it disappoints all florid expectations! This familiar, simple, home-speaking countenance is as if one should meet a friend. The knowledge of picture-dealers has its value, but listen not to their criticism when your heart is touched by genius. It was not painted for them, it was painted for you; for such as had eyes capable of being touched by simplicity and lofty emotions.

Yet when we have said all our fine things about the arts, we must end with a frank confession that the arts, as we know them, are but initial. Our best praise is given to what they aimed and promised, not to the actual result. He has conceived meanly of the resources of man, who believes that the best age of production is past. The real value of the Iliad or the Transfiguration is as signs of power; billows or ripples they are of the great stream of tendency; tokens of the everlasting effort to produce, which even in its worst estate the soul betrays. Art has not come to its maturity if it do not put itself abreast with the most potent influences of the world, if it is not practical and moral, if it do not stand in connection with the conscience, if it do not make the poor and uncultivated feel that it addresses them with a voice of lofty cheer. There is higher work for Art than the arts. They are abortive births of an imperfect or vitiated instinct. Art is the need to create; but in its essence, immense and universal, it is impatient of working with lame or tired hands, and of making cripples and monsters, such as all pictures and statues are. Nothing less than the creation of man and nature is its end. A man should find in it an outlet for his whole energy. He may paint and carve only as long as he can do that. Art should exhilarate, and throw down the walls of circumstance on every side, awakening in the beholder the same sense of universal relation and power which the work evinced in the artist, and its highest effect is to make new artists.

Already History is old enough to witness the old age and disappearance of particular arts. The art of sculpture is long ago perished to any real effect. It was originally an useful art, a mode of writing, a savage's record of gratitude or devotion, and among a people possessed of a wonderful perception of form this childish carving was refined to the utmost splendor of effect. But it is the game of a rude and youthful people, and not the manly labor of a wise and spiritual nation. Under an oak-tree loaded with leaves and nuts, under a sky full of eternal eyes, I stand in a thoroughfare. Cut in the works of our plastic arts and especially of sculpture, creation is driven into a corner. I cannot hide from myself that there is a certain appearance of paltriness, as of toys and the trumpery of a theatre, in sculpture. Nature transcends all our moods of thought, and its secret we do not yet find. But the gallery stands at the mercy of our moods, and there is a moment when it becomes frivolous. I do not wonder that Newton, with an attention habitually engaged on the paths of planets and suns, should have wondered what the Earl of Pembroke found to admire in "stone dolls." Sculpture may serve to teach the pupil how deep is the secret of form, how purely the spirit can translate its meanings into that eloquent dialect. But the statue will look cold and false before that new activity which needs to roll through all things, and is impatient of counterfeits and things not alive. Picture and sculpture are the celebrations and festivities of form. But true art is never fixed, but always flowing. The sweetest music is not in the oratorio, but in the human voice when it speaks from its instant life tones of tenderness, truth, or courage. The oratorio has already lost its relation to the morning, to the sun, and the earth, but that persuading voice is in tune with these. All works of art should not be detached, but extempore performances. A great man is a new statue in every attitude and action. A beautiful woman is a picture which drives all beholders nobly mad. Life may be lyric or epic, as well as a poem or a romance.

A true announcement of the law of creation, if a man were found worthy to declare it, would carry art up into the kingdom of nature, and destroy its separate and contrasted existence. The fountains of invention and beauty in modern society are all but dried up. A popular novel, a theatre, or a ballroom makes us feel that we are all paupers in the almshouse of this world, without dignity, without skill or industry. Art is as poor and low. The old tragic Necessity, which lowers on the brows even of the Venuses and the Cupids of the antique, and furnishes the sole apology for the intrusion of such anomalous figures into nature,— namely that they were inevitable; that the artist was drunk with a passion for form which he could not resist, and which vented itself in these fine extravagancies,—no longer dignifies the chisel or the pencil. But the artist and the connoisseur now seek in art the exhibition of their talent, or an asylum from the evils of life. Men are not well pleased with the figure they make in their own imaginations, and they flee to art, and convey their better sense in an oratorio, a statue, or a picture. Art makes the same effort which a sensual prosperity makes; namely to detach the beautiful from the useful, to do up the work as unavoidable, and, hating it, pass on to enjoyment. These solaces and compensations, this division of beauty from use, the laws of nature do not permit. As soon as beauty is sought, not from religion and love but for pleasure, it degrades the seeker. High beauty is no

longer attainable by him in canvas or in stone in sound,
or in lyrical construction; an effeminate, prudent, sickly
beauty, which is not beauty, is all that can be formed:
for the hand can never execute any thing higher than
the character can inspire.

The art that thus separates is itself first separated.
Art must not be a superficial talent, but must begin
farther back in man.   Now men do not see nature to
be beautiful, and they go to make a statue which shall
be.   They abhor men as tasteless, dull, and inconvert-
ible, and console themselves with color-bags and blocks
of marble.   They reject life as prosaic, and create a
death which they call poetic.   They despatch the day's
weary chores, and fly to voluptuous reveries.   They
eat and drink, that they may afterwards execute the
ideal.   Thus is art vilified; the name conveys to the
mind its secondary and bad senses; it stands in the imagination as somewhat contrary to nature, and struck
with death from the first.   Would it not be better to
begin higher up,—to serve the ideal before they eat and
drink; to serve the ideal in eating and drinking, in
drawing the breath, and in the functions of life?
Beauty must come back to the useful arts, and the distinction between the fine and the useful arts be forgotten.   If history were truly told, if life were nobly
spent, it would be no longer easy or possible to distinguish the one from the other.   In nature, all is useful, all is beautiful.   It is therefore beautiful because
it is alive, moving, reproductive; it is therefore useful
because it is symmetrical and fair.   Beauty will not
come at the call of a legislature, nor will it repeat in
England or America its history in Greece.   It will

come, as always, unannounced, and spring up between the feet of brave and earnest men. It is in vain that we look for genius to reiterate its miracles in the old arts; it is its instinct to find beauty and holiness in new and necessary facts, in the field and roadside, in the shop and mill. Proceeding from a religious heart it will raise to a divine use the railroad, the insurance office, the joint-stock company; our law, our primary assemblies, our commerce, the galvanic battery, the electric jar, the prism, and the chemist's retort; in which we seek now only an economical use. Is not the selfish and even cruel aspect which belongs to our great mechanical works, to mills, railways, and machinery, the effect of the mercenary impulses which these works obey? When its errands are noble and adequate, a steamboat bridging the Atlantic between Old and New England and arriving at its ports with the punctuality of a planet,—is a step of man into harmony with nature. The boat at St. Petersburg, which plies along the Lena by magnetism, needs little to make it sublime. When science is learned in love, and its powers are wielded by love, they will appear the supplements and continuations of the material creation.

ESSAY I

THE POET

A moody child and wildly wise
Pursued the game with joyful eyes,
Which chose, like meteors, their way,
And rived the dark with private ray:
They overleapt the horizon's edge,
Searched with Apollo's privilege;
Through man, and woman, and sea, and star,
Saw the dance of nature forward far;
Through worlds, and races, and terms, and times,
Saw musical order, and pairing rhymes.

Olympian bards who sung
Divine ideas below,
Which always find us young,
And always keep us so.

THOSE who are esteemed umpires of taste,
are often persons who have acquired some
knowledge of admired pictures or sculptures,
and have an inclination for whatever is elegant; but
if you inquire whether they are beautiful souls, and
whether their own acts are like fair pictures, you learn
that they are selfish and sensual. Their cultivation is
local, as if you should rub a log of dry wood in one
spot to produce fire, all the rest remaining cold. Their

knowledge of the fine arts is some study of rules and
particulars, or some limited judgment of color or form,
which is exercised for amusement or for show.   It is
a proof of the shallowness of the doctrine of beauty,
as it lies in the minds of our amateurs, that men seem
to have lost the perception of the instant dependence
of form upon soul.   There is no doctrine of forms in
our philosophy.   We were put into our bodies, as fire
is put into a pan, to be carried about; but there is no
accurate adjustment between the spirit and the organ,
much less is the latter the germination of the former.
So in regard to other forms, the intellectual men do
not believe in any essential dependence of the material world on thought and volition.   Theologians
think it a pretty air-castle to talk of the spiritual meaning of a ship or a cloud, of a city or a contract,
but they prefer to come again to the solid ground of
historical evidence; and even the poets are contented
with a civil and conformed manner of living, and to
write poems from the fancy, at a safe distance from
their own experience.   But the highest minds of the
world have never ceased to explore the double meaning, or, shall I say, the quadruple, or the centuple, or
much more manifold meaning, of every sensuous fact:
Orpheus, Empedocles, Heraclitus, Plato, Plutarch,
Dante, Swedenborg, and the masters of sculpture,
picture, and poetry.   For we are not pans and barrows,
nor even porters of the fire and torchbearers, but children of the fire, made of it, and only the same divinity
transmuted, and at two or three removes, when we
know least about it.   And this hidden truth, that the
fountains whence all this river of Time, and its crea-

tures, floweth, are intrinsically ideal and beautiful,
draws us to the consideration of the nature and functions of the Poet, or the man of Beauty, to the means
and materials he uses, and to the general aspect of the
art in the present time.

The breadth of the problem is great, for the poet is
representative. He stands among partial men for
the complete man, and apprises us not of his wealth,
but of the commonwealth. The young man reveres
men of genius, because, to speak truly, they are more
himself than he is. They receive of the soul as he
also receives, but they more. Nature enhances her
beauty, to the eye of loving men, from their belief
that the poet is beholding her shows at the same time.
He is isolated among his contemporaries, by truth and
by his art, but with his consolation in his pursuits, that
they will draw all men sooner or later. For all men
live by truth, and stand in need of expression. In love,
in art, in avarice, in politics, in labor, in games, we
study to utter our painful secret. The man is only
half himself, the other half is his expression.

Notwithstanding this necessity to be published,
adequate expression is rare. I know not how it is
that we need an interpreter: but the great majority
of men seem to be minors, who have not yet come
into possession of their own, or mutes, who cannot
report the conversation they have had with nature.
There is no man who does not anticipate a super-
sensual utility in the sun, and stars, earth, and water.
These stand and wait to render him a peculiar service. But there is some obstruction, or some excess
of phlegm in our constitution, which does not suffer

them to yield the due effect. Too feeble fall the impressions of nature on us to make us artists. Every touch should thrill. Every man should be so much an artist, that he could report in conversation what had befallen him. Yet, in our experience, the rays or appulses have sufficient force to arrive at the senses, but not enough to reach the quick, and compel the reproduction of themselves in speech. The poet is the person in whom these powers are in balance, the man without impediment, who sees and handles that which others dream of, traverses the whole scale of experience, and its representative of man, in virtue of being the largest power to receive and to impart.

For the Universe has three children, born at one time, which reappear, under different names, in every system of thought, whether they be called cause, operation, and effect; or, more poetically, Jove, Pluto, Neptune; or, theologically, the Father, the Spirit, and the Son; but which we will call here, the Knower, the Doer, and the Sayer. These stand respectively for the love of truth, for the love of good, and for the love of beauty. These three are equal. Each is that which he is essentially, so that he cannot be surmounted or analyzed, and each of these three has the power of the others latent in him, and his own patent.

The poet is the sayer, the namer, and represents beauty. He is a sovereign, and stands on the centre. For the world is not painted, or adorned, but is from the beginning beautiful; and God has not made some beautiful things, but Beauty is the creator of the universe. Therefore the poet is not any permissive potentate, but is emperor in his own right. Criticism

is infested with a cant of materialism, which assumes
that manual skill and activity is the first merit of all
men, and disparages such as say and do not, overlooking the fact, that some men, namely, poets, are
natural sayers, sent into the world to the end of expression, and confounds them with those whose province is action, but who quit it to imitate the sayers.
But Homer's words are as costly and admirable to
Homer, as Agamemnon's victories are to Agamemnon.
The poet does not wait for the hero or the sage, but,
as they act and think primarily, so he writes primarily
what will and must be spoken, reckoning the others,
though primaries also, yet, in respect to him, secondaries
and servants; as sitters or models in the studio of a
painter, or as assistants who bring building materials
to an architect.

For poetry was all written before time was, and
whenever we are so finely organized that we can pene-
trate into that region where the air is music, we hear
those primal warblings, and attempt to write them
down, but we lose ever and anon a word, or a verse, and
substitute something of our own, and thus miswrite the
poem. The men of more delicate ear write down
these cadences more faithfully, and these transcripts,
though imperfect, become the songs of the nations.
For nature is as truly beautiful as it is good, or as it is
reasonable, and must as much appear, as it must be
done, or be known. Words and deeds are quite indifferent modes of the divine energy. Words are also
actions, and actions are a kind of words.

The sign and credentials of the poet are, that he
announces that which no man foretold. He is the

true and only doctor; he knows and tells; he is the only teller of news, for he was present and privy to the appearance which he describes. He is a beholder of ideas, and an utterer of the necessary and causal. For we do not speak now of men of poetical talents, or of industry and skill in metre, but of the true poet. I took part in a conversation the other day, concerning a recent writer of lyrics, a man of subtle mind, whose head appeared to be a music-box of delicate tunes and rhythms, and whose skill, and command of language, we could not sufficiently praise. But when the question arose, whether he was not only a lyrist, but a poet, we were obliged to confess that he is plainly a contemporary, not an eternal man. He does not stand out of our low limitations, like a Chimborazo under the line, running up from the torrid base through all the climates of the globe, with belts of the herbage of every latitude on its high and mottled sides; but this genius is the landscape-garden of a modern house, adorned with fountains and statues, with well-bred men and women standing and sitting in the walks and terraces. We hear, through all the varied music, the ground-tone of conventional life. Our poets are men of talents who sing, and not the children of music. The argument is secondary, the finish of the verses is primary.

For it is not metres, but a metre-making argument, that makes a poem,—a thought so passionate and alive, that, like the spirit of a plant or an animal, it has an architecture of its own, and adorns nature with a new thing. The thought and the form are equal in the order of time, but in the order of genesis the thought is prior to the form. The poet has a new thought: he has

a whole new experience to unfold; he will tell us how
it was with him, and all men will be the richer in his
fortune. For, the experience of each new age requires
a new confession, and the world seems always waiting
for its poet. I remember, when I was young, how
much I was moved one morning by tidings that genius
had appeared in a youth who sat near me at table. He
had left his work, and gone rambling none knew
whither, and had written hundreds of lines, but could
not tell whether that which was in him was therein told:
he could tell nothing but that all was changed,—man,
beast, heaven, earth, and sea. How gladly we listened!
how credulous! Society seemed to be compromised.
We sat in the aurora of a sunrise which was to put out
all the stars. Boston seemed to be at twice the distance it had the night before, or was much farther than
that. Rome,—what was Rome? Plutarch and
Shakspeare were in the yellow leaf, and Homer no
more should be heard of. It is much to know that
poetry has been written this very day, under this very
roof by your side. What! that wonderful spirit has
not expired! these stony moments are still sparkling
and animated! I had fancied that the oracles were all
silent, and nature had spent her fires, and behold! all
night, from every pore, these fine auroras have been
streaming. Every one has some interest in the advent
of the poet, and no one knows how much it may concern him. We know that the secret of the world is
profound, but who or what shall be our interpreter, we
know not. A mountain ramble, a new style of face,
a new person, may put the key into our hands. Of
course, the value of genius to us is in the veracity of its

report. Talent may frolic and juggle; genius realizes and adds. Mankind, in good earnest, have availed so far in understanding themselves and their work, that the foremost watchman on the peak announces his news. It is the truest word ever spoken, and the phrase will be the fittest, most musical, and the unerring voice of the world for that time.

All that we call sacred history attests that the birth of a poet is the principal event in chronology. Man, never so often deceived, still watches for the arrival of a brother who can hold him steady to a truth, until he has made it his own. With what joy I begin to read a poem, which I confide in as an inspiration! And now my chains are to be broken; I shall mount above these clouds and opaque airs in which I live, —opaque, though they seem transparent,—and from the heaven of truth I shall see and comprehend my relations. That will reconcile me to life, and renovate nature, to see trifles animated by a tendency, and to know what I am doing. Life will no more be a noise; now I shall see men and women, and know the signs by which they may be discerned from fools and satans. This day shall be better than my birthday: then I became an animal: now I am invited into the science of the real. Such is the hope, but the fruition is postponed. Oftener it falls, that this winged man, who will carry me into the heaven, whirls me into the clouds, then leaps and frisks about with me from cloud to cloud, still affirming that he is bound heavenward; and I, being myself a novice, and slow in perceiving that he does not know the way into the heavens, and is merely bent that I should admire his skill to rise,

like a fowl or a flying fish, a little way from the ground
or the water; but the all-piercing, all-feeding, and
ocular air of heaven, that man shall never inhabit. I
tumble down again soon into my old nooks, and lead
the life of exaggerations as before, and have lost my
faith in the possibility of any guide who can lead me
thither where I would be.

But leaving these victims of vanity, let us, with new
hope, observe how nature, by worthier impulses, has
ensured the poet's fidelity to his office of announcement
and affirming, namely, by the beauty of things, which
becomes a new, and higher beauty, when expressed.
Nature offers all her creatures to him as a picture-
language. Being used as a type, a second wonderful
value appears in the object, far better than its old
value, as the carpenter's stretched cord, if you hold your
ear close enough, is musical in the breeze.

"Things more excellent than every image," says
Jamblichus, "are expressed through images." Things
admit of being used as symbols, because nature is a
symbol, in the whole, and in every part. Every line
we can draw in the sand, has expression; and there is
no body without its spirit of genius. All form is an
effect of character; all condition, of the quality of the
life; all harmony, of health; (and for this reason, a
perception of beauty should be sympathetic, or proper
only to the good). The beautiful rests on the foundations of the necessary. The soul makes the body, as
the wise Spenser teaches:—

> So every spirit, as it is most pure,
> And hath in it the more of heavenly light,

So it the fairer body doth procure
To habit in, and it more fairly dight,
With cheerful grace and amiable sight.
For, of the soul, the body form doth take,
For soul is form, and doth the body make.

Here we find ourselves, suddenly, not in a critical spec-
ulation, but in a holy place, and should go very warily
and reverently. We stand before the secret of the
world, there where Being passes into Appearance, and
Unity into Variety.

The Universe is the externization of the soul.
Wherever the life is, that bursts into appearance around
it. Our science is sensual, and therefore superficial.
The earth, and the heavenly bodies, physics, and chemistry, we sensually treat, as if they were self-existent;
but these are the retinue of that Being we have. "The
mighty heaven," said Proclus, "exhibits, in its trans-
figurations, clear images of the splendor of intellectual
perceptions; being moved in conjunction with the un-
apparent periods of intellectual natures." Therefore,
science always goes abreast with the just elevation of
the man, keeping step with religion and metaphysics;
or, the state of science is an index of our self-
knowledge. Since every thing in nature answers to
a moral power, if any phenomenon remains brute and
dark, it is that the corresponding faculty in the observer
is not yet active.

No wonder, then, if these waters be so deep, that we
hover over them with a religious regard. The beauty
of the fable proves the importance of the sense; to the
poet, and to all others; or if you please, every man is
so far a poet as to be susceptible of these enchantments

of nature: for all men have the thoughts whereof the universe is the celebration. I find that the fascination resides in the symbol. Who loves nature? Who does not? Is it only poets, and men of leisure and cultivation, who live with her? No; but also hunters, farmers, grooms, and butchers, though they express their affection in their choice of life, and not in their choice of words. The writer wonders what the coachman or the hunter values in riding, in horses, and dogs. It is not superficial qualities. When you talk with him, he holds these at as slight a rate as you. His worship is sympathetic; he has no definitions, but he is commanded in nature, by the living power which he feels to be there present. No imitation, or playing of these things, would content him; he loves the earnest of the northwind, of rain, of stone, and wood, and iron. A beauty not explicable, is dearer than a beauty which we can see to the end of. It is nature the symbol, nature certifying the supernatural, body overflowed by life, which he worships, with coarse, but sincere rites.

The inwardness and mystery of this attachment, drives men of every class to the use of emblems. The schools of poets, and philosophers, are not more intoxicated with their symbols, than the populace with theirs. In our political parties, compute the power of badges and emblems. See the great ball which they roll from Baltimore to Bunker Hill! In the political processions, Lowell goes in a loom, and Lynn in a shoe, and Salem in a ship. Witness the cider-barrel, the log cabin, the hickory-stick, the palmetto, and all the cognizances of party. See the power of national emblems. Some stars, lilies, leopards, a crescent, a lion, an eagle, or other figure, which came into credit God knows how. on an old rag of bunting, blowing in the wind, on a fort, at the ends of the earth, shall make the blood tingle under the rudest, or the most conventional exterior.   The people fancy they hate poetry, and they are all poets and mystics!

Beyond this universality of the symbolic language, we are apprised of the divineness of this superior use of things, whereby the world is a temple, whose walls are covered with emblems, pictures, and commandments of the Deity, in this, that there is no fact in nature which does not carry the whole sense of nature; and the distinctions which we make in events, and in affairs, of low and high, honest and base, disappear when nature is used as a symbol.   Thought makes every thing fit for use.   The vocabulary of an omniscient man would embrace words and images excluded from polite conversation.   What would be base, or even obscene, to the obscene, becomes illustrious, spoken in a new connection of thought.   The piety of the Hebrew prophets purges their grossness.   The circumcision is an example of the power of poetry to raise the low and offensive.   Small and mean things serve as well as great symbols.   The meaner the type by which a law is expressed, the more pungent it is, and the more lasting in the memories of men: just as we choose the smallest box, or case, in which any needful utensil can be carried.   Bare lists of words are found suggestive, to an imaginative and excited mind; as it is related of Lord Chatham, that he was accustomed to read in Bailey's Dictionary, when he was preparing to speak in Parliament.   The poorest experience is rich

enough for all the purposes of expressing thought.
Why covet a knowledge of new facts? Day and night,
house and garden, a few books, a few actions, serve us
as well as would all trades and all spectacles. We are
far from having exhausted the significance of the few
symbols we use. We can come to use them yet with a
terrible simplicity. It does not need that a poem should
be long. Every word was once a poem. Every new
relation is a new word. Also, we use defects and
deformities to a sacred purpose, so expressing our sense
that the evils of the world are such only to the evil eye.
In the old mythology, mythologists observe, defects are
ascribed to divine natures, as lameness to Vulcan, blindness to Cupid, and the like, to signify exuberances.

For, as it is dislocation and detachment from the life
of God, that makes things ugly, the poet, who re-
attaches things to nature and the Whole,—re-attaching
even artificial things and violations of nature, to nature, by a deeper insight—disposes very easily of the
most disagreeable facts. Readers of poetry see the
factory-village, and the railway, and fancy that the
poetry of the landscape is broken up by these; for these
works of art are not yet consecrated in their readings;
but the poet sees them fall within the great Order
not less than the bee-hive, or the spider's geometrical
web. Nature adopts them very fast into her vital circles, and the gliding train of cars she loves like her
own. Besides, in a centred mind, it signifies nothing
how many mechanical inventions you exhibit. Though
you add millions, and never so surprising, the fact of
mechanics has not gained a grain's weight. The spiritual fact remains unalterable, by many or by few

particulars; as no mountain is of any appreciable height to break the curve of the sphere. A shrewd country-boy goes to the city for the first time, and the complacent citizen is not satisfied with his little wonder. It is not that he does not see all the fine houses, and know that he never saw such before, but he disposes of them as easily as the poet finds place for the railway. The chief value of the new fact, is to enhance the great and constant fact of Life, which can dwarf any and every circumstance, and to which the belt of wampum, and the commerce of America, are alike.

The world being thus put under the mind for verb and noun, the poet is he who can articulate it. For, though life is great, and fascinates, and absorbs,—and though all men are intelligent of the symbols through which it is named,—yet they cannot originally use them. We are symbols, and inhabit symbols; workman, work, and tools, words and things, birth and death, all are emblems; but we sympathize with the symbols, and, being infatuated with the economical uses of things, we do not know that they are thoughts. The poet, by an ulterior intellectual perception, gives them a power which makes their old use forgotten, and puts eyes, and a tongue into every dumb and inanimate object. He perceives the independence of the thought on the symbol, the stability of the thought, the accidency and fugacity of the symbol. As the eyes of Lyncæus were said to see through the earth, so the poet turns the world to glass, and shows us all things in their right series and procession. For, through that better perception, he stands one step nearer to things, and sees the flowing or metamorphosis; perceives that thought is multiform; that within the form of every creature is a force impelling it to ascend into a higher form; and, following with his eyes the life, uses the forms which express that life, and so his speech flows with the flowing of nature. All the facts of the animal economy, sex, nutriment, gestation, birth, growth, are symbols of the passage of the world into the soul of man, to suffer there a change, and reappear a new and higher fact. He uses forms according to the life, and not according to the form. This is true science. The poet alone knows astronomy, chemistry, vegetation, and animation, for he does not stop at these facts, but employs them as signs. He knows why the plain, or meadow of space, was strown with these flowers we call suns, and moons, and stars; why the great deep is adorned with animals, with men, and gods; for, in every word he speaks he rides on them as the horses of thought.

By virtue of this science the poet is the Namer, or Language-maker, naming things sometimes after their appearance, sometimes after their essence, and giving to every one its own name and not another's, thereby rejoicing the intellect, which delights in detachment or boundary. The poets made all the words, and therefore language is the archives of history, and, if we must say it, a sort of tomb of the muses. For, though the origin of most of our words is forgotten, each word was at first a stroke of genius, and obtained currency, because for the moment it symbolized the world to the first speaker and to the hearer. The etymologist finds the deadest word to have been once a brilliant picture. Language is fossil poetry. As the limestone of the continent consists of infinite masses of the shells of animalcules, so language is made up of images, or tropes, which now, in their secondary use, have long ceased to remind us of their poetic origin. But the poet names the thing because he sees it, or comes one step nearer to it than any other. This expression or naming, is not art, but a second nature, grown out of the first, as a leaf out of a tree. What we call nature, is a certain self-regulated motion, or change; and nature does all things by her own hands, and does not leave another to baptize her, but baptizes herself; and this through the metamorphosis again. I remember that a certain poet described it to me thus:

Genius is the activity which repairs the decays of things, whether wholly or partly of a material and finite kind. Nature, through all her kingdoms, insures herself. Nobody cares for planting the poor fungus: so she shakes down from the gills of one agaric countless spores, any one of which, being preserved, transmits new billions of spores to-morrow or next day. The new agaric of this hour has a chance which the old one had not. This atom of seed is thrown into a new place, not subject to the accidents which destroyed its parent two rods off. She makes a man; and having brought him to ripe age, she will no longer run the risk of losing this wonder at a blow, but she detaches from him a new self, that the kind may be safe from accidents to which the individual is exposed. So when the soul of the poet has come to ripeness of thought she detaches and sends away from it its poems or songs,—a fearless, sleepless, deathless progeny, which

is not exposed to the accidents of the weary kingdom
of time : a fearless, vivacious offspring, clad with wings
(such was the virtue of the soul out of which they
came), which carry them fast and far, and infix them
irrecoverably into the hearts of men.   These wings are
the beauty of the poet s soul.   The songs, thus flying
immortal from their mortal parent, are pursued by
clamorous flights of censures, which swarm in far
greater numbers, and threaten to devour them; but
these last are not winged.   At the end of a very short
leap they fall plump down, and rot, having received
from the souls out of which they came no beautiful
wings.   But the melodies of the poet ascend, and leap,
and pierce into the deeps of infinite time.

So far the bard taught me, using his freer speech.
But nature has a higher end, in the production of new
individuals, than security, namely, *ascension,* or, the
passage of the soul into higher forms.   I knew, in my
younger days, the sculptor who made the statue of
the youth which stands in the public garden.   He
was, as I remember, unable to tell directly, what made
him happy, or unhappy, but by wonderful indirections
he could tell.   He rose one day, according to his habit,
before the dawn, and saw the morning break, grand as
the eternity out of which it came, and, for many days
after, he strove to express this tranquillity, and, lo!
his chisel had fashioned out of marble the form of a
beautiful youth, Phosphorus, whose aspect is such, that,
it is said, all persons who look on it become silent.
The poet also resigns himself to his mood, and that
thought which agitated him is expressed, but *alter idem*

in a manner totally new. The expression is organic, or, the new type which things themselves take when liberated. As, in the sun, objects paint their images on the retina of the eye, so they, sharing the aspiration of the whole universe, tend to paint a far more delicate copy of their essence in his mind. Like the metamorphosis of things into higher organic forms, is their change into melodies. Over every thing stands its dæmon, or soul, and, as the form of the thing is reflected by the eye, so the soul of the thing is reflected by a melody. The sea, the mountain-ridge, Niagara, and every flower-bed, pre-exist, or super-exist, in pre-cantations, which sail like odors in the air, and when any man goes by with an ear sufficiently fine, he overhears them, and endeavors to write down the notes, without diluting or depraving them. And herein is the legitimation of criticism, in the mind's faith, that the poems are a corrupt version of some text in nature, with which they ought to be made to tally. A rhyme in one of our sonnets should not be less pleasing than the iterated nodes of a sea-shell, or the resembling difference of a group of flowers. The pairing of the birds is an idyl, not tedious as our idyls are; a tempest is a rough ode, without falsehood or rant: a summer, with its harvest sown, reaped, and stored, is an epic song, subordinating how many admirably executed parts. Why should not the symmetry and truth that modulates these, glide into our spirits, and we participate the invention of nature?

This insight, which expresses itself by what is called Imagination, is a very high sort of seeing, which does not come by study, but by the intellect being where

and what it sees, by sharing the path, or circuit of things
through forms, and so making them translucid to
others. The path of things is silent. Will they suffer
a speaker to go with them? A spy they will not suffer; a lover, a poet, is the transcendency of their own
nature,—him they will suffer. The condition of true
naming, on the poet's part, is his resigning himself to
the divine *aura* which breathes through forms, and
accompanying that.

It is a secret which every intellectual man quickly
learns, that, beyond the energy of his possessed and
conscious intellect, he is capable of a new energy (as
of an intellect doubled on itself), by abandonment to
the nature of things; that, beside his privacy of power
as an individual man, there is a great public power, on
which he can draw, by unlocking, at all risks, his human
doors, and suffering the ethereal tides to roll and circulate through him: then he is caught up into the
life of the Universe, his speech is thunder, his thought
is law, and his words are universally intelligible as
the plants and animals. The poet knows that he speaks
adequately, then, only when he speaks somewhat wildly,
or, "with the flower of the mind"; not with the intellect,
used as an organ, but with the intellect released from
all service, and suffered to take its direction from its
celestial life; or, as the ancients were wont to express
themselves, not with intellect alone, but with the intellect inebriated by nectar. As the traveller who has
lost his way, throws his reins on his horse's neck, and
trusts to the instinct of the animal to find his road, so
must we do with the divine animal who carries us
through this world. For if in any manner we can

stimulate this instinct, new passages are opened for us into nature, the mind flows into and through things hardest and highest, and the metamorphosis is possible.

This is the reason why bards love wine, mead, narcotics, coffee, tea, opium, the fumes of sandal-wood and tobacco, or whatever other species of animal exhilaration. All men avail themselves of such means as they can, to add this extraordinary power to their normal powers; and to this end they prize conversation, music, pictures, sculpture, dancing, theatres, travelling, war, mobs, fires, gaming, politics, or love, or science, or animal intoxication, which are several coarser or finer *quasi*-mechanical substitutes for the true nectar, which is the ravishment of the intellect by coming nearer to the fact. These are auxiliaries to the centrifugal tendency of a man, to his passage out into free space, and they help him to escape the custody of that body in which he is pent up, and of that jail-yard of individual relations in which he is enclosed. Hence a great number of such as were professionally expressors of Beauty, as painters, poets, musicians, and actors, have been more than others wont to lead a life of pleasure and indulgence; all but the few who received the true nectar; and, as it was a spurious mode of obtaining freedom, an emancipation not into the heavens, but into the freedom of baser places, they were punished for that advantage they won, by a dissipation and deterioration. But never can any advantage be taken of nature by a trick. The spirit of the world, the great calm presence of the creator, comes not forth to the sorceries of opium or of wine. The sublime vision comes to the pure and simple soul in a clean and chaste body. That is not an inspiration which we owe to narcotics, but some counterfeit excitement and fury. Milton says, that the lyric poet may drink wine and live generously, but the epic poet, he who shall sing of the gods, and their descent unto men, must drink water out of a wooden bowl.

For poetry is not "Devil's wine," but God's wine. It is with this as it is with toys. We fill the hands and nurseries of our children with all manner of dolls, drums, and horses, withdrawing their eyes from the plain face and sufficing object of nature, the sun, and moon, the animals, the water, and stones, which should be their toys. So the poet's habit of living should be set on a key so low and plain, that the common influences should delight him. His cheerfulness should be the gift of the sunlight; the air should suffice for his inspiration, and he should be tipsy with water. That spirit which suffices quiet hearts, which seems to come forth to such from every dry knoll of sere grass, from every pine-stump, and half-imbedded stone, on which the dull March sun shines, comes forth to the poor and hungry, and such as are of simple taste. If thou fill thy brain with Boston and New York, with fashion and covetousness, and wilt stimulate thy jaded senses with wine and French coffee, thou shalt find no radiance of wisdom in the lonely waste of the pinewoods.

If the imagination intoxicates the poet, it is not inactive in other men. The metamorphosis excites in the beholder an emotion of joy.

The use of symbols has a certain power of emancipation and exhilaration for all men. We seem to be touched by a wand, which makes us dance and run

about happily, like children.   We are like persons who
come out of a cave or cellar into the open air.   This is
the effect on us of tropes, fables, oracles, and all poetic
forms.   Poets are thus liberating gods.   Men have
really got a new sense, and found within their world,
another world or nest of worlds; for the metamorphosis
once seen, we divine that it does not stop.   I will not
now consider how much this makes the charm of algebra
and the mathematics, which also have their tropes, but
it is felt in every definition; as, when Aristotle defines
space to be an immovable vessel, in which things are
contained;—or, when Plato defines a *line* to be a flowing point; or, *figure* to be a bound of solid; and many
the like.   What a joyful sense of freedom we have,
when Vitruvius announces the old opinion of artists,
that no architect can build any house well, who does not
know something of anatomy.   When Socrates, in
Charmides, tells us that the soul is cured of its maladies
by certain incanations, and that these incantations are
beautiful reasons, from which temperance is generated
in souls; when Plato calls the world an animal; and
Timæus affirms that the plants also are animals; or affirms a man to be a heavenly tree, growing with his
root, which is his head, upward; and, as George Chap-
man, following him, writes,—

> So in our tree of man, whose nervie root
> Springs in his top;

when Orpheus speaks of hoariness as "that white flower
which marks extreme old age"; when Proclus calls the
universe the statue of the intellect; when Chaucer, in
his praise of "Gentilesse," compares good blood in mean

condition to fire, which, though carried to the darkest
house betwixt this and the mount of Caucasus, will
yet hold its natural office, and burn as bright as if
twenty thousand men did it behold; when John saw, in
the apocalypse, the ruin of the world through evil, and
the stars fall from heaven, as the figtree casteth her
untimely fruit; when Æsop reports the whole catalogue
of common daily relations through the masquerade of
birds and beasts;—we take the cheerful hint of the immortality of our essence, and its versatile habit and
escapes, as when the gypsies say, "it is vain to hang
them, they cannot die."

The poets are thus liberating gods. The ancient
British bards had for the title of their order, "Those
who are free throughout the world." They are free,
and they make free. An imaginative book renders us
much more service at first, by stimulating us through
its tropes, than afterward, when we arrive at the precise sense of the author. I think nothing is of any
value in books, excepting the transcendental and extraordinary. If a man is inflamed and carried away by
his thought, to that degree that he forgets the authors
and the public, and heeds only this one dream, which
holds him like an insanity, let me read his paper, and
you may have all the arguments and histories and criticism. All the value which attaches to Pythagoras,
Paracelsus, Cornelius Agrippa, Cardan, Kepler, Swedenborg, Schelling, Oken, or any other who introduces
questionable facts into his cosmogony, as angels, devils,
magic, astrology, palmistry, mesmerism, and so on, is
the certificate we have of departure from routine, and
that here is a new witness. That also is the best suc-

cess in conversation, the magic of liberty, which puts the world like a ball, in our hands. How cheap even the liberty then seems; how mean to study, when an emotion communicates to the intellect the power to sap and upheave nature: how great the perspective! nations, times, systems, enter and disappear like threads in tapestry of large figure and many colors; dream delivers us to dream, and, while the drunkenness lasts, we will sell our bed, our philosophy, our religion, in our opulence.

There is good reason why we should prize this liberation. The fate of the poor shepherd, who, blinded and lost in the snow-storm, perishes in a drift within a few feet of his cottage door, is an emblem of the state of man. On the brink of the waters of life and truth, we are miserably dying. The inaccessibleness of every thought but that we are in, is wonderful. What if you come near to it,—you are as remote, when you are nearest, as when you are farthest. Every thought is also a prison; every heaven is also a prison. Therefore we love the poet, the inventor, who in any form, whether in an ode, or in an action, or in looks and behavior, has yielded us a new thought. He unlocks our chains, and admits us to a new scene.

This emancipation is dear to all men, and the power to impart it, as it must come from greater depth and scope of thought, is a measure of intellect. Therefore all books of the imagination endure, all which ascend to that truth, that the writer sees nature beneath him, and uses it as his exponent. Every verse or sentence, possessing this virtue, will take care of its own immortality. The religions of the world are the ejaculations of a few imaginative men.

But the quality of the imagination is to flow, and not to freeze. The poet did not stop at the color, or the form, but read their meaning; neither may he rest in this meaning; but he makes the same objects exponents of his new thought. Here is the difference betwixt the poet and the mystic, that the last nails a symbol to one sense, which was a true sense for a moment, but soon becomes old and false. For all symbols are fluxional; all language is vehicular and transitive, and is good, as ferries and horses are, for conveyance, not as farms and houses are, for homestead. Mysticism consists in the mistake of an accidental and individual symbol for an universal one. The morning-redness happens to be the favorite meteor to the eyes of Jacob Behman, and comes to stand to him for truth and faith; and he believes should stand for the same realities to every reader. But the first reader prefers as naturally the symbol of a mother and child, or a gardener and his bulb, or a jeweller polishing a gem. Either of these, or of a myriad more, are equally good to the person to whom they are significant. Only they must be held lightly, and be very willingly translated into the equivalent terms which others use. And the mystic must be steadily told,—All that you say is just as true without the tedious use of that symbol as with it. Let us have a little algebra, instead of this trite rhetoric,— universal signs, instead of these village symbols,—and we shall both be gainers. The history of hierarchies seems to show, that all religious error consisted in making the symbol too stark and solid, and, at last, nothing but an excess of the organ of language.

Swedenborg, of all men in the recent ages, stands eminently for the translator of nature into thought. I do not know the man in history to whom things stood so uniformly for words. Before him the metamorphosis continually plays. Every thing on which his eye rests, obeys the impulses of moral nature. The figs become grapes whilst he eats them. When some of his angels affirmed a truth, the laurel twig which they held blossomed in their hands. The noise which, at a distance, appeared like gnashing and thumping, on coming nearer was found to be the voice of disputants. The men, in one of his visions, seen in heavenly light, appeared like dragons, and seemed in darkness: but, to each other, they appeared as men, and, when the light from heaven shone into their cabin, they complained of the darkness, and were compelled to shut the window that they might see.

There was this perception in him, which makes the poet or seer, an object of awe and terror, namely, that the same man, or society of men, may wear one aspect to themselves and their companions, and a different aspect to higher intelligences. Certain priests, whom he describes as conversing very learnedly together, appeared to the children, who were at some distance, like dead horses: and many the like misappearances. And instantly the mind inquires, whether these fishes under the bridge, yonder oxen in the pasture, those dogs in the yard, are immutably fishes, oxen, and dogs, or only so appear to me. and perchance to themselves appear upright men; and whether I appear as a man to all eyes.

The Brahims and Pythagoras propounded the same question, and if any poet has witnessed the transformation, he doubtless found it in harmony with various experiences. We have all seen changes as considerable in wheat and caterpillars. He is the poet, and shall draw us with love and terror, who sees, through the flowing vest, the firm nature, and can declare it.

I look in vain for the poet whom I describe. We do not, with sufficient plainness, or sufficient profoundness, address ourselves to life, nor dare we chant our own times and social circumstance. If we filled the day with bravery, we should not shrink from celebrating it. Time and nature yield us many gifts, but not yet the timely man, the new religion, the reconciler, whom all things await. Dante's praise is, that he dared to write his autobiography in colossal cipher, or into universality. We have yet had no genius in America, with tyrannous eye, which knew the value of our incomparable materials, and saw, in the barbarism and materialism of the times, another carnival of the same gods whose picture he so much admires in Homer; then in the middle age; then in Calvinism. Banks and tariffs, the newspaper and caucus, methodism and unitarianism, are flat and dull to dull people, but rest on the same foundations of wonder as the town of Troy, and the temple of Delphos, and are as swiftly passing away. Our logrolling, our stumps and their politics, our fisheries, our Negroes, and Indians, our boats, and our repudiations, the wrath of rogues, and the pusillanimity of honest men, the northern trade, the southern planting, the western clearing, Oregon, and Texas, are yet unsung. Yet America is a poem in our eyes: its

ample geography dazzles the imagination, and it will
not wait long for metres. If I have not found that
excellent combination of gifts in my countrymen which
I seek, neither could I aid myself to fix the idea of the
poet by reading now and then in Chalmers's collection
of five centuries of English poets. These are wits,
more than poets, though there have been poets among
them. But when we adhere to the ideal of the poet,
we have our difficulties even with Milton and Homer.
Milton is too literary, and Homer too literal and historical.

But I am not wise enough for a national criticism,
and must use the old largeness a little longer, to discharge my errand from the muse to the poet concerning his art.

Art is the path of the creator to his work. The
paths, or methods, are ideal and eternal, though few
men ever see them, not the artist himself for years, or
for a lifetime, unless he come into the conditions. The
painter, the sculptor, the composer, the epic rhapsodist,
the orator, all partake one desire, namely, to express
themselves symmetrically and abundantly, not dwarf-
ishly and fragmentarily. They found or put themselves in certain conditions, as, the painter and sculptor
before some impressive human figures; the orator, into
the assembly of the people; and the others, in such
scenes as each has found exciting to his intellect; and
each presently feels the new desire. He hears a voice,
he sees a beckoning. Then he is apprised, with wonder, what herds of dæmons hem him in. He can no
more rest; he says, with the old painter, "By God, it is
in me, and must go forth of me." He pursues a beauty,

half seen, which flies before him. The poet pours out
verses in every solitude. Most of the things he says
are conventional, no doubt; but by and by he says something which is original and beautiful. That charms
him. He would say nothing else but such things. In
our way of talking, we say, "That is yours, this is
mine"; but the poet knows well that it is not his; that
it is as strange and beautiful to him as to you; he would
fain hear the like eloquence at length. Once having
tasted this immortal ichor, he cannot have enough of
it, and, as an admirable creative power exists in these
intellections, it is of the last importance that these things
get spoken. What a little of all we know is said!
What drops of all the sea of our science are baled up!
and by what accident it is that these are exposed, when
so many secrets sleep in nature! Hence the necessity
of speech and song; hence these throbs and heart-
beatings in the orator, at the door of the assembly, to
the end, namely, that thought may be ejaculated as
Logos, or Word.

Doubt not, O poet, but persist. Say, "It is in me,
and shall out." Stand there, balked and dumb, stut-
tering and stammering, hissed and hooted, stand and
strive, until, at last, rage draw out of thee that *dream-*
power which every night shows thee is thine own; a
power transcending all limit and privacy, and by virtue
of which a man is the conductor of the whole river of
electricity. Nothing walks, or creeps, or grows, or
exists, which must not in turn arise and walk before
him as exponent of his meaning. Comes he to that
power, his genius is no longer exhaustible. All the
creatures, by pairs and by tribes, pour into his mind

as into a Noah's ark, to come forth again to people a
new world.   This is like the stock of air for our
respiration, or for the combustion of our fireplace, not
a measure of gallons, but the entire atmosphere if
wanted.   And therefore the rich poets, as Homer,
Chaucer, Shakspeare, and Raphael, have obviously no
limits to their works, except the limits of their lifetime,
and resemble a mirror carried through the street, ready
to render an image of every created thing.

O poet! a new nobility is conferred in groves and
pastures, and not in castles, or by the sword-blade, any
longer.   The conditions are hard, but equal.   Thou
shalt leave the world, and know the muse only.   Thou
shalt not know any longer the times, customs, graces,
politics, or opinions of men, but shalt take all from the
muse.   For the time of towns is tolled from the world
by funeral chimes, but in nature the universal hours
are counted by succeeding tribes of animals and plants,
and by growth of joy on joy.   God wills also that thou
abdicate a manifold and duplex life, and that thou be
content that others speak for thee.   Others shall be
thy gentlemen, and shall represent all courtesy and
worldly life for thee; others shall do the great and re-
sounding actions also.   Thou shalt lie close hid with
nature, and canst not be afforded to the Capitol or the
Exchange.   The world is full of renunciations and ap-
prenticeships, and this is thine: thou must pass for a
fool and a churl for a long season.   This is the screen
and sheath in which Pan has protected his well-beloved
flower, and thou shalt be known only to thine own,
and they shall console thee with tenderest love.   And
thou shalt not be able to rehearse the names of thy

friends in thy verse, for an old shame before the holy ideal. And this is the reward: that the ideal shall be real to thee, and the impressions of the actual world shall fall like summer rain, copious, but not troublesome, to thy invulnerable essence. Thou shalt have the whole land for thy park and manor, the sea for thy bath and navigation, without tax and without envy; the woods and the rivers thou shalt own; and thou shalt possess that wherein others are only tenants and boarders. Thou true land-lord! sea-lord! air-lord! Wherever, snow falls, or water flows, or birds fly, wherever day and night meet in twilight, wherever the blue heaven is hung by clouds, or sown with stars, wherever are forms with transparent boundaries, wherever are outlets into celestial space, wherever is danger, and awe, and love, there is Beauty, plenteous as rain, shed for thee, and though thou shouldest walk the world over, thou shalt not be able to find a condition inopportune or ignoble.

EXPERIENCE

THE lords of life, the lords of life,
I saw them pass,
In their own guise,
Like and unlike,
Portly and grim,
Use and Surprise,
Surface and Dream,
Succession swift, and spectral Wrong,
Temperament without a tongue,
And the inventor of the game
Omnipresent without name;—
Some to see, some to be guessed,
They marched from east to west:
Little man, least of all,
Among the legs of his guardians tall,
Walked about with puzzled look:—
Him by the hand dear nature took;
Dearest nature, strong and kind,
Whispered, 'Darling, never mind!
To-morrow they will wear another face,
The founder thou! these are thy race!'

WHERE do we find ourselves? In a series of which we do not know the extremes, and believe that it has none. We wake and find ourselves on a stair; there are stairs below us, which we seem to have ascended, there are stairs above us, many a one, which go upward and out of sight. But the

Genius which, according to the old belief, stands at the
door by which we enter, and gives us the lethe to drink,
that we may tell no tales, mixed the cup too strongly,
and we cannot shake off the lethargy now at noonday.
Sleep lingers all our lifetime about our eyes, as night
hovers all day in the boughs of the fir-tree. All things
swim and glitter. Our life is not so much threatened
as our perception. Ghostlike we glide through nature
and should not know our place again. Did our birth
fall in some fit of indigence and frugality in nature,
that she was so sparing of her fire and so liberal of
her earth, that it appears to us that we lack the affirmative principle, and though we have health and
reason, yet we have no superfluity of spirit for new
creation? We have enough to live and bring the year
about, but not an ounce to impart or to invest. Ah
that our Genius were a little more of a genius! We
are like millers on the lower levels of a stream, when
the factories above them have exhausted the water.
We too fancy that the upper people must have raised
their dams.

If any of us knew what we were doing or where we
are going, then when we think we best know! We do
not know to-day whether we are busy or idle. In
times when we thought ourselves indolent we have
afterwards discovered, that much was accomplished,
and much was begun in us. All our days are so un-
profitable while they pass, that 'tis wonderful where
or when we ever got anything of this which we call
wisdom, poetry, virtue. We never got it on any dated
calendar day. Some heavenly days must have been
intercalated somewhere, like those that Hermes won

with dice of the Moon, that Osiris might be born.   It
is said, all martyrdoms looked mean when they were
suffered.   Every ship is a romantic object, except that
we sail in.   Embark, and the romance quits our vessel, and hangs on every other sail on the horizon.   Our
life looks trivial, and we shun to record it.   Men seem
to have learned of the horizon the art of perpetual re-
treating and reference.   "Yonder uplands are rich
pasturage, and my neighbor has fertile meadow, but
my field," says the querulous farmer, "only holds the
world together."   I quote another man's saying; unluckily, that other withdraws himself in the same way,
and quotes me.   'Tis the trick of nature thus to degrade to-day; a good deal of buzz, and somewhere a
result slipped magically in.   Every roof is agreeable to
the eye, until it is lifted; then we find tragedy and
moaning women, and hard-eyed husbands, and deluges
of lethe, and the men ask "What's the news?" as if the
old were so bad.   How many individuals can we count
in society? how many actions? how many opinions?
So much of our time is preparation, so much is routine,
and so much retrospect, that the pith of each man's
genius contracts itself to a very few hours.   The history of literature—take the net result of Tiraboschi,
Warton, or Schlegel,—is a sum of very few ideas, and
of very few original tales,—all the rest being variation
of these.   So in this great society wide lying around us,
a critical analysis would find very few spontaneous actions.   It is almost all custom and gross sense.   There
are even few opinions, and these seem organic in the
speakers, and do not disturb the universal necessity.

What opium is instilled into all disaster!   It shows

formidable as we approach it, but there is at last no
rough rasping friction, but the most slippery sliding
surfaces. We fall soft on a thought. *Ate Dea* is
gentle,

> Over men's heads walking aloft,
> With tender feet treading so soft.

People grieve and bemoan themselves, but it is not half
so bad with them as they say. There are moods in
which we court suffering, in the hope that here, at least,
we shall find reality, sharp peaks and edges of truth.
But it turns out to be scene-painting and counterfeit.
The only thing grief has taught me, is to know how
shallow it is. That, like all the rest, plays about the
surface, and never introduces me into the reality, for
contact with which, we would even pay the costly price
of sons and lovers. Was it Boscovich who found out
that bodies never come in contact? Well, souls never
touch their objects. An innavigable sea washes with
silent waves between us and the things we aim at and
converse with. Grief too will make us idealists. In
the death of my son, now more than two years ago,
I seem to have lost a beautiful estate,—no more. I
cannot get it nearer to me. If to-morrow I should be
informed of the bankruptcy of my principal debtors,
the loss of my property would be a great inconvenience
to me, perhaps, for many years; but it would leave
me as it found me,—neither better nor worse. So it is
with this calamity: it does not touch me: some thing
which I fancied was a part of me, which could not be
torn away without tearing me, nor enlarged without
enriching me, falls off from me, and leaves no scar.

It was caducous. I grieve that grief can teach me nothing, nor carry me one step into real nature. The Indian who was laid under a curse, that the wind should not blow on him, nor water flow to him, nor fire burn him, is a type of us all. The dearest events are summer-rain, and we the Para coats that shed every drop. Nothing is left us now but death. We look to that with a grim satisfaction, saying, there at least is reality that will not dodge us.

I take this evanescence and lubricity of all objects, which lets them slip through our fingers then when we clutch hardest, to be the most unhandsome part of our condition. Nature does not like to be observed, and likes that we should be her fools and playmates. We may have the sphere for our cricket-ball, but not a berry for our philosophy. Direct strokes she never gave us power to make; all our blows glance, all our hits are accidents. Our relations to each other are oblique and casual.

Dream delivers us to dream, and there is no end to illusion. Life is a train of moods like a string of beads, and, as we pass through them, they prove to be many-colored lenses which paint the world their own hue, and each shows only what lies in its focus. From the mountain you see the mountain. We animate what we can, and we see only what we animate. Nature and books belong to the eyes that see them. It depends on the mood of the man, whether he shall see the sunset or the fine poem. There are always sunsets, and there is always genius; but only a few hours so serene that we can relish nature or criticism. The more or less depends on structure or temperament. Temperament is

the iron wire on which the beads are strung. Of what
use is fortune or talent to a cold and defective nature?
Who cares what sensibility or discrimination a man has
at some time shown, if he falls asleep in his chair? or
if he laugh and giggle? or if he apologize? or is affected with egotism? or thinks of his dollar? or cannot go by food? or has gotten a child in his boyhood?
Of what use is genius, if the organ is too convex or
too concave, and cannot find a focal distance within the
actual horizon of human life? Of what use, if the
brain is too cold or too hot, and the man does not
care enough for results, to stimulate him to experiment,
and hold him up in it? or if the web is too finely woven,
too irritable by pleasure and pain, so that life stagnates
from too much reception, without due outlet? Of
what use to make heroic vows of amendment, if the
same old law-breaker is to keep them? What cheer
can the religious sentiment yield, when that is suspected
to be secretly dependent on the seasons of the year, and
the state of the blood? I knew a witty physician who
found theology in the biliary duct, and used to affirm
that if there was disease in the liver, the man became
a Calvinist, and if that organ was sound, he became a
Unitarian. Very mortifying is the reluctant experience that some unfriendly excess or imbecility
neutralizes the promise of genius. We see young men
who owe us a new world, so readily and lavishly they
promise, but they never acquit the debt; they die young
and dodge the account: or if they live, they lose themselves in the crowd.

Temperament also enters fully into the system or
illusions, and shuts us in a prison of glass which we

cannot see. There is an optical illusion about every person we meet. In truth, they are all creatures of given temperament, which will appear in a given character, whose boundaries they will never pass: but we look at them, they seem alive, and we presume there is impulse in them. In the moment it seems impulse; in the year, in the lifetime, it turns out to be a certain uniform tune which the revolving barrel of the music-box must play. Men resist the conclusion in the morning, but adopt it as the evening wears on, that temper prevails over every thing of time, place and condition, and is inconsumable in the flames of religion. Some modifications the moral sentiment avails to impose, but the individual texture holds its dominion, if not to bias the moral judgments, yet to fix the measure of activity and of enjoyment.

I thus express the law as it is read from the platform of ordinary life, but must not leave it without noticing the capital exception. For temperament is a power which no man willingly hears any one praise but himself. On the platform of physics, we cannot resist the contracting influences of so-called science. Temperament puts all divinity to rout. I know the mental proclivity of physicians. I hear the chuckle of the phrenologists. Theoretic kidnappers and slave-drivers, they esteem each man the victim of another, who winds him round his finger by knowing the law of his being, and by such cheap signboards as the color of his beard, or the slope of his occiput, reads the inventory of his fortunes and character. The grossest ignorance does not disgust like this impudent knowingness. The physicians say, they are not materialists;

but they are:—Spirit is matter reduced to an extreme
thinness: O *so* thin!—But the definition of *Spiritual*
should be, *that which is its own evidence.* What no-
tions do they attach to love! what to religion! One
would not willingly pronounce these words in their
hearing, and give them the occasion to profane them.
I saw a gracious gentleman who adapts his conversation to the form of the head of the man he talks with!
I had fancied that the value of life lay in its inscrutable
possibilities; in the fact that I never know, in address-
ing myself to a new individual, what may befall me.
I carry the keys of my castle in my hand, ready to throw
them at the feet of my lord, whenever and in what disguise soever he shall appear. I know he is in the neighborhood hidden among vagabonds. Shall I preclude
my future, by taking a high seat and kindly adapting
my conversation to the shape of heads? When I come
to that, the doctors shall buy me for a cent.——"But,
sir, medical history; the report to the institute; the
proven facts!"—I distrust the facts and the inferences.
Temperament is the veto or limitation-power in the constitution, very justly applied to restrain an opposite excess in the constitution, but absurdly offered as a bar to
original equity. When virtue is in presence, all subordinate powers sleep. On its own level, or in view of
nature, temperament is final. I see not, if one be once
caught in this trap of so-called sciences, any escape for
the man from the links of the chain of physical necessity. Given such an embryo, such a history must follow. On this platform, one lives in a sty of sensualism,
and would soon come to suicide. But it is impossible
that the creative power should exclude itself. Into

every intelligence there is a door which is never closed, through which the creator passes. The intellect, seeker of absolute truth, or the heart, lover of absolute good, intervenes for our succor, and at one whisper of these high powers, we awake from ineffectual struggles with this nightmare. We hurl it into its own hell, and cannot again contract ourselves to so base a state.

The secret of the illusoriness is in the necessity of a succession of moods or objects. Gladly we would anchor, but the anchorage is quicksand. This onward trick of nature is too strong for us: *Pero si muove.* When, at night, I look at the moon and stars, I seem stationary, and they to hurry. Our love of the real draws us to permanence, but health of body consists in circulation, and sanity of mind in variety or facility of association. We need change of objects. Dedication to one thought is quickly odious. We house with the insane, and must humor them; then conversation dies out. Once I took such delight in Montaigne, that I thought I should not need any other book; before that, in Shakespeare; then in Plutarch; then in Plotinus; at one time in Bacon; afterwards in Goethe; even in Bettine; but now I turn the pages of either of them languidly, whilst I still cherish their genius. So with pictures; each will bear an emphasis of attention once, which it cannot retain, though we fain would continue to be pleased in that manner. How strongly I have felt of pictures, that when you have seen one well, you must take your leave of it; you shall never see it again. I have had good lessons from pictures, which I have since seen without emotion or remark. A deduction must be

made from the opinion, which even the wise express of
a new book or occurrence.   Their opinion gives me tidings of their mood, and some vague guess at the new
fact, but is nowise to be trusted as the lasting relation between that intellect and that thing.   The child
asks "Mamma, why don't I like the story as well as
when you told it me yesterday?"   Alas, child, it is even
so with the oldest cherubim of knowledge.   But will it
answer thy question to say, Because thou wert born
to a whole, and this story is a particular?   The reason
of the pain this discovery causes us (and we make it late
in respect to works of art and intellect), is the plaint of
tragedy which murmurs from it in regard to persons,
to friendship and love.

That immobility and absence of elasticity which we
find in the arts, we find with more pain in the artist.
There is no power of expansion in men.   Our friends
early appear to us as representatives of certain ideas,
which they never pass or exceed.   They stand on the
brink of the ocean of thought and power, but they never
take the single step that would bring them there.   A
man is like a bit of Labrador spar, which has no lustre
as you turn it in your hand, until you come to a particular angle; then it shows deep and beautiful colors.
There is no adaptation or universal applicability in men,
but each has his special talent, and the mastery of successful men consists in adroitly keeping themselves
where and when that turn shall be oftenest to be
practised.   We do what we must, and call it by the
best names we can, and would fain have the praise of
having intended the result which ensues.   I cannot recall any form of man who is not superfluous sometimes.

But is not this pitiful? Life is not worth the taking to do tricks in.

Of course, it needs the whole society, to give the symmetry we seek. The parti-colored wheel must revolve very fast to appear white. Something is learned too by conversing with so much folly and defect. In fine, whoever loses, we are always of the gaining party. Divinity is behind our failures and follies also. The plays of children are nonsense, but very educative nonsense. So it is with the largest and solemnest things, with commerce, government, church, marriage, and so with the history of every man's bread, and the ways by which he is to come by it. Like a bird which alights nowhere, but hops perpetually from bough to bough, is the Power which abides in no man and in no woman, but for a moment speaks from this one, and for another moment from that one.

But what help from these fineries or pedantries? What help from thought? Life is not dialectics. We, I think, in these times, have had lessons enough of the futility of criticism. Our young people have thought and written much on labor and reform, and for all that they have written, neither the world nor themselves have got on a step. Intellectual tasting of life will not supersede muscular activity. If a man should consider the nicety of the passage of a piece of bread down his throat, he would starve. At Education-Farm the noblest theory of life sat on the noblest figures of young men and maidens, quite powerless and melancholy. It would not rake or pitch a ton of hay; it would not rub down a horse; and the men and maidens it left pale and hungry. A political orator wittily compared our party

promises to western roads, which opened stately enough,
with planted trees on either side, to tempt the traveller,
but soon became narrow and narrower, and ended in
a squirrel-track, and ran up a tree. So does culture
with us; it ends in head-ache. Unspeakably sad and
barren does life look to those, who a few months ago
were dazzled with the splendor of the promise of the
times. "There is now no longer any right course of
action, nor any self-devotion left among the Iranis."
Abjections and criticism we have had our fill of.
There are objections to every course of life and action,
and the practical wisdom infers an indifferency, from
the omnipresence of objection. The whole frame of
things preaches indifferency. Do not craze yourself
with thinking, but go about your business anywhere.
Life is not intellectual or critical, but sturdy. Its chief
good is for well-mixed people who can enjoy what they
find, without question. Nature hates peeping, and our
mothers speak her very sense when they say, "Children,
eat your victuals, and say no more of it." To fill the
hour,—that is happiness; to fill the hour, and leave no
crevice for a repentance or an approval. We live amid
surfaces, and the true art of life is to skate well on
them. Under the oldest mouldiest conventions, a man
of native force prospers just as well as in the newest
world, and that by skill of handling and treatment.
He can take hold anywhere. Life itself is a mixture of
power and form, and will not bear the least excess of
either. To finish the moment, to find the journey's end
in every step of the road, to live the greatest number
of good hours, is wisdom. It is not the part of men,
but of fanatics, or of mathematicians, if you will, to

say, that, the shortness of life considered, it is not worth
caring whether for so short a duration we were sprawl-
ing in want, or sitting high.   Since our office is with
moments, let us husband them.   Five minutes of to-day
are worth as much to me, as five minutes in the next
millennium.   Let us be poised, and wise, and our own,
to-day.   Let us treat the men and women well: treat
them as if they were real: perhaps they are.   Men live
in their fancy, like drunkards whose hands are too soft
and tremulous for successful labor.   It is a tempest of
fancies, and the only ballast I know, is a respect to
the present hour.   Without any shadow of doubt,
amidst this vertigo of shows and politics, I settle myself ever the firmer in the creed, that we should not
postpone and refer and wish, but do broad justice where
we are, by whomsoever we deal with, accepting our
actual companions and circumstances, however humble
or odious, as the mystic officials to whom the universe
has delegated its whole pleasure for us.   If these are
mean and malignant, their contentment, which is the
last victory of justice, is a more satisfying echo to the
heart, than the voice of poets and the casual sympathy
of admirable persons.   I think that however a thoughtful man may suffer from the defects and absurdities of
his company, he cannot without affectation deny to any
set of men and women, a sensibility to extraordinary
merit.   The coarse and frivolous have an instinct of
superiority, if they have not a sympathy, and honor it
in their blind capricious way with sincere homage.

The fine young people despise life, but in me, and
in such as with me are free from dyspepsia, and to
whom a day is a sound and solid good, it is a great

excess of politeness to look scornful and to cry for
company. I am grown by sympathy a little eager and
sentimental, but leave me alone, and I should relish
every hour and what it brought me, the pot-luck of
the day, as heartily as the oldest gossip in the bar-room.
I am thankful for small mercies. I compared notes
with one of my friends who expects every thing of the
universe, and is disappointed when any thing is less
than the best, and I found that I begin at the other extreme, expecting nothing, and am always full of thanks
for moderate goods. I accept the clangor and jangle
of contrary tendencies. I find my account in sots and
bores also. They give a reality to the circumjacent
picture, which such a vanishing meteorous appearance
can ill spare. In the morning I awake, and find the old
world, wife, babes, and mother, Concord and Boston,
the dear old spiritual world, and even the dear old devil
not far off. If we will take the good we find, asking
no questions, we shall have heaping measures. The
great gifts are not got by analysis. Every thing good
is on the highway. The middle region of our being is
the temperate zone. We may climb into the thin and
cold realm of pure geometry and lifeless science, or
sink into that of sensation. Between these extremes is
the equator of life, of thought, of spirit, of poetry,—
a narrow belt. Moreover, in popular experience every
thing good is on the highway. A collector peeps into
all the picture-shops of Europe, for a landscape of
Poussin, a crayon-sketch of Salvator; but the Transfiguration, the Last Judgment, the Communion of St.
Jerome, and what are as transcendent as these, are on
the walls of the Vatican, the Uffizii, or the Louvre,

where every footman may see them; to say nothing of nature's pictures in every street, of sunsets and sunrises every day, and the sculpture of the human body never absent. A collector recently bought at public auction, in London, for one hundred and fifty-seven guineas, an autograph of Shakspeare: but for nothing a schoolboy can read Hamlet, and can detect secrets of highest concernment yet unpublished therein. I think I will never read any but the commonest books,—the Bible, Homer, Dante, Shakspeare, and Milton. Then we are impatient of so public a life and planet, and run hither and thither for nooks and secrets. The imagination delights in the woodcraft of Indians, trappers, and bee-hunters. We fancy that we are strangers, and not so intimately domesticated in the planet as the wild man, and the wild beast and bird. But the exclusion reaches them also; reaches the climbing, flying, gliding, feathered and four-footed man. Fox and woodchuck, hawk and snipe, and bittern, when nearly seen, have no more root in the deep world than man, and are just such superficial tenants of the globe. Then the new molecular philosophy shows astronomical interspaces betwixt atom and atom, shows that the world is all outside: it has no inside.

The mid-world is best. Nature, as we know her, is no saint. The lights of the church, the ascetics, Gentoos and Grahamites, she does not distinguish by any favor. She comes eating and drinking and sinning. Her darlings, the great, the strong, the beautiful, are not children of our law, do not come out of the Sunday School, nor weigh their food, nor punctually keep the commandments. If we will be strong with her strength, we must not harbor such disconsolate consciences, borrowed too from the consciences of other nations. We must set up the strong present tense against all the rumors of wrath, past or to come. So many things are unsettled which it is of the first importance to settle,—and, pending their settlement, we will do as we do. Whilst the debate goes forward on the equity of commerce, and will not be closed for a century or two, New and Old England may keep shop. Law of copyright and international copyright is to be discussed, and, in the interim, we will sell our books for the most we can. Expediency of literature, reason of literature, lawfulness of writing down a thought, is questioned; much is to say on both sides, and, while the fight waxes hot, thou, dearest scholar, stick to thy foolish task, add a line every hour, and between whiles add a line. Right to hold land, right of property, is disputed, and the conventions convene, and before the vote is taken, dig away in your garden, and spend your earnings as a waif or godsend to all serene and beautiful purposes. Life itself is a bubble and a scepticism, and a sleep within a sleep. Grant it, and as much more as they will,—but thou, God's darling! heed thy private dream: thou wilt not be missed in the scorning and scepticism: there are enough of them: stay there in thy closet, and toil, until the rest are agreed what to do about it. Thy sickness, they say, and thy puny habit, require that thou do this or avoid that, but know that thy life is a flitting state, a tent for a night, and do thou, sick or well, finish that stint. Thou art sick, but shalt not be worse, and the universe, which holds thee dear, shall be the better.

Human life is made up of the two elements, power and form, and the proportion must be invariably kept if we would have it sweet and sound. Each of these elements in excess makes a mischief as hurtful as its defect. Every thing runs to excess: every good quality is noxious, if unmixed, and, to carry the danger to the edge of ruin, nature causes each man's peculiarity to superbound. Here, among the farms, we adduce the scholars as examples of this treachery. They are nature's victims of expression. You who see the artist, the orator, the poet, too near, and find their life no more excellent than that of mechanics or farmers, and themselves victims of partiality, very hollow and haggard, and pronounce them failures,—not heroes, but quacks,—conclude very reasonably, that these arts are not for man, but are disease. Yet nature will not bear you out. Irresistible nature made men such, and makes legions more of such, every day. You love the boy reading in a book, gazing at a drawing, or a cast: yet what are these millions who read and behold, but incipient writers and sculptors? Add a little more of that quality which now reads and sees, and they will seize the pen and chisel. And if one remembers how innocently he began to be an artist, he perceives that nature joined with his enemy. A man is a golden impossibility. The line he must walk is a hair's breadth. The wise through excess of wisdom is made a fool.

How easily, if fate would suffer it, we might keep forever these beautiful limits, and adjust ourselves, once for all, to the perfect calculation of the kingdom of known cause and effect. In the street and in the newspapers, life appears so plain a business, that manly resolution and adherence to the multiplication-table through all weathers, will insure success. But ah! presently comes a day, or it is only a half-hour, with its angel-whispering,—which discomfits the conclusions of nations and of years! To-morrow again, everything looks real and angular, the habitual standards are reinstated, common sense is as rare as genius,—is the basis of genius, and experience is hands and feet to every enterprise;—and yet, he who should do his business on this understanding, would be quickly bankrupt. Power keeps quite another road than the turnpikes of choice and will, namely, the subterranean and invisible tunnels and channels of life. It is ridiculous that we are diplomatists, and doctors, and considerate people: there are no dupes like these. Life is a series of surprises, and would not be worth taking or keeping, if it were not. God delights to isolate us every day, and hide from us the past and the future. We should look about us, but with grand politeness he draws down before us an impenetrable screen of purest sky, and another behind us of purest sky. "You will not remember," he seems to say, "and you will not expect." All good conversation, manners, and action, come from a spontaneity which forgets usages, and makes the moment great. Nature hates calculators; her methods are saltatory and impulsive. Man lives by pulses; our organic movements are such; and the chemical and ethereal agents are undulatory and alternate; and the mind goes antagonizing on, and never prospers but by fits. We thrive by casualties. Our chief experiences have been casual. The most attractive class of people are those who are powerful obliquely, and not by the direct stroke: men of genius, but not yet accredited: one gets the cheer of their light, without paying too great a tax. Theirs is the beauty of the bird, or the morning light, and not of art. In the thought of genius there is always a surprise; and the moral sentiment is well called "the newness," for it is never other; as new to the oldest intelligence as to the young child,— "the kingdom that cometh without observation." In like manner, for practical success, there must not be too much design. A man will not be observed in doing that which he can do best. There is a certain magic about his properest action, which stupefies your powers of observation, so that though it is done before you, you wist not of it. The art of life has a pudency, and will not be exposed. Every man is an impossibility, until he is born; every thing impossible, until we see a success. The ardors of piety agree at last with the coldest scepticism,—that nothing is of us or our works,—that all is of God. Nature will not spare us the smallest leaf of laurel. All writing comes by the grace of God, and all doing and having. I would gladly be moral, and keep due metes and bounds, which I dearly love, and allow the most to the will of man, but I have set my heart on honesty in this chapter, and I can see nothing at last, in success or failure, than more or less of vital force supplied from the Eternal. The results of life are uncalculated and uncalculable. The years teach much which the days never know. The persons who compose our company, converse, and come and go, and design and execute many things, and somewhat comes of it all, but an unlooked for result. The individual is always mistaken. He designed many things, and drew in other persons as coadjutors, quarrelled with some or all, blundered much, and something is done; all are a little advanced, but the individual is always mistaken. It turns out somewhat new, and very unlike what he promised himself.

The ancients, struck with this irreducibleness of the elements of human life to calculation, exalted Chance into a divinity, but that is to stay too long at the spark,—which glitters truly at one point,—but the universe is warm with the latency of the same fire. The miracle of life which will not be expounded, but will remain a miracle, introduces a new element. In the growth of the embryo, Sir Everard Home, I think, noticed that the evolution was not from one central point, but co-active from three or more points. Life has no memory. That which proceeds in succession might be remembered, but that which is co-existent, or ejaculated from a deeper cause, as yet far from being conscious, knows not its own tendency. So is it with us, now sceptical, or without unity, because immersed in forms and effects all seeming to be of equal yet hostile value, and now religious, whilst in the reception of spiritual law. Bear with these distractions, with this coetaneous growth of the parts: they will one day be *members,* and obey one will. On that one will, on that secret cause, they nail our attention and hope. Life is hereby melted into an expectation or a religion. Underneath the inharmonious and trivial particulars, is a musical perfection, the Ideal journeying always with us, the heaven without rent or seam. Do but observe the mode of our illumination. When I converse with a profound mind, or if at any time being alone I have good thoughts, I do not at once arrive at satisfactions, as when, being thirsty, I drink water, or go to the fire, being cold: no! but I am at first apprised of my vicinity to a new and excellent region of life. By persisting to read or to think, this region gives further sign of itself, as it were in flashes of light, in sudden discoveries of its profound beauty and repose, as if the clouds that covered it parted at intervals, and showed the approaching traveller the inland mountains, with the tranquil eternal meadows spread at their base, whereon flocks graze, and shepherds pipe and dance. But every insight from this realm of thought is felt as initial, and promises a sequel. I do not make it; I arrive there, and behold what was there already. I make! O, no! I clap my hands in infantile joy and amazement, before the first opening to me of this august magnificence, old with the love and homage of innumerable ages, young with the life of life, the sunbright Mecca of the desert. And what a future it opens! I feel a new heart beating with the love of the new beauty. I am ready to die out of nature, and be born again into this new yet unapproachable America I have found in the West.

> Since neither now nor yesterday began
> These thoughts, which have been ever, nor yet can
> A man be found who their first entrance knew.

If I have described life as a flux of moods, I must now add, that there is that in us which changes not, and which ranks all sensations and states of mind. The consciousness in each man is a sliding scale which identifies him now with the First Cause, and now with the flesh of his body; life above life, in infinite degrees. The sentiment from which it sprung determines the dignity of any deed, and the question ever is, not, what you have done or forborne, but, at whose command you have done or forborne it.

Fortune, Minerva, Muse, Holy Ghost,—these are quaint names, too narrow to cover this unbounded substance. The baffled intellect must still kneel before this cause, which refuses to be named,—ineffable cause, which every fine genius has essayed to represent by some emphatic symbol, as, Thales by water, Anaximenes by air, Anaxagoras by (Νοῦς) thought, Zoroaster by fire, Jesus and the moderns by love: and the metaphor of each has become a national religion. The Chinese Mencius has not been the least successful in his generalization. "I fully understand language," he said, "and nourish well my vast-flowing vigor."— "I beg to ask what you call vast-flowing vigor?"—said his companion. "The explanation," replied Mencius, "is difficult. This vigor is supremely great, and in the highest degree unbending. Nourish it correctly, and do it no injury, and it will fill up the vacancy between heaven and earth. This vigor accords with and assists justice and reason, and leaves no hunger."—In our more correct writing, we give to this generalization the name of Being, and thereby confess that we have arrived as far as we can go. Suffice it for the joy of the universe, that we have not arrived at a wall, but at interminable oceans. Our life seems not present, so much as prospective; not for the affairs on which it is wasted, but as a hint of this vast-flowing vigor. Most of life seems to be mere advertisement of faculty: information is given us not to sell ourselves cheap; that we are very great. So, in particulars, our greatness is always in a tendency or direction, not in an action. It is for us to believe in the rule, not in the exception. The noble are thus known from the ignoble. So in accepting the leading of the sentiments, it is not what we believe concerning the immortality of the soul, or the like, but *the universal impulse to believe,* that is the material circumstance, and is the principal fact in the history of the globe. Shall we describe this cause as that which works directly? The spirit is not helpless or needful of mediate organs. It has plentiful powers and direct effects. I am explained without explaining, I am felt without acting, and where I am not. Therefore all just persons are satisfied with their own praise. They refuse to explain themselves, and are content that new actions should do them that office. They believe that we communicate without speech, and above speech, and that no right action of ours is quite unaffecting to our friends, at whatever distance; for the influence of action is not to be measured by miles. Why should I fret myself, because a circumstance has occurred, which hinders my presence where I was expected? If I am not at the meeting, my presence where I am, should be as useful to the commonwealth of friendship and wisdom, as would be my presence in that place. I exert the same quality of power in all places. Thus journeys the mighty Ideal before us; it never was known to fall into the rear. No man ever came to an experience which was satiating, but his good is tidings of a better.

Onward and onward! In liberated moments, we know that a new picture of life and duty is already possible; the elements already exist in many minds around you, of a doctrine of life which shall transcend any written record we have. The new statement will comprise the scepticisms, as well as the faiths of society, and out of unbeliefs a creed shall be formed. For, scepticisms are not gratuitous or lawless, but are limitations of the affirmative statement, and the new philosophy must take them in, and make affirmations outside of them, just as much as it must include the oldest beliefs.

It is very unhappy, but too late to be helped, the discovery we have made, that we exist. That discovery is called the Fall of Man. Ever afterwards, we suspect our instruments. We have learned that we do not see directly, but mediately, and that we have no means of correcting these colored and distorting lenses which we are, or of computing the amount of their errors. Perhaps these subject-lenses have a creative power; perhaps there are no objects. Once we lived in what we saw; now, the rapaciousness of this new power, which threatens to absorb all things, engages us. Nature, art, persons, letters, religions,—objects, successively tumble in, and God is but one of its ideas. Nature and literature are subjective phenomena; every evil and every good thing is a shadow which we cast. The street is full of humiliations to the proud. As the fop contrived to dress his bailiffs in his livery, and make them wait on his guests at table, so the chagrins which the bad heart gives off as bubbles, at once take form as ladies and gentlemen in the street, shopmen or barkeepers in hotels, and threaten or insult whatever is threat-

enable and insultable in us. 'Tis the same with our
idolatries.   People forget that it is the eye which makes
the horizon, and the rounding mind's eye which makes
this or that man a type or representative of humanity
with the name of hero or saint.   Jesus the "providen-
tial man," is a good man on whom many people are
agreed that these optical laws shall take effect.   By
love on one part, and by forbearance to press objection
on the other part, it is for a time settled, that we will
look at him in the centre of the horizon, and ascribe
to him the properties that will attach to any man so
seen.   But the longest love or aversion has a speedy
term.   The great and crescive self, rooted in absolute
nature, supplants all relative existence, and ruins the
kingdom of mortal friendship and love.   Marriage (in
what is called the spiritual world) is impossible, because of the inequality between every subject and
every object.   The subject is the receiver of God-head,
and at every comparison must feel his being enhanced
by that cryptic might.   Though not in energy, yet by
presence, this magazine of substance cannot be otherwise than felt: nor can any force of intellect attribute
to the object the proper deity which sleeps or wakes
forever in every subject.   Never can love make consciousness and ascription equal in force.   There will
be the same gulf between every me and thee, as between the original and the picture.   The universe is
the bride of the soul.   All private sympathy is partial.
Two human beings are like globes, which can touch
only in a point, and, whilst they remain in contact, all
other points of each of the spheres are inert; their turn
must also come, and the longer a particular union lasts,

the more energy of appetency the parts not in union acquire.

Life will be imaged, but cannot be divided nor doubled. Any invasion of its unity would be chaos. The soul is not twin-born, but the only-begotten, and though revealing itself as child in time, child in appearance, is of a fatal and universal power, admitting no co-life. Every day, every act betrays the ill-concealed deity. We believe in ourselves, as we do not believe in others. We permit all things to ourselves, and that which we call sin in others, is experiment for us. It is an instance of our faith in ourselves, that men never speak of crime as lightly as they think: or, every man thinks a latitude safe for himself, which is nowise to be indulged to another. The act looks very differently on the inside, and on the outside; in its quality, and in its consequences. Murder in the murderer is no such ruinous thought as poets and romancers will have it; it does not unsettle him, or fright him from his ordinary notice of trifles: it is an act quite easy to be contemplated, but in its sequel, it turns out to be a horrible jangle and confounding of all relations. Especially the crimes that spring from love, seem right and fair from the actor's point of view, but, when acted, are found destructive of society. No man at last believes that he can be lost, nor that the crime in him is as black as in the felon. Because the intellect qualifies in our own case the moral judgments. For there is no crime to the intellect. That is antinomian or hypernomian, and judges law as well as fact. "It is worse than a crime, it is a blunder," said Napoleon, speaking the language of the intellect.

To it, the world is a problem in mathematics or the science of quantity, and it leaves out praise and blame, and all weak emotions. All stealing is comparative. If you come to absolutes, pray who does not steal? Saints are sad, because they behold sin, (even when they speculate,) from the point of view of the conscience, and not of the intellect; a confusion of thought. Sin seen from the thought, is a diminution or *less:* seen from the conscience or will, it is pravity or *bad.* The intellect names it shade, absence of light, and no essence. The conscience must feel it as essence, essential evil. This it is not: it has an objective existence, but no subjective.

Thus inevitably does the universe wear our color, and every object fall successively into the subject itself. The subject exists, the subject enlarges; all things sooner or later fall into place. As I am, so I see; use what language we will, we can never say any thing but what we are; Hermes, Cadmus, Columbus, Newton, Buonaparte, are the mind's ministers. Instead of feeling a poverty when we encounter a great man, let us treat the new comer like a travelling geologist, who passes through our estate, and shows us good slate, or limestone, or anthracite, in our brush pasture. The partial action of each strong mind in one direction, is a telescope for the objects on which it is pointed. But every other part of knowledge is to be pushed to the same extravagance, ere the soul attains her due sphericity. Do you see that kitten chasing so prettily her own tail? If you could look with her eyes, you might see her surrounded with hundreds of figures performing complex dramas, with tragic and comic issues, long conversations, many characters, many ups and downs of fate,—and meantime it is only puss and her tail. How long before our masquerade will end its noise of tamborines, laughter, and shouting, and we shall find it was a solitary performance?—A subject and an object,—it takes so much to make the galvanic circuit complete, but magnitude adds nothing. What imports it whether it is Kepler and the sphere; Columbus and America; a reader and his book; or puss with her tail?

It is true that all the muses and love and religion hate these developments, and will find a way to punish the chemist, who publishes in the parlor the secrets of the laboratory. And we cannot say too little of our constitutional necessity of seeing things under private aspects, or saturated with our humors. And yet is the God the native of these bleak rocks. That need makes in morals the capital virtue of self-trust. We must hold hard to this poverty, however scandalous, and by more vigorous self-recoveries, after the sallies of action, possess our axis more firmly. The life of truth is cold, and so far mournful; but it is not the slave of tears, contritions, and perturbations. It does not attempt another's work, nor adopt another's facts. It is a main lesson of wisdom to know your own from another's. I have learned that I cannot dispose of other people's facts; but I possess such a key to my own, as persuades me against all their denials, that they also have a key to theirs. A sympathetic person is placed in the dilemma of a swimmer among drowning men, who all catch at him, and if he gives so much as a leg or a finger, they will drown him. They wish to be saved from the mischiefs of their vices, but not from their vices. Charity would be wasted on this poor waiting on the symptoms. A wise and hardy physician will say, *Come out of that,* as the first condition of advice.

In this our talking America, we are ruined by our good nature and listening on all sides. This compliance takes away the power of being greatly useful. A man should not be able to look other than directly and forthright. A preoccupied attention is the only answer to the importunate frivolity of other people: an attention, and to an aim which makes their wants frivolous. This is a divine answer, and leaves no appeal, and no hard thoughts. In Flaxman's drawing of the Eumenides of Æschylus, Orestes supplicates Apollo, whilst the Furies sleep on the threshold. The face of the god expresses a shade of regret and compassion, but calm with the conviction of the irreconcilableness of the two spheres. He is born into other politics, into the eternal and beautiful. The man at his feet asks for his interest in turmoils of the earth, into which his nature cannot enter. And the Eumenides there lying express pictorially this disparity. The god is surcharged with his divine destiny.

Illusion, Temperament, Succession, Surface, Surprise, Reality, Subjectiveness,—these are threads on the loom of time, these are the lords of life. I dare not assume to give their order, but I name them as I find them in my way. I know better than to claim any completeness for my picture. I am a fragment, and this is a fragment of me. I can very confidently

announce one or another law, which throws itself into
relief and form, but I am too young yet by some
ages to compile a code. I gossip for my hour concerning the eternal politics. I have seen many fair
pictures not in vain. A wonderful time I have lived
in. I am not the novice I was fourteen, nor yet seven
years ago. Let who will ask, where is the fruit? I
find a private fruit sufficient. This is a fruit,—that
I should not ask for a rash effect from meditations,
counsels, and the hiving of truths. I should feel it
pitiful to demand a result on this town and county, an
overt effect on the instant month and year. The effect is deep and secular as the cause. It works on periods in which mortal lifetime is lost. All I know is
reception; I am and I have: but I do not get, and when
I have fancied I had gotten anything, I found I did
not. I worship with wonder the great Fortune. My
reception has been so large, that I am not annoyed by
receiving this or that superabundantly. I say to the
Genius, if he will pardon the proverb, *In for a mill, in
for a million.* When I receive a new gift, I do not
macerate my body to make the account square, for, if
I should die, I could not make the account square.
The benefit overran the merit the first day, and has
overrun the merit ever since. The merit itself, so-
called, I reckon part of the receiving.

Also, that hankering after an overt or practical effect
seems to me an apostasy. In good earnest, I am willing to spare this most unnecessary deal of doing. Life
wears to me a visionary face. Hardest, roughest action is visionary also. It is but a choice between soft
an1 turbulent dreams. People disparage knowing and

the intellectual life, and urge doing.   I am very content
with knowing, if only I could know.   That is an august entertainment, and would suffice me a great while.
To know a little, would be worth the expense of this
world.   I hear always the law of Adrastia, "that every
soul which had acquired any truth, should be safe
from harm until another period."

I know that the world I converse with in the city
and in the farms, is not the world I *think*.   I observe
that difference, and shall observe it.   One day, I shall
know the value and law of this discrepance.   But I
have not found that much was gained by manipular
attempts to realize the world of thought.   Many eager
persons successively make an experiment in this way,
and make themselves ridiculous.   They acquire democratic manners, they foam at the mouth, they hate and
deny.   Worse, I observe, that, in the history of mankind, there is never a solitary example of success,—
taking their own tests of success.   I say this polemi-
cally, or in reply to the inquiry, why not realize your
world?   But far be from me the despair which pre-
judges the law by a paltry empiricism,—since there
never was a right endeavor, but it succeeded.   Patience
and patience, we shall win at the last.   We must be
very suspicious of the deceptions of the element of
time.   It takes a good deal of time to eat or to sleep,
or to earn a hundred dollars, and a very little time to
entertain a hope and an insight which becomes the light
of our life.   We dress our garden, eat our dinners,
discuss the household with our wives, and these things
make no impression, are forgotten next week; but in
the solitude to which every man is always returning, he

has a sanity and revelations, which in his passage into new worlds he will carry with him. Never mind the ridicule, never mind the defeat: up again, old heart! —it seems to say,—there is victory yet for all justice; and the true romance which the world exists to realize, will be the transformation of genius into practical power.

CHARACTER

The sun set; but set not his hope:
Stars rose; his faith was earlier up:
Fixed on the enormous galaxy,
Deeper and older seemed his eye:
And matched his sufferance sublime
The taciturnity of time.
He spoke, and words more soft than rain
Brought the Age of Gold again:
His action won such reverence sweet,
As hid all measure of the feat.

———

Work of his hand
He nor commends nor grieves:
Pleads for itself the fact;
As unrepenting Nature leaves
Her every act.

I HAVE read that those who listened to Lord Chatham felt that there was something finer in the man, than anything which he said. It has been complained of our brilliant English historian of the French Revolution, that when he has told all his facts about Mirabeau, they do not justify his estimate of his genius. The Gracchi, Agis, Cleomenes, and others of Plutarch's heroes, do not in the record of facts equal their own fame. Sir Philip Sidney, the Earl of Essex, Sir Walter Raleigh, are men of great figure, and of few deeds. We cannot find the smallest part of the personal weight of Washington, in the narrative of his exploits. The authority of the name of Schiller is too great for his books. This inequality of the reputation to the works or the anecdotes, is not accounted for by saying that the reverberation is longer than the thunder-clap; but somewhat resided in these men which begot an expectation that outran all their performance. The largest part of their power was latent. This is that which we call Character,—a reserved force which acts directly by presence, and without means. It is conceived of as a certain undemonstrable force, a Familiar or Genius, by whose impulses the man is guided, but whose counsels he cannot impart; which is company for him, so that such men are often solitary, or if they chance to be social, do not need society, but can entertain themselves very well alone. The purest literary talent appears at one time great, at another time small, but character is of a stellar and undiminishable greatness. What others effect by talent or by eloquence this man accomplishes by some magnetism. "Half his strength he put not forth." His victories are by demonstration of superiority, and not by crossing of bayonets. He conquers, because his arrival alters the face of affairs. " 'O Iole! how did you know that Hercules was a god?' 'Because,' answered Iole, 'I was content the moment my eyes fell on him. When I beheld Theseus, I desired that I might see him offer battle, or at least guide his horses in the chariot-race; but Hercules did not wait for a contest; he conquered whether he stood, or walked, or sat, or whatever thing he did.' " Man, ordinarily a pendant to events, only half attached, and that awkwardly, to the world he lives in, in these examples appears to share the life of things, and to be an expression of the same laws which control the tides and the sun, numbers and quantities.

But to use a more modest illustration, and nearer home, I observe, that in our political elections, where this element, if it appears at all, can only occur in its coarsest form, we sufficiently understand its incomparable rate. The people know that they need in their representative much more than talent, namely, the power to make his talent trusted. They cannot come at their ends by sending to Congress a learned, acute, and fluent speaker, if he be not one, who, before he was appointed by the people to represent them, was appointed by Almighty God to stand for a fact,— invincibly persuaded of that fact in himself,—so that the most confident and the most violent persons learn that here is resistance on which both impudence and terror are wasted, namely, faith in a fact. The men who carry their points do not need to inquire of their constituents what they should say, but are themselves the country which they represent: nowhere are its emotions or opinions so instant and true as in them; nowhere so pure from a selfish infusion. The constituency at home hearkens to their words, watches the color of their cheek, and therein, as in a glass, dresses its own. Our public assemblies are pretty good tests of manly force. Our frank countrymen of the west and south have a taste for character, and like to know whether the New Englander is a substantial man, or whether the hand can pass through him.

The same motive force appears in trade. There

are geniuses in trade, as well as in war, or the state, or letters; and the reason why this or that man is fortunate, is not to be told. It lies in the man: that is all anybody can tell you about it. See him, and you will know as easily why he succeeds, as, if you see Napoleon, you would comprehend his fortune. In the new objects we recognize the old game, the habit of fronting the fact, and not dealing with it at second-hand, through the perceptions of somebody else. Nature seems to authorize trade, as soon as you see the natural merchant, who appears not so much a private agent, as her factor and Minister of Commerce. His natural probity combines with his insight into the fabric of society, to put him above tricks, and he communicates to all his own faith, that contracts are of no private interpretation. The habit of his mind is a reference to standards of natural equity and public advantage; and he inspires respect, and the wish to deal with him, both for the quiet spirit of honor which attends him, and for the intellectual pastime which the spectacle of so much ability affords. This immensely stretched trade, which makes the capes of the Southern Ocean his wharves, and the Atlantic Sea his familiar port, centres in his brain only; and nobody in the universe can make his place good. In his parlor, I see very well that he has been at hard work this morning, with that knitted brow, and that settled humor, which all his desire to be courteous cannot shake off. I see plainly how many firm acts have been done; how many valiant *noes* have this day been spoken, when others would have uttered ruinous *yeas*. I see, with the pride of art, and skill of masterly arithmetic and power of remote combination, the consciousness of being an agent and play-fellow of the original laws of the world. He too believes that none can supply him, and that a man must be born to trade, or he cannot learn it.

This virtue draws the mind more, when it appears in action to ends not so mixed. It works with most energy in the smallest companies and in private relations. In all cases, it is an extraordinary and incomputable agent. The excess of physical strength is paralyzed by it. Higher natures overpower lower ones by affecting them with a certain sleep. The faculties are locked up, and offer no resistance. Perhaps that is the universal law. When the high cannot bring up the low to itself, it benumbs it, as man charms down the resistance of the lower animals. Men exert on each other a similar occult power. How often has the influence of a true master realized all the tales of magic! A river of command seemed to run down from his eyes into all those who beheld him, a torrent of strong sad light, like an Ohio or Danube, which pervaded them with his thoughts, and colored all events with the hue of his mind. "What means did you employ?" was the question asked of the wife of Concini, in regard to her treatment of Mary of Medici; and the answer was, "Only that influence which every strong mind has over a weak one." Cannot Cæsar in irons shuffle off the irons, and transfer them to the person of Hippo or Thraso the turnkey? Is an iron handcuff so immutable a bond? Suppose a slaver on the coast of Guinea should take on board a gang of negroes, which should contain persons of the stamp of Toussaint L'Ouverture: or, let us fancy, under these swarthy masks he has a gang of Washingtons in chains. When they arrive at Cuba, will the relative order of the ship's company be the same? Is there nothing but rope and iron? Is there no love, no reverence? Is there never a glimpse of right in a poor slave-captain's mind; and cannot these be supposed available to break, or elude, or in any manner overmatch the tension of an inch or two of iron ring?

This is a natural power, like light and heat, and all nature coöperates with it. The reason why we feel one man's presence, and do not feel another's, is as simple as gravity. Truth is the summit of being: justice is the application of it to affairs. All individual natures stand in a scale, according to the purity of this element in them. The will of the pure runs down from them into other natures, as water runs down from a higher into a lower vessel. This natural force is no more to be withstood, than any other natural force. We can drive a stone upward for a moment into the air, but it is yet true that all stones will forever fall; and whatever instances can be quoted of unpunished theft, or of a lie which somebody credited, justice must prevail, and it is the privilege of truth to make itself believed. Character is this moral order seen through the medium of an individual nature. An individual is an encloser. Time and space, liberty and necessity, truth and thought, are left at large no longer. Now, the universe is a close or pound. All things exist in the man tingled with the manners of his soul. With what quality is in him, he infuses all nature that he can reach; nor does he tend to lose himself in vastness, but at how long a curve soever, all his regards return

into his own good at last.   He animates all he can, and
he sees only what he animates.   He encloses the world,
as the patriot does his country, as a material basis
for his character, and a theatre for action.   A healthy
soul stands united with the Just and the True, as the
magnet arranges itself with the pole, so that he stands
to all beholders like a transparent object betwixt them
and the sun, and whoso journeys towards the sun,
journeys towards that person.   He is thus the medium
of the highest influence to all who are not on the same
level.   Thus men of character are the conscience of the
society to which they belong.

The natural measure of this power is the resistance
of circumstances.   Impure men consider life as it is reflected in opinions, events, and persons.   They cannot
see the action, until it is done.   Yet its moral element
pre-existed in the actor, and its quality as right or
wrong, it was easy to predict.   Everything in nature
is bipolar, or has a positive and negative pole.   There
is a male and a female, a spirit and a fact, a north and
a south.   Spirit is the positive, the event is the negative.   Will is the north, action the south pole.   Character may be ranked as having its natural place in the
north.   It shares the magnetic currents of the system.
The feeble souls are drawn to the south or negative
pole.   They look at the profit or hurt of the action.
They never behold a principle until it is lodged in a
person.   They do not wish to be lovely, but to be
loved.   The class of character like to hear of their
faults: the other class do not like to hear of faults;
they worship events; secure to them a fact, a connection, a certain chain of circumstances, and they will

ask no more. The hero sees that the event is ancillary: it must follow *him.* A given order of events has no power to secure to him the satisfaction which the imagination attaches to it; the soul of goodness escapes from any set of circumstances, whilst prosperity belongs to a certain mind, and will introduce that power and victory which is its natural fruit, into any order of events. No change of circumstances can repair a defect of ·character. We boast our emancipation from many superstitions; but if we have broken any idols, it is through a transfer of the idolatry. What have I gained, that I no longer immolate a bull to Jove, or to Neptune, or a mouse to Hecate; that I do not tremble before the Eumenides, or the Catholic Purgatory, or the Calvinistic Judgment-day,—if I quake at opinion, the public opinion, as we call it; or at the threat of assault, or contumely, or bad neighbors, or poverty, or mutilation, or at the rumor of revolution, or of murder? If I quake, what matters it what I quake at? Our proper vice takes form in one or another shape, according to the sex, age, or temperament of the person, and, if we are capable of fear, will readily find terrors. The covetousness or the malignity which saddens me, when I ascribe it to society, is my own. I am always environed by myself. On the other part, rectitude is a perpetual victory, celebrated not by cries of joy, but by serenity, which is joy fixed or habitual. It is disgraceful to fly to events for confirmation of our truth and worth. The capitalist does not run every hour to the broker, to coin his advantages into current money of the realm; he is satisfied to read in the quotations of the market, that his stocks have risen. The same transport which the occurrence of the best events in the best order would occasion me, I must learn to taste purer in the perception that my position is every hour meliorated, and does already command those events I desire. That exultation is only to be checked by the foresight of an order of things so excellent, as to throw all our prosperities into the deepest shade.

The face which character wears to me is self-sufficingness. I revere the person who is riches; so that I cannot think of him as alone, or poor, or exiled, or unhappy, or a client, but as perpetual patron, benefactor, and beatified man. Character is centrality, the impossibility of being displaced or overset. A man should give us a sense of mass. Society is frivolous, and shreds its day into scraps, its conversation into ceremonies and escapes. But if I go to see an ingenious man, I shall think myself poorly entertained if he give me nimble pieces of benevolence and etiquette; rather he shall stand stoutly in his place, and let me apprehend, if it were only his resistance; know that I have encountered a new and positive quality;—great refreshment for both of us. It is much, that he does not accept the conventional opinions and practices. That nonconformity will remain a goad and remembrancer, and every inquirer will have to dispose of him, in the first place. There is nothing real or useful that is not a seat of war. Our houses ring with laughter and personal and critical gossip, but it helps little. But the uncivil, unavailable man, who is a problem and a threat to society, whom it cannot let pass in silence, but must either worship or hate,—and to whom all parties feel related, both the leaders of opinion, and the obscure and eccentric,—he helps; he puts America and Europe in the wrong, and destroys the scepticism which says, "man is a doll, let us eat and drink, 'tis the best we can do," by illuminating the untried and unknown. Acquiescence in the establishment, and appeal to the public, indicate infirm faith, heads which are not clear, and which must see a house built, before they can comprehend the plan of it. The wise man not only leaves out of his thought the many, but leaves out the few. Fountains, fountains, the self-moved, the absorbed, the commander because he is commanded, the assured, the primary,—they are good; for these announce the instant presence of supreme power.

Our action should rest mathematically on our substance. In nature, there are no false valuations. A pound of water in the ocean-tempest has no more gravity than in a midsummer pond. All things work exactly according to their quality, and according to their quantity; attempt nothing they cannot do, except man only. He has pretension: he wishes and attempts things beyond his force. I read in a book of English memoirs, "Mr. Fox (afterwards Lord Holland) said, he must have the Treasury; he had served up to it, and would have it."—Xenophon and his Ten Thousand were quite equal to what they attempted, and did it; so equal, that it was not suspected to be a grand and inimitable exploit. Yet there stands that fact unrepeated, a high-water-mark in military history. Many have attempted it since, and not been equal to it. It is only on reality, that any power of action can be based. No institution will be better than the institutor. I knew an amiable and accomplished person

who undertook a practical reform, yet I was never able
to find in him the enterprise of love he took in hand.
He adopted it by ear and by the understanding from the
books he had been reading.   All his action was tenta-
tive, a piece of the city carried out into the fields, and
was the city still, and no new fact, and could not inspire enthusiasm.   Had there been something latent in
the man, a terrible undemonstrated genius agitating
and embarrassing his demeanor, we had watched for
its advent.   It is not enough that the intellect should
see the evils, and their remedy.   We shall still postpone our existence, nor take the ground to which we
are entitled, whilst it is only a thought and not a spirit
that incites us.   We have not yet served up to it.

These are properties of life, and another trait is the
notice of incessant growth.   Men should be intelligent
and earnest.   They must also make us feel, that they
have a controlling happy future, opening before them,
which sheds a splendor on the passing hour.   The hero
is misconceived and misreported: he cannot therefore
wait to unravel any man's blunders: he is again on his
road, adding new powers and honors to his domain,
and new claims on your heart, which will bankrupt
you, if you have loitered about the old things, and
have not kept your relation to him, by adding to your
wealth.   New actions are the only apologies and ex-
planations of old ones, which the noble can bear to offer
or to receive.   If your friend has displeased you, you
shall not sit down to consider it, for he has already
lost all memory of the passage, and has doubled his
power to serve you, and, ere you can rise up again, will
burden you with blessings.

We have no pleasure in thinking of a benevolence that is only measured by its works. Love is inexhaustible, and if its estate is wasted, its granary emptied, still cheers and enriches, and the man, though he sleep, seems to purify the air, and his house to adorn the landscape and strengthen the laws. People always recognize this difference. We know who is benevolent, by quite other means than the amount of subscription to soup-societies. It is only low merits that can be enumerated. Fear, when your friends say to you what you have done well, and say it through; but when they stand with uncertain timid looks of respect and half-dislike, and must suspend their judgment for years to come, you may begin to hope. Those who live to the future must always appear selfish to those who live to the present. Therefore it was droll in the good Riemer, who has written memoirs of Goethe, to make out a list of his donations and good deeds, as, so many hundred thalers given to Stilling, to Hegel, to Tischbein: a lucrative place found for Professor Voss, a post under the Grand Duke for Herder, a pension for Meyer, two professors recommended to foreign universities, &c., &c. The longest list of specifications of benefit, would look very short. A man is a poor creature, if he is to be measured so. For, all these, of course, are exceptions; and the rule and hodiernal life of a good man is benefaction. The true charity of Goethe is to be inferred from the account he gave Dr. Eckermann, of the way in which he had spent his fortune. "Each bon-mot of mine has cost a purse of gold. Half a million of my own money, the fortune I inherited, my salary, and the large income derived from my writings for fifty years back, have been expended to instruct me in what I now know. I have besides seen," &c.

I own it is but poor chat and gossip to go to enumerate traits of this simple and rapid power, and we are painting the lightning with charcoal; but in these long nights and vacations, I like to console myself so. Nothing but itself can copy it. A word warm from the heart enriches me. I surrender at discretion. How death-cold is literary genius before this fire of life! These are the touches that reanimate my heavy soul, and give it eyes to pierce the dark of nature. I find, where I thought myself poor, there was I most rich. Thence comes a new intellectual exaltation, to be again rebuked by some new exhibition of character. Strange alternation of attraction and repulsion! Character repudiates intellect, yet excites it; and character passes into thought, is published so, and then is ashamed before new flashes of moral worth.

Character is nature in the highest form. It is of no use to ape it, or to contend with it. Somewhat is possible of resistance, and of persistence, and of creation, to this power, which will foil all emulation.

This masterpiece is best where no hands but nature's have been laid on it. Care is taken that the greatly-destined shall slip up into life in the shade, with no thousand-eyed Athens to watch and blazon every new thought, every blushing emotion of young genius Two persons lately,—very young children of the most high God,—have given me occasion for thought. When I explored the source of their sanctity, and charm for the imagination, it seemed as if each an-

swered, "From my non-conformity: I never listened to
your people's law, or to what they call their gospel,
and wasted my time. I was content with the simple
rural poverty of my own; hence this sweetness: my
work never reminds you of that;—is pure of that."
And nature advertises me in such persons, that, in democratic America, she will not be democratized. How
cloistered and constitutionally sequestered from the
market and from scandal! It was only this morning,
that I sent away some wild flowers of these wood-
gods. They are a relief from literature,—these fresh
draughts from the sources of thought and sentiment;
as we read, in an age of polish and criticism, the first
lines of written prose and verse of a nation. How
captivating is their devotion to their favorite books,
whether Æschylus, Dante, Shakespeare, or Scott, as
feeling that they have a stake in that book: who touches
that, touches them;—and especially the total solitude
of the critic, the Patmos of thought from which he
writes, in unconsciousness of any eyes that shall ever
read this writing. Could they dream on still, as angels, and not wake to comparisons, and to be flattered!
Yet some natures are too good to be spoiled by praise,
and wherever the vein of thought reaches down into
the profound, there is no danger from vanity. Solemn
friends will warn them of the danger of the head's
being turned by the flourish of trumpets, but they can
afford to smile. I remember the indignation of an eloquent Methodist at the kind admonitions of a Doctor
of Divinity,—"My friend, a man can neither be praised
nor insulted." But forgive the counsels; they are very
natural. I remember the thought which occurred to

me when some ingenious and spiritual foreigners came
to America, was, Have you been victimized in being
brought hither?—or, prior to that, answer me this,
"Are you victimizable?"

As I have said, nature keeps these sovereignties in
her own hands, and however pertly our sermons and
disciplines would divide some share of credit, and teach
that the laws fashion the citizen, she goes her own gait,
and puts the wisest in the wrong. She makes very
light of gospels and prophets, as one who has a great
many more to produce, and no excess of time to spare
on any one. There is a class of men, individuals of
which appear at long intervals, so eminently endowed
with insight and virtue, that they have been unanimously
saluted as *divine,* and who seem to be an accumulation
of that power we consider. Divine persons are character born, or, to borrow a phrase from Napoleon, they
are victory organized. They are usually received with
ill-will, because they are new, and because they set a
bound to the exaggeration that has been made of the
personality of the last divine person. Nature never
rhymes her children, nor makes two men alike. When
we see a great man, we fancy a resemblance to some
historical person, and predict the sequel of his character and fortune, a result which he is sure to disappoint.
None will ever solve the problem of his character according to our prejudice, but only in his own high unprecedented way. Character wants room; must not
be crowded on by persons, nor be judged from glimpses
got in the press of affairs or on few occasions. It needs
perspective, as a great building. It may not, probably
does not, form relations rapidly; and we should not

require rash explanation, either on the popular ethics, or on our own, of its action.

I look on Sculpture as history. I do not think the Apollo and the Jove impossible in flesh and blood. Every trait which the artist recorded in stone, he had seen in life, and better than his copy. We have seen many counterfeits, but we are born believers in great men. How easily we read in old books, when men were few, of the smallest action of the patriarchs. We require that a man should be so large and columnar in the landscape, that it should deserve to be recorded, that he arose, and girded up his loins, and departed to such a place. The most credible pictures are those of majestic men who prevailed at their entrance, and convinced the senses; as happened to the eastern magian who was sent to test the merits of Zertusht or Zoroaster. When the Yunani sage arrived at Balkh, the Persians tell us, Gushtasp appointed a day on which the mobeds of every country should assemble, and a golden chair was placed for the Yunani sage. Then the beloved Yezdam, the prophet Zertusht, advanced into the midst of the assembly. The Yunani sage, on seeing that chief, said "This form and this gait cannot lie, and nothing but truth can proceed from them." Plato said, it was impossible not to believe in the children of the gods, "though they should speak without probable or necessary arguments." I should think myself very unhappy in my associates, if I could not credit the best things in history. "John Bradshaw," says Milton, "appears like a consul, from whom the fasces are not to depart with the year; so that not on the tribunal only but throughout his life, you would re-

gard him as sitting in judgment upon kings." I find
it more credible, since it is anterior information, that
one man should *know heaven,* as the Chinese say, than
that so many men should know the world. "The virtuous prince confronts the gods, without any misgiving. He waits a hundred ages till a sage comes, and
does not doubt. He who confronts the gods, without
any misgiving, knows heaven; he who waits a hundred
ages until a sage comes, without doubting, knows men.
Hence the virtuous prince moves, and for ages shows
empire the way." But there is no need to seek remote
examples. He is a dull observer whose experience has
not taught him the reality and force of magic, as well
as of chemistry. The coldest precisian cannot go
abroad without encountering inexplicable influences.
One man fastens an eye on him, and the graves of the
memory render up their dead; the secrets that make
him wretched either to keep or to betray, must be
yielded;—another, and he cannot speak, and the bones
of his body seem to lose their cartilage; the entrance
of a friend adds grace, boldness, and eloquence to him;
and there are persons, he cannot choose but remember,
who gave a transcendant expansion to his thought, and
kindled another life in his bosom.

What is so excellent as strict relations of amity, when
they spring from this deep root? The sufficient reply
to the sceptic, who doubts the power and the furniture
of man, is in that possibility of joyful intercourse with
persons, which makes the faith and practice of all reasonable men. I know nothing which life has to offer
so satisfying as the profound good understanding,
which can subsist, after much exchange of good offices,

between two virtuous men, each of whom is sure of himself, and sure of his friend. It is a happiness which postpones all other gratifications, and makes politics, and commerce, and churches, cheap. For, when men shall meet as they ought, each a benefactor, a shower of stars, clothed with thoughts, with deeds, with accomplishments, it should be the festival of nature which all things announce. Of such friendship, love in the sexes is the first symbol, as all other things are symbols of love. Those relations to the best men, which, at one time, we reckoned the romances of youth, become, in the progress of the character, the most solid enjoyment.

If it were possible to live in right relations with men! —if we could abstain from asking anything of them, from asking their praise, or help, or pity, and content us with compelling them through the virtue of the eldest laws! [3] Could we not deal with a few persons,— with one person,—after the unwritten statutes, and make an experiment of their efficacy? Could we not pay our friend the compliment of truth, of silence, of forbearing? Need we be so eager to seek him? If we are related, we shall meet. It was a tradition of the ancient world, that no metamorphosis could hide a god from a god; and there is a Greek verse which runs,

> The Gods are to each other not unknown.

Friends also follow the laws of divine necessity; they gravitate to each other, and cannot otherwise:—

> When each the other shall avoid
> Shall each by each be most enjoyed.

Their relation is not made, but allowed. The gods must seat themselves without seneschal in our Olympus, and as they can install themselves by seniority divine. Society is spoiled if pains are taken, if the associates are brought a mile to meet. And if it be not society, it is a mischievous, low, degrading jangle, though made up of the best. All the greatness of each is kept back, and every foible in painful activity, as if the Olympians should meet to exchange snuff-boxes.

Life goes headlong. We chase some flying scheme, or we are hunted by some fear or command behind us. But if suddenly we encounter a friend we pause; our heat and hurry look foolish enough; now pause, now possession, is required, and the power to swell the moment from the resources of the heart. The moment is all, in all noble relations.

A divine person is the prophecy of the mind; a friend is the hope of the heart. Our beatitude waits for the fulfilment of these two in one. The ages are opening this moral force. All force is the shadow or symbol of that. Poetry is joyful and strong, as it draws its inspiration thence. Men write their names on the world, as they are filled with this. History has been mean; our nations have been mobs; we have never seen a man: that divine form we do not yet know, but only the dream and prophecy of such: we do not know the majestic manners which belong to him, which appease and exalt the beholder. We shall one day see that the most private is the most public energy, that quality atones for quantity, and grandeur of character acts in the dark, and succors them who never saw it. What greatness has yet appeared, is beginnings and encouragements to us in this direction. The history of those gods and saints which the world has written, and then worshipped, are documents of character. The ages have exulted in the manners of a youth who owed nothing to fortune, and who was hanged at the Tyburn of his nation, who, by the pure quality of his nature, shed an epic splendor around the facts of his death, which has transfigured every particular into an universal symbol for the eyes of mankind. This great defeat is hitherto our highest fact. But the mind requires a victory to the senses, a force of character which will convert judge, jury, soldier, and king; which will rule animal and mineral virtues, and blend with the courses of sap, of rivers, of winds, of stars, and of moral agents.

If we cannot attain at a bound to these grandeurs at least, let us do them homage. In society, high advantages are set down to the possessor, as disadvantages. It requires the more wariness in our private estimates. I do not forgive in my friends the failure to know a fine character, and to entertain it with thankful hospitality. When at last, that which we have always longed for, is arrived, and shines on us with glad rays out of that far celestial land, then to be coarse, then to be critical, and treat such a visitant with the jabber and suspicion of the streets, argues a vulgarity that seems to shut the doors of heaven. This is confusion, this the right insanity, when the soul no longer knows its own, nor where its allegiance, its religion, are due. Is there any religion but this, to know, that. wherever in the wide desert of being, the holy sentiment we cherish has opened into a flower, it blooms for me? if none sees it I see it; I am aware, if I alone, of the greatness of the fact. Whilst it blooms, I will keep sabbath or holy time, and suspend my gloom, and my folly and jokes. Nature is indulged by the presence of this guest. There are many eyes that can detect and honor the prudent and household virtues; there are many that can discern Genius on his starry track, though the mob is incapable; but when that love which is all-suffering, all-abstaining, all-aspiring, which has vowed to itself, that it will be a wretch and also a fool in this world, sooner than soil its white hands by any compliances, comes into our streets and houses,—only the pure and aspiring can know its face, and the only compliment they can pay it, is to own it.

MANNERS

How near to good is what is fair!
  Which we no sooner see,
But with the lines and outward air
  Our senses taken be.

    ———

  Again yourselves compose,
And now put all the aptness on
  Of Figure, that Proportion
    Or Color can disclose;
That if those silent arts were lost,
Design and Picture, they might boast
    From you a newer ground,
Instructed by the heightening sense
Of dignity and reverence
    In their true motions found.

                BEN JONSON.

HALF the world, it is said, knows not how the other half live. Our Exploring Expedition saw the Feejee islanders getting their dinner off human bones; and they are said to eat their own wives and children. The husbandry of the modern inhabitants of Gournou (west of old Thebes) is philosophical to a fault. To set up their housekeeping, nothing is requisite but two or three earthen pots, a stone to grind meal, and a mat which is the bed. The house, namely, a tomb, is ready without rent or taxes.

No rain can pass through the roof, and there is no door, for there is no want of one, as there is nothing to lose. If the house do not please them, they walk out and enter another, as there are several hundreds at their command. "It is somewhat singular," adds Belzoni, to whom we owe this account, "to talk of happiness among people who live in sepulchres, among the corpses and rags of an ancient nation which they know nothing of." In the deserts of Borgoo, the rock-Tibboos still dwell in caves, like cliff-swallows, and the language of these negroes is compared by their neighbors to the shrieking of bats, and to the whistling of birds. Again, the Bornoos have no proper names; individuals are called after their height, thickness, or other accidental quality, and have nick-names merely. But the salt, the dates, the ivory, and the gold, for which these horrible regions are visited, find their way into countries, where the purchaser and consumer can hardly be ranked in one race with these cannibals and man-stealers; countries where man serves himself with metals, wood, stone, glass, gum, cotton, silk, and wool; honors himself with architecture; writes laws, and contrives to execute his will through the hands of many nations; and, especially, establishes a select society, running through all the countries of intelligent men, a self-constituted aristocracy, or fraternity of the best, which, without written law or exact usage of any kind, perpetuates itself, colonizes every new-planted island, and adopts and makes its own whatever personal beauty or extraordinary native endowment anywhere appears.

What fact more conspicuous in modern history, than the creation of the gentleman? Chivalry is that, and loyalty is that, and, in English literature, half the drama, and all the novels, from Sir Philip Sidney to Sir Walter Scott, paint this figure. The word *gentleman,* which, like the word Christian, must hereaftet characterize the present and the few preceding centuries, by the importance attached to it, is a homage to personal and incommunicable properties. Frivolous and fantastic additions have got associated with the name, but the steady interest of mankind in it must be attributed to the valuable properties which it designates. An element which unites all the most forcible persons of every country; makes them intelligible and agreeable to each other, and is somewhat so precise, that it is at once felt if an individual lack the masonic sign, cannot be any casual product, but must be an average result of the character and faculties universally found in men. It seems a certain permanent average; as the atmosphere is a permanent composition, whilst so many gases are combined only to be decompounded. *Comme il faut,* is the Frenchman's description of good society, *as we must be.* It is a spontaneous fruit of talents and feelings of precisely that class who have most vigor, who take the lead in the world of this hour, and, though far from pure, far from constituting the gladdest and highest tone of human feeling, is as good as the whole society permits it to be. It is made of the spirit, more than of the talent of men, and is a compound result, into which every great force enters as an ingredient, namely, virtue, wit, beauty, wealth, and power.

There is something equivocal in all the words in use to express the excellence of manners and social cultivation, because the quantities are fluctional, and the last effect is assumed by the senses as the cause. The word *gentleman* has not any correlative abstract to express the quality. *Gentility* is mean, and *gentilesse* is obsolete. But we must keep alive in the vernacular, the distinction between *fashion,* a word of narrow and often sinister meaning, and the heroic character which the gentleman imports. The usual words, however, must be respected: they will be found to contain the root of the matter. The point of distinction in all this class of names, as courtesy, chivalry, fashion, and the like, is, that the flower and fruit, not the grain of the tree, are contemplated. It is beauty which is the aim this time, and not worth. The result is now in question, although our words intimate well enough the popular feeling, that the appearance supposes a substance. The gentleman is a man of truth, lord of his own actions, and expressing that lordship in his behavior, not in any maner dependent and servile either on persons, or opinions, or possessions. Beyond this fact of truth and real force, the word denotes good-nature or benevolence; manhood first, and then gentleness. The popular notion certainly adds a condition of ease and fortune; but that is a natural result of personal force and love, that they should possess and dispense the goods of the world. In times of violence, every eminent person must fall in with many opportunities to approve his stoutness and worth; therefore every man's name that emerged at all from the mass in the feudal ages, rattles in our ear like a flourish of trumpets. But personal force never goes out of fashion. That is still paramount to-day, and, in the moving crowd of good society, the men of valor and reality are known, and rise to their natural place. The competition is transferred from war to politics and trade, but the personal force appears readily enough in these new arenas.

Power first, or no leading class. In politics and in trade, bruisers and pirates are of better promise than talkers and clerks. God knows that all sorts of gentlemen knock at the door; but whenever used in strictness, and with any emphasis, the name will be found to point at original energy. It describes a man standing in his own right, and working after untaught methods. In a good lord, there must first be a good animal, at least to the extent of yielding the incomparable advantage of animal spirits. The ruling class must have more, but they must have these, giving in every company the sense of power, which makes things easy to be done which daunt the wise. The society of the energetic class, in their friendly and festive meetings, is full of courage, and attempts, which intimidate the pale scholar. The courage which girls exhibit is like a battle of Lundy's Lane, or a sea fight. The intellect relies on memory to make some supplies to face these extemporaneous squadrons. But memory is a base mendicant with basket and badge, in the presence of these sudden masters. The rulers of society must be up to the work of the world, and equal to their versatile office: men of the right Cæsarian pattern, who have great range of affinity. I am far from believing the timid maxim of Lord Falkland, ("that for ceremony there must go two to it; since a bold fellow will go through the cunningest forms,") and am of opinion that the gentleman is the bold fellow whose forms are not to be broken through; and only that plenteous nature is rightful master, which is the complement of whatever person it converses with.   My gentleman gives the law where he is; he will outpray saints in chapel, outgeneral veterans in the field, and outshine all courtesy in the hall. He is good company for pirates, and good with academicians; so that it is useless to fortify yourself against him; he has the private entrance to all minds, and I could as easily exclude myself, as him.   The famous gentlemen of Asia and Europe have been of this strong type; Saladin, Sapor, the Cid, Julius Cæsar, Scipio, Alexander, Pericles, and the lordliest personages.   They sat very carelessly in their chairs, and were too excellent themselves to value any condition at a high rate.

A plentiful fortune is reckoned necessary, in the popular judgment, to the completion of this man of the world: and it is a material deputy which walks through the dance which the first has led.   Money is not essential, but this wide affinity is, which transcends the habits of clique and caste, and makes itself felt by men of all classes.   If the aristocrat is only valid in fashionable circles, and not with truckmen, he will never be a leader in fashion; and if the man of the people cannot speak on equal terms with the gentleman, so that the gentleman shall perceive that he is already really of his own order, he is not to be feared.   Diogenes, Socrates, and Epaminondas, are gentlemen of the best blood, who have chosen the condition of poverty, when that of wealth was equally open to them. I use these old names, but the men I speak of are my

contemporaries. Fortune will not supply to every generation one of these well-appointed knights, but every
collection of men furnishes some example of the class:
and the politics of this country, and the trade of every
town, are controlled by these hardy and irresponsible
doers, who have invention to take the lead, and a broad
sympathy which puts them in fellowship with crowds,
and makes their action popular.

The manners of this class are observed and caught
with devotion by men of taste. The association of
these masters with each other, and with men intelligent
of their merits, is mutually agreeable and stimulating.
The good forms, the happiest expressions of each, are
repeated and adopted. By swift consent, everything
superfluous is dropped, everything graceful is renewed.
Fine manners show themselves formidable to the uncultivated man. They are a subtler science of defence
to parry and intimidate; but once matched by the skill
of the other party, they drop the point of the sword,—
points and fences disappear, and the youth finds himself in a more transparent atmosphere, wherein life is
a less troublesome game, and not a misunderstanding
rises between the players. Manners aim to facilitate
life, to get rid of impediments, and bring the man pure
to energize. They aid our dealing and conversation, as
a railway aids travelling, by getting rid of all avoidable
obstructions of the road, and leaving nothing to be conquered but pure space. These forms very soon become
fixed, and a fine sense of propriety is cultivated with the
more heed, that it becomes a badge of social and civil
distinction. Thus grows up Fashion, an equivocal
semblance, the most puissant, the most fantastic and

frivolous, the most feared and followed, and which morals and violence assault in vain.

There exists a strict relation between the class of power, and the exclusive and polished circles. The last are always filled or filling from the first. The strong men usually give some allowance even to the petulances of fashion, for that affinity they find in it. Napoleon, child of the revolution, destroyer of the old noblesse, never ceased to court the Faubourg St. Germain: doubtless with the feeling, that fashion is a homage to men of his stamp. Fashion, though in a strange way, represents all manly virtue. It is virtue gone to seed: it is a kind of posthumous honor. It does not often caress the great, but the children of the great: it is a hall of the Past. It usually sets its face against the great of this hour. Great men are not commonly in its halls: they are absent in the field: they are working, not triumphing. Fashion is made up of their children; of those, who, through the value and virtue of somebody, have acquired lustre to their name, marks of distinction, means of cultivation and generosity, and, in their physical organization, a certain health and excellence, which secures to them, if not the highest power to work, yet high power to enjoy. The class of power, the working heroes, the Cortez, the Nelson, the Napoleon, see that this is the festivity and permanent celebration of such as they; that fashion is funded talent; is Mexico, Marengo, and Trafalgar beaten out thin; that the brilliant names of fashion run back to just such busy names as their own, fifty or sixty years ago. They are the sowers, their sons shall be the reapers, and *their* sons, in the ordinary course of things, must yield the possession of the harvest to new competitors with keener eyes and stronger frames. The city is recruited from the country. In the year 1805, it is said, every legitimate monarch in Europe was imbecile. The city would have died out, rotted, and exploded long ago, but that it was reinforced from the fields. It is only country which came to town day before yesterday, that is city and court to-day.

Aristocracy and fashion are certain inevitable results. These mutual selections are indestructible. If they provoke anger in the least favored class, and the excluded majority revenge themselves on the excluding minority, by the strong hand, and kill them, at once a new class finds itself at the top, as certainly as cream rises in a bowl of milk: and if the people should destroy class after class, until two men only were left, one of these would be the leader, and would be involuntarily served and copied by the other. You may keep this minority out of sight and out of mind, but it is tenacious of life, and is one of the estates of the realm. I am the more struck with this tenacity, when I see its work. It respects the administration of such unimportant matters, that we should not look for any durability in its rule. We sometimes meet men under some strong moral influence, as, a patriotic, a literary, a religious movement, and feel that the moral sentiment rules man and nature. We think all other distinctions and ties will be slight and fugitive, this of caste or fashion, for example; yet come from year to year, and see how permanent that is, in this Boston or New York life of man, where, too, it has not the least countenance from the law of the land. Not in Egypt or in India a firmer or more impassable line. Here are associations whose ties go over, and under, and through it, a meeting of merchants, a military corps, a college-class, a fire-club, a professional association, a political, a religious convention;—the persons seem to draw inseparably near; yet, that assembly once dispersed, its members will not in the year meet again. Each returns to his degree in the scale of good society, porcelain remains porcelain, and earthen earthen. The objects of fashion may be frivolous, or fashion may be objectless, but the nature of this union and selection can be neither frivolous nor accidental. Each man's rank in that perfect graduation depends on some symmetry in his structure, or some agreement in his structure to the symmetry of society. Its doors unbar instantaneously to a natural claim of their own kind. A natural gentleman finds his way in, and will keep the oldest patrician out, who has lost his intrinsic rank. Fashion understands itself; good-breeding and personal superiority of whatever country readily fraternize with those of every other. The chiefs of savage tribes have distinguished themselves in London and Paris, by the purity of their tournure.

To say what good of fashion we can,—it rests on reality, and hates nothing so much as pretenders;—to exclude and mystify pretenders, and send them into everlasting "Coventry," is its delight. We contemn, in turn, every other gift of men of the world; but the habit even in little and the least matters, of not appealing to any but our own sense of propriety, constitutes the foundation of all chivalry. There is almost no kind of self-reliance, so it be sane and proportioned, which fashion does not occasionally adopt, and give it the freedom of its saloons. A sainted soul is always elegant, and, if it will, passes unchallenged into the most guarded ring. But so will Jock the teamster pass, in some crisis that brings him thither, and find favor, as long as his head is not giddy with the new circumstance, and the iron shoes do not wish to dance in waltzes and cotillons. For there is nothing settled in manners, but the laws of behavior yield to the energy of the individual. The maiden at her first ball, the countryman at a city dinner, believes that there is a ritual according to which every act and compliment must be performed, or the failing party must be cast out of this presence. Later, they learn that good sense and character make their own forms every moment, and speak or abstain, take wine or refuse it, stay or go, sit in a chair or sprawl with children on the floor, or stand on their head, or what else soever, in a new and aboriginal way: and that strong will is always in fashion, let who will be unfashionable. All that fashion demands is composure, and self-content. A circle of men perfectly well-bred would be a company of sensible persons, in which every man's native manners and character appeared. If the fashionist have not this quality, he is nothing. We are such lovers of self-reliance, that we excuse in a man many sins, if he will show us a complete satisfaction in his position, which asks no leave to be, or mine, or any man's good opinion. But any deference to some eminent man or woman of the world, forfeits all privilege of nobility. He is an underling: I have nothing to do with him; I will speak with his master. A man should not go where he cannot carry his whole sphere or society with him,—not bodily, the whole circle of his friends, but atmospherically. He should preserve in a new company the same attitude of mind and reality of relation, which his daily associates draw him to, else he is shorn of his best beams, and will be an orphan in the merriest club. "If you could see Vich Ian Vohr with his tail on!——" But Vich Ian Vohr must always carry his belongings in some fashion, if not added as honor, then severed as disgrace.

There will always be in society certain persons who are mercuries of its approbation, and whose glance will at any time determine for the curious their standing in the world. These are the chamberlains of the lesser gods. Accept their coldness as an omen of grace with the loftier deities, and allow them all their privilege. They are clear in their office, nor could they be thus formidable, without their own merits. But do not measure the importance of this class by their pretension, or imagine that a fop can be the dispenser of honor and shame. They pass also at their just rate; for how can they otherwise, in circles which exist as a sort of herald's office for the sifting of character?

As the first thing man requires of man, is reality, so, that appears in all the forms of society. We pointedly, and by name, introduce the parties to each other. Know you before all heaven and earth, that this is Andrew, and this Gregory;—they look each other in the eye; they grasp each other's hand, to identify and signalize each other. It is a great satisfaction. A gentleman never dodges: his eyes look straight forward, and he assures the other party, first of all, that he has been met. For what is it that we seek, in so many visits and hospitalities? Is it your draperies, pictures, and decorations? Or, do we not insatiably ask, Was a man in the house? I may easily go into a great household where there is much substance, excellent provision for comfort, luxury, and taste, and yet not encounter there any Amphitryon, who shall subordinate these appendages. I may go into a cottage, and find a farmer who feels that he is the man I have come to see, and fronts me accordingly. It was therefore a very natural point of old feudal etiquette, that a gentleman who received a visit, though it were of his sovereign, should not leave his roof, but should wait his arrival at the door of his house. No house, though it were the Tuileries, or the Escurial, is good for anything without a master. And yet we are not often gratified by this hospitality. Every body we know surrounds himself with a fine house, fine books, conservatory, gardens, equipage, and all manner of toys, as screens to interpose between himself and his guest. Does it not seem as if man was of a very sly, elusive nature, and dreaded nothing so much as a full rencontre front to front with this fellow? It were unmerciful, I know, quite to abolish the use of these screens, which are of eminent convenience, whether the guest is too great, or too little. We call together many friends who keep each other in play, or, by luxuries and ornaments we amuse the young people, and guard our retirement. Or if, perchance, a searching realist comes to our gate, before whose eye we have no care to stand, then again we run to our curtain, and hide ourselves as Adam at the voice of the Lord God

in the garden. Cardinal Capara, the Pope's legate at
Paris, defended himself from the glances of Napoleon, by an immense pair of green spectacles. Napoleon remarked them, and speedily managed to rally
them off: and yet Napoleon, in his turn, was not great
enough with eight hundred thousand troops at his back,
to face a pair of freeborn eyes, but fenced himself with
etiquette, and within triple barriers of reserve: and,
as all the world knows from Madame de Staël, was
wont, when he found himself observed, to discharge his
face of all expression. But emperors and rich men
are by no means the most skilful masters of good
manners. No rent-roll nor army-list can dignify
skulking and dissimulation: and the first point of
courtesy must always be truth, as really all the forms of
good-breeding point that way.

I have just been reading, in Mr. Hazlitt's transla-
tion, Montaigne's account of his journey into Italy, and
am struck with nothing more agreeably than the self-
respecting fashions of the time. His arrival in each
place, the arrival of a gentleman of France, is an event
of some consequence. Wherever he goes, he pays a
visit to whatever prince or gentleman of note resides
upon his road, as a duty to himself and to civilization.
When he leaves any house in which he has lodged for
a few weeks, he causes his arms to be painted and hung
up as a perpetual sign to the house, as was the custom
of gentlemen.

The complement of this graceful self-respect, and
that of all the points of good breeding I most require
and insist upon, is deference. I like that every chair
should be a throne, and hold a king. I prefer a ten-

dency to stateliness, to an excess of fellowship. Let
the incommunicable objects of nature and the metaphysical isolation of man teach us independence. Let
us not be too much acquainted. I would have a man
enter his house through a hall filled with heroic and
sacred sculptures, that he might not want the hint of
tranquillity and self-poise. We should meet each morning, as from foreign countries, and spending the day
together, should depart at night, as into foreign countries. In all things I would have the island of a man
inviolate. Let us sit apart as the gods, talking from
peak to peak all around Olympus. No degree of affection need invade this religion. This is myrrh and rose-
mary to keep the other sweet. Lovers should guard
their strangeness. If they forgive too much, all slides
into confusion and meanness. It is easy to push this
deference to a Chinese etiquette; but coolness and absence of heat and haste indicate fine qualities. A
gentleman makes no noise: a lady is serene. Propor-
tionate is our disgust at those invaders who fill a
studious house with blast and running, to secure some
paltry convenience. Not less I dislike a low sympathy
of each with his neighbor's needs. Must we have a
good understanding with one another's palates? as
foolish people who have lived long together, know when
each wants salt or sugar. I pray my companion, if he
wishes for bread, to ask me for bread, and if he wishes
for sassafras or arsenic, to ask me for them, and not
to hold out his plate, as if I knew already. Every
natural function can be dignified by deliberation and
privacy. Let us leave hurry to slaves. The compliments and ceremonies of our breeding should signify,

however remotely, the recollection of the grandeur of our destiny.

The flower of courtesy does not very well bide, handling, but if we dare to open another leaf, and explore what parts go to its conformation, we shall find also an intellectual quality. To the leaders of men, the brain as well as the flesh and the heart must furnish a proportion. Defect in manners is usually the defect of fine perceptions. Men are too coarsely made for the delicacy of beautiful carriage and customs. It is not quite sufficient to good breeding, a union of kindness and independence. We imperatively require a perception of, and a homage to beauty in our companions. Other virtues are in request in the field and workyard, but a certain degree of taste is not to be spared in those we sit with. I could better eat with one who did not respect the truth or the laws, than with a sloven and unpresentable person. Moral qualities rule the world, but at short distances, the senses are despotic. The same discrimination of fit and fair runs out, if with less rigor, into all parts of life. The average spirit of the energetic class is good sense, acting under certain limitations and to certain ends. It entertains every natural gift. Social in its nature, it respects everything which tends to unite men. It delights in measure. The love of beauty is mainly the love of measure or proportion. The person who screams, or uses the superlative degree, or converses with heat, puts whole drawing-rooms to flight. If you wish to be loved, love measure. You must have genius, or a prodigious usefulness, if you will hide the want of measure. This perception comes in to polish and perfect the parts of the social instruments. Society will pardon much to genius and special gifts, but, being in its nature a convention, it loves what is conventional, or what belongs to coming together. That makes the good and bad of manners, namely, what helps or hinders fellowship. For, fashion is not good sense absolute, but relative; not good sense private, but good sense entertaining company. It hates corners and sharp points of character, hates quarrelsome, egotistical, solitary, and gloomy people; hates whatever can interfere with total blending of parties; whilst it values all peculiarities as in the highest degree refreshing, which can consist with good fellowship. And besides the general infusion of wit to heighten civility, the direct splendor of intellectual power is ever welcome in fine society as the costliest addition to its rule and its credit.

The dry light must shine in to adorn our festival, but it must be tempered and shaded, or that will also offend. Accuracy is essential to beauty, and quick perceptions to politeness, but not too quick perceptions. One may be too punctual and too precise. He must leave the omniscience of business at the door, when he comes into the palace of beauty. Society loves creole natures, and sleepy, languishing manners, so that they cover sense, grace, and goodwill; the air of drowsy strength, which disarms criticism; perhaps because such a person seems to reserve himself for the best of the game, and not spend himself on surfaces; an ignoring eye, which does not see the annoyances, shifts and inconvenience, that cloud the brow and smother the voice of the sensitive.

Therefore, besides personal force and so much per-

ception as constitutes unerring taste, society demands
in its patrician class, another element already intimated,
which it significantly terms good-nature, expressing all
degrees of generosity, from the lowest willingness and
faculty to oblige, up to the heights of magnanimity and
love. Insight we must have, or we shall run against
one another, and miss the way to our food; but intellect is selfish and barren. The secret of success in
society, is a certain heartiness and sympathy. A man
who is not happy in the company, cannot find any word
in his memory that will fit the occasion. All his information is a little impertinent. A man who is happy
there, finds in every turn of the conversation equally
lucky occasions for the introduction of that which he
has to say. The favorites of society and what it calls
whole souls, are able men, and of more spirit than wit,
who have no uncomfortable egotism, but who exactly
fill the hour and the company, contented and contenting,
at a marriage or a funeral, a ball or a jury, a water-
party or a shooting-match. England, which is rich
in gentlemen, furnished, in the beginning of the present
century, a good model of that genius which the world
loves, in Mr. Fox, who added to his great abilities the
most social disposition, and real love of men. Parlia-
mentary history has few better passages than the debate, in which Burke and Fox separated in the House
of Commons; when Fox urged on his old friend the
claims of old friendship with such tenderness, that the
house was moved to tears. Another anecdote is so
close to my matter, that I must hazard the story. A
tradesman who had long dunned him for a note of
three hundred guineas, found him one day counting

gold, and demanded payment: "No," said Fox, "I owe this money to Sheridan: it is a debt of honor: if an accident should happen to me, he has nothing to show." "Then," said the creditor, "I change my debt into a debt of honor," and tore the note in pieces. Fox thanked the man for his confidence, and paid him, saying, "his debt was of older standing, and Sheridan must wait." Lover of Liberty, friend of the Hindoo, friend of the African slave, he possessed a great personal popularity; and Napoleon said of him on the occasion of his visit to Paris, in 1805, "Mr. Fox will always hold the first place in an assembly at the Tuileries."

We may easily seem ridiculous in our eulogy of courtesy, whenever we insist on benevolence as its foundation. The painted phantasm Fashion rises to cast a species of derision on what we say. But I will neither be driven from some allowance to Fashion as a symbolic institution, nor from the belief that love is the basis of courtesy. We must obtain *that,* if we can; but by all means we must affirm *this.* Life owes much of its spirit to these sharp contrasts. Fashion which affects to be honor, is often, in all men's experience, only a ballroom-code. Yet, so long as it is the highest circle, in the imagination of the best heads on the planet, there is something necessary and excellent in it; for it is not to be supposed that men have agreed to be the dupes of anything preposterous; and the respect which these mysteries inspire in the most rude and sylvan characters, and the curiosity with which details of high life are read, betray the universality of the love of cultivated manners. I know that a comic disparity would be felt, if we should enter the acknowledged "first circles" and apply these terrific standards of justice, beauty, and benefit to the individuals actually found there. Monarchs and heroes, sages and lovers, these gallants are not. Fashion has many classes and many rules of probation and admission; and not the best alone. There is not only the right of conquest, which genius pretends,—the individual, demonstrating his natural aristocracy best of the best;—but less claims will pass for the time; for Fashion loves lions, and points like Circe, to her horned company. This gentleman is this afternoon arrived from Denmark; and that is my Lord Ride, who came yesterday from Bagdat; here is Captain Friese, from Cape Turnagain; and Captain Symmes, from the interior of the earth; and Monsieur Jovaire, who came down this morning in a balloon; Mr. Hobnail, the reformer; and Reverend Jul Bat, who has converted the whole torrid zone in his Sunday-school; and Signor Torre del Greco, who extinguished Vesuvius by pouring into it the Bay of Naples; Spahi, the Persian ambassador; and Tul Wil Shan, the exiled nabob of Nepaul, whose saddle is the new moon.—But these are monsters of one day, and to-morrow will be dismissed to their holes and dens; for, in these rooms, every chair is waited for. The artist, the scholar, and, in general, the clerisy, wins its way up into these places, and gets represented here, somewhat on this footing of conquest. Another mode is to pass through all the degrees, spending a year and a day in St. Michael's Square, being steeped in Cologne water, and perfumed, and dined, and introduced, and properly grounded in all the biography, and politics, and anecdotes of the boudoirs.

Yet these fineries may have grace and wit. Let there be grotesque sculpture about the gates and offices of temples. Let the creed and commandments even have the saucy homage of parody. The forms of politeness universally express benevolence in superlative degrees. What if they are in the mouths of selfish men, and used as means of selfishness? What if the false gentleman almost bows the true out of the world? What if the false gentleman contrives so to address his companion, as civilly to exclude all others from his discourse, and also to make them feel excluded? Real service will not lose its nobleness. All generosity is not merely French and sentimental; nor is it to be concealed, that living blood and a passion of kindness does at last distinguish God's gentleman from Fashion's. The epitaph of Sir Jenkin Grout is not wholly unintelligible to the present age. "Here lies Sir Jenkin Grout, who loved his friend, and persuaded his enemy: what his mouth ate, his hand paid for: what his servants robbed, he restored: if a woman gave him pleasure, he supported her in pain: he never forgot his children: and whoso touched his finger, drew after it his whole body." Even the line of heroes is not utterly extinct. There is still ever some admirable person in plain clothes, standing on the wharf, who jumps in to rescue a drowning man; there is still some absurd inventor of charities; some guide and comforter of runaway slaves; some friend of Poland; some Philhellene; some fanatic who plants shade-trees for the second and third generation, and orchards when he is grown old; some well-concealed piety; some just man happy in an ill-fame; some youth ashamed of the favors of fortune, and impatiently casting them on other shoulders. And these are the centres of society, on which it returns for fresh impulses. These are the creators of Fashion, which is an attempt to organize beauty of behavior. The beautiful and the generous are, in the theory, the doctors and apostles of this church: Scipio, and the Cid, and Sir Philip Sidney, and Washington, and every pure and valiant heart, who worshipped Beauty by word and by deed. The persons who constitute the natural aristocracy, are not found in the actual aristocracy, or, only on its edge; as the chemical energy of the spectrum is found to be greatest just outside of the spectrum. Yet that is the infirmity of the seneschals, who do not know their sovereign, when he appears. The theory of society supposes the existence and sovereignty of these. It divines afar off their coming. It says with the elder gods,—

As Heaven and Earth are fairer far
Than Chaos and blank Darkness, though once chiefs;
And as we show beyond that Heaven and Earth,
In form and shape compact and beautiful;
So, on our heels a fresh perfection treads;
A power, more strong in beauty, born of us,
And fated to excel us, as we pass
In glory that old Darkness:
———————— for, 'tis the eternal law,
That first in beauty shall be first in might.

Therefore, within the ethnical circle of good society, there is a narrower and higher circle, concentration of its light, and flower of courtesy, to which there is always a tacit appeal of pride and reference, as to its inner and imperial court, the parliament of love and chivalry. And this is constituted of those persons in whom heroic dispositions are native, with the love of beauty, the delight in society, and the power to embellish the passing day. If the individuals who compose the purest circles of aristocracy in Europe, the guarded blood of centuries, should pass in review, in such manner as that we could, at leisure, and critically inspect their behavior, we might find no gentleman, and no lady; for, although excellent specimens of courtesy and high-breeding would gratify us in the assemblage, in the particulars, we should detect offence. Because, elegance comes of no breeding, but of birth. There must be romance of character, or the most fastidious exclusion of impertinencies will not avail. It must be genius which takes that direction: it must be not courteous, but courtesy. High behavior is as rare in fiction, as it is in fact. Scott is praised for the fidelity with which he painted the demeanor and conversation of the superior classes. Certainly, kings and queens, nobles and great ladies, had some right to complain of the absurdity that had been put in their mouths, before the days of Waverley; but neither does Scott's dialogue bear criticism. His lords brave each other in smart epigrammatic speeches, but the dialogue is in costume, and does not please on the second reading: it is not warm with life. In Shakspeare alone, the speakers do not strut and bridle, the dialogue is easily great, and he adds to so many titles that of being the best-bred man in England and in Christendom. Once or twice in a lifetime we are permitted to enjoy the charm of noble manners, in the presence of a man or woman who have no bar in their nature, but whose character emanates freely in their word and gesture.   A beautiful form is better than a beautiful face; a beautiful behavior is better than a beautiful form: it gives a higher pleasure than statues or pictures; it is the finest of the fine arts.   A man is but a little thing in the midst of the objects of nature, yet, by the moral quality radiating from his countenance, he may abolish all considerations of magnitude, and in his manners equal the majesty of the world.   I have seen an individual, whose manners, though wholly within the conventions of elegant society, were never learned there, but were original and commanding, and held out protection and prosperity; one who did not need the aid of a court-suit, but carried the holiday in his eye; who exhilarated the fancy by flinging wide the doors of new modes of existence; who shook off the captivity of etiquette, with happy, spirited bearing, good-natured and free as Robin Hood; yet with the port of an emperor,—if need be, calm, serious, and fit to stand the gaze of millions.

The open air and the fields, the street and public chambers, are the places where Man executes his will; let him yield or divide the sceptre at the door of the house.   Woman, with her instinct of behavior, instantly detects in man a love of trifles, any coldness or imbecility, or, in short, any want of that large, flowing, and magnanimous deportment, which is indispensable as an exterior in the hall.   Our American institutions have been friendly to her, and at this moment, I esteem it a chief felicity of this country, that it excels in women. A certain awkward consciousness of inferiority in the men, may give rise to the new chivalry in behalf of Woman's Rights. Certainly, let her be as much better placed in the laws and in social forms, as the most zealous reformer can ask, but I confide so entirely in her inspiring and musical nature, that I believe only herself can show us how she shall be served. The wonderful generosity of her sentiments raises her at times into heroical and godlike regions, and verifies the pictures of Minerva, Juno, or Polymnia; and, by the firmness with which she treads her upward path, she convinces the coarsest calculators that another road exists, than that which their feet know. But besides those who make good in our imagination the place of muses and of Delphic Sibyls, are there not women who fill our vase with wine and roses to the brim, so that the wine runs over and fills the house with perfume; who inspire us with courtesy; who unloose our tongues, and we speak; who anoint our eyes, and we see? We say things we never thought to have said; for once, our walls of habitual reserve vanished, and left us at large; we were children playing with children in a wide field of flowers. Steep us, we cried, in these influences, for days, for weeks, and we shall be sunny poets, and will write out in many-colored words the romance that you are. Was it Hafiz or Firdousi that said of his Persian Lilla, She was an elemental force, and astonished me by her amount of life, when I saw her day after day radiating, every instant, redundant joy and grace on all around her. She was a solvent powerful to reconcile all heterogeneous persons into one society: like air or water, an element of such a great range of affinities, that it combines readily with a thousand substances. Where she is present, all others will be more than they are wont. She was a unit and whole, so that whatsoever she did, became her. She had too much sympathy and desire to please, than that you could say, her manners were marked with dignity, yet no princess could surpass her clear and erect demeanor on each occasion. She did not study the Persian grammar, nor the books of the seven poets, but all the poems of the seven seemed to be written upon her. For, though the bias of her nature was not to thought, but to sympathy, yet was she so perfect in her own nature, as to meet intellectual persons by the fulness of her heart, warming them by her sentiments; believing, as she did, that by dealing nobly with all, all would show themselves noble.

I know that this Byzantine pile of chivalry or Fashion, which seems so fair and picturesque to those who look at the contemporary facts for science or for entertainment, is not equally pleasant to all spectators. The constitution of our society makes it a giant's castle to the ambitious youth who have not found their names enrolled in its Golden Book, and whom it has excluded from its coveted honors and privileges. They have yet to learn that its seeming grandeur is shadowy and relative: it is great by their allowance: its proudest gates will fly open at the approach of their courage and virtue. For the present distress, however, of those who are predisposed to suffer from the tyrannies of this caprice, there are easy remedies. To remove your residence a couple of miles, or at most four, will com-

monly relieve the most extreme susceptibility. For,
the advantages which fashion values, are plants which
thrive in very confined localities, in a few streets,
namely. Out of this precinct, they go for nothing; are
of no use in the farm, in the forest, in the market, in
war, in the nuptial society, in the literary or scientific
circle, at sea, in friendship, in the heaven of thought
or virtue.

But we have lingered long enough in these painted
courts. The worth of the thing signified must vindicate our taste for the emblem. Everything that is
called fashion and courtesy humbles itself before the
cause and fountain of honor, creator of titles and dig-
nities, namely, the heart of love. This is the royal
blood, this is the fire, which, in all countries and con-
tingencies, will work after its kind, and conquer and
expand all that approaches it. This gives new meanings to every fact. This impoverishes the rich, suffering no grandeur but its own. What *is* rich? Are
you rich enough to help anybody? to succor the unfashionable and the eccentric? rich enough to make the
Canadian in his wagon, the itinerant with his consul's
paper which commends him "To the charitable," the
swarthy Italian with his few broken words of English, the lame pauper hunted by overseers from town to
town, even the poor insane or besotted wreck of man
or woman, feel the noble exception of your presence
and your house, from the general bleakness and stoni-
ness; to make such feel that they were greeted with a
voice which made them both remember and hope?
What is vulgar, but to refuse the claim on acute and
conclusive reasons? What is gentle, but to allow it,

and give their heart and yours one holiday from the national caution? Without the rich heart, wealth is an ugly beggar. The king of Schiraz could not afford to be so bountiful as the poor Osman who dwelt at his gate. Osman had a humanity so broad and deep, that although his speech was so bold and free with the Koran, as to disgust all the dervishes, yet was there never a poor outcast, eccentric, or insane man, some fool who had cut off his beard, or who had been mutilated under a vow, or had a pet madness in his brain, but fled at once to him,—that great heart lay there so sunny and hospitable in the centre of the country, that it seemed as if the instinct of all sufferers drew them to his side. And the madness which he harbored, he did not share. Is not this to be rich? this only to be rightly rich?

But I shall hear without pain, that I play the courtier very ill, and talk of that which I do not well understand. It is easy to see, that what is called by distinction society and fashion, has good laws as well as bad, has much that is necessary, and much that is absurd. Too good for banning, and too bad for blessing, it reminds us of a tradition of the pagan mythology, in any attempt to settle its character. "I overheard Jove, one day," said Silenus, "talking of destroying the earth; he said, it had failed; they were all rogues and vixens, who went from bad to worse, as fast as the days succeeded each other. Minerva said, she hoped not; they were only ridiculous little creatures, with this odd circumstance, that they had a blur, or indeterminate aspect, seen far or seen near; if you called them bad, they would appear so; if you called them good, they would appear so; and there was no one person or action among them, which would not puzzle her owl, much all Olympus, to know whether it was fundamentally bad or good."

GIFTS

Gifts of one who loved me,—
'Twas high time they came;
When he ceased to love me,
Time they stopped for shame.

IT is said that the world is in a state of bankruptcy,
that the world owes the world more than the world
can pay, and ought to go into chancery, and be
sold. I do not think this general insolvency, which in-
volves in some sort all the population, to be the reason
of the difficulty experienced at Christmas and New
Year, and other times, in bestowing gifts; since it is
always so pleasant to be generous, though very vex-
atious to pay debts. But the impediment lies in the
choosing. If, at any time, it comes into my head, that
a present is due from me to somebody, I am puzzled
what to give, until the opportunity is gone. Flowers
and fruits are always fit presents; flowers, because they
are a proud assertion that a ray of beauty outvalues
all the utilities of the world. These gay natures contrast with the somewhat stern countenance of ordinary nature: they are like music heard out of a work-
house. Nature does not cocker us: we are children,
not pets: she is not fond: everything is dealt to us
without fear or favor, after severe universal laws. Yet

these delicate flowers look like the frolic and interference of love and beauty. Men use to tell us that we
love flattery, even though we are not deceived by it,
because it shows that we are of importance enough to
be courted. Something like that pleasure, the flowers
give us: what am I to whom these sweet hints are addressed? Fruits are acceptable gifts, because they are
the flower of commodities, and admit of fantastic values being attached to them. If a man should send to
me to come a hundred miles to visit him, and should
set before me a basket of fine summer-fruit, I should
think there was some proportion between the labor and
the reward.

For common gifts, necessity makes pertinences and
beauty every day, and one is glad when an imperative
leaves him no option, since if the man at the door
have no shoes, you have not to consider whether you
could procure him a paint box. And as it is always
pleasing to see a man eat bread, or drink water, in the
house or out of doors, so it is always a great satisfaction to supply these first wants. Necessity does everything well. In our condition of universal dependence,
it seems heroic to let the petitioner be the judge of his
necessity, and to give all that is asked, though at great
inconvenience. If it be a fantastic desire, it is better
to leave to others the office of punishing him. I can
think of many parts I should prefer playing to that of
the Furies. Next to things of necessity, the rule for
a gift, which one of my friends prescribed, is, that we
might convey to some person that which properly be-
longed to his character, and was easily associated with
him in thought. But our tokens of compliment and

love are for the most part barbarous. Rings and other jewels are not gifts, but apologies for gifts. The only gift is a portion of thyself. Thou must bleed for me. Therefore the poet brings his poem; the shepherd, his lamb; the farmer, corn; the miner, a gem; the sailor, coral and shells; the painter, his picture; the girl, a handkerchief of her own sewing. This is right and pleasing, for it restores society in so far to its primary basis, when a man's biography is conveyed in his gifts, and every man's wealth is an index of his merit. But it is a cold, lifeless business when you go to the shops to buy me something, which does not represent your life and talent, but a goldsmith's. This is fit for kings, and rich men who represent kings, and a false state of property, to make presents of gold and silver stuffs, as a kind of symbolical sin-offering, or payment of black-mail.

The law of benefits is a difficult channel, which requires careful sailing, or rude boats. It is not the office of a man to receive gifts. How dare you give them? We wish to be self-sustained. We do not quite forgive a giver. The hand that feeds us is in some danger of being bitten. We can receive anything from love, for that is a way of receiving it from ourselves; but not from any one who assumes to bestow. We sometimes hate the meat which we eat, because there seems something of degrading dependence in living by it.

> Brother, if Jove to thee a present make,
> Take heed that from his hands thou nothing take.

We ask the whole. Nothing less will content us. We arraign society, if it do not give us besides earth, and fire, and water, opportunity, love, reverence, and objects of veneration.

He is a good man, who can receive a gift well. We are either glad or sorry at a gift, and both emotions are unbecoming. Some violence, I think, is done, some degradation borne, when I rejoice or grieve at a gift. I am sorry when my independence is invaded, or when a gift comes from such as do not know my spirit, and so the act is not supported; and if the gift pleases me overmuch, then I should be ashamed that the donor should read my heart, and see that I love his commodity and not him. The gift, to be true, must be the flowing of the giver unto me, correspondent to my flowing unto him. When the waters are at level, then my goods pass to him, and his to me. All his are mine, all mine his. I say to him, How can you give me this pot of oil, or this flagon of wine, when all your oil and wine is mine, which belief of mine this gift seems to deny? Hence the fitness of beautiful, not useful things for gifts. This giving is flat usurpation, and therefore when the beneficiary is ungrateful, as all beneficiaries hate all Timons, not at all considering the value of the gift, but looking back to the greater store it was taken from, I rather sympathize with the beneficiary, than with the anger of my lord Timon. For, the expectation of gratitude is mean, and is continually punished by the total insensibility of the obliged person. It is a great happiness to get off without injury and heart-burning, from one who has had the ill luck to be served by you.   It is a very onerous business, this of being served, and the debtor naturally wishes to give you a slap.   A golden text for these gentlemen is that which I so admire in the Buddhist, who never thanks, and who says, "Do not flatter your benefactors."

The reason of these discords I conceive to be, that there is no commensurability between a man and any gift.   You cannot give anything to a magnanimous person.   After you have served him, he at once puts you in debt by his magnanimity.   The service a man renders his friend is trivial and selfish, compared with the service he knows his friend stood in readiness to yield him, alike before he had begun to serve his friend, and now also.   Compared with that good-will I bear my friend, the benefit it is in my power to render him seems small.   Besides, our action on each other, good as well as evil, is so incidental and at random, that we can seldom hear the acknowledgments of any person who would thank us for a benefit, without some shame and humiliation.   We can rarely strike a direct stroke, but must be content with an oblique one; we seldom have the satisfaction of yielding a direct benefit, which is directly received.   But rectitude scatters favors on every side without knowing it, and receives with wonder the thanks of all people.

I fear to breathe any treason against the majesty of love, which is the genius and god of gifts, and to whom we must not affect to prescribe.   Let him give kingdoms or flower-leaves indifferently.   There are persons, from whom we always expect fairy tokens; let us not cease to expect them.   This is prerogative, and

not to be limited by our municipal rules. For the rest,
I like to see that we cannot be bought and sold. The
best of hospitality and of generosity is also not in the
will but in fate. I find that I am not much to you;
you do not need me; you do not feel me; then am I
thrust out of doors, though you proffer me house and
lands. No services are of any value, but only likeness.
When I have attempted to join myself to others by
services, it proved an intellectual trick,—no more.
They eat your service like apples, and leave you out.
But love them, and they feel you, and delight in you
all the time.

NATURE

The rounded world is fair to see,
Nine times folded in mystery:
Though baffled seers cannot impart
The secret of its laboring heart,
Throb thine with Nature's throbbing breast
And all is clear from east to west.
Spirit that lurks each form within
Beckons to spirit of its kin;
Self-kindled every atom glows,
And hints the future which it owes.

THERE are days which occur in this climate, at almost any season of the year, wherein the world reaches its perfection, when the air, the heavenly bodies, and the earth, make a harmony, as if nature would indulge her offspring; when, in these bleak upper sides of the planet, nothing is to desire that we have heard of the happiest latitudes, and we bask in the shining hours of Florida and Cuba; when everything that has life gives sign of satisfaction, and the cattle that lie on the ground seem to have great and tranquil thoughts. These halcyons may be looked for with a little more assurance in that pure October weather, which we distinguish by the name of the Indian Summer. The day, immeasurably long, sleeps over the broad hills and warm wide fields. To have lived through all its sunny hours, seems longevity enough. The solitary places do not seem quite lonely. At the gates of the forest, the surprised man of the world is forced to leave his city estimates of great and small, wise and foolish. The knapsack of custom falls off his back with the first step he makes into these precincts. Here is sanctity which shames our religions, and reality which discredits our heroes. Here we find nature to be the circumstance which dwarfs every other circumstance, and judges like a god all men that come to her. We have crept out of our close and crowded houses into the night and morning, and we see what majestic beauties daily wrap us in their bosom. How willingly we would escape the barriers which render them comparatively impotent, escape the sophistication and second thought, and suffer nature to entrance us. The tempered light of the woods is like a perpetual morning, and is stimulating and heroic. The anciently reported spells of these places creep on us. The stems of pines, hemlocks, and oaks, almost gleam like iron on the excited eye. The incommunicable trees begin to persuade us to live with them, and quit our life of solemn trifles. Here no history, or church, or state, is interpolated on the divine sky and the immortal year. How easily we might walk onward into the opening landscape, absorbed by new pictures, and by thoughts fast succeeding each other, until by degrees the recollection of home was crowded out of the mind, all memory obliterated by the tyranny of the present, and we were led in triumph by nature.

These enchantments are medicinal, they sober and heal us. These are plain pleasures, kindly and native to us. We come to our own, and make friends with matter, which the ambitious chatter of the schools would persuade us to despise. We never can part with it; the mind loves its old home: as water to our thirst, so is the rock, the ground, to our eyes, and hands, and feet. It is firm water: it is cold flame: what health, what affinity! Ever an old friend, ever like a dear friend and brother, when we chat affectedly with strangers, comes in this honest face, and takes a grave liberty with us, and shames us out of our nonsense. Cities give not the human senses room enough. We go out daily and nightly to feed the eyes on the horizon, and require so much scope, just as we need water for our bath. There are all degrees of natural influence, from these quarantine powers of nature, up to her dearest and gravest ministrations to the imagination and the soul. There is the bucket of cold water from the spring, the wood-fire to which the chilled traveller rushes for safety,—and there is the sublime moral of autumn and of noon. We nestle in nature, and draw our living as parasites from her roots and grains, and we receive glances from the heavenly bodies, which call us to solitude, and foretell the remotest future. The blue zenith is the point in which romance and reality meet. I think, if we should be rapt away into all that we dream of heaven, and should converse with Gabriel and Uriel, the upper sky would be all that would remain of our furniture.

It seems as if the day was not wholly profane, in which we have given heed to some natural object. The fall of snowflakes in a still air, preserving to each crystal its perfect form; the blowing of sleet over

a wide sheet of water, and over plains, the waving
rye-field, the mimic waving of acres of houstonia,
whose innumerable florets whiten and ripple before the
eye; the reflections of trees and flowers in glassy lakes;
the musical steaming odorous south wind, which converts all trees to windharps; the crackling and spurting
of hemlock in the flames; or of pine logs, which yield
glory to the walls and faces in the sitting-room,—
these are the music and pictures of the most ancient
religion. My house stands in low land, with limited
outlook, and on the skirt of the village. But I go with
my friend to the shore of our little river; and with one
stroke of the paddle, I leave the village politics and
personalities, yes, and the world of villages and personalities behind, and pass into a delicate realm of sunset and moonlight, too bright almost for spotted man
to enter without noviciate and probation. We pene-
trate bodily this incredible beauty: we dip our hands in
this painted element: our eyes are bathed in these lights
and forms. A holiday, a villeggiatura, a royal revel,
the proudest, most heart-rejoicing festival that valor
and beauty, power and taste, ever decked and enjoyed,
establishes itself on the instant. These sunset clouds,
these delicately emerging stars, with their private and
ineffable glances, signify it and proffer it. I am taught
the poorness of our invention, the ugliness of towns
and palaces. Art and luxury have early learned that
they must work as enchantment and sequel to this original beauty. I am over-instructed for my return.
Henceforth I shall be hard to please. I cannot go
back to toys. I am grown expensive and sophisticated.
I can no longer live without elegance: but a countryman

shall be my master of revels.   He who knows the most, he who knows what sweets and virtues are in the ground, the waters, the plants, the heavens, and how to come at these enchantments, is the rich and royal man.   Only as far as the masters of the world have called in nature to their aid, can they reach the height of magnificence.   This is the meaning of their hanging-gardens, villas, garden-houses, islands, parks, and preserves, to back their faulty personality with these strong accessories.   I do not wonder that the landed interest should be invincible in the state with these dangerous auxiliaries.   These bribe and invite; not kings, not palaces, not men, not women, but these tender and poetic stars, eloquent of secret promises.   We heard what the rich man said, we knew of his villa, his grove, his wine, and his company, but the provocation and point of the invitation came out of these beguiling stars.   In their soft glances, I see what men strove to realize in some Versailles, or Paphos, or Ctesiphon.   Indeed, it is the magical lights of the horizon, and the blue sky for the background, which save all our works of art, which were otherwise bawbles. When the rich tax the poor with servility and obsequiousness, they should consider the effect of men reputed to be the possessors of nature, on imaginative minds. Ah! if the rich were rich as the poor fancy riches! A boy hears a military band play on the field at night, and he has kings and queens, and famous chivalry palpably before him.   He hears the echoes of a horn in a hill country, in the Notch Mountains, for example, which converts the mountains into an Æolian harp, and this supernatural *tiralira* restores to him the Dorian mythology, Apollo, Diana, and all divine hunters and huntresses. Can a musical note be so lofty, so haughtily beautiful! To the poor young poet, thus fabulous is his picture of society; he is loyal; he respects the rich; they are rich for the sake of his imagination; how poor his fancy would be, if they were not rich! That they have some high-fenced grove, which they call a park; that they live in larger and better-garnished saloons than he has visited, and go in coaches, keeping only the society of the elegant, to watering-places, and to distant cities, are the groundwork from which he has delineated estates of romance, compared with which their actual possessions are shanties and paddocks. The muse herself betrays her son, and enhances the gifts of wealth and well-born beauty, by a radiation out of the air, and clouds, and forests that skirt the road,—a certain haughty favor, as if from patrician genii to patricians, a kind of aristocracy in nature, a prince of the power of the air.

The moral sensibility which makes Edens and Tempes so easily, may not be always found, but the material landscape is never far off. We can find these enchantments without visiting the Como Lake, or the Madeira Islands. We exaggerate the praises of local scenery. In every landscape, the point of astonishment is the meeting of the sky and the earth, and that is seen from the first hillock as well as from the top of the Alleghanies. The stars at night stoop down over the brownest, homeliest common, with all the spiritual magnificence which they shed on the Campagna, or on the marble deserts of Egypt. The uprolled clouds and the colors of morning and evening, will transfigure maples and alders. The difference between landscape and landscape is small, but there is great difference in the beholders. There is nothing so wonderful in any particular landscape, as the necessity of being beautiful under which every landscape lies. Nature cannot be surprised in undress. Beauty breaks in everywhere.

But it is very easy to outrun the sympathy of readers on this topic, which schoolmen called *natura naturata,* or nature passive. One can hardly speak directly of it without excess. It is as easy to broach in mixed companies what is called "the subject of religion." A susceptible person does not like to indulge his tastes in this kind, without the apology of some trivial necessity: he goes to see a wood-lot, or to look at the crops, or to fetch a plant or a mineral from a remote locality, or he carries a fowling-piece, or a fishing-rod. I suppose this shame must have a good reason. A dilettantism in nature is barren and unworthy. The fop of fields is no better than his brother of Broadway. Men are naturally hunters and inquisitive of wood-craft, and I suppose that such a gazetter as wood-cutters and Indians should furnish facts for, would take place in the most sumptuous drawing-rooms of all the "Wreaths" and "Flora's chaplets" of the bookshops; yet ordinarily, whether we are too clumsy for so subtle a topic, or from whatever cause, as soon as men begin to write on nature, they fall into euphuism. Frivolity is a most unfit tribute to Pan, who ought to be represented in the mythology as the most continent of gods. I would not be frivolous before the admirable reserve and prudence of time, yet I cannot renounce

the right of returning often to this old topic. The
multitude of false churches accredits the true religion.
Literature, poetry, science, are the homage of man to
this unfathomed secret, concerning which no sane man
can affect an indifference or incuriosity. Nature
is loved by what is best in us. It is loved as the city
of God, although, or rather because there is no citizen. The sunset is unlike anything that is underneath it: it wants men. And the beauty of nature
must always seem unreal and mocking, until the landscape has human figures, that are as good as itself.
If there were good men, there would never be this
rapture in nature. If the king is in the palace, nobody
looks at the walls. It is when he is gone, and the
house is filled with grooms and gazers, that we turn
from the people, to find relief in the majestic men that
are suggested by the pictures and the architecture.
The critics who complain of the sickly separation of
the beauty of nature from the thing to be done, must
consider that our hunting of the picturesque is inseparable from our protest against false society. Man is
fallen; nature is erect, and serves as a differential ther-
mometer, detecting the presence or absence of the divine
sentiment in man. By fault of our dullness and selfishness, we are looking up to nature, but when we are
convalescent, nature will look up to us. We see the
foaming brook with compunction: if our own life
flowed with the right energy, we should shame the
brook. The stream of zeal sparkles with real fire, and
not with reflex rays of sun and moon. Nature may
be selfishly studied as trade. Astronomy to the selfish

becomes astrology.   Psychology, mesmerism (with intent to show where our spoons are gone) ; and anatomy
and physiology, become phrenology and palmistry.

But taking timely warning, and leaving many things
unsaid on this topic, let us not longer omit our homage to the Efficient Nature, *natura naturans,* the quick
cause, before which all forms flee as the driven snows,
itself secret, its works driven before it in flocks and
multitudes, (as the ancient represented nature by Proteus, a shepherd,) and in undescribable variety.   It
publishes itself in creatures, reaching from particles
and spicula, through transformation on transformation
to the highest symmetries, arriving at consummate results without a shock or a leap.   A little heat, that is,
a little motion, is all that differences the bald, dazzling
white, and deadly cold poles of the earth from the pro-
lific tropical climates.   All changes pass without violence, by reason of the two cardinal conditions of boundless space and boundless time.   Geology has initiated us
into the secularity of nature, and taught us to disuse
our dame-school measures, and exchange our Mosaic
and Ptolemaic schemes for her large style.   We knew
nothing rightly, for want of perspective.   Now we
learn what patient periods must round themselves before the rock is formed, then before the rock is broken,
and the first lichen race has disintegrated the thinnest
external plate into soil, and opened the door for the
remote Flora, Fauna, Ceres, and Pomona, to come in.
How far off yet is the trilobite! how far the quadruped!
how inconceivably remote is man!   All duly arrive, and
then race after race of men.   It is a long way from
granite to the oyster; farther yet to Plato, and the

preaching of the immortality of the soul. Yet all must come, as surely as the first atom has two sides.

Motion or change, and identity or rest, are the first and second secrets of nature: Motion and Rest. The whole code of her laws may be written on the thumbnail, or the signet of a ring. The whirling bubble on the surface of a brook, admits us to the secret of the mechanics of the sky. Every shell on the beach is a key to it. A little water made to rotate in a cup explains the formation of the simpler shells; the addition of matter from year to year, arrives at last at the most complex form; and yet so poor is nature with all her craft, that, from the beginning to the end of the universe, she has but one stuff,—but one stuff with its two ends, to serve up all her dream-like variety. Compound it how she will, star, sand, fire, water, tree, man, it is still one stuff, and betrays the same properties.

Nature is always consistent, though she feigns to contravene her own laws. She keeps her laws, and seems to transcend them. She arms and equips an animal to find its place and living in the earth, and, at the same time, she arms and equips another animal to destroy it. Space exists to divide creatures; but by clothing the sides of a bird with a few feathers, she gives him a petty omnipresence. The direction is forever onward, but the artist still goes back for materials, and begins again with the first elements on the most advanced stage: otherwise, all goes to ruin. If we look at her work, we seem to catch a glance of a system in transition. Plants are the young of the world, vessels of health and vigor; but they grope ever upward toward consciousness; the trees are imperfect

men, and seem to bemoan their imprisonment, rooted
in the ground.   The animal is the novice and proba-
tioner of a more advanced order.   The men, though
young, having tasted the first drop from the cup of
thought, are already dissipated: the maples and ferns
are still uncorrupt; yet no doubt, when they come to
consciousness, they too will curse and swear.   Flowers so strictly belong to youth, that we adult men soon
come to feel, that their beautiful generations concern
not us: we have had our day; now let the children
have theirs.   The flowers jilt us, and we are old
bachelors with our ridiculous tenderness.

Things are so strictly related, that according to the
skill of the eye, from any one object the parts and
properties of any other may be predicted.   If we
had eyes to see it, a bit of stone from the city wall
would certify us of the necessity that man must exist,
as readily as the city.   That identity makes us all one,
and reduces to nothing great intervals on our customary scale.   We talk of deviations from natural life,
as if artificial life were not also natural.   The smooth-
est curled courtier in the boudoirs of a palace has an an
imal nature, rude and aboriginal as a white bear, om
nipotent to its own ends, and is directly related, there
amid essences and billets-doux, to Himmaleh mountain-
chains, and the axis of the globe.   If we consider how
much we are nature's, we need not be superstitious about
towns, as if that terrific or benefic force did not find us
there also, and fashion cities.   Nature who made the
mason, made the house.   We may easily hear too much
of rural influences.   The cool disengaged air of natural
objects, makes them enviable to us, chafed and irritable

creatures with red faces, and we think we shall be as grand as they, if we camp out and eat roots; but let us be men instead of wookchucks, and the oak and the elm shall gladly serve us, though we sit in chairs of ivory on carpets of silk.

This guilding identity runs through all the surprises and contrasts of the piece, and characterizes every law. Man carries the world in his head, the whole astronomy and chemistry suspended in a thought. Because the history of nature is charactered in his brain, therefore is he the prophet and discoverer of her secrets. Every known fact in natural science was divined by the presentiment of somebody, before it was actually verified. A man does not tie his shoe without recognizing laws which bind the farthest regions of nature: moon, plant, gas, crystal, are concrete geometry and numbers. Common sense knows its own, and recognizes the fact at first sight in chemical experiment. The common sense of Franklin, Dalton, Davy, and Black, is the same common sense which made the arrangements which now it discovers.

If the identity expresses organized rest, the counter action runs also into organization. The astronomers said, "Give us matter, and a little motion, and we will construct the universe. It is not enough that we should have matter, we must also have a single impulse, one shove to launch the mass, and generate the harmony of the centrifugal and centripetal forces. Once heave the ball from the hand, and we can show how all this mighty order grew."—"A very unreasonable postulate," said the metaphysicians, "and a plain begging of the question. Could you not prevail to know the genesis of projection, as well as the continuation of it?" Nature, meanwhile, had not waited for the discussion, but, right or wrong, bestowed the impulse, and the balls rolled. It was no great affair, a mere push, but the astronomers were right in making much of it, for there is no end to the consequences of the act. That famous aboriginal push propagates itself through all the balls of the system, and through every atom of every ball, through all the races of creatures, and through the history and performances of every individual. Exaggeration is in the course of things. Nature sends no creature, no man into the world, without adding a small excess of his proper quality. Given the planet, it is still necessary to add the impulse; so, to every creature nature added a little violence of direction in its proper path, a shove to put it on its way; in every instance, a slight generosity, a drop too much. Without electricity the air would rot, and without this violence of direction, which men and women have, without a spice of bigot and fanatic, no excitement, no efficiency. We aim above the mark, to hit the mark. Every act hath some falsehood of exaggeration in it. And when now and then comes along some sad, sharp-eyed man, who sees how paltry a game is played, and refuses to play, but blabs the secret;—how then? is the bird flown? O no, the wary Nature sends a new troop of fairer forms, of lordlier youths, with a little more excess of direction to hold them fast to their several aim; makes them a little wrong-headed in that direction in which they are rightest, and on goes the game again with new whirl, for a generation or two

more. The child with his sweet pranks, the fool of his
senses, commanded by every sight and sound, without
any power to compare and rank his sensations, aban-
doned to a whistle or a painted chip, to a lead dragoon,
or a gingerbread-dog, individualizing everything, generalizing nothing, delighted with every new thing, lies
down at night overpowered by the fatigue, which this
day of continual pretty madness has incurred. But
Nature has answered her purpose with the curly, dim-
pled lunatic. She has tasked every faculty, and has
secured the symmetrical growth of the bodily frame,
by all these attitudes and exertions,—an end of the
first importance, which could not be trusted to any
care less perfect than her own. This glitter, this opaline lustre plays round the top of every toy to his eye, to
ensure his fidelity, and he is deceived to his good. We
are made alive and kept alive by the same arts. Let
the stoics say what they please, we do not eat for the
good of living, but because the meat is savory and the
appetite is keen. The vegetable life does not content
itself with casting from the flower or the tree a single
seed, but it fills the air and earth with a prodigality of
seeds, that, if thousands perish, thousands may plant
themselves, that hundreds may come up, that tens may
live to maturity, that, at least, one may replace the parent. All things betray the same calculated profusion.
The excess of fear with which the animal frame is
hedged round, shrinking from cold, starting at sight
of a snake, or at a sudden noise, protects us, through
a multitude of groundless alarms, from some one real
danger at last. The lover seeks in marriage his pri-

vate felicity and perfection, with no prospective end;
and nature hides in his happiness her own end, namely,
progeny, or the perpetuity of the race.

But the craft with which the world is made, runs
also into the mind and character of men. No man is
quite sane; each has a vein of folly in his composition, a slight determination of blood to the head, to
make sure of holding him hard to some one point
which nature had taken to heart. Great causes are
never tried on their merits; but the cause is reduced
to particulars to suit the size of the partisans, and
the contention is ever hottest on minor matters. Not
less remarkable is the overfaith of each man in the importance of what he has to do or say. The poet,
the prophet, has a higher value for what he utters than
any hearer, and therefore it gets spoken. The strong,
self-complacent Luther declares with an emphasis, not
to be mistaken, that "God himself cannot do without
wise men." Jacob Behmen and George Fox betray
their egotism in the pertinacity of their controversial
tracts, and James Naylor once suffered himself to be
worshipped as the Christ. Each prophet comes presently to identify himself with his thought, and to esteem
his hat and shoes sacred. However this may discredit
such persons with the judicious, it helps them with the
people, as it gives heat, pungency, and publicity to their
words. A similar experience is not infrequent in private life. Each young and ardent person writes a di-
ary, in which, when the hours of prayer and penitence
arrive, he inscribes his soul. The pages thus written
are, to him, burning and fragrant: he reads them on
his knees by midnight and by the morning star; he

wets them with his tears: they are sacred; too good for the world, and hardly yet to be shown to the dearest friend. This is the man-child that is born to the soul, and her life still circulates in the babe. The umbilical cord has not yet been cut. After some time has elapsed, he begins to wish to admit his friend to this hallowed experience, and with hesitation, yet with firmness, exposes the pages to his eye. Will they not burn his eyes? The friend coldly turns them over, and passes from the writing to conversation, with easy transition, which strikes the other party with astonishment and vexation. He cannot suspect the writing itself. Days and nights of fervid life, of communion with angels of darkness and of light, have engraved their shadowy characters on that tear-stained book. He suspects the intelligence or the heart of his friend. Is there then no friend? He cannot yet credit that one may have impressive experience, and yet may not know how to put his private fact into literature; and perhaps the discovery that wisdom has other tongues and ministers than we, that though we should hold our peace, the truth would not the less be spoken, might check injuriously the flame of our zeal. A man can only speak, so long as he does not feel his speech to be partial and inadequate. It is partial, but he does not see it to be so, whilst he utters it. As soon as he is released from the instinctive and particular, and sees its partiality, he shuts his mouth in disgust. For, no man can write anything, who does not think that what he writes is for the time the history of the world; or do anything well, who does not esteem his work to be of importance. My work may be of none, but I must not think it of none, or I shall not do it with impunity.

In like manner, there is throughout nature something mocking, something that leads us on and on, but arrives nowhere, keeps no faith with us. All promise outruns the performance. We live in a system of approximations. Every end is prospective of some other end, which is also temporary; a round and final success nowhere. We are encamped in nature, not domesticated. Hunger and thirst lead us on to eat and to drink; but bread and wine, mix and cook them how you will, leave us hungry and thirsty, after the stomach is full. It is the same with all our arts and performances. Our music, our poetry, our language itself are not satisfactions, but suggestions. The hunger for wealth, which reduces the planet to a garden, fools the eager pursuer. What is the end sought? Plainly to secure the ends of good sense and beauty, from the intrusion of deformity or vulgarity of any kind. But what an operose method! What a train of means to secure a little conversation! This palace of brick and stone, these servants, this kitchen, these stables, horses and equipage, this bank-stock, and file of mortgages; trade to all the world, country-house and cottage by the waterside, all for a little conversation, high, clear, and spiritual! Could it not be had as well by beggars on the highway? No, all these things came from successive efforts of these beggars to remove friction from the wheels of life, and give opportunity. Conversation, character, were the avowed ends; wealth was good as it appeased the animal cravings, cured the smoky chimney, silenced the creaking door, brought friends together in a warm and quiet room, and kept the children and the dinner-table in a different apartment. Thought, virtue, beauty, were the ends; but it was known that men of thought and virtue sometimes had the headache, or wet feet, or could lose good time whilst the room was getting warm in winter days. Unluckily, in the exertions necessary to remove these inconveniences, the main attention has been diverted to this object; the old aims have been lost sight of, and to remove friction has come to be the end. That is the ridicule of rich men, and Boston, London, Vienna, and now the governments generally of the world, are cities and governments of the rich, and the masses are not men, but *poor men,* that is, men who would be rich; this is the ridicule of the class, that they arrive with pains and sweat and fury nowhere; when all is done, it is for nothing. They are like one who has interrupted the conversation of a company to make his speech, and now has forgotten what he went to say. The appearance strikes the eye everywhere of an aimless society, of aimless nations. Were the ends of nature so great and cogent, as to exact this immense sacrifice of men?

Quite analogous to the deceits in life, there is, as might be expected, a similar effect on the eye from the face of external nature. There is in woods and waters a certain enticement and flattery, together with a failure to yield a present satisfaction. This disappointment is felt in every landscape. I have seen the softness and beauty of the summer-clouds floating feathery overhead, enjoying, as it seemed, their height and privilege of motion, whilst yet they appeared not so much the drapery of this place and hour, as for looking to some pavilions and gardens of festivity beyond. It is an odd jealousy: but the poet finds himself not near enough to his object. The pine-tree, the river, the bank of flowers before him, does not seem to be nature. Nature is still elsewhere. This or this is but outskirt and far-off reflection and echo of the triumph that has passed by, and is now at its glancing splendor and heyday, perchance in the neighboring fields, or, if you stand in the field, then in the adjacent woods. The present object shall give you this sense of stillness that follows a pageant which has just gone by. What splendid distance, what recesses of ineffable pomp and loveliness in the sunset! But who can go where they are, or lay his hand or plant his foot thereon? Off they fall from the round world forever and ever. It is the same among the men and women, as among the silent trees, always a referred existence, an absence, never a presence and satisfaction. Is it, that beauty can never be grasped? in persons and in landscape is equally inaccessible? The accepted and betrothed lover has lost the wildest charm of his maiden in her acceptance of him. She was heaven whilst he pursued her as a star: she cannot be heaven, if she stoops to such a one as he.

What shall we say of this omnipresent appearance of that first projectile impulse, of this flattery and balking of so many well-meaning creatures? Must we not suppose somewhere in the universe a slight treachery and derision? Are we not engaged to a serious resentment of this use that is made of us? Are we tickled trout, and fools of nature? One look at the face of heaven and earth lays all petulance at rest, and soothes us to wiser convictions. To the intelligent, nature converts itself into a vast promise, and will not be rashly explained. Her secret is untold. Many and many an Œdipus arrives: he has the whole mystery teeming in his brain. Alas! the same sorcery has spoiled his skill; no syllable can he shape on his lips. Her mighty orbit vaults like the fresh rainbow into the deep, but no archangel's wing was yet strong enough to follow it, and report of the return of the curve. But it also appears, that our actions are seconded and disposed to greater conclusions than we designed. We are escorted on every hand through life by spiritual agents, and a beneficent purpose lies in wait for us. We cannot bandy words with nature, or deal with her as we deal with persons. If we measure our individual forces against hers, we may easily feel as if we were the sport of an insuperable destiny. But if, instead of identifying ourselves with the work, we feel that the soul of the workman streams through us, we shall find the peace of the morning dwelling first in our hearts, and the fathomless powers of gravity and chemistry, and, over them, of life, pre-existing within us in their highest form.

The uneasiness which the thought of our helplessness in the chain of causes occasions us, results from looking too much at one condition of nature, namely, Motion. But the drag is never taken from the wheel. Wherever the impulse exceeds, the Rest or Identity insinuates its compensation. All over the wide fields of earth grows the prunella or self-heal. After every foolish day we sleep off the fumes and furies of its hours; and though we are always engaged with par-

ticulars, and often enslaved to them, we bring with us
to every experiment the innate universal laws. These,
while they exist in the mind as ideas, stand around us
in nature forever embodied, a present sanity to expose
and cure the insanity of men. Our servitude to particulars betrays into a hundred foolish expectations. We
anticipate a new era from the invention of a locomo-
tive, or a balloon; the new engine brings with it the
old checks. They say that by electro-magnetism, your
salad shall be grown from the seed, whilst your fowl
is roasting for dinner: it is a symbol of our modern
aims and endeavors,—of our condensation and accelera-
tion of objects: but nothing is gained: nature cannot
be cheated: man's life is but seventy salads long, grow
they swift or grow they slow. In these checks and
impossibilities, however, we find our advantage, not
less than in the impulses. Let the victory fall where it
will, we are on that side. And the knowledge that
we traverse the whole scale of being, from the centre to
the poles of nature, and have some stake in every possibility, lends that sublime lustre to death, which philosophy and religion have too outwardly and literally
striven to express in the popular doctrine of the immortality of the soul. The reality is more excellent
than the report. Here is no ruin, no discontinuity, no
spent ball. The divine circulations never rest nor
linger. Nature is the incarnation of a thought, and
turns to a thought, again, as ice becomes water and gas.
The world is mind precipitated, and the volatile essence
is forever escaping again into the state of free thought.
Hence the virtue and pungency of the influence on the
᛫᛫᛫᛫, of natural objects, whether inorganic or or-

ganized. Man imprisoned, man crystallized, man vegtative, speaks to man impersonated. That power which does not respect quantity, which makes the whole and the particle its equal channel, delegates its smile to the morning, and distils its essence into every drop of rain. Every moment instructs, and every object, for wisdom is infused into every form. It has been poured into us as blood; it convulsed us as pain, it slid into us as pleasure; it enveloped us in dull, melancholy days, or in days of cheerful labor; we did not guess its essence, until after a long time.

POLITICS

Gold and iron are good
To buy iron and gold;
All earth's fleece and food
For their like are sold.
Boded Merlin wise,
Proved Napoleon great,—
Nor kind nor coinage buys
Aught above its rate.
Fear, Craft, and Avarice
Cannot rear a State.
Out of dust to build
What is more than dust,—
Walls Amphion piled
Phœbus stablish must.
When the Muses nine
With the Virtues meet,
Find to their design
An Atlantic seat,
By green orchard boughs
Fended from the heat,
Where the statesman ploughs
Furrow for the wheat;
When the Church is social worth,
When the state-house is the hearth,
Then the perfect State is come,
The republican at home.

IN dealing with the State, we ought to remember that its institutions are not aboriginal, though they existed before we were born: that they are not superior to the citizen: that every one of them was once the act of a single man: every law and usage was a man's expedient to meet a particular case; that they all are imitable, all alterable; we may make as good; we may make better. Society is an illusion to the young citizen. It lies before him in rigid repose, with certain names, men, and institutions, rooted like oak-trees to the centre, round which all arrange themselves the best they can. But the old statesman knows that society is fluid; there are no such roots and centres; but any particle may suddenly become the centre of the movement, and compel the system to gyrate round it, as every man of strong will, like Pisistratus, or Cromwell, does for a time, and every man of truth, like Plato, or Paul, does forever. But politics rest on necessary foundations, and cannot be treated with levity. Republics abound in young civilians, who believe that the laws make the city, that grave modifications of the policy and modes of living, and employments of the population, that commerce, education, and religion, may be voted in or out; and that any measure, though it were absurd, may be imposed on a people, if only you can get sufficient voices to make it a law. But the wise know that foolish legislation is a rope of sand, which perishes in the twisting; that the State must follow, and not lead the character and progress of the citizen; the strongest usurper is quickly got rid of; and they only who built on Ideas, build for eternity; and that the form of government which prevails, is the expression of what cultivation exists in the population which permits it. The law is only a memorandum. We are superstitious, and esteem the statute somewhat; so much life as it has in the character of living men, is its force. The statute stands there to say, yesterday we agreed

so and so, but how feel ye this article to-day? Our
statute is a currency, which we stamp with our own
portrait : it soon becomes unrecognizable, and in process
of time will return to the mint.   Nature is not democratic, nor limited monarchical, but despotic, and will
not be fooled or abated of any jot of her authority,
by the pertest of her sons : and as fast as the public
mind is opened to more intelligence, the code is seen
to be brute and stammering.   It speaks not articulately,
and must be made to.   Meantime the education of the
general mind never stops.   The reveries of the true
and simple are prophetic.   What the tender poetic
youth dreams, and prays, and paints to-day, but shuns
the ridicule of saying aloud, shall presently be the reso-
lutions of public bodies, then shall be carried as griev-
ance and bill of rights through conflict and war, and
then shall be triumphant law and establishment for a
hundred years, until it gives place, in turn, to new
prayers and pictures.   The history of the State sketches
in coarse outline the progress of thought, and follows
at a distance the delicacy of culture and of aspiration.

The theory of politics, which has possessed the
mind of men, and which they have expressed the best
they could in their laws and in their revolutions, con-
siders persons and property as the two objects for
whose protection government exists.   Of persons, all
have equal rights, in virtue of being identical in nature.
This interest, of course, with its whole power demands
a democracy.   Whilst the rights of all as persons are
equal, in virtue of their access to reason, their rights
in property are very unequal.   One man owns his

clothes, and another owns a county. This accident, depending, primarily, on the skill and virtue of the parties, of which there is every degree, and secondarily, on patrimony, falls unequally, and its rights, of course, are unequal. Personal rights, universally the same, demand a government framed on the ratio of the census: property demands a government framed on the ratio of owners and of owning. Laban, who has flocks and herds, wishes them looked after by an officer on the frontiers, lest the Midianites shall drive them off, and pays a tax to that end. Jacob has no flocks or herds, and no fear of the Midianites, and pays no tax to the officer. It seemed fit that Laban and Jacob should have equal rights to elect the officer, who is to defend their persons, but that Laban and not Jacob, should elect the officer who is to guard the sheep and cattle. And, if question arise whether additional officers or watch-towers should be provided, must not Laban and Isaac, and those who must sell part of their herds to buy protection for the rest, judge better of this, and with more right, than Jacob, who, because he is a youth and a traveller, eats their bread and not his own?

In the earliest society the proprietors made their own wealth, and so long as it comes to the owners in the direct way, no other opinion would arise in any equitable community, than that property should make the law for property, and persons the law for persons.

But property passes through donation or inheritance to those who do not create it. Gift, in one case, makes it as really the new owner's, as labor made it the first owner's: in the other case, of patrimony, the law makes an ownership, which will be valid in each man's view according to the estimate which he sets on the public tranquillity.

It was not, however, found easy to embody the readily admitted principle, that property should make law for property, and persons for persons: since persons and property mixed themselves in every transaction. At last it seems settled, that the rightful distinction was, that the proprietors should have more elective franchise than non-proprietors, on the Spartan principle of "calling that which is just, equal; not that which is equal, just."

That principle no longer looks so self evident. as it appeared in former times, partly, because doubts have arisen whether too much weight had not been allowed in the laws, to property, and such a structure given to our usages, as allowed the rich to encroach on the poor, and to keep them poor; but mainly, because there is an instinctive sense, however obscure and yet inarticulate, that the whole constitution of property, on its present tenures, is injurious, and its influence on persons deteriorating and degrading; that truly, the only interest for the consideration of the State, is persons; that property will always follow persons; that the highest end of government is the culture of men: and if men can be educated, the institutions will share their improvement, and the moral sentiment will write the law of the land.

If it be not easy to settle the equity of this question, the peril is less when we take note of our natural defences. We are kept by better guards than the vigilance of such magistrates as we commonly elect. Society always consists, in greatest part, of young and foolish persons. The old, who have seen through the hypocrisy of courts and statesmen, die, and leave no wisdom to their sons. They believe their own newspaper, as their fathers did at their age. With such an ignorant and deceivable majority, States would soon run to ruin, but that there are limitations beyond which the folly and ambition of governors cannot go. Things have their laws, as well as men; and things refuse to be trifled with. Property will be protected. Corn will not grow, unless it is planted and manured; but the farmer will not plant or hoe it, unless the chances are a hundred to one, that he will cut and harvest it. Under any forms, persons and property must and will have their just sway. They exert their power, as steadily as matter its attraction. Cover up a pound of earth never so cunningly, divide and subdivide it; melt it to liquid, convert it to gas; it will always weigh a pound: it will aways attract and resist other matter, by the full virtue of one pound weight;—and the attributes of a person, his wit and his moral energy, will exercise, under any law or extinguishing tyranny, their proper force,— if not overtly, then covertly; if not for the law, then against it; with right, or by might.

The boundaries of personal influence it is impossible to fix, as persons are organs of moral or supernatural force. Under the dominion of an idea, which possesses the minds of multitudes, as civil freedom, or the religious sentiment, the powers of persons are no longer subjects of calculation. A nation of men unanimously bent on freedom, or conquest, can easily confound the arithmetic of statists, and achieve extravagant actions, out of all proportion to their means;

as, the Greeks, the Saracens, the Swiss, the Americans, and the French have done.

In like manner, to every particle of property belongs its own attraction. A cent is the representative of a certain quantity of corn or other commodity. Its value is in the necessities of the animal man. It is so much warmth, so much bread, so much water, so much land. The law may do what it will with the owner of property, its just power will still attach to the cent. The law may in a mad freak say, that all shall have power except the owners of property: they shall have no vote. Nevertheless, by a higher law, the property will, year after year, write every statute that respects property. The non-proprietor will be the scribe of the proprietor. What the owners wish to do, the whole power of property will do, either through the law, or else in defiance of it. Of course, I speak of all the property, not merely of the great estates. When the rich are outvoted, as frequently happens, it is the joint treasury of the poor which exceeds their accumulations. Every man owns something, if it is only a cow, or a wheelbarrow, or his arms, and so has that property to dispose of.

The same necessity which secures the rights of person and property against the malignity or folly of the magistrate, determines the form and methods of governing, which are proper to each nation, and to its habit of thought, and nowise transferable to other states of society. In this country, we are very vain of our political institutions, which are singular in this, that they sprung, within the memory of living men, from the character and condition of the people, which they still express with sufficient fidelity,—and we ostentatiously prefer them to any other in history. They are not better, but only fitter for us. We may be wise in asserting the advantage in modern times of the democratic form but to other states of society, in which religion consecrated the monarchical, that and not this was expedient. Democracy is better for us, because the religious sentiment of the present time accords better with it. Born democrats, we are nowise qualified to judge of monarchy, which, to our fathers living in the monarchical idea, was also relatively right. But our institutions, though in coincidence with the spirit of the age, have not any exemption from the practical defects which have discredited other forms. Every actual State is corrupt. Good men must not obey the laws too well. What satire on government can equal the severity of censure conveyed in the word *politic,* which now for ages has signified *cunning,* intimating that the State is a trick?

The same benign necessity and the same practical abuse appear in the parties into which each State divides itself, of opponents and defenders of the administration of the government. Parties are also founded on instincts, and have better guides to their own humble aims than the sagacity of their leaders. They have nothing perverse in their origin, but rudely mark some real and lasting relation. We might as wisely reprove the east wind, or the frost, as a political party, whose members, for the most part, could give no account of their position, but stand for the defence of those interests in which they find themselves. Our quarrel with them begins, when they quit this deep natural ground at the bidding of some leader, and, obeying personal considerations, throw themselves into the maintenance and defence of points, nowise belonging to their system. A party is perpetually corrupted by personality. Whilst we absolve the association from dishonesty, we cannot extend the same character to their leaders. They reap the rewards of the docility and zeal of the masses which they direct. Ordinarily, our parties are parties of circumstance, and not of principle; as, the planting interest in conflict with the commercial; the party of capitalists, and that of operatives; parties which are identical in their moral character, and which can easily change ground with each other, in the support of many of their measures. Parties of principle, as, religious sects, or the party of free-trade, of universal suffrage, of abolition of slavery, of abolition of capital punishment, degenerate into personalities, or would inspire enthusiasm. The vice of our leading parties in this country (which may be cited as a fair specimen of these societies of opinion) is, that they do not plant themselves on the deep and necessary grounds to which they are respectively entitled, but lash themselves to fury in the carrying of some local and momentary measure, nowise useful to the commonwealth. Of the two great parties, which, at this hour, almost share the nation between them, I should say, that, one has the best cause, and the other contains the best men. The philosopher, the poet, or the religious man, will of course, wish to cast his vote with the democrat, for free-trade, for wide suffrage, for the abolition of legal cruelties in the penal code, and for facilitating in every manner the access of the young and the poor to the sources of wealth

and power.   But he can rarely accept the persons whom
the so-called popular party propose to him as representatives of these liberalities.   They have not at heart the
ends which give to the name of democracy what hope
and virtue are in it.   The spirit of our American
radicalism is destructive and aimless : it is not loving,
it has no ulterior and divine ends; but is destructive
only out of hatred and selfishness.   On the other side,
the conservative party, composed of the most moderate,
able, and cultivated part of the population, is timid,
and merely defensive of property.   It vindicates no
right, it aspires to no real good, it brands no crime, it
proposes no generous policy, it does not build, nor write,
nor cherish the arts, nor foster religion, nor establish
schools, nor encourage science, nor emancipate the slave,
nor befriend the poor, or the Indian, or the immigrant.
From neither party, when in power, has the world any
benefit to expect in science, art, or humanity, at all commensurate with the resources of the nation.

I do not for these defects despair of our republic.
We are not at the mercy of any waves of chance.   In
the strife of ferocious parties, human nature always
finds itself cherished, as the children of the convicts
at Botany Bay are found to have as healthy a moral
sentiment as other children.   Citizens of feudal states
are alarmed at our democratic institutions lapsing into
anarchy; and the older and more cautious among ourselves are learning from Europeans to look with some
terror at our turbulent freedom.   It is said that in our
license of construing the Constitution, and in the des-
potism of public opinion, we have no anchor; and one
foreign observer thinks he has found the safeguard in

the sanctity of Marriage among us; and another thinks
he has found it in our Calvinism. Fisher Ames expressed the popular security more wisely, when he compared a monarchy and a republic, saying, "that a monarchy is a merchantman, which sails well, but will sometimes strike on a rock, and go to the bottom; whilst a
republic is a raft, which would never sink, but then your
feet are always in water." No forms can have any
dangerous importance, whilst we are befriended by the
laws of things. It makes no difference how many tons
weight of atmosphere presses on our heads, so long as
the same pressure resists it within the lungs. Aug-
ment the mass a thousand fold, it cannot begin to crush
us, as long as reaction is equal to action. The fact of
two poles, of two forces, centripetal and centrifugal, is
universal, and each force by its own activity develops
the other. Wild liberty develops iron conscience.
Want of liberty, by strengthening law and decorum,
stupefies conscience. "Lynch-law" prevails only where
there is greater hardihood and self-subsistency in the
leaders. A mob cannot be a permanency: everybody's
interest requires that it should not exist, and only
justice satisfies all.

We must trust infinitely to the beneficent necessity
which shines through all laws. Human nature expresses itself in them as characteristically as in statues,
or songs, or railroads, and an abstract of the codes of
nations would be a transcript of the common conscience. Governments have their origin in the moral
identity of men. Reason for one is seen to be reason
for another, and for every other. There is a middle
measure which satisfies all parties, be they never so

many, or so resolute for their own.   Every man finds a
sanction for his simplest claims and deeds in decisions
of his own mind, which he calls Truth and Holiness.
In these decisions all the citizens find a perfect agreement, and only in these; not in what is good to eat, good
to wear, good use of time, or what amount of land, or
of public aid, each is entitled to claim.   This truth and
justice men presently endeavor to make application of,
to the measuring of land, the apportionment of service,
the protection of life and property.   Their first endeavors, no doubt, are very awkward.   Yet absolute
right is the first governor; or, every government is an
impure theocracy.   The idea, after which each community is aiming to make and mend its law, is, the will
of the wise man.   The wise man, it cannot find in nature, and it makes awkward but earnest efforts to secure
his government by contrivance; as, by causing the entire people to give their voices on every measure; or,
by a double choice to get the representation of the whole;
or, by a selection of the best citizens; or, to secure the
advantages of efficiency and internal peace, by confiding the government to one, who may himself select his
agents.   All forms of government symbolize an immortal government, common to all dynasties and independent of numbers, perfect where two men exist,
perfect where there is only one man.

Every man's nature is a sufficient advertisement to
him of the character of his fellows.   My right and my
wrong, is their right and their wrong.   Whilst I do
what is fit for me, and abstain from what is unfit, my
neighbor and I shall often agree in our means, and
work together for a time to one end.   But whenever I

find my dominion over myself not sufficient for me, and undertake the direction of him also, I overstep the truth, and come into false relations to him. I may have so much more skill or strength then he, that he cannot express adequately his sense of wrong, but it is a lie, and hurts like a lie both him and me. Love and nature cannot maintain the assumption: it must be executed by a practical lie, namely, by force. This undertaking for another, is the blunder which stands in colossal ugliness in the governments of the world. It is the same thing in numbers, as in a pair, only not quite so intelligible. I can see well enough a great difference between my setting myself down to a self-control, and my going to make somebody else act after my views: but when a quarter of the human race assume to tell me what I must do, I may be too much disturbed by the circumstances to see so clearly the absurdity of their command. Therefore, all public ends look vague and quixotic beside private ones. For, any laws but those which men make for themselves, are laughable. If I put myself in the place of my child, and we stand in one thought, and see that things are thus or thus, that perception is law for him and me. We are both there, both act. But if, without carrying him into the thought, I look over into his plot, and guessing how it is with him, ordain this or that, he will never obey me. This is the history of governments,—one man does something which is to bind another. A man who cannot be acquainted with me, taxes me; looking from afar at me, ordains that a part of my labor shall go to this or that whimsical end, not as I, but as he happens to fancy. Behold the consequence. Of all debts, men

are least willing to pay the taxes. What a satire is
this on government! Everywhere they think they get
their money's worth, except for these.

Hence, the less government we have, the better,—the
fewer laws, and the less confided power. The antidote
to this abuse of formal Government, is, the influence of
private character, the growth of the Individual; the
reappearance of the principal to supersede the proxy;
the appearance of the wise man, of whom the existing
government, is, it must be owned, but a shabby imitation. That which all things tend to educe, which freedom, cultivation, intercourse, revolutions, go to form
and deliver, is character; that is the end of nature, to
reach unto this coronation, of her king. To educate
the wise man, the State exists; and with the appearance
of the wise man, the State expires. The appearance of
character makes the State unnecessary. The wise man
is the State. He needs no army, fort, or navy,—he
loves men too well; no bribe, or feast, or palace, to
draw friends to him; no vantage grounds, no favorable
circumstance. He needs no library, for he has not done
thinking; no church, for he is a prophet; no statute
book, for he is the law-giver; no money, for he is value;
no road, for he is at home where he is; no experience,
for the life of the creator shoots through him and looks
from his eyes. He has no personal friends, for he who
has the spell to draw the prayer and piety of all men
unto him, needs not husband and educate a few, to share
with him a select and poetic life. His relation to men
is angelic; his memory is myrrh to them; his presence,
frankincense and flowers.

We think our civilization near its meridian, but we

are yet only at the cock-crowing and the morning star. In our barbarous society the influence of character is in its infancy. As a political power, as the rightful lord who is to tumble all rulers from their chairs, its presence is hardly yet suspected. Malthus and Ricardo quite omit it; the Annual Register is silent; in the Conversations' Lexicon, it is not set down; the President's Message, the Queen's Speech, have not mentioned it; and yet it is never nothing. Every thought which genius and piety throw into the world, alters the world. The gladiators in the lists of power feel, through all their frocks of force and simulation, the presence of worth. I think the very strife of trade and ambition are confession of this divinity; and successes in those fields are the poor amends, the fig-leaf with which the shamed soul attempts to hide its nakedness. I find the like unwilling homage in all quarters. It is because we know how much is due from us, that we are impatient to show some petty talent as a substitute for worth. We are haunted by a conscience of this right to grandeur of character, and are false to it. But each of us has some talent, can do somewhat useful, or graceful, or formidable, or amusing, or lucrative. That we do, as an apology to others and to ourselves, for not reaching the mark of a good and equal life. But it does not satisfy us, whilst we thrust it on the notice of our companions. It may throw dust in their eyes, but does not smooth our own brow, or give us the tranquillity of the strong when we walk abroad. We do penance as we go. Our talent is a sort of expiation, and we are constrained to reflect on our splendid moment, with a certain humiliation, as somewhat too fine.

and not as one act of many acts, a fair expression of our permanent energy. Most persons of ability meet in society with a kind of tacit appeal. Each seems to say, "I am not all here." Senators and presidents have climbed so high with pain enough, not because they think the place specially agreeable, but as an apology for real worth, and to vindicate their manhood in our eyes. This conspicuous chair is their compensation to themselves for being of a poor, cold, hard nature. They must do what they can. Like one class of forest animals, they have nothing but a prehensile tail: climb they must, or crawl. If a man found himself so rich-natured that he could enter into strict relations with the best persons, and make life serene around him by the dignity and sweetness of his behavior, could he afford to circumvent the favor of the caucus and the press, and covet relations so hollow and pompous, as those of a politician? Surely nobody would be a charlatan, who could afford to be sincere.

The tendencies of the times favor the idea of self-government, and leave the individual, for all code, to the rewards and penalties of his own constitution, which work with more energy than we believe, whilst we depend on artificial restraints. The movement in this direction has been very marked in modern history. Much has been blind and discreditable, but the nature of the revolution is not affected by the vices of the revolters; for this is a purely moral force. It was never adopted by any party in history, neither can be. It separates the individual from all party, and unites him, at the same time, to the race. It promises a recognition of higher rights than those of personal freedom. or

the security of property.   A man has a right to be employed, to be trusted, to be loved, to be revered.   The
power of love, as the basis of a State, has never been
tried.   We must not imagine that all things are lapsing
into confusion, if every tender protestant be not compelled to bear his part in certain social conventions: nor
doubt that roads can be built, letters carried, and the
fruit of labor secured, when the government of force is
at an end.   Are our methods now so excellent that all
competition is hopeless?   Could not a nation or friends
even devise better ways?   On the other hand, let not
the most conservative and timid fear anything from a
premature surrender of the bayonet, and the system of
force.   For, according to the order of nature, which is
quite superior to our will, it stands thus; there will
always be a government of force, where men are selfish;
and when they are pure enough to adjure the code of
force, they will be wise enough to see how these public
ends of the post-office, of the highway, of commerce,
and the exchange of property, of museums and libraries,
of institutions of art and science, can be answered.

We live in a very low state of the world, and pay
unwilling tribute to governments founded on force.
There is not, among the most religious and instructed
men of the most religious and civil nations, a reliance on the moral sentiment, and a sufficient belief in
the unity of things to persuade them that society can be
maintained without artificial restraints, as well as the
solar system; or that the private citizen might be reasonable, and a good neighbor, without the hint of a jail
or a confiscation.   What is strange too, there never was
in any man sufficient faith in the power of rectitude,

to inspire him with the broad design of renovating the State on the principle of right and love. All those who have pretended this design, have been partial reformers, and have admitted in some manner the supremacy of the bad State. I do not call to mind a single human being who has steadily denied the authority of the laws, on the simple ground of his own moral nature. Such designs, full of genius and full of fate as they are, are not entertained except avowedly as air-pictures. If the individual who exhibits them, dare to think them practicable, he disgusts scholars and churchmen; and men of talent, and women of superior sentiments, cannot hide their contempt. Not the less does nature continue to fill the heart of youth with suggestions of this enthusiasm, and there are now men,—if indeed I can speak in the plural number,—more exactly, I will say, I have just been conversing with one man, to whom no weight of adverse experience will make it for a moment appear impossible, that thousands of human being might exercise towards each other the grandest and simplest sentiments, as well as a knot of friends, or a pair of lovers.

NOMINALIST AND REALIST

In countless upward-striving waves
The moon-drawn tide-wave strives;
In thousand far-transplanted grafts
The parent fruit survives;
So, in the new-born millions,
The perfect Adam lives.
Not less are summer-mornings dear
To every child they wake,
And each with novel life his sphere
Fills for his proper sake.

I CANNOT often enough say, that a man is only a relative and representative nature. Each is a hint of the truth, but far enough from being that truth, which yet he quite newly and inevitably suggests to us. If I seek it in him, I shall not find it. Could any man conduct into me the pure stream of that which he pretends to be! Long afterwards, I find that quality elsewhere which he promised me. The genius of the Platonists is intoxicating to the student, yet how few particulars of it can I detach from all their books. The man momentarily stands for the thought, but will not bear examination; and a society of men will cursorily represent well enough a certain quality and culture, for example, chivalry or beauty of manners, but separate them, and there is no gentleman and no lady in the group. The least hint sets us on the pursuit of a character, which no man realizes. We have such exorbitant eyes, that on seeing the smallest arc, we complete the curve, and when the curtain is lifted from the diagram which it seemed to veil, we are vexed to find that no more was drawn, than just that fragment of an arc which we first beheld. We are greatly too liberal in our construction of each other's faculty and promise. Exactly what the parties have already done, they shall do again; but that which we inferred from their nature and inception, they will not do. That is in nature, but not in them. That happens in the world, which we often witness in a public debate. Each of the speakers expresses himself imperfectly: no one of them hears much that another says, such is the preoccupation of mind of each; and the audience, who have only to hear and not to speak, judge very wisely and superiorly how wrongheaded and unskilful is each of the debaters to his own affair. Great men or men of great gifts you shall easily find, but symmetrical men never. When I meet a pure intellectual force, or a generosity of affection, I believe, here then is man; and am presently mortified by the discovery, that this individual is no more available to his own or to the general ends, than his companions; because the power which drew my respect, is not supported by the total symphony of his talents. All persons exist to society by some shining trait of beauty or utility, which they have. We borrow the proportions of the man from that one fine feature, and finish the portrait symmetrically; which is false; for the rest of his body is small or deformed. I observe a person who makes a good public appearance, and conclude

thence the perfection of his private character, on which
this is based; but he has no private character. He is a
graceful cloak or lay-figure for holidays. All our poets,
heroes, and saints, fail utterly in some one or in many
parts to satisfy our idea, fail to draw our spontaneous
interest, and so leave us without any hope of realization
but in our own future. Our exaggeration of all fine
characters arises from the fact, that we identify each in
turn with the soul. But there are no such men as we
fable; no Jesus, nor Pericles, nor Cæsar, nor Angelo,
nor Washington, such as we have made. We conse-
crate a great deal of nonsense, because it was allowed
by great men. There is none without his foible. I
verily believe if an angel should come to chant the
chorus of the moral law, he would eat too much ginger-
bread, or take liberties with private letters, or do some
precious atrocity. It is bad enough, that our geniuses
cannot do anything useful, but it is worse that no man
is fit for society, who has fine traits. He is admired
at a distance, but he cannot come near without appearing a cripple. The men of fine parts protect themselves
by solitude, or by courtesy, or by satire, or by an acid
worldly manner, each concealing, as he best can, his incapacity for useful association, but they want either love
or self-reliance.

Our native love of reality joins with this experience to teach us a little reserve, and to dissuade a too
sudden surrender to the brilliant qualities of persons.
Young people admire talents or particular excellence;
as we grow older, we value total powers and effects, as,
the impression, the quality, the spirit of men and things.
The genius is all. The man,—it is his system: we do

not try a solitary word or act, but his habit. The acts which you praise, I praise not, since they are departures from his faith, and are mere compliances. The magnetism which arranges tribes and races in one polarity, is alone to be respected; the men are steel-filings. Yet we unjustly select a particle, and say, "O steel-filing number one! what heart-drawings I feel to thee! what prodigious virtues are these of thine! how constitutional to thee, and incommunicable."

Whilst we speak, the loadstone is withdrawn; down falls our filing in a heap with the rest, and we continue our mummery to the wretched shaving. Let us go for universals; for the magnetism, not for the needles. Human life and its persons are poor empirical pretensions. A personal influence is an *ignis fatuus*. If they say, it is great, it is great; if they say, it is small, it is small; you see it, and you see it not, by turns; it borrows all its size from the momentary estimation of the speakers: the Will-of-the-wisp vanishes, if you go too near, vanishes if you go too far, and only blazes at one angle. Who can tell if Washington be a great man, or no? Who can tell if Franklin be? Yes, or any but the twelve, or six, or three great gods of fame? And they too, loom and fade before the eternal.

We are amphibious creatures, weaponed for two elements, having two sets of faculties, the particular and the catholic. We adjust our instrument for general observation, and sweep the heavens as easily as we pick out a single figure in the terrestrial landscape. We are practically skilful in detecting elements, for which we have no place in our theory, and no name. Thus we are very sensible of an atmospheric influence in men and in bodies of men, not accounted for in an arithmetical addition of all their measurable properties. There is a genius of a nation, which is not to be found in the numerical citizens, but which characterizes the society. England, strong, punctual, practical, well-spoken England, I should not find, if I should go to the island to seek it. In the parliament, in the playhouse, at dinnertables, I might see a great number of rich, ignorant, book-read, conventional, proud men,—many old women, —and not anywhere the Englishman who made the good speeches, combined the accurate engines, and did the bold and nervous deeds. It is even worse in America, where, from the intellectual quickness of the race, the genius of the country is more splendid in its promise, and more slight in its performance. Webster cannot do the work of Webster. We conceive distinctly enough the French, the Spanish, the German genius, and it is not the less real, that perhaps we should not meet in either of those nations, a single individual who corresponded with the type. We infer the spirit of the nation in great measure from the language, which is a sort of monument, to which each forcible individual in a course of many hundred years has contributed a stone. And, universally, a good example of this social force, is the veracity of language, which cannot be debauched. In any controversy concerning morals, an appeal may be made with safety to the sentiments, which the language of the people expresses. Proverbs, words and grammar inflections convey the public sense with more purity and precision, than the wisest individual.

In the famous dispute with the Nominalists, the Realists had a good deal of reason. General ideas are

essences. They are our gods: they round and ennoble
the most partial and sordid way of living. Our proclivity to details cannot quite degrade our life, and di-
vest it of poetry. The day-laborer is reckoned as standing at the foot of the social scale, yet he is saturated with
the laws of the world. His measures are the hours;
morning and night, solstice and equinox, geometry,
astronomy, and all the lovely accidents of nature play
through his mind. Money, which represents the prose
of life, and which is hardly spoken of in parlors without
an apology, is, in its effects and laws, as beautiful as
roses. Property keeps the accounts of the world, and
is always moral. The property will be found where
the labor, the wisdom, and the virtue have been in nations, in classes, and (the whole life-time considered,
with the compensations) in the individual also. How
wise the world appears, when the laws and usages of nations are largely detailed, and the completeness of the
municipal system is considered! Nothing is left out.
If you go into the markets, and the custom-houses, the
insurers and notaries' offices, the offices of sealers of
weights and measures, of inspection of provisions,—it
will appear as if one man had made it all. Wherever
you go, a wit like your own has been before you, and
has realized its thought. The Eleusinian mysteries,
the Egyptian architecture, the Indian astronomy, the
Greek sculpture, show that there always were seeing
and knowing men in the planet. The world is full of
masonic ties, of guilds of secret and public legions of
honor; that of scholars, for example: and that of gentlemen fraternizing with the upper class of every country and every culture.

I am very much struck in literature by the appearance, that one person wrote all the books; as if the editor of a journal planted his body of reporters in different parts of the field of action, and relieved some by others from time to time; but there is such equality and identity both of judgment and point of view in the narrative, that it is plainly the work of one all-seeing, all-hearing gentleman.   I looked into Pope's Odyssey yesterday: it is as correct and elegant after our canon of to-day, as if it were newly written.   The modernness of all good books seems to give me an existence as wide as man.   What is well done, I feel as if I did; what is ill-done, I reck not of.   Shakspeare's passages of passion (for example, in Lear and Hamlet) are in the very dialect of the present year.   I am faithful again to the whole over the members in my use of books. I find the most pleasure in reading a book in a manner least flattering to the author.   I read Proclus, and sometimes Plato, as I might read a dictionary, for a mechanical help to the fancy and the imagination.   I read for the lustres, as if one should use a fine picture in a chromatic experiment, for its rich colors.   'Tis not Proclus, but a piece of nature and fate that I explore. It is a greater joy to see the author's author, than himself.   A higher pleasure of the same kind I found lately at a concert, where I went to hear Handel's Messiah.   As the master overpowered the littleness and incapableness of the performers, and made them conductors of his electricity, so it was easy to observe what efforts nature was making through so many hoarse, wooden, and imperfect persons, to produce beautiful voices, fluid and soul-guided men and women. The genius of nature was paramount at the oratorio.

This preference of the genius to the parts is the secret of that deification of art, which is found in all superior minds. Art, in the artist, is proportion, or, a habitual respect to the whole by an eye loving beauty in details. And the wonder and charm of it is the sanity in insanity which it denotes. Proportion is almost impossible to human beings. There is no one who does not exaggerate. In conversation, men are encumbered with personality, and talk too much. In modern sculpture, picture, and poetry, the beauty is miscellaneous; the artist works here and there, and at all points, adding and adding, instead of unfolding the unit of his thought. Beautiful details we must have, or no artist: but they must be means and never other. The eye must not lose sight for a moment of the purpose. Lively boys write to their ear and eye, and the cool reader finds nothing but sweet jingles in it. When they grow older, they respect the argument.

We obey the same intellectual integrity, when we study in exceptions the law of the world. Anomalous facts, as the never quite obsolete rumors of magic and demonology, and the new allegations of phrenologists and neurologists, are of ideal use. They are good indications. Homœopathy is insignificant as an art of healing, but of great value as criticism on the hygeia or medical practice of the time. So with Mesmerism, Swedenborgism, Fourierism, and the Millennial Church; they are poor pretensions enough, but good criticism on the science, philosophy, and preaching of the day. For these abnormal insights of the adepts, ought to be normal, and things of course.

All things show us, that on every side we are very near to the best. It seems not worth while to execute with too much pains some one intellectual, or æsthetical, or civil feat, when presently the dream will scatter, and we shall burst into universal power. The reason of idleness and of crime is the deferring of our hopes. Whilst we are waiting, we beguile the time with jokes, with sleep, with eating, and with crimes.

Thus we settle it in our cool libraries, that all the agents with which we deal are subalterns, which we can well afford to let pass, and life will be simpler when we live at the centre, and flout the surfaces. I wish to speak with all respect of persons, but sometimes I must pinch myself to keep awake, and preserve the due decorum. They melt so fast into each other, that they are like grass and trees, and it needs an effort to treat them as individuals. Though the uninspired man certainly finds persons a conveniency in household matters, the divine man does not respect them: he sees them as a rack of clouds, or a fleet of ripples which the wind drives over the surface of the water. But this is flat rebellion. Nature will not be Buddhist: she resents generalizing, and insults the philosopher in every moment with a million of fresh particulars. It is all idle talking: as much as a man is a whole, so is he also a part; and it were partial not to see it. What you say in your pompous distribution only distributes you into your class and section. You have not got rid of parts by denying them, but are the more partial. You are one thing, but nature is *one thing and the other thing,* in the same moment. She will not remain orbed in a thought, but rushes into persons: and when each person, inflamed to a fury of personality, would conquer all things to his poor crotchet, she raises up against him another person, and by many persons incarnates again a sort of whole. She will have all. Nick Bottom cannot play all the parts, work it how he may: there will be somebody else, and the world will be round. Every thing must have its flower or effort at the beautiful, coarser or finer according to its stuff. They relieve and recommend each other, and the sanity of society is a balance of a thousand insanities. She punishes abstractionists, and will only forgive an induction which is rare and casual. We like to come to a height of land and see the landscape, just as we value a general remark in conversation. But it is not the intention of nature that we should live by general views. We fetch fire and water, run about all day among the shops and markets, and get our clothes and shoes made and mended, and are the victims of these details, and once in a fortnight we arrive perhaps at a rational moment. If we were not thus infatuated, if we saw the real from hour to hour, we should not be here to write and to read, but should have been burned or frozen long ago. She would never get anything done, if she suffered admirable Crichtons, and universal geniuses. She loves better a wheelwright who dreams all night of wheels, and a groom who is part of his horse: for she is full of work, and these are her hands. As the frugal farmer takes care that his cattle shall eat down the rowan, and swine shall eat the waste of his house, and

poultry shall pick the crumbs, so our economical mother
despatches a new genius and habit of mind into every
district and condition of existence, plants an eye
wherever a new ray of light can fall, and gathering up
into some man every property in the universe, establishes thousandfold occult mutual attractions among her
offspring, that all this wash and waste of power may
be imparted and exchanged.

Great dangers undoubtedly accrue from this incarnation and distribution of the godhead, and hence nature has her maligners, as if she were Circe; and Al-
phonso of Castille fancied he could have given useful
advice.   But she does not go unprovided; she has helle-
bore at the bottom of the cup.   Solitude would ripen a
plentiful crop of despots.   The recluse thinks of men
as having his manner, or as not having his manner;
and as having degrees of it, more and less.   But when
he comes into a public assembly, he sees that men have
very different manners from his own, and in their way
admirable.   In his childhood and youth, he has had
many checks and censures, and thinks modestly enough
of his own endowment.   When afterwards he comes
to unfold it in propitious circumstance, it seems the only
talent: he is delighted with his success, and accounts
himself already the fellow of the great.   But he goes
into a mob, into a banking-house, into a mechanic's
shop, into a mill, into a laboratory, into a ship, into a
camp, and in each new place he is no better than an
idiot: other talents take place, and rule the hour.   The
rotation which whirls every leaf and pebble to the
meridian, reaches to every gift of man, and we all
take turns at the top.

For nature, who abhors mannerism, has set her heart on breaking up all styles and tricks, and it is so much easier to do what one has done before, than to do a new thing, that there is a perpetual tendency to a set mode. In every conversation, even the highest, there is a certain trick, which may be soon learned by an acute person, and then that particular style continued indefinitely. Each man, too, is a tyrant in tendency, because he would impose his idea on others; and their trick is their natural defence. Jesus would absorb the race; but Tom Paine or the coarsest blasphemer helps humanity by resisting this exuberance of power. Hence the immense benefit of party in politics, as it reveals faults of character in a chief, which the intellectual force of the persons, with ordinary opportunity and not hurled into aphelion by hatred, could not have seen. Since we are all so stupid, what benefit that there should be two stupidities! It is like that brute advantage so essential to astronomy, of having the diameter of the earth's orbit for a base of its triangles. Democracy is morose, and runs to anarchy, but in the state, and in the schools, it is indispensable to resist that consolidation of all men into a few men. If John was perfect, why are you and I alive? As long as any man exists, there is some need of him; let him fight for his own. A new poet has appeared; a new character approached us; why should we refuse to eat bread, until we have found his regiment and section in our old army-files? Why not a new man? Here is a new enterprise of Brook Farm, of Skeneateles, of Northampton: why so impatient to baptize them Essences, or Port-Royalists, or Shakers, or by any known and effete name? Let it be a new way of living. Why have only two or three ways of life, and not thousands? Every man is wanted, and no man is wanted much. We came this time for condiments, not for corn. We want the great genius only for joy; for one star more in our constellation, for one tree more in our grove. But he thinks we wish to belong to him, as he wishes to occupy us. He greatly mistakes us. I think I have done well, if I have acquired a new word from a good author; and my business with him is to find my own, though it were only to melt him down into an epithet or an image for daily use.

Into paint will I grind thee, my bride!

To embroil the confusion, and make it impossible to arrive at any general statement, when we have insisted on the imperfection of individuals, our affections and our experience urge that every individual is entitled to honor, and a very generous treatment is sure to be repaid. A recluse sees only two or three persons, and allows them all their room; they spread themselves at large. The man of state looks at many, and compares the few habitually with others, and these look less. Yet are they not entitled to this generosity of reception? and is not munificence the means of insight? For though gamesters say, that the cards beat all the players, though they were never so skilful, yet in the contest we are now considering, the players are also the game, and share the power of the cards. If you criticise a fine genius, the odds are that you are out of your reckoning, and, instead of the poet, are censuring your own caricature of him. For there is somewhat spheral

and infinite in every man, especially in every genius,
which, if you can come very near him, sports with all
your limitations. For, rightly, every man is a channel
through which heaven floweth, and, whilst I fancied I
was criticising him, I was censuring or rather terminat-
ing my own soul. After taxing Goethe as a courtier,
artificial, unbelieving, worldly,—I took up this book of
Helena, and found him an Indian of the wilderness, a
piece of pure nature like an apple or an oak, large as
morning or night, and virtuous as a briar-rose.

But care is taken that the whole tune shall be played.
If we were not kept among surfaces, every thing would
be large and universal: now the excluded attributes
burst in on us with the more brightness, that they have
been excluded. "Your turn now, my turn next," is
the rule of the game. The universality being hindered
in its primary form, comes in the secondary form of
all sides: the points come in succession to the meridian,
and by the speed of rotation, a new whole is formed.
Nature keeps herself whole and her representation complete in the experience of each mind. She suffers no
seat to be vacant in her college. It is the secret of the
world that all things subsist, and do not die, but
only retire a little from sight, and afterwards return
again. Whatever does not concern us, is concealed
from us. As soon as a person is no longer related to
our present well-being, he is concealed, or *dies,* as we
say. Really, all things and persons are related to us,
but according to our nature, they act on us not at once,
but in succession, and we are made aware of their presence one at a time. All persons, all things which we
have known, are here present, and many more than we

see; the world is full. As the ancient said, the world is a *plennum* or solid; and if we saw all things that really surround us, we should be imprisoned and unable to move. For, though nothing is impassable to the soul, but all things are pervious to it, and like highways, yet this is only whilst the soul does not see them. As soon as the soul sees any object, it stops before that object. Therefore, the divine Providence, which keeps the universe open in every direction to the soul, conceals all the furniture and all the persons that do not concern a particular soul from the senses of that individual. Through solidest eternal things, the man finds his road, as if they did not subsist, and does not once suspect their being. As soon as he needs a new object, suddenly he beholds it and no longer attempts to pass through it, but takes another way. When he has exhausted for the time the nourishment to be drawn from any one person or thing, that object is withdrawn from his observation, and though still in his immediate neighborhood, he does not suspect its presence.

Nothing is dead: men feign themselves dead, and endure mock funerals and mournful obituaries, and there they stand looking out of the window, sound and well, in some new and strange disguise. Jesus is not dead: he is very well alive: nor John, nor Paul, nor Mahomet, nor Aristotle; at times we believe we have seen them all, and could easily tell the names under which they go.

If we cannot make voluntary and conscious steps in the admirable science of universals, let us see the parts wisely, and infer the genius of nature from the best particulars with a becoming charity. What is best in each kind is an index of what should be the average of that thing.   Love shows me the opulence of nature, by disclosing to me in my friend a hidden wealth, and I infer an equal depth of good in every other direction. It is commonly said by farmers, that a good pear or apple costs no more time or pains to rear, than a poor one; so I would have no work of art, no speech, or action, or thought, or friend, but the best.

The end and the means, the gamester and the game, —life is made up of the intermixture and reaction of these two amicable powers, whose marriage appears beforehand monstrous, as each denies and tends to abolish the other.   We must reconcile the contradictions as we can, but their discord and their concord introduce wild absurdities into our thinking and speech. No sentence will hold the whole truth, and the only way in which we can be just, is by giving ourselves the lie; Speech is better than silence; silence is better than speech;—All things are in contact; every atom has a sphere of repulsion;—Things are, and are not, at the same time;—and the like.   All the universe over, there is but one thing, this old-Two-Face, creator-creature, mind-matter, right-wrong, of which any proposition may be affirmed or denied.   Very fitly, therefore, I assert, that every man is a partialist, that nature secures him as an instrument by self-conceit, preventing the tendencies to religion and science; and now further assert, that, each man's genius being nearly and affectionately explored, he is justified in his individuality, as his nature is found to be immense; and now I add, that every man is a universalist also, and as our earth, whilst it spins on its own axis, spins all the time round the sun through the celestial spaces, so the least of its rational children, the most dedicated to his private affair, works out, though as it were under a disguise, the universal problem. We fancy men are individuals; so are pumpkins; but every pumpkin in the field, goes through every point of pumpkin history. The rabid democrat, as soon as he is senator and rich man, has ripened beyond possibility of sincere radicalism and unless he can resist the sun, he must be conservative the remainder of his days. Lord Eldon said in his old age, "that, if he were to begin life again, he would be damned but he would begin as agitator."

We hide this universality, if we can, but it appears at all points. We are as ungrateful as children. There is nothing we cherish and strive to draw to us, but in some hour we turn and rend it. We keep a running fire of sarcasm at ignorance and the life of the senses; then goes by, perchance, a fair girl, a piece of life, gay and happy, and making the commonest offices beautiful, by the energy and heart with which she does them, and seeing this, we admire and love her and them, and say, "Lo! a genuine creature of the fair earth, not dissipated, or too early ripened by books, philosophy, religion, society, or care!" insinuating a treachery and contempt for all we had so long loved and wrought in ourselves and others.

If we could have any security against moods! If the profoundest prophet could be holden to his words, and the hearer who is ready to sell all and join the crusade, could have any certificate that to-morrow his prophet shall not unsay his testimony! But the Truth sits veiled there on the Bench, and never interposes an adamantine syllable; and the most sincere and revolutionary doctrine, put as if the ark of God were carried forward some furlongs, and planted there for the succor of the world, shall in a few weeks be coldly set aside by the same speaker, as morbid; "I thought I was right, but I was not,"—and the same immeasurable credulity demanded for new audacities. If we were not of all opinions! if we did not in any moment shift the platform on which we stand, and look and speak from another! if there could be any regulation, any "one-hour-rule," that a man should never leave his point of view, without sound of trumpet. I am always insincere, as always knowing there are other moods.

How sincere and confidential we can be, saying all that lies in the mind, and yet go away feeling that all is yet unsaid, from the incapacity of the parties to know each other, although they use the same words! My companion assumes to know my mood and habit of thought, and we go on from explanation to explanation, until all is said which words can, and we leave matters just as they were at first, because of that vicious assumption. Is it that every man believes every other to be an incurable partialist, and himself an universalist? I talked yesterday with a pair of philosophers: I endeavored to show my good men that I love every thing by turns, and nothing long; that I loved the centre, but doated on the superficies; that I loved man, if men seemed to me mice and rats; that I revered saints, but woke up glad that the old pagan world stood its ground, and died hard; that I was glad of men of every gift and nobility, but would not live in their arms. Could they but once understand, that I loved to know that they existed; and heartily wished them Godspeed, yet, out of my poverty of life and thought, had no word of welcome for them when they came to see me, and could well consent to their living in Oregon, for any claim I felt on them, it would be a great satisfaction.

THE END